# WINTER'S WRATH

Printed in the United States of America

First printing, 2024

ISBN: 978-1-7381402-1-3

Imprint: Elgin House Press

Cover Design: Moor Books Design

Editor: Richard's Corrections

**www.emmacouetteauthor.com**

Emma K. C. Couette

# WINTER'S WRATH

THE FIDALIAN CHRONICLES
BOOK 2

ELGIN HOUSE
— PRESS —

# ALSO BY EMMA K. C. COUETTE

**The Guild Trilogy**

Silent Night
Sacred Ruse
Solemn Vow
Assassins Below

**The Fidalian Chronicles**

Summer's Revenge
Winter's Wrath

# AUTHOR'S NOTE

**For the best reading** experience, please reference the below two guides at the back of the book for information that is not discussed in depth by characters in the story.

**The Noble Families of Summer:** page 434
**Magic in Fidalia:** page 436

# PRONUNCIATION GUIDE

**Appalachia:** app-a-lay-shia (Capital city of Winter)
**Areevia:** a -ree-vee-a (Isan and Sky's mother)
**Arkenier:** are-ken-yay (King of Summer)
**Asmund:** az-mund (Son of Lord Arrath)
**Cahir:** ca-hear (Shadow Watch member)
**Fidal:** fee-dal (Creator of Fidalia)
**Fidalia:** fee-dal-ee-a (The name of the realm)
**Gwyneth:** gwin-eth (Daughter of Lord Norwell)
**Icaria:** eye-sair-ee-a (Princess of Winter)
**Isanfier:** eyes-an-fire (Prince of Summer)
**Kainda:** cane-da (Daughter of Lord Norwell)
**Kallen:** kal-lin (King Frost's general)
**Sancia:** san-see-a (Goddess of Summer)
**Soleia:** sol-ay-ah (Daughter of Lord Lachlan)
**Snowdon:** snow-done (Prince of Winter)
**Skiansy:** sky-an-zee (Princess of Summer)
**Tamise:** ta-mees (City in Winter)
**Weylyn:** -way-lin (Son of Lord Norwell)
**Widonia:** wid-own-ee-a (Capital city of Summer)
**Wylla:** will-a (Goddess of Winter)

Map Created By Rachael Ward

*To my granny,*
*who has only asked me a few times if this book is ready yet*
*(and who will be very upset I called her granny in a published*
*book)*

*It's finally here!*
*And no, I don't know when book three will be done,*
*but I promise you'll be the first to know*

Once, an old God had a fear
Of a land that would be forever at war.
This God's name was Fidal,
And he created the Curse of Fidalia.

Fidalia was wondrous
But its people were falling from grace and light.
A war had torn them apart,
And Fidal could no longer trust their motives.

The kingdoms stood divided,
The Edgewood now a sentinel between them,
And Fidal could not allow
Another battle to ruin the balance.

And so, Fidal made a Curse,
A prophecy to guide new generations,
An omen of disaster,
A chance to change the fate of Fidalia.

When the realm is unbalanced,
Four champions will be born to correct it:
A set of twins for each land,
Destined to be each other's end or the realm's.

Two shall survive the battle,
If they follow the destiny of the stars,
And the actions required
To win the war will save the realm from itself.

But if they ignore their fate,
They will doom Fidalia to destruction.
All four of them shall perish,
And the entire realm will follow in their wake.

# *Part One: Shadows*

"Someone I loved one gave me a box full of darkness. It took me years to understand that this too, was a gift."

—Mary Oliver

# 1
# Wounds of War

**A chill settled into** my bones as I rode my horse through the gates of Widonia, the Summer army a sea at my back and Sky a rock at my side to anchor me to the world. Even after five weeks of leading them, I still found it hard to call them my men. I was detached from the idea that I was the one in charge now, that the Summer throne was empty and I would have to take up the crown much sooner than anticipated.

Darkenier's fallen sword was a hollow weight on my right hip, one I would be glad to shed.

The sun shone down on us, glinting off our armour as we rode through the streets towards the castle, a complete reversal of our departure months ago. The people cheered for us, waving flags and flowers, and I reminded myself to smile. This was the moment I had longed for, the moment I had dreamed of, but victory is usually bittersweet.

People seldom worry about the right things. I had been so terrified of never seeing Widonia again when we left that I hadn't stopped to consider what it would be like to return without certain people at our side.

I wondered how the citizens of Widonia were reacting to Darkenier's absence, how long before the cheers would dissolve into restless whispers.

*The King is dead. Is the Prince ready to lead us? How could they let him die?*

Something brushed my arm, and I jumped in the saddle, half turning in that direction.

Sky gave me a look and dropped her hand, her brown eyes boring into me. "Smile, Isan," she said. "We're home. We survived. We won."

I took a deep breath and nodded. "I know, I just...never imagined this moment."

"You should enjoy it while it lasts. These next few weeks won't be so pleasant." She gave me one last smile and then turned to give the people an even wider one.

She was so good at projecting happiness, at giving people something to hope for, but then again, it was much easier to spread joy when you weren't pretending to possess it. Even so, I took another deep breath and followed her example.

The people would be receiving enough bad news in the next couple days; the least I could do was put on a brave face and lead them through it.

The knights dispersed into the city as we went, some towards the barracks and others towards home. By the time we reached the castle, there was only Sky, Asmund, Silas, me, and an entourage of ten knights. When our armies had parted ways north of the Edgewood, Asmund had chosen not to go home to Skar with his father, saying he was needed more in Widonia. I wasn't sure if that was strictly true, but I didn't blame him. Lord Arrath had been frosty with him ever since his defiance in Appalachia.

Sir Kent met us at the castle doors, and I was beyond grateful to see him. He would know how to proceed, what meetings had to be held and such, though I did wonder how he would react to the King's demise.

I dismounted my horse, and the others followed my lead. We walked fourteen strong up the stairs to join Kent, who ushered us inside.

"Your Highnesses," Kent exclaimed, "I am so glad to see you both! It has been agony awaiting your return. The people have been growing restless." He beamed at us, but there was a sadness in his eyes. "Where is the King?"

My heart constricted, and I could only shake my head.

His eyes widened, and his voice was almost impossible to hear when he said, "He is dead?"

Asmund brushed past me. "Worse than dead, Captain. He betrayed us all. There is quite a story to tell, but we are all weary. Perhaps we could hold a dinner later to discuss the ramifications?"

Kent blinked at Asmund, some of the colour draining from his face. "He...what?"

"He betrayed us," Asmund repeated. "Disappeared in the battle when we needed him most, beheaded King Frost, and then made an attempt on Isanfier's life. Should I go on?"

Kent looked like he might be sick, and I stepped in to save him from more suffering. It would not be easy for him to accept the truth about Darkenier; they had been close friends for as long as I could remember.

"That's enough, Asmund," I said, placing a hand on his shoulder. "We can give Sir Kent the details later. We know full well it is a lot to take in."

Asmund took a step back, and Kent nodded. "Some time to process would be best, I think. You sound genuine, but...Fidal's breath, I do not possess the words to address the matter. We will discuss it in depth at dinner tonight, but for now, you all should rest. I know the journey is long."

I gave him a smile. "Thank you, Sir Kent. I'm sorry we return with such somber news."

He sighed. "It is not your fault, Your Highness. Conflict brings out the worst in people. It's in struggle that you see who they really are, that their true colours are brought to light. War seldom hides the truth."

I nodded. That was the understatement of a lifetime.

The silence following his words was broken by an exclamation to our right. "Isan? Sky? Oh, Sancia's breath, you made it home!"

Sky and I turned to see Aunt Mag barreling toward us, as fast as she could while still maintaining her ladylike demeanor. We were in motion almost instantly, rushing to meet her. The three of us collided, and I finally felt at home again as she squeezed us against her and whispered a prayer of thanks to the stars.

"Oh, I was so worried," Aunt Mag gasped. "I've been beside myself since the moment you left, but I never lost faith. I knew the two of you would do everything you could."

"We promised you we'd come back, didn't we?" I asked as she finally let us go.

She smiled at me, tears running down her weathered face. "That you did, child. That you did."

She and Sky took a moment to wipe their eyes, and I turned back to the waiting men in the foyer. "You are relieved from duty for now, men. Go see your families and rest up. We shall reconvene at dusk for dinner and discuss the details of our journey. Sancia be with you."

The men took their leave one by one until only Silas remained.

I looked at him. "Afraid to go home?"

He smiled. "Not at all, son. I want to make sure you have no further need of me before I head out."

I smiled back. "I'm sure your wisdom would be welcomed at all hours, but your family needs you more right now. Your wife must miss you terribly."

"As I do her. Thank you, Your Highness. It has been a pleasure to ride by your side."

"This isn't the end of our journey together, Silas," I replied, "though the choice lies with you. I would like to formally invite you to join the Council of Knights here at the palace. We seem to have an empty seat."

A whirlwind of emotions passed across his face until he settled on shock and said, "Your Highness...that's too kind. I really couldn't..."

I waved a hand. "You belong on the Council, Silas. The kingdom is changing, and I need someone like you on my side, someone with strength and wisdom and humility. I will not force you, but don't deny it because you think you don't deserve it. That is the farthest thing from the truth. Think about it this afternoon. Discuss it with your family, and give me your answer tonight at dinner."

His old face was red as he looked at his feet and said, "Thank you, son. I don't know what to say, but I shall think about it and give you an answer soon."

I smiled. "Good, now go. See your family."

He nodded, and the others waved goodbye as he finally took his leave. I sincerely hoped he would take my offer. I needed someone I could trust on the Council; after everything that had happened, I couldn't be sure who was with me and who was against me anymore.

"Well, Your Highnesses," Sir Kent said, "I shall go make the dinner preparations and attend to some housekeeping matters. I will reconvene with you later."

"Of course, Sir Kent," I replied. "Thank you."

That left Aunt Mag, Sky, Asmund, and me in the foyer. Aunt Mag was looking at the three of us rather inquisitively, and I knew what she was thinking. I knew how smug she would be when she discovered our new alliance. I should probably say something before she did.

"Well, I don't know about you boys," Sky said, giving her shoulders a stretch, "but I would like to get off my feet for a bit and have a proper bath. I'll see you two at dinner."

"I'll walk with you," Aunt Mag offered. "I found this beautiful dress while you were away, and it would be perfect for this evening."

Sky beamed, and the two of them walked off down the hall arm in arm, already chatting away. I could almost see a weight lift off of Sky's shoulders as she let the past few months go. I wished I could do the same.

"And then there were two," Asmund said. "How are you holding up?"

I shrugged. "As well as can be expected. This dinner tonight should be riveting." I heaved a sigh.

Asmund put a hand on my shoulder. "At least I saved you from an endless meeting. The men won't be able to talk long with full stomachs and a few glasses of wine."

"I suppose you're right. I just hope I can last long enough. Do you think you can steer the conversation away from delicate topics?"

"I'll do what I can. Have you made any progress?"

I shook my head. "It hasn't been easy with all the soldiers around. I'm counting on having some free time and privacy in the next few weeks."

He nodded. "You'll get it, Isanfier, and in the meantime, we'll do what we can to keep it hidden. Are you sure you don't want to tell—"

"No," I interrupted him. "She's been through enough."

He rolled his eyes. "As you wish, but don't say I didn't tell you so when that backfires horribly."

I waved a hand. "Sky will forgive me, eventually."

He shrugged. "If you say so. Now if you don't mind, I'm going to have a bath of my own. My hair hasn't felt right in months."

Indeed he was right. His dreadlocks were quite matted, sticks and leaves stuck between the strands in some places. He hadn't rebraided them in weeks, and I shuddered to think how long it would take him to untangle them.

Thank Fidal I kept my hair short. I had enough problems to deal with.

He gave me a quick parting remark and then left me alone with the remnants of our conversation.

Asmund was still the only one who knew about my magic, and I intended to keep it that way for as long as possible. Darkenier may be dead, but magic was still outlawed, and I did not yet possess the power to revoke his policies. There were undoubtedly many who supported his choice.

My magic had been quiet since our fight. I had spent many nights on the way back to Widonia trying to conjure it, sitting in silence in my tent until my fingernails drew lines on my closed fists and sweat beaded on my forehead. Nothing would come, not even a wisp of smoke, but I could feel it, lingering beneath my skin.

It flared up along with my anger, a slow simmer in my veins, and I knew it was only a matter of time before it broke free again, especially now that I had returned to the castle. I prayed I could learn to control it before it hurt me, or someone else.

• • •

My room was not how I remembered it. Everything was in the same place—my desk against the wall between the windows, my wardrobe to the left, my bed beside the door—but they weren't how I had left them. My bed was made, my wardrobe was shut tight, and the papers on my desk were stacked neatly in one corner, my quill pens safely tucked in their jar.

It was not the room I had left, and I was not the boy who had left it. There was a weight on my shoulders I feared I would never be rid of.

I threw my cloak on the bed and dropped Darkenier's sword on my desk. It hit the wood with a dull thud, and I felt like my room was tainted further by its presence. Shadows had killed my parents, had destroyed this kingdom so irrevocably that I wasn't sure I would ever be able to put the pieces back together. Darkenier's death was a start, but it was far from the end.

I walked away from the sword and pulled open my shutters, letting the Summer breeze air out my room and put my mind at rest. The coming months wouldn't be easy, but I had to take them one day at a time. The first thing to tackle would be tonight's dinner. We had to fill Sir Kent in on everything that had happened and begin planning our next steps.

A Regent would have to be chosen, to rule in my stead until my eighteenth birthday, but I couldn't stand idle and let others make decisions about my kingdom anymore. I would be crowned King in just over a year, and it was time to start acting like it.

I wouldn't let another man take too much power, become another tyrant. I took one last glance at the sword on my desk before heading into the bathing room to get ready for dinner. Its weight seemed to follow me in, and I had a feeling it would be a long time before the consequences of Darkenier's death truly left me.

## 2
## Treachery and Truth

**The sun had begun** to set by the time I left my room for dinner, its dying light bathing my room in an orange glow. I closed the shutters on my windows and attached both *Ember* and *Shadows* to my belt, the former out of habit and the latter out of fear. Something told me I shouldn't let Darkenier's sword out of my sight until I laid it to rest in Widonia's cemetery.

Sky was waiting outside my room, and I nearly jumped out of my boots at the sight of her.

"Sancia's breath, Sky," I gasped. "Are you vying for the throne?"

She gave me a quizzical look. "What do you mean?"

I scowled. "Lurking outside my room is going to send me to an early grave."

She waved a gloved hand and half turned away. "Maybe that's a good thing. If you can't handle me, you won't stand a chance as King."

"Very funny," I replied. "You look nice this evening," I added as I followed her down the hall.

Her long hair was piled atop her head in a dark braided bun, a few strands hanging loose to frame her face, and the dress Aunt Mag had picked was indeed perfect. It was a pale green with yellow flowers running around the skirt—simple yet elegant.

Sky smiled. "Thank you. I dare say I have missed wearing a dress. One without a corset, that is."

"I know I'm glad to be free of my armour and chainmail, but formal attire… I'm not desperate enough for that." I had changed into a fresh tunic in a chestnut brown colour and my usual black pants, going against my instincts to wear all black in hopes of putting the men at ease tonight.

She shrugged. "Men can get away with a little less frivolity, but Aunt Mag was devastated when she saw the state I was in, especially my hair. She's been pruning me for the past three hours."

I winced. "Could've been worse, I suppose. You could be Asmund. I swear he'll need to go bald to fix his hair."

Sky smirked. "I think that would make my entire year."

I smiled back. "I think he'd probably ask me to kill him."

We laughed then, and for the first time in weeks, I didn't feel like it was forced.

Sky and I were two of the last people to enter the dining hall, and the table was half full, a sight I hdn't seen since I was a child. On the left, Aunt Mag sat beside Sky's empty seat, Silas on her other side. On the right, Asmund sat beside the head with Sir Kent beside him. There were seven other chairs reserved for the knighted members of the Council, though I noticed the one directly beside Sir Kent was still empty. A quick study of the men present proved Sir Quinton was missing. His absence was odd, as he usually prided himself on impeccable manners, and I noticed a few of the other knights glancing at his empty seat as well.

Sky quickly took her seat beside Aunt Mag, greeting everyone at the table in turn, but I stood in the doorway, staring at the empty chair that had once belonged to Darkenier. It was mine now. I had every right to take it, but it felt wrong somehow, like I wasn't worthy of it.

We might be electing a Regent to rule in my stead for the next year and a half, but he wouldn't be given the same power and authority Darkenier once had. I was essentially the King already, albeit without the official title and heavy crown.

Could I lead these men, this kingdom, like he once had, like my father and grandfather before him? Darkenier might have had terrible intentions, but at least the kingdom had been strong under his rule.

Could I follow in his footsteps, or was I destined to destroy Summer and everything my ancestors had worked towards?

*You can't know until you try,* I reminded myself. *Don't discount yourself before then.*

I took a deep breath.

*One step at a time.*

I crossed the room and took my place at the head of the table, pulling my chair in tight before I could change my mind. The chatter around me died instantly, and I felt exposed, like the whole kingdom had its eyes on me. I looked over at Sky, and her encouraging smile put me at ease, if only a little. I took one last deep breath before addressing the room.

"Thank you all for coming," I said, forcing a smile onto my face. "It is an honour to have you at our dinner table. Gatherings such as these have been long overdue. I hope we can all enjoy the food and company, even as we discuss some delicate matters."

Asmund raised his glass, half full of red wine, and the table followed suit as he toasted to my words.

"I'm sure we are all honoured to be here," Kent replied. "It certainly is a pleasure to have everyone in the Capital again, but tell me, Your Highness, what is the whole story behind King Arkenier's death? Spare us no details."

I sighed. "It is not a happy tale, Captain, but it is one that must be told."

The next few minutes passed slowly as I recounted the events of the war and the final attack on Appalachia. The colour drained from Kent's face with each word I said, and Aunt Mag gasped out loud as I explained my and Sky's harrowing escape from Snowdon.

When I reached the part about Darkenier's betrayal, I was careful to keep my story the same as the one I'd given the men in the Winter palace, not once using his true name or mentioning that he was a Wyllan. It wasn't that I didn't trust Kent with the truth about Darkenier's identity, but I knew his trust in my story was already thin. Adding anything else might make him dismiss it entirely.

"Arkenier betrayed us all," I finished, "and nearly brought the entire realm down with him." I unclipped *Shadows* from my belt and set it gently on the table, careful not to upset any dishes. "This is all that is left of our late King."

Kent was silent, gaping at me and the sword, an expression I'd never seen him wear. I couldn't tell if he was more shocked or scared, but his eyes held a deep, irrevocable caution.

The servants entered the room with our first course then, saving him from the need to offer an immediate reply, and I removed *Shadows* from the table to give them space. Large bowls of orange soup were laid out before us, and we ate in silence for a few minutes, warmth seeping into our stomachs.

Finally, Kent found his words again. "I am so sorry, Your Highness. I feel as though I have failed this kingdom. How could I have not seen his treachery? How could I have swallowed his lies?"

I shook my head. "We cannot sink into despair; he was exceptional at what he did. The best way to give ourselves grace is to move on, move forward. Summer needs us to continue the fight, even in the face of adversity. Arkenier's death will sit with me for the rest of my days, but I would be doing this kingdom a disservice by wallowing in my apparent shortcomings. As would you, or any of us at this table, for that matter.

"We survived the war," I went on. "We avenged King Oaden and Queen Areevia. Now we must bring Summer into a new era, to show Winter that this betrayal has not destroyed us."

Several at the table raised their glasses again, and Kent gave me a small smile. "I believe the kingdom is in good hands with you, Your Highness, and I am eager to help in any way I can, though I would caution against revealing your tale to the masses."

I frowned. "What do you mean?"

Kent shifted in his seat. "I mean that learning of their King's death will be hard enough on the citizens of Summer, let alone trying to swallow the fact that their King betrayed them. It would only sow seeds of distrust. We can't have them questioning whether or not you will do the same."

I could see where he was coming from, but his words left an unsettled feeling in the pit of my stomach. I was already lying to the council about Darkenier's true identity and exactly how he had died; if I sold the people yet another story, I would run the risk of getting caught up in my own lies. Aside from that, Summer had a right to know the truth—as much of it as I could give them, anyway.

"Your concern has merit, Sir Kent," I replied, "but I will not lie to my people in the name of trust. I know some of them will not believe me. I know some of them may hate me for it, but the truth is bound to be discovered someday. What will the people think then? There will always be those who stand against the monarchy; I can't afford to lose the ones who *do* stand by me now."

"Your Highness—" Kent tried again, but I held up a hand.

"I will not entertain the idea further," I told him, "but your opinion is valued. It is important for ideas to be voiced and actions to be questioned. Which is why I would like to appoint you as my Regent, until I come of age."

Kent's eyes widened in surprise, and there were murmurs of dissent around the table, but I raised my glass for silence, and the whispers died out.

"There will be time to counter my words," I told them, "but please hear me out before you dismiss them entirely." I paused and surveyed each man in turn before continuing. "I understand this is not the natural way, that there is meant to be a vote cast by all members of the Council after days of intense debate, but I believe Sir Kent has proven his worth for this position. The castle did not fall apart in our absence. The kingdom continued to flourish under his guiding hand. I may be young and untried, and I understand the need to postpone my crowning until my eighteenth birthday, but I also understand the war left us vulnerable.

"Our King is dead, and it will not take Winter long to exploit that, if they haven't made plans already. We can't afford to waste time conferring over possible candidates when the perfect one is sitting before us already."

The knights glanced between each other, sharing looks of unease and annoyance yet with an underlying feel of acceptance, as if knowing I was right but not wanting to admit it.

I knew I was pushing my limits, that I had already asked a lot of them tonight, but I couldn't budge on this request. The future of Summer depended on the new Regent being someone I could trust, and Sir Silas definitely wouldn't be on the table. I had to meet the Council in the middle.

The men remained silent until Sir Delwyn stood up and looked in my direction. "Your Highness," he said, "if I may add to your speech?"

I nodded, praying he wasn't about to condemn me.

Delwyn glanced around at his comrades and took a deep breath before beginning. "I can sense your unease, men, but there is merit in His Highness's words. Perhaps, in this new dawn of Summer, some traditions will have to be broken. It was the Council's poor judgment in the past which led to the traitor's kingship in the first place, so I do not see how there can be any fault in letting Prince Isanfier choose his own Regent. Besides, how many of us were planning to recommend Sir Kent anyway? How many of us would've voted for him?"

Several men raised their hands, and Delwyn nodded.

"Then, if there are no further objections, I believe we have our answer."

"No further objections to what?"

Everyone turned to face the voice, and we watched as Sir Quinton waltzed into the dining hall as if nothing was amiss and we were all early instead of him late.

"Ah," Sir Saxon said, "so good of you to finally join us, Sir Quinton." There was a tone of distaste beneath his words I was sure Quinton didn't miss.

"My apologies for being late," Quinton replied. "Something came up."

Saxon raised a brow. "Something more important than this dinner? You do realize this is a discussion to solidify the future of our kingdom, correct?"

I could sense Quinton's urge to roll his eyes, but he held it back. "I understand your concern, Sir Saxon, but I assure you, I had my reasons, and I am here now. Have I missed much?"

Saxon opened his mouth to protest again, but Kent held up a hand. "That will be enough, Sir Saxon. Sir Quinton accompanied you all to the war, so I doubt there was much need for him to be present for the regaling of the tale. Please, Sir Quinton, have a seat. We were deciding on the matter of regency, and His Highness has appointed me, with the blessing of the rest of the men."

Quinton was moving to his empty seat but stopped short at Kent's words, giving me a sidelong glance. "His Highness *appointed* you? That's hardly in accordance with tradition."

"And yet, it has been decided," Sir Delwyn replied, a rough edge to his voice. "Perhaps if you were on time..." He let the rest of his sentence hang in midair, and Quinton took his seat with a scowl but without another word.

"Now that the matter is settled," I said, sensing it was time to turn the conversation elsewhere, "we should work on our next steps. Does anyone have any issues they'd like to bring to the table?"

Sky raised a hand, and I nodded. "We should start by arranging a memorial for the dead," she said. "Our people need closure. They need to know we are willing to acknowledge what they have lost."

Sir Saxon nodded solemnly. "Many good men were taken far too early; we need to honour their sacrifice."

"I agree," I replied. "Can I rely on you to arrange that, Sir Saxon?"

"Of course, Your Majesty. It'll be ready by the end of the week."

At the other end of the table, Sir Warmund raised his hand. "Go ahead," I told him.

"We also need to establish an improved, if not new, defence system. I suggest instating border patrols along the Edgewood and sending more untried youth to Skar for training. They need not become knights, but we will need more skilled fighters in the event of another war."

"More fighters are all well and good," Sir Delwyn countered, "but will the training be mandatory? How will the people receive such news after the family they've already lost?"

"Well, their sons will be more prepared should there be a next time. I believe that would be enough motivation."

Asmund raised his hand. "If I may interject?"

Warmund nodded.

"If it would help ease people's minds, I could perhaps train some boys here, at the barracks? I spent my childhood under the direct tutelage of Lord Arrath himself and was knighted this past spring. The idea of training may be more well received if the boys can still return home on days off."

Delwyn gave Asmund an appreciative look; even I was impressed by his generosity. "That could be an excellent compromise, Master Asmund. We shall have to discuss it further before making a decision."

Asmund nodded.

There was a lull in the conversation as the servants came to clear our plates, dish out the second course, and pour more wine. Our second course was a roast pig and several dishes of boiled and spiced vegetables.

The men dug into the meal with an unparalleled vigour, all but starving for real food after the months of dried meat, nuts, and the occasional rabbit or deer.

I ate slow, careful not to overwhelm my stomach, and watched the men around me, searching for anything amiss. It was going to be hard to trust anyone now, to look them in the eyes and believe their words as truth. Even giving the regency to Kent put me on edge, but the kingdom would certainly not accept me as King at sixteen years old. That was the one tradition I knew they wouldn't break.

As the men began to clean their plates and lean back in their chairs, Sir Kent stood up, clinking a spoon against his wine glass to grab everyone's attention. All eyes were on him as he spoke.

"I want to start by thanking you, Your Highness, for appointing me to the position of Regent," he said, looking at me. "It is a great honour and a responsibility I will not take lightly. As Regent, it is my duty to ensure and strengthen the future of our kingdom. Thus, I would like to propose we begin preparations for a Festival of Honour."

Murmurs rose up around the table, and I almost dropped my wine glass.

*A Festival of Honour? Now?*

I snuck a glance at Sky, and she looked as sick as I felt. We both knew it was coming, had been fearing it for years now, and yet, I always thought we would have more time.

Aunt Mag put an arm around Sky, as if sensing her discomfort, and said, "Are you sure the timing is wise, Sir Kent? Their Highnesses have barely returned from war. That can take some time to recover from."

"That is exactly why I have chosen now, Governess Magnolia. As our Prince said, Summer is vulnerable. We cannot wait any longer, especially now that the royal family has been reduced to two. His Highness must marry, start fathering children, and prepare to become King himself in a few years. We must solidify the future of this kingdom." He looked around the table. "Is anyone else opposed?"

No one raised a hand. Of course, Sky and I wouldn't get a vote in the matter. Our only consolation, I supposed, was that Darkenier's death had given us the gift of being able to choose our own bride and groom at the end of the Festival. Still, it wasn't much of a choice when our candidates were already set in stone and saying no wasn't an option.

"Then it is settled," Sir Kent went on. "I will send invitations out to our lords and ladies in the morning, and we shall begin preparations to host their eligible children. It will be a Festival of Honour to remember, a symbol of unity even after dark times."

Sir Delwyn raised his glass. "For the prosperity of Summer. Fidalia forever."

The others raised their glasses and repeated his words in unison. Sky and I followed suit but without the same excitement. It wasn't that I didn't agree with Sir Kent's sentiments; Summer did need more heirs, but it was horrible timing. The last thing I needed with unpredictable magic flowing through my veins was a castle full of people.

• • •

Later, Sky sat on her bed as I paced the room. The rest of dinner had passed amicably, with plans made for Darkenier's "burial" and an announcement scheduled for tomorrow morning, but I couldn't get my mind off Kent's proposal.

"Isan," Sky said finally, "would you please sit down? You're going to wear a hole through the floor. There's nothing we can do about it now."

I forced myself to stand still. "That's just it, though, isn't it? The traitor's dead, Summer is free, and yet the two of us still have no say over our future. Are you prepared to be wed before your seventeenth birthday and be with child soon after? Sancia knows I'm far from ready to be a father; I can barely manage myself."

Sky winced at my words. "Maybe we can postpone having children? I don't think any of my suitors would be cruel enough to force..." She grimaced. "Fidal's breath, you're right, Isan, but I don't know what to do. I'm honestly surprised I wasn't married off sooner."

"We probably would've been, if more Sancian heirs hadn't been the exact opposite of Darkenier's plans."

Sky took a deep breath. "We'll have to see how everything plays out. At least you have some decent options."

I gave her a skeptical look. "The one thing we don't have is options, Sky. I barely know any of them. When was the last time the Norwells came to call?"

"I'm not sure," she replied. "They didn't exactly get along with Uncle, but at least Kainda and Gywneth are a decent age. Weylyn is twelve. What am I supposed to do with him?"

"You keep track of how old they are?"

She frowned. "We're expected to. It's a part of our lessons, keeping all the noble families straight."

I ran a hand through my hair. "I think I'm going to need a review."

Sky sighed. "You know, someday I may not be around to be your brain." Before I could come up with a good retort, she rambled on. "There's Kainda, Gwyneth, and Weylyn from Ne-Trol; Penelope and Tamsen from Fortude; Soleia and Raina from Laurel; Jasper and Rosetta from Mensden; Dorin, Orella, Diera, Elena, and Euric from Cargoff, though Dorin is the only one who's of age; and, of course, Asmund and Aramina from Skar. Arran is off the table because he's already been appointed as Lord Arrath's heir."

My head spun at the influx of information. "And is there anyone we hate?

"Not entirely, but I don't particularly wish to spend the rest of my life with any of them either." She groaned. "I feel so *selfish* for saying that, but it's the truth. What's the point of being royal if we can't even choose our partners? I am thankful for the freedom this war brought us, but I also curse it. We were given a taste of what could be, and now... It's hard to turn back."

I returned to pacing the room, my thoughts racing as I searched for a way out, but it looked like we were sincerely out of options. We couldn't run away from this problem and deal with the consequences later. We couldn't refuse to host the Festival of Honour without bringing the wrath of the Council and the noble families down upon us. The only thing we could do was stall, and even that wouldn't last long.

"Fidal's breath, Sky," I breathed, running a hand through my hair yet again. "I don't think I can get us out of this one. I could... I could ask to prioritize my own engagement, buy you some more time..."

Sky stood up and walked over, taking my hands in hers and stopping my pacing once more. "I can't ask you to do that, Isan. It would be incredibly selfish, and I don't want you to have to go through it alone. Besides, the Council isn't going to invite everyone here twice, not when we're the same age, and especially not after everything the war cost us." She squeezed my hand and met my sad eyes with her own. "If there's no way out of this, we're in it together."

Anger welled up in me at the thought of being forced to accept our fate, but I pushed it down before it could take hold of me.

*That's the last thing I need right now.*

"I guess, if nothing else, the festivities should distract us from our war trauma," I said.

She laughed, letting go of my hands. "I suppose it might be a welcome change—a castle full of people, vibrant decorations, music..." She closed her eyes and began to hum a slow tune.

It took me a minute, but I recognized it as *Whispers of Wisteria*, and Echo's face flashed through my mind. I wondered how she was doing, if she worried about us, if she knew what had happened in Winter, that Prince Snowdon and King Frost were dead.

"Isan? Are you okay?"

I realized then that Sky had stopped humming, and I shook my head to clear it. "I'm fine," I replied, "just lots on my mind. I wish there was some way to send a message to Echo, to let her know we're all right. Going to see her will be out of the question for now."

Sky's face fell again. "Sancia's breath, I forgot about that. She's going to be beside herself."

I sighed. "Unfortunately, there's not much we can do about it. I'd send Asmund, but his presence is required at the Festival, and I'm not entirely certain Echo wouldn't kill him on sight if he showed up alone."

Sky smiled. "Unlike you, Echo isn't that rash."

"I'll let that insult slide," I replied, "but you better stay on your toes."

She huffed a breath and wandered back over to the bed where she flopped down, rather unceremoniously, onto the voluptuous sheets. "Well," she said, "if we're actually doing this, are there any of them you fancy?"

I gave her a look she didn't see. "You can't be serious."

"What? I'm trying to make some fun out of it."

"As if *you'd* answer that question truthfully."

"I might, if there was an answer to give. As I said, my options are limited. Tamsen and Dorin are nice enough, but they're younger than me, which I think would be a strange dynamic. Jasper is older, but he's from Mensden, and I don't want to marry into Lord Byron's family if I can help it; they're insufferable."

I snorted. "That's the understatement of the year. I guarantee you Rosetta will be all over me as soon as she gets here." I shuddered at the thought. The girl was beautiful, I could admit, but that was her only redeeming quality. I swear arrogance was bred into her body so thoroughly there was no room for brains or passion.

"I suppose there's always Asmund," Sky mused after a few moments of silence.

"Absolutely not," I replied, irritation seeping back into my veins.

Sky sat up, swinging her legs over the bed to face me. "Why? You two are friends now."

"More like tentative allies," I countered. "We've learned to tolerate each other, but that doesn't erase years of ridicule and every ugly word he ever said to you. Don't you remember what he was like?" I could feel my fire rising from the emotions my memories brought to the surface. If only I'd had magic back then; I would've put him in his place.

"Isan, calm down," Sky coaxed me. "You're shaking."

I looked down at my hands and was startled to see she was right. I clenched my fists and took a couple deep breaths to dispel the rage.

*That was a close one.*

"I'm only saying there will be people—half the Council at least—who will expect that of me," Sky said. "I know Uncle is gone now, but I'm not foolish enough to believe my betrothal is truly in our hands now."

My chest tightened at her words. "I'll do the best I can, Sky, to keep you safe."

"I know," she answered, looking at her feet. "I'm not getting my hopes up, though."

"What about Tamsen?" I asked her, trying to lighten the mood. "He's only one year younger, and you two were always thick as thieves when we were little. He'd make a good Prince Consort, with a little more combat training."

She gave me another look. "We were only so close because you and Penelope were, and if I marry him, that means Penelope isn't available for you."

"So?"

"So you've always fancied her, Isan. Now is your chance."

I shook my head as dread settled in the pit of my stomach.

She narrowed her eyes. "Why not? What didn't you tell me?"

"Nothing," I replied, turning away and walking over to the window.

"I know that look, Isan. Something happened."

I gripped the back of her desk chair as I said, "I, uh… kind of already took my chance, and she said no."

"What? When?"

"It was a few years ago, okay?" I replied without looking back at her. "I don't want to talk about it, and I'm not interested in asking her again. It was embarrassing enough the first time."

A long stretch of silence followed my words. I stared out the window as I remembered the day in question: the exhilaration on her face after the two of us had snuck out to the gardens unnoticed, my attempt to kiss her in what I'd thought was a perfect moment, and her ensuing tears as she'd explained she didn't feel that way about me. Her family had left the following day, and I hadn't seen her since, but the mistake still haunted me.

I felt a hand on my shoulder and turned to see Sky standing behind me. "I understand, Isan," she said. "There are certain memories I keep to myself too, but I'm always here for you, okay?"

"I know," I replied.

"We should get some sleep," she went on. "We have a long day ahead of us tomorrow. I'm not going to say it'll look better in the morning, but perhaps we will have some better ideas."

I shrugged, and her hand fell. "I suppose it's worth trying. To be honest, it feels a little weird to have a bed to sleep in again."

She laughed. "I'm looking forward to easing my bruised muscles and battered bones. I've felt like an old lady for months now."

"Well, as long as you don't look like one, you'll be fine."

"Ha ha, hilarious."

"All right," I said, finally walking away from the window. "I'll get out of your hair. Whether or not I'll actually sleep is another matter entirely."

A look of concern flashed across her face. "The nightmare hasn't come back, has it?"

I shook my head. "No, but there's still a lot on my mind. I feel like I haven't slept properly in months, probably not since we left Echo's treehouse."

She sighed. "I wish there was something I could do, but..."

"It's okay, Sky. I'm strong enough to handle it, and besides, it might be better now that we're home."

"I hope so," she replied, fiddling with the end of her braid. "Let me know if you need me."

"I will. Goodnight."

"Goodnight. May Sancia be with you, and Wylla too, I suppose, for sleep."

I frowned at that as I left the room.

Throughout all my sleepless nights from that Fidal-forsaken nightmare, I'd never once reached out to Wylla to ask for a peaceful sleep. Though Echo had helped to ease my distrust of Winter, Darkenier had thrown my walls back up, and the thought of turning to Wylla to solve my problems felt like a betrayal, a slap in the face of everything Summer had suffered at the hands of the Winter royals.

No, I would suffer in silence, and if anything, I would pray to Stella for healing and Fidal for strength.

# 3
# A Fragile Trust

**Widonia was a blur** all around me as I sprinted down the streets as if being chased by a soulless monster, but there was no one behind me. The only threat was myself.

The sun was beginning to set, and the sight of its fiery orange tendrils spreading through the sky quickened the beat of my already racing heart, reminding me what was running through my veins and begging to be released.

Children were playing on the side of the road and stopped to watch as I ran by.

I wanted to scream at them to run, to go for help, but I didn't have the breath to spare. I had to get as far away from the city as I could before...

Before it...

The fire rose up, scorching my skin even as it still lurked beneath the surface.

I clenched my teeth against the pain.

A little further, *I urged myself.* You can't give in here, not around all these people.

What if they see you?

What if they die?

*I had to get out of Widonia, or I would burn it to the ground. I could feel it, the power scorching in my blood, and it would not be easily quenched. It was terrifying.*

*My brain was racing, but my legs were starting to fade, screaming at me to slow down, to rest.*

No, keep going, keep going.

*My blood boiled, and the fire roared within me.*

Not now. Not yet. It's not safe.

*But it was coming, and I knew I couldn't stop it.*

*I lurched to a stop as my legs gave out, and I collapsed to my knees in the middle of the street, defeated. A part of me knew I couldn't stay there, but the fire was stronger, the magic invincible.*

*My hands ignited in the space of a breath, and the fire raced up my arms, ate away at my shoulders—*

*In a blast of light and heat, I exploded into a pillar of flame, sending fire in every direction. Every inch of my skin burned, from my toes to the tips of my hair. I caught sight of my reflection in a shop window across the street and was horrified. I looked like a harbinger of death, and my eyes... Their blue had been replaced with red tongues of fire.*

*I screamed, but I couldn't move a muscle, couldn't suppress my magic, even as the whole street went up in flames and the city burnt to ash.*

• • •

I woke up screaming and thrashed around in my bed for a few minutes before I realized it was over.

*You're awake, I told myself as I took gulping breaths to calm myself down. It was only a nightmare.*

And yet, I knew firsthand that nightmares weren't always mere figments of my imagination, and this one gave off the same aura as the last one that had plagued me. It had felt real—the fear, the urgency to flee the city—and I was still burning up. My sheets were clinging to my skin like my cloak after a heavy storm, slick with my sweat instead of rain.

I peeled them off me and jumped out of bed, the cold rush of the floor beneath my feet grounding me in reality. Still, I couldn't help glancing over at the mirror and letting out a sigh of relief when I saw my normal blue eyes staring back at me.

I wasn't in danger yet, but I knew that nightmare was an omen of what could come to pass if I didn't learn to control the magic burning inside me. The last thing Widonia needed after the war and the betrayal of its King was for its Prince to burn it to the ground. I needed training, but there was no one left in the city or kingdom to teach me—not anyone who would admit their connection to magic, anyway.

Darkenier had banned magic to eliminate all threats, but I wondered if he had ever stopped to consider the repercussions, people like me who would have no one to turn to and few able to stop them if necessary.

Not for the first time since we left Appalachia, I was left wondering what in Fidal's name I was supposed to do, and the hardest part was that my magic was somehow the worst and least of my problems all at once.

A knock sounded on my door then, dragging me from my thoughts, and I groaned. I didn't want company. "Go away, Sky," I called out.

"Don't worry, child," Aunt Mag's voice answered. "It's not Skiansy coming to torment you. May I come in?"

I straightened up, surprised. It had been a while since Aunt Mag had sought me out in my rooms. She tended to focus on Sky more as I rarely needed help doing my hair or choosing which outfit to wear.

"Of course, Aunt Mag," I replied, after taking a quick glance around the room to make sure it was presentable.

The door swung open a moment later, and she swept in with a blur of green.

"Good morning," I said, turning away from the mirror. I tried not to glance at the bed, hoping she wouldn't notice the wet covers and ask me what was wrong.

She smiled, the action lighting up her whole face. "Good morning, child."

"To what do I owe the pleasure?" I asked. My brows furrowed. "Is something wrong?"

"Oh no," she replied, waving her hands. "No, not at all. I… Well, I thought you might need a new outfit for today's announcement."

I groaned again. *Right, the announcement.*

I'd forgotten about it, though I wasn't surprised. My memory was short of late, my mental space taken up by so much stress I feared my skull would burst at the seams.

"Are you sure I have to go?" I asked her.

"You must," she replied with a stern look. "It is essential that the people know the truth before rumours are allowed to spread, and you must be the one to tell them. They will look to you for guidance now, Isanfier; you must steady them in this turbulent time."

I sighed. *No pressure or anything.*

"I know, Aunt Mag, but it's not easy."

She gave me a small smile. "I didn't say it was, but that's the thing about leadership; if it's easy, you're heading in the wrong direction."

"I suppose."

"Oh, I don't suppose, child. I know for certain. I practically grew up in this palace; I've seen more than one monarch come and go. I've learned much over the years, and it is my duty to pass that knowledge down to you."

"I trust you," I told her and then decided to change the subject before she could pry further into my troubles. "What was that you said about a new outfit?"

"Why don't you try it on?" She handed me a parcel wrapped in brown paper, and I did as she said. It was a perfect fit, but then again, Aunt Mag was seldom wrong when it came to me and Sky.

She clasped her hands when she finished with my buttons, unable to keep from helping even in her old age. "You look handsome." She steered me toward the mirror, and I took my first proper look at myself.

*Handsome?*

"I look ridiculous," I said. Green was as foreign on me as I imagined cropped hair would look on Asmund, and the gold buttons and epaulettes made the whole ensemble garish. The black pants I could stomach, though they, too, were adorned with gold stitching and buttons. My pale skin wasn't meant for the colours of my kingdom, never had been and never would.

"Nonsense," Aunt Mag retorted, cuffing me lightly on the arm. "You look dashing. Any young lady would say the same and more."

I met her steady green eyes in the mirror as my shoulders drooped. "What do you see in me that I can't?"

"I see a Summer Prince, a warrior, a leader." She paused. "Isanfier, I know you don't fancy it, but it is vital you wear our colours when speaking of King Arkenier's death." I flinched at the name, though she didn't notice. "There will be those who don't believe your account—there are some in every crowd—and you will only add more coals to their rebellious fire if you wear Winter black."

I cringed. Why did everything always come back to fire when it was the one thing I was trying to forget?

"For once, my child, I ask you to trust me," Aunt Mag finished.

I turned to look at her. "I always trust you," I replied. "I'll try to make it work. Thank you for thinking of me."

She smiled, squeezing my shoulder. "You're welcome, child. I will see you out there. Good luck, and may Sancia be with you."

•  •  •

The ride to the town square was a quiet affair with both Sir Kent and Asmund accompanying Sky and me in the Royal Carriage. Kent had insisted we travel together for safety, though he had raised an eyebrow at my request for Asmund to join us. I still wasn't sure what I made of our relationship. Did I invite him because I feared what he would do if left to his own devices, or because I had grown used to his presence, because I actually wanted him there?

Sky, to her credit, had said nothing, but I knew she was remembering our conversation last night where I had quashed the idea of her choosing Asmund as her future husband. I just couldn't wrap my head around it, couldn't reconcile the years of hatred and mistrust to the tentative alliance we now held.

I couldn't shake the feeling I was being played for a fool.

I braced myself for the task ahead as the carriage wheeled to a halt and my company got to their feet. This would be much different than the last gathering. I would be delivering terrible news, and like Aunt Mag had said, not everyone would receive it well.

Sky reached out and squeezed my hand as Asmund and Kent walked out ahead of us, presumably to scout for any dangers. "You can do this, Isan," she said, "and I'll be by your side throughout."

"I know," I replied. "I just... I've never spoken in front of a crowd before, much less with the intent to tell them I killed the

King." I winced. "What if they riot? What if I get an arrow in the chest?"

Her eyes narrowed. "Then they better hope they can run faster than *my* arrow, because I won't rest until they pay. But no one is going to let anything happen to us, Isan. We are the future of this kingdom, and I would hope the people would at least give you a chance to prove yourself before condemning you."

I sighed. "I would hope so too, but after everything we've been through, I'm inclined to be skeptical."

"Whatever happens, we'll get through it."

"Your Highness," Sir Kent's voice called out from outside. "The herald is ready for you."

I took a deep breath. *Sancia save me.*

I opened the door of the carriage and stepped into the shade of the pavilion to the watchful gaze of over a hundred eyes crowding the square and open windows along the street edges.

Nerves danced along my skin and made my stomach jump, but I did my best to ignore them, walking to the edge of the pavilion as the herald announced my arrival for all to hear. Sky and Asmund followed suit behind me, and I realized it was the first time in my life Sky and I had not been announced together, as a pair.

Our lives were already changing in Darkenier's absence, and my heart clenched at the yawning stretch of responsibility opening in front of me. In less than two years, I would be King, and Skiansy would be cast in my shadow, a spare should something ever happen to me but never a choice.

The thought boiled my blood, but I shut it down before the fire could latch on to my anger and use it to stoke its flames.

I took another deep breath and faced my people. "I want to begin by thanking you all for coming," I started. "We have gathered here today to discuss the events and consequences of the recent war on Winter and what the future looks like for both Widonia and Summer as a whole. The first thing I must announce is that King Arkenier is no longer of this realm."

I paused as cries of outrage and despair swept through the square. People threw their fists in the air, screamed hateful words in the name of Winter, and bemoaned our horrible luck. I let each emotion run its course and then held up a hand for silence.

"I know you are saddened at this news. I know you are angry, but vengeance is not the answer. We will not be marching back into Winter for his sake. King Arkenier died a traitor on my own blade, after he confessed to the murders of our late King Oaden and Queen Areevia and threatened to kill me."

I could've used a blade to cut it, so heavy was the sudden silence in the square.

"I understand the truth is hard to swallow. It can be easy to live in the past, in the reality you once knew, but it is my job now, as Crown Prince of this kingdom, to make the hard decisions, and though I do not carry the burden of my uncle's death lightly, I know it had to be done.

"He was not the King we thought he was," I went on after a pause. "Maybe he started out with good intentions, but he became power hungry. He wanted the throne for himself and only him, and he had every intention of cutting down whoever stood in his way. I would've fallen victim to his hate too, if Master Asmund hadn't been there." I nodded to Asmund standing behind me. "It was with his aid that I was able to bring an end to the threat and closure to a war Arkenier had started to further his own means.

"We have no quarrel with Winter at this time as for once, we are the ones who have wronged them. I will not pretend we are free from them forever, as their King and Prince were killed in our blind tirade through Appalachia. Winter may yet seek retribution for what they lost, and so we must be vigilant. We must strengthen our kingdom while we wait to see what will come of our late King's actions."

I looked back at Sir Kent and motioned him to come forward. "And so it is with great honour that I introduce to you, Sir Kent, as the new Regent of Summer."

There was a pause as the people absorbed my words, but then a few cheers erupted in the silence along with subdued applause. I was pleased to see there was some reservation in their reaction, that they weren't welcoming their temporary protector with completely open arms. Sir Kent would have to earn their trust, the same as I would, the same as any monarch should. Widonia had learned its lesson, and I hoped it would never make the mistake again.

Sir Kent took a few steps in front of me and waved to the people. "Thank you, thank you," he called out. "It is a great honour to take up this position, and I only hope I can do it justice and give all of you the support you need after the turbulent times we have been through.

"As Regent, I would like to make a few announcements before we part ways today. As His Highness said, the threat from Winter still lingers, and because of that, it is our wish to continue training the untried men of Widonia, so that we may be able to protect the innocent of this city in the case of an attack. Typically, our young would-be soldiers would be sent to Skar to train under the watchful eye of Lord Arrath, but in light of the recent war, the Council has decided to keep them here, in the city. They will train at the barracks under Sir Saxon, who built his skills in Skar when he was a young lad."

There were many murmurs through the crowd at this request, but I could tell we had made the right choice to train the men here. I could sense only the slightest amount of anger in the air, mixed in with trepidation and purpose.

Asmund's offer to train the boys himself had ultimately been overturned with the introduction of the Festival of Honour, as he wouldn't have the time to spare.

"The second announcement I would like to make," Sir Kent continued, "is that I have appointed Sir Quinton to be my substitute as Captain of the Royal Guard, until my time as Regent has come to its end. Many of you know Sir Quinton already, but for those of you who do not, he should be waving to you now."

The crowd followed his gaze to see Sir Quinton waving to them from atop his horse to the west of the pavilion, surveying the crowd for any suspicious activity during the announcement.

I had my trepidations when Sir Kent told me his choice the previous night, but Quinton did seem to be taking his job of ensuring our safety seriously.

"Our final announcement today," Sir Kent said, "is that Widonia will be hosting a Festival of Honour for the first time in decades. We will be welcoming the young nobles of Widonia's sister cities to the castle to secure the future of this kingdom in matrimony with our young Prince and Princess. In a few short months, we will be able to put the darkness of the past behind us and celebrate a new chapter of our lives as we host not one but two royal weddings and welcome our future Queen to Widonia."

Another cheer rose up in the crowd, but all I could feel was the nausea building in my stomach, threatening to spill over. It was an unhealthy mixture of disgust, fear, and anger. There would be no backing out now that the whole city knew about it, and I was sure that was Sir Kent's plan. I knew the old man cared for Sky and me in some way. I was sure a part of him would sympathize with our plight, but like I'd said, it was up to leaders to make the hard decisions.

Still, I didn't have to be happy about it.

Sir Kent explained a few more issues to the crowd and then motioned for me to take centre stage again, likely to close the gathering and bid everyone farewell. I plastered a smile on my face and did as he wanted.

"Thank you all for joining us here today and listening to our words," I called out. "We will need to work together to bring Summer back to its former glory, but I have no doubt in my mind it can be done. May Sancia watch over us and Fidal lend us strength in the following days. Fidalia forever."

The square echoed my prayer, and I gave a short bow before turning back to the carriage.

Sky's hand found my shoulder before I stepped inside. "You did well, Isan."

I nodded. "We can only hope they trust me, that my words are enough to quell any distaste."

"I'm sure your actions will speak louder than any words. Show them they can trust you, and all will be forgiven."

She was right, as usual, but unfortunately, it would be easier said than done. I had to be given the opportunity to show them before they made their decision, and with the Festival of Honour poised to take up most of my time for the next few months, I wasn't sure I would get the chance Summer and I desperately needed.

# 4
# Threat and Throne

**The sun was past** its zenith as Sky and I circled each other in the courtyard. Our swords were up, our eyes tracing each other's every move, searching for an opening. We had improved immensely during the course of the war, and I knew this wouldn't be like our previous duels.

It had been a week since the gathering in the town square, and our time had been filled with meetings, lessons in Festival traditions, and endless tailor appointments. Sky said she'd been fitted for over two dozen dresses and didn't know where she was going to put them amongst the hundred or so she already owned.

I knew if one more tailor accidentally poked me in the arm with their pin, they would be met with a blaze of fire I would be hard-pressed to stop.

The only thing left to do was wait for our suitors to arrive. Lord Byron's children would be here within the next day or so, their city being the closest to Widonia, and the Norwells were at least another week out with their trek halfway across the kingdom.

Sky and I had managed to escape this afternoon between to-do list items for a much-needed reprieve, and the feel of my sword hilt in my hand again eased my nerves, if only a little.

I'd been suffering from the same nightmare again, and the constant fear of my magic was a heavy weight on my shoulders, but so far, none of my fears had been realized, and I thanked Fidal every day for that.

I lunged at Sky, ending our stalemate, but she blocked and swung at me. I ducked and danced back, recognizing her feint as she changed direction.

"You thought I'd fall for that?" I laughed.

"It was worth a try."

I reached for her, hoping to find her distracted, and she dodged.

"And did *you* think I'd fall for *that*?"

I shrugged and doubled my efforts.

The clang of metal soon became the courtyard's symphony, and we danced to the music, our feet moving faster and faster, our swords drawing brilliant patterns through the air. My soul hadn't felt so alive in days, and I could tell Sky felt the same, a smile lighting up her face and mischief dancing in her eyes.

The impending doom of the Festival was starting to get to her, and it angered me to no end that I didn't know how to ease her pain.

Finally, I began to wear her down, my swings becoming sharper as hers declined in strength. Our swords locked, and we strained, her grip slipping until I threw her sword aside, and then...

She tripped me.

I thudded to the ground, my sword flying out of my hand and the breath forcing from my lungs in a whoosh. I lay there stunned for a moment before I was able to suck in a ragged breath.

"Nice trick," I gasped.

Sky stood over me, sword resting against my sternum. "I thought it was pretty clever," she said, grinning.

A slow clap started somewhere behind us, and we looked over to find Sir Quinton standing in the archway to the courtyard.

"Bravo, Your Highness," he said to Sky as he approached. "I didn't know the Prince could be bested."

Sky held out her hand, and I took it. She hoisted me to my feet before answering.

"Sir Quinton," she said, nodding. "It's the great secret of our family that Isan is not invincible. I show him his place when I can." She grinned again and I swatted at her, but she danced away, laughing.

"Charming," Sir Quinton replied, though I sensed disapproval in his gaze.

I narrowed my eyes. "To what do we owe the pleasure, Sir Quinton?"

"I was actually looking for you, Your Highness," he said to me. "I hoped we could have a word."

His tone of voice sent unease through me. He had been sour since Sir Kent was chosen as Regent, always questioning my input in meetings, doing everything he could to remind me I wasn't yet King.

Still, I forced a smile and said, "Of course."

"Shall we?" He gestured to the hall, and I realized that whatever he wanted to say, he didn't want Sky to hear it.

I admired his effort, but it was misguided. I didn't keep secrets from Sky—at least, not when the secret concerned her. Whatever he said, Sky would definitely hear about it.

I picked my sword up from where it had fallen and sheathed it before turning to Sky. "I'll see you at dinner, then." She nodded, and I followed Quinton back into the castle.

We walked down the hall side by side, though I had to work hard to keep up with his long stride, which probably brought him great joy.

"Your sister is quite the warrior," he said.

"She is," I replied. "Do you have an issue with that?"

"I respect her commitment to this kingdom, but there are other ways she can show that. She needn't throw herself into the gruesome fray of battle. War, as I'm sure you've learned, is a perilous endeavour."

I gave him a look. "Is this a bid for her safety, Sir Quinton, or are you questioning her place on the battlefield?"

He held up a hand. "I would never question, but it's our duty to ensure the strength of our army and—"

"It is also Sky's *right* to fight for what she believes in," I countered. "I would never keep her from doing what she sees fit, and as far as the strength of our army goes, Skiansy is anything but fragile. You may not have witnessed her prowess with a bow firsthand, but I have. She struck not only arrows but fear into the hearts of the men she faced."

"I am aware of her apparent skills, Your Highness," Quinton assured me, "but your sister has other responsibilities now, and it's high time she started focusing on them, instead of pretending to be a man."

I bristled at the insult, fire sizzling in my veins, but I took a deep breath to quell it before speaking. "You are treading on dangerous ground, Sir Quinton. I would suggest you choose your next words carefully."

"I do not wish to cause you discomfort, Your Highness. Sir Kent was too weak to have this conversation with you, but it needs to be said. Your sister is to be married soon. It will be her duty then to have and raise children. She will not be respected by her husband-to-be if she is intent on running off to the battlefield, or if she is seen in this courtyard dueling with our future King. And the noble families will certainly not respect *you* if they see her defeating you."

I narrowed my eyes. "What are you insinuating?"

"Oh, I'm *insinuating* nothing. You know exactly what I'm talking about. If you want to protect your sister, you'll put a stop to this training. You'll remind her she is a lady, and she'll soon have a husband to protect her instead."

I swallowed the lump in my throat as my anger dissipated. "I will talk with her, Sir Quinton, but I can't make any promises. I will not force her into anything."

He shrugged. "That is your choice, I suppose. We can only pray that her future husband will be so understanding."

I shuddered at the thought, a dozen gruesome scenarios running through my head, and I vowed to protect Sky at all costs, even if I had to kill every single one of her suitors to spare her the pain of an ugly marriage.

"Consider my words, Your Highness," Sir Quinton continued. "The first of our guests are set to arrive tomorrow, and I would hate for everyone to get off on the wrong foot."

"Thank you for your advice," I replied, though I was anything but grateful for his words. "I shall see you at the Welcoming."

"Indeed you shall. Good day, Your Highness."

He walked away in a swirl of green robes, and I clenched my fist against the fire building in my veins. I doubted he had run this conversation by Sir Kent before seeking me out, but I couldn't doubt the truth in his words.

The worst that could happen to me was being tied to an annoying wife for the rest of my days. Sky stood to lose so much more, not the least of which was her freedom. I still didn't know what I could do, but I was resolved to do my best.

No one would bring harm to Sky on my watch, and if they did, my wrath would know no bounds. I would burn this city to the ground in retribution.

• • •

The next day dawned with thick clouds blocking out the sun, which set my mood somewhere inside the bounds of grey misery. I dressed without much thought to the action and was finished before I realized I hadn't picked any of the new outfits that had been made for me. Aunt Mag had brought me the first three last night, saying the rest would arrive within the week.

I let out a large sigh as I studied myself, clad in the black attire everyone frowned upon, in the mirror.

*You'll be King soon enough*, I reminded myself, *and then you'll be able to wear whatever you want without question.*

The thought formed a heavy knot in my stomach. I tried my best to ignore the feeling as I set about getting changed. I kept my boots and pants but switched the plain black tunic and cloak for a green tunic with gold trim and the cape Aunt Mag had set out for me. A stylized gold Summer sun was expertly stitched into the back of it, set amongst the silky green.

The cape was weightless, and I felt rather exposed with it around my shoulders instead of my heavy cloak. Still, I guessed it wouldn't hurt to give myself a little break. Sancia only knew how heavy my crown was to bear on its own.

I eyed the gold circlet, sitting atop my dusty dresser yet again, and grimaced as I considered how much use it was going to get during this Festival. Maybe my first decree as King would be to eliminate the use of the forsaken things, or at least commission a more comfortable one.

I dragged my feet over to the dresser and set the crown atop my head, the metal instantly digging into my temples. Darkenier used to insist the edges would wear smooth if I wore it long enough, but I'd never believed him, and I certainly wouldn't be heeding his advice now.

With another reluctant sigh, I faced myself in the mirror and, like the other night, saw a complete stranger looking back. The only familiar aspect was the reassuring presence of *Ember* at my hip, but that wasn't enough to convince me. I didn't look like that. Maybe it's what a Prince of Summer should've looked like. Maybe this was what everyone so desperately wanted to see, but my blue eyes shone out like beacons, and my pale skin could not be hidden behind greenery and Summer symbols.

I was still myself—a once-sick child and colossal disappointment to the monarchs who came before me.

Heavy footsteps interrupted my thoughts, and I turned to see Asmund enter the room. He was dressed in his best as well, minus a cape and crown. His braided hair shone like he'd polished it, and a spark of envy shot through me as I studied him.

"Why do both you and Sky insist on making me look like I'm playing dress-up?" I sighed.

He raised a dark eyebrow. "Maybe because you are?" I scowled and he held up a hand, a hint of alarm reaching his eyes. "I didn't mean it like that. You're not an imposter, but you don't usually try to look the part of a Prince, so it's bound to be...jarring. I'm only this put-together because my father doesn't accept anything short of my best, ever."

"Even back in Skar?"

He nodded. "I mean, you did see Arran when he was here, right?"

"Well, yes, but I just thought he'd been taking his studies more seriously."

"That was part of it, but honestly, I'm glad to be away from the harshness of my father's gaze. It's exhausting. I can only imagine the pressure you're under."

I narrowed my eyes. "Are you being...sympathetic?"

He gave me a look. "I am capable of it, yes, if that's what you're asking."

"Sure took you long enough to showcase the skill," I replied with a snort. "Why are you here?"

"I told you, I'm avoiding my father, and I—"

I held up a hand. "No, no, I mean right now. Why are you in my room?"

"Oh, Sir Kent said it would be prudent for us to arrive at the throne room together. He says I'm to be considered your bodyguard. He wanted to send a pair of knights, but I said you wouldn't like that. I know you don't want a lot of people around right now, given your...condition."

My face softened. "You're right about that, but it's not like I have much of a choice, do I?" I was grateful for his intervention on my behalf, but I wasn't ready to completely let my guard down with him. If I said thank you, if I acknowledged it, he might claim I owed him a debt.

"Have you thought about who you might choose?"

I shook my head, automatically moving to run my hand through my hair as I answered before I remembered my crown. I clenched my fists at my sides instead. "I always had this ridiculous notion that this was still years ahead of me. It's not that I don't want a wife. I'd like a family some day, a legacy to pass on, but that's just it. I want it *someday*, not right now. I don't want to be a father within a year. What in Fidal's name am I going to do with a baby? I've barely figured out my own path."

He grimaced at my words. "It's not easy being royalty; you don't often get what you want."

I sighed. "I'm starting to realize that. Maybe it would've been better if I'd died and Darkenier had appointed someone else as his heir."

"All right," Asmund said, "that's enough of the pity party. I'm sure one of the lovely ladies will catch your eye, and *maybe* you'll loosen up and have a little fun. You might be able to hold off on having children, at least until you're officially King."

"Maybe," I allowed.

And maybe I would also learn how to fly.

I walked around Asmund to the door then, not risking another glance at my awful reflection. "Let's get this Welcoming party over with. Who is escorting Sky, do you know?"

He fell into step beside me as I shut my bedroom door and strode down the hall.

"I believe Governess Magnolia volunteered."

I nodded, glad Sky would be in good hands, someone to keep her safe and to quell the nerves.

We spoke little the rest of the way to the throne room, and I almost missed the right hall in my mental musings—that, and the fact that I hadn't set foot in the place since before I could remember. The last time had been for Darkenier's coronation, and I had only been four years old.

Asmund led me through a side chamber into the space, and my eyes took it all in before settling on Sky and Aunt Mag lingering by the far wall. After seeing Frost's domain in Appalachia, our throne room was vastly underwhelming.

The room was large, with a tall ceiling ending in a turret, but it was still dwarfed by the Winter version. A few gold stained-glass windows let in sunlight behind the throne, and there were rows of benches filling the room opposite it, on either side of a stone pathway carved with intricate swirls. The path was the most eye-catching detail present, but my heart ached looking at it. It reminded me of the door leading to my parents' room, and the last thing I needed to feel right then was pain.

Despite its lacklustre wooden appearance, the throne demanded my attention, if only because I knew it now belonged to me. How many monarchs had sat in it over the years? How was I supposed to make them proud when I had inherited a broken kingdom, when I had let treachery into my family and failed to protect my people until it was almost too late?

My stomach convulsed, but Sky's eyes met mine across the room, and she sent me a reassuring smile that calmed my nerves, though only slightly.

She and Aunt Mag crossed the room to join us, and I tried not to gape at Sky's massive green dress. Gown? It billowed around her like a huge bell with layers of mesh and silk, and beaded needlework formed a Summer sun around the skirt, as if Sky was standing in the middle of it.

It was a work of art, but it wasn't her any more than my outfit was me.

"Why, don't you look like a handsome young man," Aunt Mag exclaimed. "You could be a King." She winked at me, and I laughed.

"Clever," I replied before turning to Sky. "Can you breathe in that thing?"

She shrugged. "It's surprisingly loose, but this skirt *is* rather heavy, and I'm afraid I'm going to trip over something and ruin it."

Aunt Mag touched her hand. "Oh, hush, child. It'll be fine. You only need to sit and stand, go through the formalities, and then you can retire for the day. The Byrons won't expect to see either of you outside of dinner until all the suitors have arrived."

Sky sighed. "I know, but I can't shake the anxiety. What if… What if we screw it all up and become the laughing stock of the kingdom? What if none of them even *want* to wed me?"

I frowned, and Asmund snorted behind me before saying, "I think that will be the least of your worries, Sky. Boys are simple creatures. Fancy clothes and proper manners are more than enough for some, but we all know there's more to you than that."

Sky looked at Asmund like he'd grown a second head, and so did I. Even Aunt Mag seemed shocked. I think it was the nicest thing he'd ever said to her, and he had called her Sky too, in front of Aunt Mag. Now she would be asking me prying questions until I divulged everything we'd been through.

Luckily, the awkward moment was cut short as the door swung open and Sir Kent swept into the room. "The Byrons have arrived, Your Highnesses," he called out. "Please take your places."

Two smaller thrones sat on either side of the main throne, the one on the left reserved for the Queen and the smallest one on the right reserved for the heir to the throne. I took my mother's vacant seat as Sky took mine. Under normal circumstances, Sky wouldn't have a seat. She would stand beside my mother, and if we had had younger brothers, they would stand beside me. As it was, the Festival was for both of us, and I would not have her start off being looked down upon.

Still, the wood against my back felt strange, the chair too big, as if meant to swallow me whole. It was a sensation I didn't think I'd ever get used to, but I took a deep breath, straightened my crown, and prepared myself to act like I had.

Asmund and Sir Kent came to stand at my side as Sir Kent signaled for our guests to join us. Trumpets blared a moment later, and the arched wooden doors opened to allow in a line of knights with Summer flags who marched down the aisle and fanned out to stand guard on either side, Sir Quinton in the lead.

Our earlier conversation flashed in my mind, but I tamped down the annoyance before it could distract me. I didn't want to show my magic to any of the noble families, but if I'd been forced to pick one, the Byrons would've been at the bottom of my list.

The room held its breath as we waited for our guests to present themselves, but then the herald's voice cut through the silence and broke the spell. "Presenting Master Jasper and Mistress Rosetta of Mensden."

The trumpets flared again, setting my teeth on edge, and Sky and I stood as Lord Byron's children waltzed into the room like they owned the place.

# 5
# Flames of Fear

**Rosetta was wearing a** green dress that nearly rivaled Sky's, save for the absence of gold details, as it was highly frowned upon for anyone but the royal family to wear Summer gold. Her dark brown hair was piled high above her head in a braided bun, and a deep green emerald sat in the hollow of her throat on a silver chain, accentuating her exposed collarbones. Any man would be delighted to have her as a wife… until the first time they heard her speak.

Jasper, on the other hand, was the picture of his father, albeit three decades younger. He wore a crisp military suit complete with a metal pauldron and breast plate, which, while impressive, seemed out of place. A long sword hung at his belt, its tip nearly brushing the floor at his boots. I wondered if he had to walk at a slight angle to avoid being knocked off balance. His braided hair was impeccable, but not nearly as impressive as Asmund's.

I cut a glance at Sky as they approached through the ranks of knights. Her expression was neutral, but I bet she was about as impressed as I was. She and Rosetta had little in common and never developed any sort of friendship over the years. Jasper, on the other hand, was three years our senior and probably one of the most boring people I'd ever met.

"Your Highnesses," they said in unison as they dropped to a bow and curtsy while we took our seats again.

"We are honoured to have been called to Widonia for such a momentous occasion," Jasper went on. "We hope to be worthy of your affections."

Rosetta beamed up at me, but my eyes were on Jasper as he gave Sky a look that made my skin crawl. My hand moved to my sword before I caught myself.

*Easy. Now is not the time.*

"We are pleased you could join us," I replied, reciting the words I'd been taught as I fought to keep my voice light. "The future of this kingdom will be decided in the coming weeks, and we look forward to seeing your strengths while also allowing you to work on your weaknesses. May both Sancia and Fidal be with you in your quests, and may Audria guide your hearts."

"We would be delighted if you would join us for dinner tonight so we can discuss the upcoming festivities," Sky added.

"Again, we would be honoured," Jasper replied, his eyes never leaving Sky. "I have fond memories of dinner here and don't doubt I'll be impressed once more."

Rosetta nodded. "We look forward to it, Your Highnesses."

She was playing nice for our current audience, and it irked me to no end, but for once, she was the tamer of the two. Jasper's voice was grating on my eardrums, attempting to spark the fire beneath my skin.

Sir Kent stepped forward before an awkward silence could ensue and gave the two instructions about who would show them to their rooms, when they would be expected for dinner, and who would brief them on the schedules for the upcoming days.

They both thanked him, and then Sky and I stood once more as they approached the thrones to give the customary farewells.

Jasper reached me first, giving another low bow and saying, "Always a pleasure, Your Highness." Then he moved on to Sky, and Rosetta held out her hand to me.

I took it gently and kissed the back, watching Jasper out of the corner of my eye as he did the same with Sky. His eyes didn't break her gaze as he kissed her hand, and it might have been my imagination, but it looked like he was crushing her fingers.

I might've been able to swallow my anger if I hadn't made the mistake of looking at Sky to see her reaction. To anyone else, she was the picture of calm, but I could see the discomfort written in her eyes and posture, and my resolve withered.

My magic rushed to the surface, and though it was rude of me, I dropped Rosetta's hand, afraid she would feel the heat. It wasn't the first time since Uncle's death that my anger had riled my magic, but I could tell this time was different. I had only minutes to get away.

Schooling my expression into neutrality despite the anger and heat writhing within, I nodded to Rosetta and said, "I look forward to seeing you tonight, but forgive me, I've been suffering from the most terrible headache this morning and must retire."

She looked at me with concern. "I pray for a swift recovery, Your Highness. Please, go rest."

Without further words or ceremony, I fled the throne room, keeping an even pace until the door was shut behind me and then making a mad dash for my chambers, taking every shortcut I knew of and a route that would avoid as many people as possible.

All the while, the look in Jasper's eyes kept flashing through my mind.

I felt the fire's energy running through my nerves like a lightning strike, fast and powerful with the promise to consume. The heat raced through my veins, and I ran like I never had before, reaching my room with seconds to spare.

I grabbed the door handle with my white-hot hands and wrenched it open, leaving a burn mark on the metal. Then I slammed it behind me, collapsing in a heap on the floor as the fire ignited.

Flames engulfed my hands in a blaze of orange and yellow, a colour so bright and rich it hurt to look at for a minute. I supposed it would've been natural for me to react emotionally to such a sight, but I felt calm in that moment, more at peace than I had in months. I sat there in the middle of my carpet and merely watched the flames licking at my skin, marvelling at how I had burned my metal doorknob with my hands, but now, as the fire raged, I couldn't feel the heat.

Magic was certainly a strange thing.

I had planned to wait for it to burn out—that's what I'd done with Darkenier—but then the fire began to spread up my arms. It was slow at first, so much so that I thought I was imagining it climbing up my wrist, but as it reached a third of the way up my forearm, there was no denying it any longer.

The fire was growing, and I didn't know how to stop it.

Panic set in, my heart starting to race and my breaths getting heavier as my mind spun with a host of terrible consequences.

*What if I explode like in my new dream? What if I set the whole room on fire—the whole castle, even? Everyone is going to find out my secret, and then I'm a dead man, Prince or no Prince. Where will I go if I'm exiled? Will they even let me live?*

The panic built alongside my fire, and before I knew it, the flames were at my elbows with no sign of stopping anytime soon.

*Oh Sancia, help me. Please somebody help me,* I pleaded in my head.

And then, like both a blessing and a curse, someone knocked on my door.

I debated ignoring it, but then I remembered I'd told Rosetta I was retiring, and anyone present at that time would know I was now in my room, even if they didn't know I was lying about the reason.

"Who is it?" I called out, fighting to keep my voice calm.

"It's Asmund," my visitor replied. "Is everything okay?"

I didn't answer for a minute, debating what I would say even as the flames grew, but then I realized I couldn't do this alone, even if it meant asking Asmund for help. He already knew about my curse anyway. The worst that could happen was him getting hurt, and if I was being honest, there was still a part of him that might deserve that.

"No, I'm—" I started, then half gasped as the flames reached my biceps. "Just get in here, and lock the door behind you."

I looked up as he came in and saw a trace of concern in his eyes, though it was soon masked by a serious expression as he locked the door and faced me, arms crossed.

"I told you this would happen."

I scowled. "Oh, that's really helpful right now, Asmund. Thank you so much for your insightful magic-ridding strategy."

He rolled his eyes. "You know, I could easily stand here in silence and let you suffer."

"That would be nothing new, then, would it? But you obviously came up here for a reason, so..."

He sighed. "I had a feeling you didn't have a headache. I saw the way you were looking at Jasper, the way he was…looking at Sky. I didn't care for it either. Sky looked concerned when you left, but I figured you wouldn't want her following you in your state, so here I am."

I snorted but bit back my retort for a later time. I was still on fire. "What should I do?"

"Have you tried reaching within for the source and shutting it down?"

The first night on our trek home from Winter, Asmund had told me everything his mother had taught him about magic. Her lessons had been only theory, not practice, as Asmund was too young to exhibit any magic himself, and likely never would. Magic was hereditary, but not guaranteed. Of course, the meagre lessons had stopped when he was eight years old and my parents' death brought about the ban on magic, so he didn't know much. Still, she had apparently always talked about magic as if it was a place in her head or chest.

I shook my head at his words. "I've been trying that for weeks, to tap into this supposed inner well of magic, but nothing works. It's not talking to me."

"Try it again."

"Asmund—"

"You don't have much choice, do you?" he snapped. "Try it again."

My flames flickered and rose at the instant fury his tone brought up in me, but I clenched my fists and took a deep breath.

*He's not here to hurt you. You're going to be okay. Breathe.*

And so I did, taking deep lungfuls of air in through the mouth and out through the nose as I searched myself for the magic fuelling my fire, but my mind was an endless void, and try as I might, the magic remained out of reach. It was like there was a wall or a door separating us. Frustrating as it was, though, I knew if that door was *open,* my fire would do much more than set my own skin alight.

If that door was open, there would be no telling what I would do.

I opened my eyes to find Asmund still standing over me and the fire approaching my neck. The panic returned, and though flames burned on every inch of my skin, I felt cold. "It's not working, Asmund. What am I going to do?" My hands were shaking.

"Well," Asmund said, a certain humour lacing his words. "There is one more thing we can try, though I can't guarantee it'll work."

"What do I have to lose?"

I watched as he walked around my bed and returned with one of my small floor mats.

"Asmund—"

But before I could protest further, he was already beating me with it.

I threw my hands up to protect my face and let out a slew of curses as the fabric scratched my skin, but then Asmund was cursing too.

"The carpet's caught fire!" he yelled as he stopped hitting me with it. "Ow!" He dropped the flaming fabric to the floor.

"Sancia's breath, Asmund," I snapped. "You're going to set the whole room ablaze! Throw it in the fireplace."

He ignored me as he nursed a burnt hand, eyebrows furrowed in pain, so I rushed to my feet, grabbed the mat, and threw it in the fireplace across the room where it smoldered for a few moments before going out in a puff of smoke.

I looked back at Asmund. "What in Fidal's name is wrong with you? You could've seriously injured me, not to mention yourself. It's your own fault you got burnt, and that was an expensive rug. Aunt Mag is going to kill me when she finds it missing."

He shrugged. "It worked, though, didn't it?"

"What—" I started, but then I looked down at myself and saw he was right. The flames were gone, and no sign remained to say they were ever there in the first place, except for the smoking carpet and Asmund's burn. My skin was as pale and pristine as ever, and my tunic remained untouched.

I glanced at Asmund. "How did you know that would work?"

"I didn't," he replied with another shrug as he stood up. "I just thought a magical fire could be put out with the same principles as a traditional fire, but I don't think that's what did it." He scratched his chin. "I think you transferred the flames to the mat instead; that's why it's gone."

"So you're saying it needs to burn something to go out?"

"It needs to be *fed*," he emphasized. "Can you still feel it?"

I closed my eyes for a second to centre myself, but he was right. I couldn't feel the anger or heat lingering below the surface like I usually could. It was like the magic had been put to sleep. "So that's my answer, then? Feed the fire, and it will go away?"

He shook his head. "It's nothing more than a short-term solution. I don't know enough about the subject to give you more insight, but it's only going to get worse, get hungrier, and if you don't feed it enough to satisfy, it's going to start sucking the life out of you."

I nodded. "If you don't balance magic and life equally, as nature intended, one will take from the other."

Asmund blinked. "What?"

"It's something Echo said when she was telling me about the origins of magic," I replied, "but it confirms your theory. If I don't get this under control, there's a chance it could kill me."

We stood there in silence for a minute as the weight of my words hung in the air. I was walking a dangerous path, but there was no one I could go to for advice, no one here in

Summer who would dare to train me. Even dead, Darkenier was still endangering my life with his decisions.

"You're going to have to go back to the Edgewood," Asmund said finally.

"Why?"

"Echo is the only person we know and trust who knows enough about magic to help you."

"And since when do you trust Echo?"

He gave me a look. "Would it kill you to let that go? I apologized. I meant it. I'm not the same person who first walked into that forest and neither are you, but you can't let go of the past. You're content to drag it behind you like you enjoy the pain."

I wrapped my arms around myself. "That's not—"

"Isn't it?" he snapped back. "Face it, Isanfier; you are far from perfect too, but at least I'll admit my faults. I am sorry for how I used to treat you, I truly am, but I thought… I thought we were past the hatred."

I sat down on the bed with a sigh. "I don't hate you, Asmund. I'm not sure if I ever truly did, deep down. Hatred was just…easier than disappointment, I guess. I had thought you were my friend, one of the few I'd managed to make." I clenched my fists. "You endangering Sky's life and blaming it on me was one thing, but then you started looking at Sky the way Jasper was earlier, and I couldn't see a trace of my friend behind your eyes anymore."

I took a deep breath. "I know you've changed, but it's hard to let go. It's hard to let myself trust you, especially after the betrayal of the man I thought to be my uncle. I'm still in shock, Asmund, and there's a part of me that is scared that if I let my guard down, you will stab me or Sky in the back, and I couldn't live with that.

"I want to trust you again," I told him as I met his eyes, "but we're not…there yet. I'm sorry if I took it too far, but my wounds are still there."

He was silent again, and for a moment I thought he would leave me there without another word, as if none of this had ever happened, but then his face softened, and he said, "I want to earn your trust again, Prince. I've missed having you as a friend too."

And just like that, the tension in the room lifted, and I felt like I could breathe again.

"This is going to be a long few months, isn't it?" I asked him.

"Especially if you're going to set fire to yourself every time one of the boys looks at Sky funny."

I scowled. "He didn't look at her funny; he looked at her like she could give him the sun, like if she did, he would crush it just to watch the world burn. If I had the means, I would send him right back to Mensden, but as it is, I'll have to learn to live with his insolence."

"Sky has other options," Asmund reminded me.

"But Jasper is the best one in the eyes of the Council, and I worry that, in the end, they won't give either of us a say in the matter."

"Then we fight," he replied, "with whatever power we have to our names. We might not be close, but if there's one thing I know about you, Isanfier, it's that you don't give up when it comes to family. You would burn down the entire realm to keep Sky safe."

"I know," I said, glancing warily at my hands. "That's what I'm afraid of."

He gave me a serious look. "We'll figure it out. We'll find a way to get back to the Edgewood, but for now, you're going to have to try your best to keep calm. The more you call your magic to the surface, the harder it's going to be to keep it locked away."

I nodded. "Much easier said than done, though, isn't it?"

He shrugged. "Personally, I think we've faced much worse."

"I suppose fighting the goblin horde should make magic look like a stroll through the gardens," I replied with a laugh.

"I wish you'd had it back then. They wouldn't have dared to challenge us."

"They certainly wouldn't have lived to regret it."

He took a breath, glancing at the door. "Well, I should leave you now. Wouldn't want the Byrons to accuse me of monopolizing all your time, or for Sky to worry about what we might be planning together."

I smiled. "Oh, Sky will do that anyway, and her concerns are usually justified. I'll see you at dinner, then. Don't let me kill Jasper—unless, of course, he deserves it."

He put a hand to his chest. "I promise to do my best."

# 6
## Solitude

*Echo*

**The biting wind of** Winter was even harsher than usual as Echo made her way down the cobbled streets of Tamise, powdery snow whipping about the ankles of her boots. Not much had changed visually since her last visit, a few months before the war, but something felt off. She wondered if the city was feeling the absence of its King for good or for ill.

Frost may have been a tyrant, but at least the people knew what to expect under his rule, knew what was expected of them. Freedom was only as good as the knowledge of what to do with it.

Echo pulled her hood tighter around her face as she stepped into the first shop on her route. The last thing she needed was for someone to recognize her and wonder what the princess was doing away from the capital, or worse, try to kill her and bring about the end of her family's reign.

The idea of dying in Icaria's stead didn't sit well with her.

Echo heaved a happy sigh as the warmer air of the bakery hit her face and the sweet aroma of fresh bread and squares made its way to her nose. The shop was small, but baked goods were stacked on every square inch of the shelves around her. They lined each wall with one row dividing the space in two. To her right, the baker stood at a counter, gently rolling dough with a cylinder of wood.

The man looked up briefly at the sound of the bell as the door shut behind Echo, and then he returned to his work. The only sound in the shop was that of his kneading and a clock somewhere Echo couldn't see.

As much as she would've liked to stay there forever, time was precious to her, and Wyllans seldom lingered anywhere for long. She grabbed a few loaves of fresh bread and decided to splurge with a package of snow cookies, a delicious treat with a chocolate centre and sugar-powdered shell.

She dropped her chosen goods on the counter beside where the baker was still kneading his dough. He rolled it a few more times before looking up at her again.

"Will that be all?" he asked her, pushing his spectacles back up his nose.

"Yes," Echo replied, biting down the urge to add a thank you at the end. The average Wyllan didn't have the time of day to be polite and it was seen as a sign of weakness. "Could you wrap the bread? I have a long walk home."

"It'll be extra," the man reminded her, as he did every time, though she doubted he remembered her visits.

"I'm willing to pay for it," she assured him. "Name your price."

"For the whole lot and the wrapping..." He pinched his chin. "A Copper Crown and three Bronze Buttons."

Echo sucked in a breath. The price had gone up since her last visit. She dreaded the thought, but she might have to acquire more funds if she hoped to get everything she needed in Tamise. Still, she didn't argue with the man and handed him the exact change from the pouch in her cloak pocket, careful not to disturb her hood in the process.

He wrapped her bread without another word, and she placed it in her basket with the cookies before heading back out into the cold.

•  •  •

Several hours later, Echo found herself hurrying down a back alley towards the main street, trying to shake off her guilt along with her invisibility. She hated stealing, even if it *was* for survival, but she had no other choice. She couldn't work anywhere, both because she shared a face with Icaria and because if she strayed too long from the Edgewood, she would die.

So she used her magic to steal money from people she knew wouldn't miss it. Stealing directly from the merchants she went to was out of the question. On the one hand, it didn't sit well with her, and on the other, it was a lot more difficult to nab a loaf of bread than a handful of coins, even when invisible.

This time, her mark had been a noblewoman who had left her coin purse wide open on the counter while she argued with the tailor on the colour of the dress she'd ordered. She was the only patron in the shop, so Echo had been able to grab a large handful of coins with no one the wiser.

Echo's heart rate began to slow down to a more natural pace as she turned onto the main street and joined the usual crowd of shoppers. If the noblewoman noticed she was short on coins, she'd be hard-pressed to find Echo now, and Echo would soon be on her way out of Tamise.

She'd been able to afford everything on her list with the coin she'd brought, but she didn't like to leave the city empty-handed, in case she needed something urgently the next time she visited and didn't have time to search for money.

Echo was loath to leave Tamise, even though she knew there was no reason to linger. The treehouse had been awfully quiet in the past few months without Sky's laughter and Isan and Asmund's quarrelling. She had thought she would get used to the silence again, the emptiness, but their absence had left a hole in her heart, and each day spent alone in the forest since they'd left had felt like a life sentence.

Tamise was cold and dangerous—there was no doubt in Echo's mind about that—but at least it offered the illusion of community, the illusion she was normal.

Echo took a different route towards the North Gate, hoping to postpone her inevitable departure. The shops on that side of the city were much nicer, more unique and artisanal. She passed by a dressmaking shop that rivaled the tailor where she'd stolen the noblewoman's money tenfold. The ballgowns in the window looked fit for royalty, and she wondered if this was where her Aunt Celeste purchased her finery, or if she had them sent from the Capital.

She glanced longingly towards the southeast quarter of the city, where Lady Celeste's white marble manor house presumably still stood. It had been so long since Echo had been there that she scarcely remembered it. She'd visited once to see her cousin Clarice before her and Icaria separated, and though she'd travelled to Tamise countless times in the past decade, she had never been able to muster up the courage to walk by that piece of her past.

Echo tried to distract herself from her sudden melancholy by window shopping as she made her way to the edge of town. She passed by another bakery, an elegant cobbler shop, and a bookstore. She gazed longingly at the thick volumes on display but didn't stop, knowing her basket was already heavy enough.

Finally, she saw the gate and was about to pick up her pace when the clouds shifted and a shard of light glanced off something across the street, blinding her for a moment.

Echo winced and covered her eyes, pivoting out of the direct line of the beam as she blinked away tears.

*What in Fidalia* was *that?*

She turned towards the culprit and was struck breathless at the sword on display in the window of a swordsmith shop.

The blade was the same style as Isan's, but the hilt was a deep black that would be nearly invisible in the dead of night, and there was a sapphire the size of a Bronze Button sparkling on the pommel. It was a weapon fit for the most prestigious warrior, and never in her life had Echo wanted something so fervently.

In that moment, she understood why Isanfier gravitated towards *Ember*, why he spent so many hours working to keep the blade in pristine condition. She understood why it was his most treasured possession.

At that moment, Echo mentally counted the coin in her pouch and started walking, almost absentmindedly, towards the shop.

7

# A Sneaking Suspicion

*Isan*

**The next week passed** in a blur of more meetings, tailor fittings, Welcome gatherings in the throne room, and dinners as we welcomed Penelope and Tamsen from Fortude, Raina and Soleia from Laurel, and the entire brood of Cargoff accompanied by Lady Katya herself, as Euric was only three years old. Why she brought all her children when Dorin was the only one of age was beyond me, but I supposed it was better than leaving them at their manor without their mother.

The castle had become stifling with all the guests, extra servants, and knights posted everywhere. Soon, there would be few places I could truly hide if I needed to, and we were still waiting on Aramina and the Norwells. They were due to arrive any day, and then the true torture would begin: massive feasts, shows of strength, endless dancing. It was enough to make my head spin.

To make matters worse, I hadn't slept properly since we'd arrived back in Widonia, the new nightmare plaguing me as much, if not more, than the last one. Each morning, it ended with me exploding in a pillar of light and setting the whole city ablaze, and I woke, scorching hot and breathless, feeling like I'd run a race halfway to Mensden.

My magic hadn't flared up since the arrival of Lord Byron's progeny, but I'd avoided Jasper as best I could. Now, with the start of the Festival fast approaching, I feared I wouldn't be able to stay free of it much longer, but there was only so much I could do. I felt like I was being pulled apart from both ends, and soon there wouldn't be enough left of me to support my own weight.

Still, I pulled on one of my new tunics and situated my crown, preparing myself to greet another set of suitors like there was nothing wrong, like I wanted this. I was met with a pleasant surprise, however, when the royal herald announced that Aramina had arrived at the castle.


Sky and I abandoned our thrones and all sense of decorum as she entered the throne room, all but running to her side.

"Oh, Aramina," Sky exclaimed as she threw her arms around her in a tight hug. "It's so good to see you! How are you? How's Arran?"

Confusion clouded Aramina's eyes for a moment at the warm welcome, but then a smile brightened her face, and she returned Sky's hug. "It's good to see you too, Your Highness." Sky let go of her finally, and she turned to me, dropping into a curtsy. "And you as well, Prince Isanfier."

It was instinct to correct her, to remind her I was only Isan, but in the presence of so many knights and royal officials, I bit my tongue. I imagined Sir Quinton was already appalled that we had left our thrones and deigned to embrace her.

"Did Father send you alone?" a voice popped up, and I realized Asmund was standing right behind me. He'd become like a shadow in the last week, and though there were moments when I found his presence comforting, it mostly annoyed me.

"Oh, hello, Asmund," Aramina said. "I didn't know you would be here."

Neither of the siblings moved to embrace each other, and I remembered what Asmund had been like when Aramina had left the castle before the war. She wasn't going to believe everything that had happened.

"And to answer your question," she went on, "of course not. He sent me with an official escort and five of his best knights, but they've returned home now. He says I'm 'to remain under your watchful eye for the duration of my time here,' though he also said he wasn't sure how sound a decision it was, whatever that means."

Asmund took the insult in stride and merely said, "I'm glad you're here, Mina."

She raised an eyebrow at that, but someone in the room cleared their throat before the four of us could go on.

"I hate to break up such a wonderful family reunion," Quinton said, "but there are protocols that must be followed during the Festival of Honour, and I must implore that Their Royal Highnesses return to their places."

Sky and I shared a scowl but did as we were told, abandoning Aramina in the middle of the aisle. The rest of the ceremony continued as planned, Aramina officially presenting herself to us, and Sky and I giving the customary welcome. When the door closed behind her, Quinton motioned for his knights to leave until it was just him, Sky, Kent, Asmund, and me in the throne room.

Sir Quinton nodded to Asmund. "You may go, Master Asmund. Sir Kent and I wish to speak with Their Royal Highnesses privately."

I bristled in my seat but tried to ignore the annoyance crawling beneath my skin.

Asmund glanced at me, and I gave a curt nod, though I was sure he could see the distaste in my eyes. He left by the main doors, perhaps hoping to catch up to Aramina.

As the doors banged shut behind him, Sir Quinton and Sir Kent turned to us.

"I know this is your first Festival, and that you have been trained poorly in the art of royal events, but that kind of behaviour will not be tolerated," Quinton told us simply while Kent looked on with a serious expression.

I scowled. "Aramina is our friend."

"*Mistress* Aramina," Quinton countered, "and she *may* become your future Queen, but she is not the only suitor here, and she must prove herself like all the others."

"I didn't say I wanted her as my wife, Quinton," I shot back, my hands clenching the arms of the throne. "I was merely pointing out that she means more to me than a simple handshake and some pretty, empty words. I will not apologize for greeting her in the way that I did, and I don't suppose Sky will either. I also cannot promise it won't happen again."

He stared at me for a minute, an untold fury at my words and tone of voice burning behind his dark brown eyes, but he merely pursed his lips before answering. "You will be King someday, Prince Isanfier. I hope this defiance dies before you do. You are dismissed."

I held his gaze a moment longer, much longer than was customary, and then I stood, motioning for Sky to follow me. And, though I knew it would only stoke the fires, I took my leave through the main doors, in a dull attempt to remind him he didn't rule me, and *I* dismissed *myself*.

• • •

My skin was boiling by the time Sky caught up to me, and I fought to control my breathing and lower my heart rate before

I blew up. The last person to get so under my skin had been Asmund, but I was under no delusion that Quinton and I would become allies anytime soon. That man had an agenda; I just didn't yet know what it was.

"Isan?" Sky asked me, touching a hand to my shoulder. "Are you all right?"

I fought the urge to shrug off her hand, reminding myself that Sky was my rock and I needed her now more than ever. I took a deep breath before answering. "Sir Quinton is starting to make Uncle feel like nothing more than a pesky bird, whereas *he* is a viper."

Sky half rolled her eyes. "Oh, come now, Isan. He hasn't murdered anyone."

I gave her a look. "*Yet*, you mean. There's venom in him, Sky. I can feel it. Even though he deceived us, Uncle was kind now and again. He was gentle. Quinton is nothing but sharp edges, and he doesn't care who gets sliced. He doesn't care who sees his true colours, and that's dangerous."

Sky let out a deep sigh. "I'm certain you're jumping to conclusions, but suppose you're right. What do you plan to do about it?"

"I don't have the power to do what I want," I replied. "No one respects my influence. I would persuade Kent to make the decision on my behalf, so it held more weight, but I'm not sure he's on our side anymore either." I rubbed my forehead. "Fidal's breath, I should've let the Council have their stupid discussions and prolonged vote for Regent. I've ensured our own demise."

The doubts and fears started swirling in my head, and I clenched my eyes shut tight against the vertigo. We'd come so far since we'd left the castle for the war, and yet I couldn't help but think I had fallen far behind where I wanted and needed to be.

As usual, it was Sky who brought me out of my spiral. "Isan, you need to breathe, first of all," she said calmly as she ran a hand down my back. "And second of all, you need to stop thinking about what-ifs. What's done is done, and neither you nor I can change it. All we can do is move forward and do our best to protect our *future*. We're still here, and you need to clear your head if you want to stay that way."

She took a deep breath. "I'm not saying your suspicions aren't warranted—he makes me uneasy too—but like you said, our options at the moment are limited. We need to keep our eyes open, our ears to the ground, and wait for an opportunity. Sancia is watching over us, and I don't believe our work in this realm is done yet."

That was an understatement. I thought about the threat of the Curse still looming over me, the Winter Princess plotting her revenge in her icy domain. I wondered how I could ever hope to bring peace to the entire realm when my own kingdom still held such turmoil, but I stopped the dark thoughts before they could descend further, reminding myself of something Aunt Mag had often said when we were younger.

*Small steps on a dirt path can lead to long strides through the halls of legend. You just need to keep moving.*

I forced a smile through my lingering frustration. Damn them both for always being right.

"If this Fidal-forsaken Festival is any indication, our work in this realm is just getting started. The Norwells are due to arrive tomorrow?"

She nodded as she started down the hall again with me by her side. "And then the real fun begins."

"What abysmal task do we have to sit through first?" I asked her.

She gave me a disapproving sidelong glance. "If you bothered to pay attention to our lessons, you would know the Festival of Honour officially starts with a ceremonial parade through the city, ending in the town square where each suitor will be presented to the people. Then, we shall return to the castle for the opening feast and twilight ball, where we must dance with each of our suitors and make our first true acquaintances."

I grimaced. "That's going to be the longest night of my life."

"At least you'll be able to breathe properly."

"Not if my suitors wear as much perfume as Raina did at her Welcoming." I wrinkled my nose in disgust at the memory.

Sky huffed a laugh. "Oh, Sancia's breath, that was awful, wasn't it?"

"I thought I was going to gag right in front of her," I replied. "Took all of my strength to keep my composure."

"Well, I'm sure too much perfume is going to be the least of our worries."

I sensed a note of anxiety in her tone and glanced over at her, trying to read her expression, but she was getting better at hiding her emotions, even from me. "Are *you* doing okay? I know I've been a bit… scarce lately, but I'm always here for you if you need anything."

She gave me a small smile. "I'm okay for now. Just nervous, I guess. You know, I've never even kissed a man. I don't know what I would do. This is all so… foreign. Suitors. Parties. Weddings. Romance. I've read countless books about all of them, but I feel more unprepared than I ever have before."

I reached over and squeezed her hand. "Well, you have a better chance than me, then, having read the books."

She laughed. "Maybe, but at least you have the freedom to be yourself. I have to pretend to be smaller, weaker, and gentler. I have to laugh at their jokes even when they're not funny and turn a blind eye to their vulgar comments and lewd looks. I have to be less."

Anger flared in me at her words, and though I feared she would be able to feel the heat in my skin, I squeezed her hand harder and wrenched us to a stop in the middle of the hall. "No."

She looked at me with apprehension. "What?"

"*Never* pretend to be less, Sky, not when you will always be so much more. Not even because you're royalty, but because you are *genuine*. You are strong. You are wise. You are creative, strategic, and the reason I am still alive, still sane some days. If none of them are willing to see the real you, they don't even deserve a chance."

She hung her head, something I seldom saw her do. "I don't get a choice, Isan. I never have and likely never will. This war, as terrible as it was, was probably the only taste of freedom I'll ever have. I am to marry and have children until my body can't take it anymore, and then I'll be forgotten as some old Princess while your children take the spotlight from both of us."

She looked up at me, brown eyes burning with unshed tears. "Face it, Isan; when it truly comes down to it, I have always been—and always will be—nothing more than an extra."

I took a deep shuddering breath as my anger entwined with sorrow at her words. She always carried herself with such confidence; I never realized she felt like that, like she wasn't worth as much, if not more, than I was.

"Maybe to the eyes of the court you are, Sky. I won't deny that, but not in my eyes, not in Aunt Mag's. Fidal's breath, I don't even think Asmund sees you as an extra anymore. You have a way with people, and if they don't accept you, you carry on as you are anyway. I didn't lose you in this war, and I swear I won't lose you to this."

I squeezed her hand once more and then let it go, giving her space to absorb my words.

She was quiet for a moment as we resumed our walk, and then she said, "I doubt Sir Quinton would take kindly to me behaving like my true self."

I shrugged. "*I* doubt Sir Quinton would take kindly to me shoving *Ember* through his throat."

"Isan!" she gasped, giving me a severe look. "You *can't* say that!" But a smile pulled at the corner of her mouth, and I got the impression she'd been thinking along the same lines.

"I can say what I like," I replied, "and you know what? I've decided that's exactly what I'm going to do. I'm going to do what I want. Sure, I'll go to their feasts, attend their balls, and deal with all the Festival nonsense, but I'm not going to pretend to be happy about it. If Quinton thinks he can tame us, he's welcome to try, but I think he'll find he gets more than he bargained for."

Sky finally smiled. "Oh, you're going to make his life miserable, aren't you?"

I grinned. "I'm going to do the best I can. This is our life, Sky. We have to make the most of it, and if we don't start resisting now, we're going to get stuck. We're going to stay small, and this castle will become our prison again. Our monarchy will be stolen from us again. Our people need us to stand tall."

"Our work in this realm is not done yet," she mused.

I nodded in agreement, glad we were on the same page.

We walked in comfortable silence until we came to the section of hall where we usually parted ways to head to our separate rooms.

Sky looked over at me. "Thank you, for the encouragement. I needed the reminder of who I am and what I stand for."

"I thought as much, though it's not usually me giving the reminders, so I don't want this becoming a regular occurrence."

She cracked another smile. "Only room for one dysfunctional person in the family?"

"Exactly," I replied, "and I am *excellent* at my job."

"Oh, don't worry, I know," she said. "Well, I guess I'll see you at dinner, if the Norwells don't make a surprise appearance before then."

"A part of me wishes they would so we could get on with everything. The waiting is killing me more than the socializing will."

She rolled her eyes. "You'll be singing a different tune in a few days. You'll be so tightly wound, I'll probably be talking you down from duelling anyone who looks at you funny."

I scowled. "And here I thought you were being nice to me today."

"Sometimes I'm nice," she replied, "but I'm always honest. Your head would be twice as big otherwise."

"You're just afraid of my potential," I countered.

"Believe whatever you want, but I don't have time to argue with you at the moment. I need to get rid of this dress before it cuts off all the oxygen to my head."

I grimaced. "Is it that bad?"

"Nearly," she sighed. "I'll talk to you later. Try not to be too dysfunctional without me."

"I make no promises," I replied, and indeed I couldn't. I'd never been more dysfunctional in my life, and she didn't even know the half of it.

*You chose to keep her in the dark,* I reminded myself as I watched her walk away.

*I know.*

I hoped she could forgive me when the truth finally came out, because although I planned to keep it from her as long as possible, I knew my luck wouldn't last. I knew I was grasping on to dandelion fluff that the gentlest breeze could scatter to the four corners of the realm.

Still, I wasn't ready to let go yet.

# 8
# Friend or Foe

**I was laying on** my bed, staring at the ceiling, my mind a whirlwind of sullen thoughts, when a frantic knocking came at my door.

I sat up sharply, suspicion raising the hair on my arms, and called out, "Who is it?" though I didn't move from the bed.

"It's Asmund," a voice answered. "Something…terrible has happened, and I didn't know what to do. I didn't know who else to turn to. I… Oh, Sancia's breath."

"Okay, whoa," I replied, my anxiety heightened by his own, something I'd rarely seen in him. "Take it easy. I'm coming."

I hopped off the bed and walked over to the door, but when I turned the knob, I met resistance from the other side. I narrowed my eyes, though he couldn't see. "What are you doing? I thought you wanted me to let you in."

"I do," he shot back. "I just… Can you promise me you won't freak out?"

"Asmund," I replied, "you're starting to scare me."

"Please," he said, a raw desperation in his voice.

It was such a simple word, a single syllable, but I hadn't heard it from him in nearly a decade. I was so stunned, I told him yes and turned the knob.

At first, as my eyes landed on him, I didn't see anything amiss, but then his blue eyes met mine, and I almost fainted as I realized I was looking at my own face, albeit framed with Asmund's familiar dark braids.

My eyes were round as saucers as I dragged him through the doorway, shut the door, and slid the lock over. "Did anybody see you?"

"I don't think so," he replied.

I blinked my eyes rapidly, shaken by the strangeness of hearing his voice coming from what looked to be my own reflection. "What happened?" I asked him. "Why are you wearing my face?"

He looked away from me, which was a bit of a relief, actually. "I don't..." he tried. "I'm not sure, but I guess... I must be a Magic Wielder, Isan, and if that's the case... then this is only the beginning, and I have no idea how to change back."

I ran a hand through my hair.

*Sancia save us all; this is the last thing we need right now.*

"Are you sure?" I asked him.

He whipped his head back around and gave me a severe look. "No, I think maybe I slept wrong, and that's why I can see your face when I look in the mirror," he snapped. "Of *course* I'm sure. There's no other explanation."

I tried to remember what Echo had told me about Magic Wielders. They were mortal, I knew that, and unlike Gifted Immortals, they could use more than one magical ability, shapeshifting being one of them. Echo had also said magic was hereditary, though, and there weren't any known Magic Wielders in Asmund's family.

"I thought your mother was a Gifted Immortal," I said. "Wouldn't you have followed in her footsteps?"

"The magic could've come from another relative," Asmund replied, "or my father's bloodline, dormant for generations perhaps. There probably *are* Gifted Immortals who can shape-shift, but it's much more common in Magic Wielders. Besides, if I was a Gifted Immortal, there would be some tell in my name, like you."

I frowned. "What do you mean?"

"Your name is Isan-fier," he replied, overpronouncing it to put emphasis on the second half. "We should've seen the fire magic coming a mile away."

"Oh," I said, realizing that for the first time. I'd forgotten about that part of Echo's lessons, though I still didn't understand how it worked. "How come no one did?"

Asmund shrugged. "I guess we weren't looking for it, which probably saved your life. Darkenier wouldn't have let you live through childhood if he thought you had magic."

"And neither one of us are going to live to see my coronation if we don't figure this out and fast," I replied. "What were you doing when it happened? Can you think of anything that triggered it? Echo told me Gifted Immortals have emotional triggers, but I imagine there is something similar that coaxes out the powers of Magic Wielders too, if that is what you are."

He looked down at his feet, a dark and solemn expression crossing his face like a cloud across the sun. "I... I had an argument with Aramina. I don't want to get into the details, but she called me out on my past behaviour, and I said some things I didn't mean, and..." He put his head in his hands. "I remember thinking I ruin everything I touch, that maybe everyone's lives would be better without me in it. I remember wishing I could be anyone, anything else, if only for a moment, and..." He looked up. "By Sancia, that's it!"

I nodded, coming to the realization myself. "You asked, and the magic answered."

He gave me an incredulous look. "Is it that simple? Do I ask the magic to change me back?"

I shrugged. "How should I know? You were supposed to be *my* teacher, remember?"

He scowled. "Well, I'm not an expert. *You're* the one who's actually experienced magic, and my mother only told me what she knew. She didn't give me a handbook. So, I'm asking you, *is it that simple?*"

"In my experience, no," I replied. "You'd have a better chance of success asking the clouds for rain during a drought. If it was that easy, do you think I would still be struggling the way I am?"

"That's a fair point, but I was kind of hoping you were just, you know, really terrible at magic."

I rolled my eyes. "Very funny."

"So what do I do, Isan?" he asked, fear creeping into his voice again as his breathing picked up with a hint of panic. "I can't be seen like this!"

"Oh, so I'm that hideous?" I retorted. My voice was stern, but I couldn't manage to bite back my grin. I was enjoying the situation, actually—seeing Asmund struggle for once.

He glared at me, his eyes as cold as a Winter storm. "I'm serious! This is no time for jokes; I could be discovered at any moment, and no offense, but I don't think you would survive this Festival long without me."

I sighed. "You are *so* lucky you're not as much of a prick as you used to be." I moved over and sat on the bed so I could relax while I thought everything through. "All right, let's see... I think you have a couple options. One, you can wait for it to wear off. Obviously, not the most ideal option but probably the most likely to work. From what I learned from you and Echo, magic isn't an infinite source, so you won't be able to sustain it forever."

"Yes, but it might completely drain me before it fades out," he reminded me.

"So you'll have to take control of the magic and yourself," I said, "like I've been trying to do without success for weeks. Maybe you should try to imagine what *you* look like instead, to centre yourself."

He raised an eyebrow. "You think that will work?"

I shrugged. "Honestly, it's a theory, but it's worth a shot. Sky's the one who makes intelligent suggestions; I excel at inane plans that might get people killed."

"I've noticed," he replied. Then he leaned back in the chair and took a deep breath. "What do I have to lose? Just stay quiet so I can focus."

"My lips are sealed."

Ten minutes passed in awkward silence as he sat at my desk with his eyes closed, and I twiddled my thumbs on the bed, trying to make as little noise as possible. I couldn't believe how still he was, not to mention how dedicated, and I found myself wondering if my impatience was the only thing impeding my own success. Maybe I hadn't tried hard enough, long enough. Maybe I was too stubborn for my own good.

Case in point, I was about to groan in frustration at the silence when I noticed Asmund's skin was starting to darken again.

I sat up straight in the bed and clamped my hand over my mouth so I wouldn't gasp out loud and disturb his progress.

*Sancia's breath, it's working.*

I was honestly grasping at stray feathers when I'd told him my idea, but I guess I had a little wisdom in me after all.

I watched with bated breath over the next few minutes as his skin morphed back into the dark brown I was familiar with and the shape of his own jaw returned. It was a little unsettling, the sight of it, and I couldn't help remembering the way Darkenier's face had shifted back and forth from the man I knew to a stranger.

I hadn't thought about it before, but someone else must've maintained that magic for him. Given his ability to steal light from the room and how said ability was written directly into his name like Asmund had pointed out with me, Darkenier must've been a Gifted Immortal, and Gifted Immortals had only one power as far as I knew, which meant there was a Magic Wielder out there somewhere who'd known Darkenier's secret the whole time. Had they been loyal enough to our traitor King that he trusted them, or had he paid them enough to stay quiet?

Before I could delve deeper into the matter, Asmund finally opened his eyes, and I was relieved—though also a little miffed—to see they were back to their usual deep brown instead of my own piercing blue.

I didn't know whether I wanted to clap him on the back and congratulate him or smack him across the face for being a Fidal-forsaken show-off. "How in the name of Fidalia did you do that?" I demanded to know.

He glanced over at me. "What?"

I threw my hands in the air. "I've been trying to tame my magic for weeks, *weeks*, and you manage it in one sitting? It makes me sick."

He cracked a smile. "Jealous?"

"I'm serious, Asmund. How did you do that?"

"I don't know, I just concentrated, like you said, and I guess… I think your problem is you're fighting it too much. Magic is a gift, and you have to work with it, or it won't do anything for you. Besides, it helped that I wasn't in danger of setting the room on fire. Elemental magic isn't exactly a passive gift."

"So you're saying there's no hope for me?"

He rolled his eyes. "No, I'm saying you need more time and a place to work on it that's fireproof, preferably."

"We don't have the luxury of time," I sighed, sinking down onto my bed, "or peace and quiet, let alone a place I can practise without being seen. I'm doomed, Asmund, and we both know it. The only thing the kingdom is going to be celebrating at the end of this Festival is my execution."

"Oh, for Sancia's sake, Isanfier," Asmund snapped. "Dispense with the drama and start looking at this with a critical eye. Your life is at stake—*both* of our lives are at stake. You don't think I'm worried too? What if I turn into Aramina while I'm dancing with Sky at the ball, or into Sky while I'm talking to Sir Quinton? You think they'll give me time to explain myself? Do you think I'll somehow manage to change back in seconds and convince them they imagined it? I have no idea what I'm doing either, but you don't see me bemoaning my life and giving up.

"I know you're scared, I get that, but the Prince I knew would not have let that stand in his way. We were both given a gift, and it's our responsibility to embrace it, to find out what the realm wants us to do with it."

I stared at him in stunned silence for a minute because I knew he was right, and I hated it. There was still a part of me that cursed our new friendship, that believed he was up to no good, and that part was more than ashamed to be given a wake-up call by such a person. If even Asmund was disgusted by my attitude, what did that say about me? He was right, but I didn't know how to fix it.

I leaned over the edge of the bed and looked down at my feet as I finally answered. "I am more scared than I've ever been in my life, Asmund, and I've stood face to face with the King of Winter as he froze my sister to death beside me. The war was one of the worst experiences of my life, but in a certain sense, it was easy. Swing my sword, dodge incoming attacks, kill or be killed, and move on to the next task. Now I have no easy path. I don't have a plan. I am so very lost, and I don't know anyone who holds the map."

"You don't have to have all the answers right away, but you do need to look for them. Maybe… Maybe you should talk to Sky."

I gave him a severe look. "I already told you I'm not doing that. She has too much weight on her shoulders already with this Festival and Quinton breathing down her neck over what is 'proper.' She doesn't need this too, not now."

He crossed his arms. "How is keeping this from her better for either of you? She is going to feel hurt and betrayed *again*.

I narrowed my eyes. "Again?"

"Remember how upset she was when she found out about the nightmare? Remember how you promised her you wouldn't keep something like that from her again?"

"That's different."

"No, it's not, and you know it," he snapped, getting to his feet. "You talk all the time about how the both of you are a team, and yet you exclude her at every turn in the name of protecting her. If there's one thing I learned about Sky in our travels, it's that *she* protects *herself*. She'll decide if something is too much, and Sancia save whoever thinks they know what's best for her."

He walked up to me and stabbed his finger into my chest. "The only person you're protecting with your silence is yourself."

The rage in my eyes matched his own as I grabbed his wrist and threw it away from me without conceding a step backwards. "Don't touch me, and don't talk about Sky as if you know her. I'll deal with the consequences when they come, but I am not prepared to face her now."

He smirked, an expression akin to the ones he used to wear, the resemblance so uncanny that it lit a fire in my core, a desire to wipe it off his face with my sword.

"Why?" he snapped. "Because you're a coward? Because the almighty Prince of Summer is afraid of his own sister?"

The fire within me rose up in challenge at his words, and for the first time since my fight with Darkenier, I didn't try to suppress the urge to use my magic.

Let it come. Let Asmund burn for his treacherous words.

"I am not a coward," I spat. "I am not afraid of Sky. I'm simply worried about dragging even more people into the Fidal-forsaken mess I'm in. As of right now, Sky is innocent. The moment she knows my secret, she becomes a criminal too, and I will not resign her to that fate."

"Sky would rather *be* a criminal than be lied to, Isanfier, and you know it! She would do anything for you. Anything. You have no idea the kind of power that gives you. You have no idea how much I wish I had someone like that in my life, but you dismiss it. You are a selfish, cowardly man-child, and if you don't have the guts to tell her, then I will."

He stormed over to the door, threw open the lock, and lunged out into the hall before I could fully process his words, before the red curtain of fire behind my eyes faded enough for my brain to catch up with the conversation. Then I was flying after him, the fire building with every footstep, but I didn't care.

I didn't care who saw. I didn't care if I ruined everything. I wanted to sear that smirk off his wretched face and make him vow to never speak to me that way again.

And I wanted to stop him before he reached Sky, because I knew he was right—a notion that sent the fire in my veins writhing with fury.

The only thing worse than Sky finding out I was hiding something from her would be finding out I had told Asmund first.

# 9
# Honesty and Honour

**By the time I** caught up to Asmund, my magic had reached its limit, and when I watched him knock once and then enter the room without giving time for a reply, that was it. I stormed in after him with my sword drawn and hands ablaze, not bothering to close the door behind me as I lunged at him with a battle cry.

I realized instantly that Sky wasn't in the room, but the damage was already done.

Asmund spun around and drew his sword, his military instincts kicking in as he blocked my strike just in time. "What in Sancia's name are you doing?" he snapped as he strained against me.

"You crossed the line," I replied, aiming another blow at him.

"I did nothing," he countered, dodging my strike and running around to the other side of the bed. "You brought this upon yourself."

"You gave me no choice!" I yelled, launching myself across the bed at him.

"There is always a choice!" he screamed back as we parried back and forth, my flames dancing closer to his swinging braids but not close enough. "I chose to lie to the King about what happened in the Edgewood. I chose to save Sky's life on the battlefield. I chose to go after the traitor, and I *chose* to stand against my father when he questioned your loyalty.

"I didn't have to do any of that, and you certainly made it difficult for me to do them, but I did them for you, for the future of this kingdom, because I see something in you, Isanfier. You just have to wade through all your pain and sorrow and self-deprecation to get to it, because like it or not, this kingdom *needs* you. Not me. You!"

He aimed a kick at me as he delivered the words, and I was so distracted that I didn't see it coming in time. His foot landed square in my ribs, and I hit the ground hard, the air forcing its way out of my lungs until I gasped for breath. My arms hit the floor too, my sword clunking into the wood and my fire sputtering out into nothing.

"So wake up, Isanfier," Asmund went on without a beat, looming over me with his sword clenched in both hands, "and take a good look in the mirror, because if you don't figure yourself out soon, you might not have a sister left to save."

Then he drove his sword down, only to stick it point first into the hardwood floor between my ribcage and upper arm.

I leaned my head back as I gasped in relief, my racing heart finally finding the will to steady itself, and that's when I saw a figure standing in the still open doorway behind me.

"What in Sancia's name is going on here?"

*Sky.*

And though I knew none of the gods would spare me this time, I still prayed to whoever would listen that she would be able to forgive me.

I was still trying to catch my breath as Sky rushed in and closed the door, giving us what I could only assume was the most disappointed look she'd ever worn. It was hard to tell from the floor.

"One of you had better start talking," she snapped, "and don't think for a second, Isanfier, that your prone position is going to make me believe you're the victim."

I rubbed my eyes as I took a deep breath and tried to swallow back the nerves bubbling deep inside my gut. "I've been keeping something from you," I admitted.

Her scowl deepened. "Why am I not surprised? Is honesty really too much to ask for, Isan? After all we've been through?"

"No," I replied.

"Then what is it?" she snapped. "Are you going to tell me, or do I have to beat the truth out of Asmund?"

I swallowed hard and replied, "The truth is...I have magic."

"You what?"

I struggled into a sitting position so I could look her in the eyes, ignoring the way my head swam. "I have magic, and I didn't tell you because I was afraid of what would happen. Asmund only knows because he was there when I discovered it, and he's been trying to convince me to come clean with you, but you know how stubborn I am, and, well, tensions boiled over, and I might have tried to kill him. But Asmund is a better person than I give him credit for, and I'm glad I didn't. I'm sorry you had to find out this way. I shouldn't have pretended I was okay."

I glanced between the two of them.

"I hope both of you can forgive me, but I understand if it might take some time. I understand I am a colossal moron, and I... I need help. There, I said it. I have no idea what I'm doing, and I need help."

Sky rubbed her temples and let out a long sigh before she said, "All right, start from the beginning, and then I'll decide how angry I am with you."

Asmund held out a hand to me. "I'll forgive you if you stop being so pitiful."

"I'll do my best," I replied as I took his hand. He helped me to my feet, albeit with a tighter grip than was necessary.

Asmund leaned against the dresser, and I sat in the chair as Sky sat on the bed, and we took turns telling the story. It was getting close to dinner by the time we reached the events of the day. Sky's face cycled through the complete range of human emotion as we talked, but she stayed quiet until the end.

Finally, she crossed her arms over her green dress and said, "Well, I think you're both idiots, and it's truly a miracle you haven't brought death upon yourselves yet. Asmund is right; it was only a matter of time until I found out, and while I am extremely disappointed, I'm not exactly surprised, and we have bigger problems to worry about than how I feel about this. As for your quarrel earlier, how did either of you believe that would solve anything?"

"He tried to kill me," Asmund replied. "I was only defending myself from his attack."

"You knew anger triggered his magic," Sky countered, "so that's your own fault. You were literally playing with fire."

Asmund didn't reply, but she rounded on me next. "*You,* however, blew the whole issue out of proportion, as per usual."

I hung my head, not trusting myself to speak. I was honestly grateful she wasn't crying or throwing shoes at me.

"Unfortunately," Sky went on, "our first order of business now is dinner with our numerous guests, but we'll get started on research first thing in the morning and any free time we have after that."

I frowned. "Research?"

She rolled her eyes. "*Books*, Isanfier. We'll go to the library to see if we can find any information on magic, for either of you. Knowledge will be scarce after Uncle's policies, but I'm sure he didn't find everything. Besides, being a Gifted Immortal himself, he might have kept certain books for his own benefit. We don't have much else to go on yet, and we can't leave the castle right now either. It would raise too much suspicion, not to mention leave a weakness that Winter could potentially exploit."

"I'm worried I pose more of a threat staying here than I would leaving," I replied, "especially after the incident earlier. I could've seriously hurt Asmund or torched your entire room to ash. We were lucky today, and I'm afraid that luck won't hold for much longer."

Sky gave me a small smile. "Fortunately, you have me now, so your situation isn't as dire as it was. I'm not going to let you do anything you'll regret, and we're going to figure out a solution, okay? You don't have to suffer alone. I'll be here for you and your magic, and you'll be here for me and the inevitable…issues with my suitors."

She shuddered at the thought, and my fists clenched.

"We'll both be here for you," Asmund chimed in. "I'm about as fond of Jasper as Isan is, and it won't be as scandalous if I have to show him his place. I'd merely be a jealous fellow suitor hoping to reduce the competition."

I found myself echoing his grin, but Sky shook her head. "No one is fighting anyone. Honestly, you two are impossible. Now, if you'll excuse me, I have a dinner to prepare for, and please, take your weapons with you." She gestured to Asmund's sword still stuck in the floor.

Asmund gave her a sheepish look and said, "Right, of course. I suppose we'll see you at dinner."

Sky nodded. "Try not to kill each other between now and then, okay?"

He and I exchanged a glance, and I simply replied, "We make no promises."

We took our leave before Sky could physically shoo us out the door, Asmund grabbing his sword on the way. We walked down the first hall in silence, both of us lost in thought. We'd said some things we didn't mean, and some we truly did, and it was kind of a mess, but I knew it had somehow made our bond stronger.

"Look," I said finally, "I'm sorry for earlier. I was the one who crossed a line, and you were right, about pretty much everything."

He nodded. "Apology accepted, Prince. I just hope I won't have to use those tactics again to make you see sense."

"For what it's worth," I replied, "I'm glad I didn't kill you."

"Likewise; who would annoy Skiansy then?"

I laughed. "She would be so bored and lonely without us."

He grinned and punched me lightly in the arm. "What's life without a little bit of adventure?"

"Not one worth living, that's for sure."

•　•　•

Unfortunately, the Norwells arrived the following morning as planned, and with the Festival scheduled to begin at midday, the three of us didn't get a chance to start our research. As the hours swept past, I could feel my anxiety growing. Sky and I were whisked away after the final Welcoming by two teams of servants to bathe and change outfits for the ceremonial parade.

I was buttoned into a horribly gaudy green and gold suit that made my dark hair look even more out of place than it usually did, though they thankfully let me keep my black boots. I also had to wear gold silk gloves and a ceremonial sword that weighed nothing and would *do* nothing to protect me against any potential enemies.

Last, but certainly not least, was my crown that they placed ever so carefully on top of my painfully styled hair that two servants had spent twenty minutes trying to get to lie flat.

By the time I joined Sky in the throne room, my temper was already at its peak, and the ceremony hadn't even begun.

Sky smiled when she saw me. "How are you doing?"

"Honestly?" I replied. "I feel sick to my stomach, I'm wondering if there's still time to flee to the mountains, and I'm not sure if I'm hot because of the stress or from the magic trying to claw its way out of me. But, you know, other than that, I'm great." I flashed her a too wide smile.

She grimaced and took my hand in hers, though there wasn't as much comfort to the action with us both wearing gloves. "We'll get through this, okay? I'm apprehensive too, but now is not the time for us to give in to fear. Fear will dull our minds and weaken our resolve. We can't fight for our well-being in that state."

I sighed. "You're right, as much as it pains me. Let's get this day over with, and then we can start making plans of our own."

She held back a smile. "As long as these plans are better than the ones you had in Appalachia, we might stand a chance."

I reached over to smack her arm, but before I could, the doors to the throne room banged open and Sir Quinton entered with Sir Kent at his heels. Sky and I jumped apart and tried to sharpen our relaxed positions into something more royal, though I frowned at Quinton's lack of respect for Kent as his senior.

*What a hypocrite.*

"Are Your Highnesses ready?" Sir Quinton said by way of greeting, a fake smile plastered across his face.

I shrugged. "We have little choice, do we not?"

Quinton's eyes flashed in frustration, but Sky butted in before he could retort. "We understand our duty to the court, gentlemen, and we would not put the future of Summer in danger. However, we ask that you show us each the respect we deserve for our sacrifice."

"I'm not sure what you mean, Princess," Quinton replied, sounding both annoyed and curious.

"It is simple, Sir Quinton," Sky said. "You can take any wife you like, at any point in your life, or not at all, and that is your choice to make. Isan and I do not have that luxury, and so there is a chance we will be sacrificing our true happiness for the good of the kingdom. We're prepared to do this, as much as one can be, but I will not have you breathing down our necks the whole time or pushing us into a position we are not comfortable with."

I marvelled at Sky's sudden courage to stand up for herself, against Quinton of all people, but Asmund had been right earlier. Fidal help whoever thought they knew what was best for her.

"What are you saying exactly, Your Highness?" Quinton prodded.

"She is saying we will do what the kingdom expects of us," I replied, my control wearing thin, "what *you* expect of us, but it will be our choice in the end which suitor we choose. You can choose to respect our decision or face the consequences. Are we understood?"

Quinton gave us a blank, enraged stare for a moment, but Kent stepped up beside him and said, "We understand, and we trust you both will make the right decision. The future of Summer rests in your hands, and I know you do not take that task lightly. I hope you can find partners to strengthen both your kingdom and your own hearts. You deserve that."

Sky stepped forward and took his hand in hers. "Thank you, Sir Kent. Your loyalty means more to us than you know."

I nodded. "Summer is in good hands until our time comes. Now, I suppose we have a Festival to begin."

"Indeed, Your Highness," Kent replied. "Sancia be with you both. The knights will see you to your carriage, and Quinton and I will see you at the pavilion."

We left before Quinton could get in another word, and I imagined him fuming, his thin control vanquished by both Sky and Kent. And though I felt a rush of pride from the victory, I couldn't help but wonder how long it would last, and whether we had dug ourselves a deeper grave by speaking out.

# 10
# Green and Gold

**The carriage ride was** long, the procession weaving through nearly the entire city before filing into the town square. Sky and I rode together in the first carriage, a golden masterpiece with fine details pulled by a team of golden brown stallions. The roof had been lowered, and we smiled and waved at the citizens as we passed by. They cheered as they waved back and occasionally threw bouquets of flowers.

Sir Kent and Sir Quinton rode directly behind us as security, followed by the Byrons, the Arraths, the Maddixes, the Lachlans, the Norwells, and finally, Lady Katya and all five of the Caldwell children.

The noblechildren of Summer hadn't been gathered together all at once like this before, at least not in our lifetime. Darkenier had only ever hosted one family at a time and didn't even invite the lords to the Solstice ball. It was a great show of our newfound strength and unity; I just wished it didn't have to involve marriage.

The procession finally came to a stop at the pavilion, which looked more magnificent than it ever had, with gold garlands draped around its pillars and flower petals scattered across the floor. Gold chairs with green painted ivy snaking around them had been arranged in four rows of five on the right side of the pavilion, facing the crowd. To the left, Sky's and my wooden ceremonial thrones stood twice as high, with more gold and real ivy.

I wondered briefly how we could afford such opulence after the war, but it wasn't the time for that. I didn't need another reason to be in a foul mood.

Our suitors and their guardians descended from their carriages first and took their seats in the same order, leaving the first row with Jasper, Rosetta, Aramina, Asmund, and Tamsen. The rest followed in behind, with the Caldwells taking up the whole last row, save for Dorin.

As they each took their seats and the carriages rolled out of the square, trumpets started to sound, announcing our imminent arrival to the stage.

I squeezed Sky's hand. "Together?"

She nodded. "Together."

I stepped out of the carriage to the trumpets' crescendo and offered her my hand. Then we walked side by side to the thrones, taking our seats together as the notes of the bugles died out and the cheers of our people began. More flowers were thrown towards us, one landing at Sky's feet, and the knights hurried to regain order so the ceremony could begin.

Finally, a hush came over the square, and Sir Kent took his place at the front. "Welcome all, and thank you for coming. We are gathered here today to witness the commencement of a special festival, which has not been held in sixty years. It is our joy to announce that the Festival of Honour is upon us, and to formally introduce the young souls who may become our future Queen and Prince Consort. Trials lay ahead of them, but

Widonia welcomes them and wishes each the strength, wisdom, and compassion necessary to earn their place beside our Prince and Princess. May Sancia be with each one of them and with you all as we turn the page to the next chapter of Summer. Fidalia forever!"

The people echoed his cry, and more cheers rose up as Kent retreated to Sky's side and the herald took his place, preparing to announce each of the suitors.

I did my best to relax in my seat, but I was still on edge as the herald began.

"My dear people," he called out, "please welcome Master Jasper of Mensden, son of Lord Byron and Lady Florence."

The people clapped respectfully as Jasper stood and bowed, inclining his head completely to the crowd. Then he did the same before Sky and me, while reciting the ceremonial words. "I pledge my loyalty to the crown, to Summer, and to its people. May my heart prove true and humble, whatever my destiny may be."

I clenched my fists at my side as I fought to stay calm, knowing his heart was anything but humble.

"I am honoured to name you as one of my suitors," Sky replied, her demeanour much more composed than mine.

Jasper smiled at her like he'd already been chosen and returned to his seat, though he remained standing as the herald called Rosetta up.

"Please welcome Mistress Rosetta of Mensden, daughter of Lord Byron and Lady Florence." She followed in Jasper's footsteps, though she addressed me instead of Sky, and I replied in turn.

The next twenty minutes were the same as each noblechild was presented to the crowd and pledged allegiance to Sky or me. Jasper was the only one I remained wary of, for now. I didn't like the way Kainda looked at *me*, but I suppose she wasn't too keen to be wed to a boy five years her junior. She was here out of duty and nothing more, and I wondered if these unions would benefit any of us. Were we all doomed to misery?

"And last, but certainly not least," the herald announced finally, "please welcome Master Weylyn of Ne-Trol, son of Lord Norwell and Lady Helga."

Weylyn stumbled through the steps and fumbled the ceremonial words a bit, but Sky gave him an encouraging smile anyway, and he returned to his seat with a bit more confidence than when he'd left it. Still, I couldn't imagine Sky taking him as her husband anytime soon.

The trumpets sounded again, signalling the end of the ceremony, and Sir Kent stepped forward once more to give the parting remarks. I barely listened, my mind a swirl of thoughts. I kept sneaking glances at Jasper, looking for anything out of place, but I knew I was wasting my time. Jasper was the favoured suitor, as Mensden was the second most prosperous city aside from Widonia, and no one would dare remove him from the Festival on my word alone.

Finally, a chorus of trumpets erupted from the square, and the crowd threw their hands in the air in celebration—our cue to leave. Sky and I stood first, and I led her to our carriage, letting her enter before me as a proper gentleman. The rest followed suit, and soon the carriages were on a direct route back to the castle, the cheers and flowers of our people following in our wake.

The Festival was bringing them all hope, and that's why a part of me couldn't completely dismiss it. The people needed tradition. They needed something to look forward to, a future to live for. I just wished their happiness wasn't at the expense of my own, but I supposed that was the burden of leadership. Sacrifice for the greater good.

● ● ●

The next hour passed in a blur as we were made to change outfits *again* and prepare for the opening feast, the first of many to come. This time, the servants gave me an entirely gold coat with shiny bronze buttons and brown underclothes snaked through with ivy stitching.

The dinner was only fifteen minutes away when one of the servants set a pair of golden boots down in front of me, bowing low. "Your shoes, Your Highness. Just left the cobbler's shop this morning."

I took one look at the opulent monstrosities and said, "Absolutely not."

The man blinked. "I'm sorry, Your Highness?"

"I can't wear these," I replied, fighting to keep my voice calm and my temper under control, but my strength in both areas was waning.

"But they were made specially for this occasion, Your Highness, with the measurements the cobbler took. They'll be a perfect fit, and—"

"I said *no*." My voice was low but stern. "I'll wear my black boots from this morning."

The servant girl who was finishing my hair gave me a wry smile in the mirror. "Oh, you mustn't, Your Highness. It'll ruin your entire ensemble."

I clenched my fists around the arms of my chair and said, "I *will*. You two may go now. I'm presentable enough, and I need a few moments to myself."

The girl hesitated, and I met her eyes in the mirror, trying to look kind. "Please," I added.

She gave a solemn nod and turned away. "Come, Godwin," she said to the man. "The Prince is ready."

The two left without another word, but I did catch the annoyed glare Godwin threw at me in the mirror, and that nearly set me off. Heat sizzled beneath my palms, but I took deep breaths and tried to think of happy memories to calm myself down.

I hadn't caught fire since the argument the day before with Asmund, but with the way the day was going so far, I knew my luck wouldn't last long. I just had to hope I could prevent anyone from seeing, and prevent myself from hurting anyone.

Scarcely a minute had passed before a knock sounded on my door, and I stifled a groan as I called out, "Who is it?"

"It's Aunt Mag, child," my visitor replied. "May I come in?"

I let out a sigh. "Yes."

I watched through the mirror as she entered and came to stand behind me, resting her hands on the shoulders of my fancy new coat. "Godwin tells me you refused the boots."

"Does that surprise you? Look at them." I threw my hands out in exasperation, my resolve finally fading and my frustration lashing out. "They said it would 'ruin my ensemble,' but I don't care because quite frankly, I look ridiculous! I'm already the albino Prince of Summer; I don't need to stand out even more, but sure, dress me up like I'm some kind of candelabra.

"Besides, how in Fidalia does anyone expect me to dance properly with new shoes? I'll either be the laughing stock of the ballroom or unable to walk from the blisters I'll be sure to get. Sancia's breath, Aunt Mag, this is all too much for me, and the one thing I ask is that I can wear my own comfortable worn-in black boots. Is that so wrong?"

I blinked back angry tears as Aunt Mag squeezed my shoulders and said, "There is no shame in the familiar, Isanfier, but there *is* honour in standing up for yourself. I know I've said before that it's important to wear Summer's colours, but it's also important to be yourself. Do whatever you need to do to make this Festival easy for you, to make it your own. This is your future too, no matter what anyone else thinks or expects of you."

I sniffed and wiped my eyes with the back of my hand. "So, what, are you telling me to do whatever I want?"

She smiles. "Not whatever you want, but decide what you are willing to sacrifice and what you are not. Joy can be found in the smallest things if you have the patience to look for it." She squeezed my shoulders again. "I will see you in the dining hall, child. Be true to yourself first, and everything else will follow."

She left the room without another word, and I stared blankly in the direction of the door for a few minutes before her words sank in and my thoughts started to turn.

*Decide what I'm willing to sacrifice and what I am not.*

I smiled as I realized exactly what I needed to do, and for the first time that day, I felt confidence return to me. I was going to be okay. I was going to make the most of this.

I shrugged off the gold coat and hung it back up in my wardrobe. I chose another one of my new coats instead, one that was more of a hunter green with gold stitching. The darker colour would match my hair better and wouldn't catch the light as much. I slid my feet into my own black boots, though not my most comfortable pair, as they did look a little too worn for a ball.

Then I strapped my sword belt under my coat and slid *Ember* into her sheath. If they wanted me armed, so be it, but I wasn't going to be waltzing around the ballroom with a dainty ceremonial sword. I was a man. I had fought in a war. I deserved to show my true worth and to be able to defend myself should the need arise.

Finally, despite my misgivings, I placed my crown on my head because I knew that now, more than ever, I needed to solidify my place as Prince and future King of Summer. If Quinton wanted me to act like royalty, then that's what I would do, but I had a feeling he wasn't going to like the results. If this Festival was nothing more than a political game, then I would play it, and play it well.

# 11

## A Delicate Dance

**I met Sky in** the ante-chamber behind the dining hall, a room we hadn't used in years, though the servants had cleaned it so well, you could hardly tell. A tall window behind us let in the late afternoon sun and sent the crystal chandelier above us sparkling.

Sky was wearing another opulent green dress with a corset drawn so tight even I grimaced. I knew her waist was not that slim. She did look stunning, though, I had to admit, her braided hair spun through with golden ivy and large emeralds hanging from her ears. A gold necklace sat around her neck with a massive green pendant nestled against her dark skin.

She crossed her arms over her chest as I studied her. "I know what you're thinking."

I frowned. "What?"

She bit her lip. "It's… Oh, Isan, I know the dress is lovely and any other girl would kill for it, but it's so… tight, and I can't believe how low this neckline is. They're all going to be staring down my dress."

She threw her hands up to cover her face but stopped short, probably realizing she would ruin her cosmetics.

I walked over and pulled her against me in a half hug. "If I catch anyone staring anywhere but in your eyes or at your feet, they will face my sword." I patted *Ember's* hilt to emphasize my point.

Sky gave me a wide-eyed look. "You brought *Ember?* What if Quinton notices?"

I shrugged. "At this point, I'm kind of hoping he *does* notice. I'm not going to let them tell me what to wear and what I can and can't bring anymore, Sky, and I won't let them push you around either. This is *our* Festival too. I can stall if you want to change into a more comfortable dress."

She half smiled. "I'd love to, but I can't get this thing off by myself. Could you loosen the ties a bit? I'm already starting to feel the strain."

I nodded, and she leaned against the wall as I did just that, careful to tie the ends tight again so the dress wouldn't go anywhere.

"And this," she said, reaching up to undo her necklace, "it's like a Fidal-forsaken beacon. Do you have a pocket?"

I took the necklace from her and slipped it into the inside pocket of my coat, on the opposite side of my sword to balance me out a little.

"All right," I said. "Is that everything?"

She took a deep breath and smoothed her skirts. "I think it's the best we can do for now. Are you ready?"

"For an evening of small talk, faking interest, and trying not to get stepped on?"

She laughed. "Yes, that."

"Sancia's breath, no, but I'll try to make the most of it."

We shared a smile, and then I wrapped my arm around hers and signalled to the servant boy waiting by the doors that we were ready. He called ahead to the herald, and as the trumpets began and the double doors swung open, Sky and I walked arm in arm into the dining hall and towards our future.

The dining hall had been transformed into something out of a fairytale, so much so that I hardly knew where to look first.

A golden arch wrapped with fresh ivy stood outside the doors, and a gold velvet carpet ran through it and beneath our feet, dusted with flower petals in every colour. Round tables stood around the room with green tablecloths, massive flower centrepieces, and gleaming goblets and silverware. More flowers stood in large urns around the perimeter of the room, and all the chandeliers were lit with candles, more ivy strung between them.

I leaned over and whispered in Sky's ear, "And this is only the opening feast. How will the wedding be able to outshine it?"

She shrugged, and I led us over to the high table, a rectangular table near the far wall facing the room with only two seats for us, thank the goddesses.

Everyone stood in silence until we took our seats, and then chatter started up again as the fanfare died out.

I stared at the golden table runner in dismay as I wondered how in Fidalia I was going to get through a five-course meal without spilling something on it.

"Well, here we are," Sky said softly. "So far, so good?"

"The fun hasn't even started yet," I reminded her.

A servant filled our glasses, and I raised mine to Sky. "A toast to our happy futures?"

She huffed a laugh but raised her goblet. "A toast to making our own happiness, no matter what it takes."

We clinked glasses and then sat in nervous silence as we waited for the meal to begin. I studied the different tables, knowing we would be forced to mingle before long.

To our right sat the officials with Sir Kent, Sir Quinton, and a few other knights from the Council. To our left, Asmund and Aramina were sharing a table with Jasper and Rosetta, much to Asmund's dismay, I was sure, but I felt reassured knowing he could keep an eye on Jasper. Behind them were three rows of tables with the Maddixes sharing with the Lachlans, and the Norwells and Caldwells having tables to themselves. At the far end of the hall, I could see Aunt Mag sitting with the governesses from Ne-Trol, Fortude, and Laurel.

It was the largest gathering we'd had in a long time, and a whole slew of servants were bustling in and out of the room as they tried to make it an evening to remember. I took a gulp of wine to ease my nerves as they brought in the first course, and Sir Kent stood to make the opening toast.

"Dear honoured guests," he began as servants set steaming bowls of yellow soup in front of us, "we thank you all for coming and hope you enjoy the momentous meal that has been prepared for us in celebration of this wondrous occasion. It is not often we gather together, but I do believe the future of Summer is in good hands. Dinner will be followed by dancing in the ballroom, and then we will meet at first light tomorrow for the first challenge.

"May your stomachs be full and your hearts be light, and may this Festival instill new virtues in you, even if it does not lead to a place in this household. May Sancia be with you all. Fidalia forever."

We all raised our glasses and echoed his prayer before digging into the meal. The food was beyond delicious, but my nerves kept me from enjoying it as much as I wanted to. I kept scanning the room for suspicious activity and alternating glances between Quinton and Jasper, daring either of them to step a toe out of line.

My paranoia had dinner passing in a blur, and before I knew it, my server was asking my choice of dessert. I chose strawberry and almond pudding, though I didn't feel like anything sweet, and pushed it around my bowl until Sky gave me a pointed look and said, "Are you going to eat that?"

I sighed and said, "No."

"Well, then pass it over," she replied.

I frowned. "Didn't you already have some?"

"I did, but I want more, and it's hardly fair for it to be neglected like that when it's so scrumptious. Honestly, I'd try to convince you you're missing out, but I really want to eat it."

I cracked a smile and pushed the plate over to her side of the table. "Be my guest. I'll be sure to request it for the dessert at your wedding."

She pointed her spoon at me, already laden with pudding, and said, "You better."

"How are you not nervous?" I asked her, attempting to relax my posture a bit.

"Well, I can actually breathe, for one, thanks to your plan," she replied in between mouthfuls of dessert, "but also because right now I'm enjoying a good meal at my brother's side with friends and family around me. Like you said, we have to make this our night, Isan. Worrying about everything that might happen will do us no good. We have to trust the plans Sancia has for us."

"Then can I have your first dance?"

She smiled. "Always. Plus, it'll have the added benefit of upsetting our dear friend, Quinton."

I grinned. "Oh, that's half the reason I asked. Also, your teeth are starting to go pink."

She put her hand over her mouth, her eyes widening in embarrassment. "Sancia's breath, really?"

I let her sweat for a few more seconds and then said, "Tricked you!"

She swatted at my arm with her napkin. "You are a terrible brother, Isanfier. You will *pay* for that."

I burst into laughter, but the sound of a pointed cough off to the side had me sobering up rather quickly.

Quinton was standing to my right, giving us both a scathing look that was equal parts angry and disappointed. "The ball is about to start, so if you two are finished, I suggest you take your places. Oh, and I thought I should remind you, Your Highness," he added with a glance at Sky, "that a proper lady does not devour two servings of dessert like she hasn't seen food in weeks. The men will talk."

I shot to my feet, rattling the empty plates on our table, and was about to throw myself at the bastard when Sky spoke first.

"The *men*, Sir Quinton? I think you have the boys in this dining hall confused with some other people. And I do believe you have *me* confused with someone who takes insults sitting down, but I do not, and I will not forget your insolence. You can see yourself out."

Her words were deadly calm, but there was a storm beneath them, threatening to break free. My own fire crackled in my veins, begging to be let out, but I took deep breaths to quell my anger and focused on the way Quinton's face was turning red.

"I beg your pardon?" he choked out, a vein on his forehead pulsing with the strain of keeping himself in check.

"She said you can leave, Sir Quinton," I replied.

"But the ball—"

"I'm sure Sir Kent has it covered. He is the Regent, after all, and since he used to hold your position as well, I'm sure he can handle the guards too. Have a good night."

He stood there seething in rage for a few more moments before he turned around with a huff and stormed out of the dining hall, without another word to anyone. Sir Kent gave me a look from his table, and I motioned him over.

"Your Highness," he said, "is everything all right?"

"Sir Quinton has been making inappropriate remarks to my sister, and neither one of us wishes to tolerate them any further. If he returns to the ball tonight, please send him on his way, and remind him who he serves. He answers to Sky and me, not the other way around, and if he doesn't learn to accept that, we will no longer have need of his services as Captain, or in the Council, or even as a knight."

Kent looked at me in horror. "I do apologize on his behalf, Your Highness. I had no idea his behaviour was as such, and I will definitely speak with him later. Let me know if there is ever anything else I can do."

I squeezed his shoulder. "Thank you. Now, I believe we have a ball to join?"

Indeed, our guests had already filed out into the adjoining ballroom, and I could hear the faintest notes of a waltz starting up, stirring my weary soul. The occasion was not the most joyous affair, but I rarely said no to an opportunity for dancing.

I led Sky down another golden carpet and into the ballroom, which looked more opulent than I'd seen it since our sixteenth birthday gala, full of flowers, garland, and tiny silver stars that caught the light of the torches, setting the walls ablaze with glitter.

"Are you okay?" I asked Sky, but she had her head back, taking everything in with a look of joy on her face that I hadn't seen in a long time either, so I simply took her other hand and led her into the first dance.

Everything fell away as we danced—the decorated walls of the ballroom, the nobles and knights watching our every move, even the music.It was like we were children again, learning the moves under Aunt Mag's tutelage. We had no obligations, no reservations, just our whole lives ahead of us and the dream of greatness.

Sky laughed as I spun her beneath my arm, around and around but not enough to make her dizzy.

The memory of our childhood lessons faded, and I could feel everyone watching us again, waiting for their time in the spotlight, their chance to wrap their arms around one of us. The thought made my skin crawl, and I faltered my next step.

Thankfully, Sky caught the mistake and smoothed it over before I could make a fool of both of us, and we slid into the final pose as the final note of the violin rang out.

Our audience clapped politely, and while I wondered if they were actually impressed, I caught Aunt Mag smiling from her place at the back of the crowd. I could tell she was proud of us from the joy in her eyes and the way her smile seemed to want to break free of the boundaries of her face. She had taught us everything we'd known, and we were representing her well.

Her reaction gave me the strength I needed to release Sky, who gave my hand a squeeze before letting go.

*Together*, the action said, and I knew that no matter how poorly the night went from there, she would always be there for me, and at least we had enjoyed one dance.

The orchestra began another slow tune, the melody soft and lilting to add ambient background noise between waltzes. I could see Aramina swaying in time with the music near the edge of the crowd and smiled, deciding who my next partner would be. Quinton would've chided me for showing favouritism, but Quinton wasn't there.

I left Sky's side and walked up to Aramina, feeling everyone's eyes watching me as I passed them by. Raina gave me a coy smile which quickly morphed into a scowl when she realized who I was heading towards, but she said nothing, knowing there was nothing she could say.

Aramina's face lit up in surprise when I stopped in front of her.

I took her hand. "May I have this dance, my lady?" I asked her, my tone light.

She beamed at me. "Of course, Your Highness. It would be my pleasure."

I resisted the urge to chide her for using my title and led her onto the dance floor as the music picked up. Across the ballroom, Sky was paired with Tamsen. We both had the honour of choosing our first partners, but that was the only privilege we were allowed. Around us, the rest of our suitors paired up and began to dance as well, keeping a few feet of distance between them and where Sky and I twirled in the middle of the floor.

# 12
# Whispers of Wisteria

**Aramina was an incredibly** graceful dancer, her limbs fluid like a river and yet precise. I felt like I had two left feet dancing with her, but I was enjoying myself all the same, knowing she didn't expect anything from me, wouldn't force me into anything.

"Are you enjoying your night?" I asked her after a moment.

"Did you see the way Raina and Soleia looked at me when we passed them?" she replied, eyes alight with mischief. "This is the best day of my life."

I raised an eyebrow as I spun her around. "You're happy they hate you?"

"No," she corrected, "I'm happy they *see* me. I've been invisible most of my life, so it's nice to be noticed, to have someone think I'm good enough to be jealous of. I know it's only fabricated by this festival and because I'm dancing with you, but it's still…nice."

I nodded; I could understand that. My whole life I'd wanted to be somebody, to be worthy of my crown, of my uncle's approval. If even *I* could feel that way being born into royalty, I couldn't imagine how Aramina felt, the youngest child of three, reduced to nothing more than a girl to be married off in the hopes of garnering power for her family.

"Are *you* enjoying your night?" she asked me.

"It's had some good moments," I allowed. "Dinner was excellent, and the decorations are lovely, but I'd rather be somewhere else."

"Like where?"

I shrugged, as much as I could without breaking the flow of the dance, and replied, "I don't know. Maybe in the training yard, improving my skills, or sitting in my room doing nothing in particular with Sky and Asmund."

She wrinkled her nose. "Asmund?"

I cracked a smile. "I'm sure you think I hit my head or something, but he's not the arrogant bastard he was when he left for the war, Mina. We're not perfect yet, but we've put aside our differences and are trying to move forward."

"That's what he said," she replied, sounding distant, "but it's hard to believe."

"I heard you two had a fight," I said.

She clenched her jaw. "Something like that. He's just... Well, you know how he is. I've heard it all before, that he's changed, that he's going to do better and make our mother proud, but... I don't want to get my hopes up again, and Arran says he's not worth my generous heart. I'm glad you two are closer, but I don't know if I'm ready for that yet. The wounds are too fresh."

Her voice was so small and painful I wanted to wrap her into a hug and leave the ball entirely, but I knew we both had to keep up appearances, and I still had a long line of eligible ladies waiting on their turn. We'd probably danced too long already.

"He stood up against your father for me, back in Appalachia," I told her, hoping to bring her a measure of peace before we parted ways.

Her expression froze. "He what?"

"After I killed the King, Lord Arrath accused me of lying about my motives and doing it to take the crown. Asmund stood beside me and told his father to back down."

Her eyebrows rose. "That's...impressive."

"I'm not saying you need to change your position based on that alone, but I thought you should know. He's proven his loyalty to me, and I've given him a chance, but if he turns his back on me again, I don't think I'll be able to find it in myself to forgive him."

She nodded, and we danced in companionable silence until another song ended, and I sensed it was time for us to part ways. We came to a stop, and she curtsied while still holding my hand.

"This has been lovely, Your Highness," she said. "I am honoured to be your second dance partner tonight. Until we meet again."

I pressed my lips to her outstretched hand and replied, "The pleasure is all mine."

We shared a secret smile, and then she walked away to find another partner or perhaps take a break. The servants had set out a few chairs around the perimeter of the ballroom and a table with wine and water glasses near the doors.

As Aramina walked away, the others began to take notice, and one by one they relinquished their partners. Tamsen bowed low to Sky, and she offered him a genuine smile. Out of the corner of my eye, I watched Jasper part ways from Raina and make a beeline towards Sky. My skin crawled, and heat rushed to my hands, but I knew there was little I could do, and if he tried something, Sky could more than handle herself. She'd make him wish he'd never been born.

So I took a deep breath and waited for someone to approach me, which didn't take long. Raina and Soleia nearly tripped over each other trying to get to me, allowing Rosetta to pass them. She dropped into a low curtsy, her long braids nearly touching the floor, giving me an uninvited view down the front of her dress, which was much lower cut than Sky's.

I averted my gaze as the blood rushed to my face. As much as she annoyed me, I couldn't deny she was pretty. Her skin was about the same tone as Sky's, but her hair was black as night, and she was a bit taller. I was sure her dress cost a fortune too, with its deep magenta colour and the miniature rose insignias woven throughout the design. I had no doubt she would find a good husband some day, but it wouldn't be me.

"Your Highness," she said breathily, as if she had run a race to get to me. "May I have this dance?"

I did my best to smile at her, wanting to be as polite as I could manage to each of my suitors. It wasn't their fault I wasn't interested, and it wasn't even that. I just didn't want to be forced into a relationship I wasn't ready for, to be given away to somebody who wanted me for the status it would grant them. I wanted something more.

The rest of the night passed agonizingly slow as I drifted from partner to partner, only crossing paths with Sky briefly during a break between songs. Raina had as much perfume on as I'd expected, Gwyneth stepped on my feet more than once, and Kainda didn't say a word throughout the three waltzes we danced.

I even pulled Dorin's eight-year-old sister Orella onto the floor for one song to lighten the mood a bit. Lady Katya beamed with pride, but most of my suitors seemed less than impressed by my choice.

Penelope was my last partner of the night, and the silence between us was thankfully amicable instead of the awkwardness I had anticipated.

"I assume you've been well since we last saw each other?" Penelope asked as we twirled around the perimeter of the dance floor. Most of the noblechildren were seated in the chairs now, with only Asmund dancing with Sky, and Kainda with Weylyn, though the latter pair didn't seem to be dancing to the same beat as the rest of us.

I decided to go for gentle honesty as I looked Penelope in the eyes and said, "I have to admit, I've been better. Uncle's death has shaken me, and this Festival has put both me and Sky under a lot of stress. We haven't been given enough breathing room to properly recover from our ordeals in Winter."

She gave me a small understanding smile. "I can't imagine what it must've been like. I thank both Sancia and Audria that Tamsen wasn't old enough to go. Fidal knows what state he would've been returned to me in, if he'd come back at all."

"It is definitely more gore than glory, and I don't think I'll ever be the same boy who left these gates. I haven't decided yet if it's made me stronger."

"Do you think..." She hung her head as she let the sentence trail off.

I frowned. "What is it?"

She hesitated, her dancing almost coming to a stop, and I slowed down.

"I know we've had our differences, Elle," I went on, "but your words are safe with me. I want you to know that. I haven't lost my honour or my loyalty to those who matter."

She took a deep breath, a new determination to her gaze, and said, "Do you think the danger has passed? I want to believe we won absolutely, that we are safe and the Festival of Honour is a testament to that, but I can't. I keep thinking this is a mere distraction, that we are still far from achieving peace."

I grimaced. Penelope had always been a sharp one; it was what had drawn me to her in the first place, even when we were young. She didn't take anything at face value, always questioned and tried to get to the why instead of accepting situations as they were. She would make for a wise and just Queen, but I wouldn't consign her to this life if she didn't want it.

"I'm either right, judging from your silence," she continued, a hint of annoyance in her voice, "or you're refusing to answer the question."

"No, you're on the right path," I admitted, feeling the tension leave her limbs. "The Festival of Honour is more of a necessity than a distraction, but I wouldn't say Summer is safe. King Frost and Prince Snowdon are dead, but Princess Icaria is still out there somewhere, and she is the true heir to the Winter throne."

"Will she retaliate?"

"I don't want to worry you, but it's more a question of when, not if. The Wyllans always get even, especially when Summer is involved. She will see it as a duty to her nation and her deceased family to at least *attempt* to enact vengeance upon Summer, and Sky personally."

She raised an eyebrow. "Why Princess Skiansy?"

"Sky killed the Winter Prince; Icaria will want her blood."

Penelope raised an eyebrow. "I had no idea Her Highness came that close to the enemy. She surely enjoys more privileges than the rest of us ladies."

"I'm not sure nearly dying under the Winter King's frost spell is a privilege."

Her eyes widened. "Oh, my apologies, Your Highness. I didn't mean—"

I gave her a look. "Please don't resort to using my title, Penelope. I harbour no ill feelings towards you. I just thought I should point out the obvious. War is a perilous endeavour I would wish upon no man *or* woman, but sometimes it must be done. Sky did what she felt was right, with my support, but she put herself at great risk in doing so."

"I'm sorry, Isan. Sometimes I think before I speak, and I guess I…romanticize Sky's place in the war. I imagine her out there, riding through wide open fields with no governess breathing down her neck and no expectations, but of course I know her responsibility was great, and the experience could not have been easy. I know I wouldn't want that path for myself, but I covet the right to choose. Surely even you understand that. I mean, do you even want this Festival?"

The song changed then as I contemplated her rhetorical question, and I found myself moving from muscle memory, humming the tune absentmindedly.

And suddenly, it wasn't Penelope I was dancing with.

Her dark hair and russet skin turned white, morphing into Echo's familiar face as the melody of "Whispers of Wisteria" sent me down memory lane. Echo's soft hand was in mine, her blue eyes aglow with the joy of the moment as we danced beneath the light of the moon, the trees of the Edgewood swaying around us.

Penelope's voice brought me back, sounding distant but definitely there, snapping me out of my reverie. "Isan?"

I blinked at her, disoriented.

"Isan, are you all right?"

"Yes, I'm sorry," I replied, letting go of her hand to rub at my forehead. "I'm not sure what happened."

She gave me a worried look. "It was like you were somewhere else."

The image of Echo was still fresh in my mind, and I found myself longing to be with her instead, to leave the ballroom and castle far behind, but of course I said nothing of the sort.

Instead, I took a deep breath and said, "I think I'm growing tired. It might be time for us all to retire."

She nodded. "That would probably be wise. Sir Kent said tomorrow's challenge will begin at dawn, so I'm sure everyone will be grateful for as much rest as you can give them." I relinquished her, and she dropped into a curtsy. "I have enjoyed our time together, Isan. Thank you for your honesty."

I smiled and pressed a kiss to her hand. "Anytime, my lady."

She left me then, and I looked around the room for Kent, finally finding him conversing with Aunt Mag by the drinks table. It was a moment before I caught his eye, but when I did, I motioned him over.

He made haste towards me and dropped into a bow. "What is it I may do for you, Your Highness?"

"I would like to call an end to tonight's ball. It has been a long day for everyone, and it will be an even longer day tomorrow."

Kent nodded. "Of course, Your Highness. I also wanted to assure you that Sir Quinton has made no attempts to reenter the festivities. I apologize again for his conduct, and I will make sure it is not repeated."

"Thank you," I replied. "Your loyalty is more than appreciated, Sir Kent. I will see you at first light."

Sir Kent clapped his hands once, and the orchestra brought "Whispers of Wisteria" to an early close. I felt a pang in my heart as the notes stopped and my thoughts drifted towards Echo again, wondering how she was faring in our absence and if she'd yet learned of our victory over Winter, of the death of her brother and father.

Part of me hoped she didn't know, so she wouldn't have to be alone when she heard the news. Her father had been cruel to her, and she'd known Snowdon needed to die to save the realm, but they were still family. It would still hurt to find out they were gone, just as I had felt more defeated than victorious when Darkenier died.

All this ran through my head as I watched our guests depart the ballroom, until only Asmund and Sky remained. As they joined me in the centre of the room, I noticed they were still holding hands. Asmund saw my raised eyebrow before Sky did and let go of her hand gently, so as not to cause alarm.

I scowled at him, but said nothing. I was too tired to raise a proper argument.

"What a night," Sky groaned when the doors finally closed, breaking the tension as per usual. "I feel like my feet are going to fall off." She lifted her skirts, enough to show her golden shoes, and grimaced at her swollen feet.

Even I could tell they hurt. "Well, let's walk and talk, then, so you can give your feet a rest as soon as possible."

She nodded, and the three of us headed for the doors.

"How did you fare tonight?" I asked her.

She shrugged. "It went better than I expected, I guess. Everyone was polite enough, but Weylyn could not figure out the rhythm of any of the songs, and Dorin would not stop talking. I can still hear his voice ringing in my ears."

Asmund laughed. "Maybe they'll grow out of that."

Sky's face reddened, and I couldn't help but grin. "It's not funny, you two. How would you like to be married off to someone Aramina's age?"

Asmund made a face. "Fair point."

"What about Jasper?" I asked her.

"He was the perfect gentleman, but in a way that I could tell he was lying through his teeth, you know? I thought his smile might spread wings and fly away, it was so wide. He tried to get three dances out of me too, but Asmund cut him off the last time. The look on his face made my entire day."

I gave Asmund an approving nod and said, "Well, if he starts bothering you, let one of us know, and we'll put a stop to it. Let's just pray he fares poorly in the Festival challenges, and we won't even have to lift a finger."

"I have a feeling he's trained his whole life for this and won't give up easily."

I grimaced. "I hope you're wrong, for all our sakes."

# 13
# A Dark Discovery

**The next afternoon, the** three of us were cloistered in the corner of the dusty library, each of our heads in a book with more piled around us. The first challenge had passed that morning without major incident as each of the male suitors showed their strength against a trio of knights armed with swords.

Each boy had been allowed to choose his own weapon, and some had been much smarter than others. Dorin and Weylyn had chosen a bow and mace respectively, and while both had seemed skilled with their weapons, they'd been no match for the knights and surrendered after wounding only one opponent each.

Tamsen had run circles around the knights with his pole-axe, impressing even me with his prowess as he'd swept two of the knights off their feet hard enough to stun them and knocked the third out with the flat of the blade, though not without sustaining a few injuries of his own.

Only Asmund and Jasper had escaped their battles relatively unscathed, much to my dismay. Jasper unfortunately had the skills to back up the sword he carried, even though he'd never seen a proper battlefield. Still, Asmund had outperformed him, the three knights being nothing compared to the enemies we had faced in the Edgewood and in Winter.

Asmund was the victor of the day with the fastest time and only a marginally bruised rib. Jasper had a cut across his face I hoped would scar and knock his ego down a bit.

"What are we looking for exactly?" I groaned as I attempted to stretch out my kinked neck.

Sky didn't look up from her book as she replied, "Anything to do with magic, Isanfier. You need to keep skimming the tables of contents until you find something promising. Don't linger on a book any longer than you need to. We only have a few hours until dinner."

"Then how come you've been reading that same book for twenty minutes?"

"It's a detailed account of our ancestry, much more so than anything the scholars taught us in our lessons. I'm hoping there's some talk of magic in our lineage, something Uncle didn't want them telling us about."

Asmund sighed. "Well, I'm glad one of us is having some luck. I'm about as frustrated as Isanfier is, which is saying a lot."

I scowled. "Watch it."

"Why don't you see if you can find some different books? There's no way Uncle could have destroyed all the books on magic without it being public knowledge, so the answer has to be in here somewhere. We just need to find it."

"If you say so," I replied, getting to my feet and stretching my limbs to purge the static feeling in them. "If I don't return soon, assume I've fallen asleep from boredom."

Sky rolled her eyes. "You do realize I'm doing this for you, right? This is your life on the line and the best plan I can come up with on short notice, so some gratitude would be appreciated."

I sighed. "I know, I'm sorry. I'm just not very good at this sort of thing."

She gave me a sympathetic smile. "I know. That's why I'm sending you to get more books while I keep reading."

I headed off towards the far right aisle, leaving them to their reading, and followed the stacks of books towards the non-fiction section Sky had led us to earlier. I thanked Fidal that Sky was familiar with the place, because I knew it would take me weeks to find anything otherwise.

The library took up the entire top three floors of the northwest turret, a giant circular warren of books shelved from the floor all the way to the vaulted ceilings, in countless aisles in the center, along the walls, and piled in every nook and cranny. It was impressive, especially with all the natural light coming from the huge windows, but it was also intimidating.

A few minutes later, I found the section of shelf we'd already raided and began reading the titles on the neighbouring shelf.

*A Night of Summer, Widonian People, The Farmer's Guide to a Healthy Crop, A List of Genealogies of Ne-Trol.*

I frowned—all were completely useless to us—and moved on to the shelf at the bottom, taking a seat on the dusty wooden floor which creaked beneath me.

*The Long Line of Summer, The Life and Death of Queen Katheryn.*

I smiled. Those would be perfect.

I pulled them off the shelf, accidentally knocking another book onto the floor beside me. The cover was dark blue, but it was the symbol engraved on the cover that gave me pause: a snowflake, its design identical to the symbol that opened the spiral staircase in the Appalachian palace.

I turned the book over and read the title inked in pitch black cursive on the spine: *Into the Throes of Winter.*

I narrowed my eyes.

*What in Fidalia is a Wyllan book doing in the Summer castle? Did Darkenier bring it with him? But then why leave it here and not in his own chambers?*

In search of answers, I skimmed the pages, taking care not to rip the fragile paper, but it soon became clear the book was fiction—a romance that took place in Winter. It didn't sound entirely riveting, but who was I to judge?

Still, what was it doing beside titles on Summer lineage and royalty?

I flipped through a couple more pages and was about to close the book when something fell out of it. I cursed, thinking I'd torn a page, but as I leaned over to retrieve it, I noticed it was a folded piece of parchment.

I set the book down on the floor and unfolded it, the breath leaving my lungs as I beheld another strange discovery.

Scrawled on the paper in dark blue ink was the royal Winter family tree.

I traced my finger down the core lineage, from Lea the so called First Queen, along the right-hand side until I saw Frost's name and an additional line for his wife Cascadia. Snowdon and Icaria's names were missing, so the tree must've been done before they were born. Both of Frost's parents must've had magic too, with names like Blizzard and Iceclea.

Lea and her immediate children seemed to lack the magic gene, so I assumed they'd been married off to magic users to strengthen the bloodline and create the ruthless royals Fidalia knew today.

The left side of the tree started with Edmund and his wife Izabel, who had a daughter named Alice. Alice married Colden and had two children, Shiveera and...

The ink on the name was smudged, so it took me a moment to make out the letters, and even then, I took a second glance, hoping to prove myself wrong, but there was no denying the truth. Darkenier was a part of the royal Winter family.

# Winter Royal Family Tree

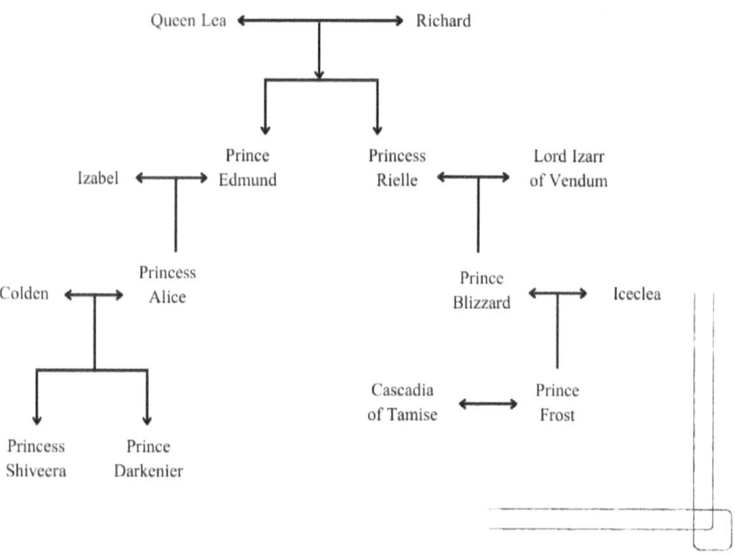


My thoughts swirled in my head until the puzzle pieces of Darkenier's masquerade and betrayal fell into place. Why Frost had called Darkenier his cousin when he'd arrived in the throne room. Why Darkenier had said he had been promised greatness but had been cheated, how Frost had stolen everything from him.

One mystery had been solved, but dozens more writhed in the shadows of its passing, and I was no closer to unraveling the mystery of my own magic.

Still, I slipped the parchment back into its book and grabbed all three to take to Sky and Asmund. They needed to know how far Darkenier's deception went too, and maybe they'd have some better ideas on how his life had gone so wrong.

"Oh, good, you're back," Sky said as she heard my footsteps returning. "What did you find?" She looked up at me from her book, and her face fell when she saw my expression. "What happened?"

I set my books down on the table beside my chair and held up the Winter book. "I found this on the shelf next to the others. It's a Wyllan romance novel, but I found a copy of a royal Winter family tree inside it." I pulled out the parchment paper and handed it to her, watching with bated breath as her eyes scanned the words.

Her eyebrows rose, and she looked over the top of the parchment at me. "Darkenier was a Prince of Winter?"

Asmund looked up from his own book in alarm. "What? Give me that." He grabbed the paper from Sky, who let him, and read through the tree quickly. "Sancia's shining light..." he breathed. "So not only was the Summer throne taken by a Wyllan, but a powerful one at that. What did he need our crown for when he had one of his own, with his own people?"

"That's just it, Asmund," I replied. "Darkenier should've been *King*. Look at the lineage."

He studied the tree again and then gave me a knowing glance. "You're right, but to be honest with you, I didn't know his side of the family existed. Not that my knowledge of Wyllan history is extensive, but still. I mean, who is Shiveera? Why wasn't she crowned Queen?"

I shrugged. "I have no idea, but it is quite curious."

"Maybe when it was all said and done, Darkenier was actually a victim?" Sky suggested.

I gave her a dark look, and she held up her hands.

"I'm definitely not saying what he did was right, but maybe his initial motives had some merit. Our ancestors were historically only children, but what would you do if Aunt Mag had a child who was crowned over you, for example?"

I crossed my arms and dropped into my chair, needing something to ground me. "I wouldn't be too thrilled," I admitted.

"Face it, Isanfier; you'd be furious," Asmund replied. "Like I was when Arran was chosen as heir over me, I'd imagine. There's few things worse than having something taken away from you that you'd waited your whole life for."

Sky narrowed her eyes in thought. "What if... What if Shiveera *was* supposed to be Queen, and Darkenier killed her for it, thus alienating himself from the family and effectively *giving* Frost the throne?"

Asmund frowned. "I suppose that's possible, but why would Frost leave him alive, if that was the case? It doesn't suit his character."

I shook my head. "No, it doesn't. Honestly, it makes more sense for *Frost* to have killed both Shiveera and Darkenier for the throne, only Darkenier lived and sought shelter in Summer?"

"That sounds more like it," Asmund agreed, "but we can only speculate, unfortunately. Neither Frost nor Darkenier will ever be able to reveal the truth, and I doubt Icaria knows or would tell us if she did."

"Echo might," Sky chimed in. "She knows a lot more about the history of the realm than anyone I've ever met, even the scholars. If we can't get your magic figured out, we'll have to ask her when we go back to the Edgewood."

"We're going back to the Edgewood someday even if we *do* figure my magic out," I replied. "Like you said when we left Appalachia, she needs to know we're okay."

Asmund elbowed me in the arm with a sly grin. "Is our Crown Prince worried about the pretty Wyllan girl?"

I scowled at him. "Yes, I'm worried," I snapped back, "but it's because I have compassion, not because she's pretty."

He raised a victorious eyebrow. "So you think she's pretty?"

I picked up one of the thinner books and smacked him with it. "You're a Fidal-forsaken thorn in my side, you know that?" I asked him as dust flew.

"Isanfier Oaden," Sky snapped. "Please tell me you did *not* just use a book as a weapon."

I glanced at her slowly, hanging my head at the fire in her eyes. "Um, no," I replied.

"Good," she said. "Now sit down and get back to work, the both of you. We'll figure out the mystery of Darkenier later. Right now, we need answers to more pressing questions. Did you find anything useful in your search?"

I held up *The Long Line of Summer* and *The Life and Death of Queen Katheryn*.

Sky cracked a smile. "Perfect; you get started on *The Life and Death of Queen Katheryn*, and I'll get to *The Long Line of Summer* as soon as I've finished *Royalty Through the Ages*."

I groaned inwardly as I noticed how thick the book Sky had chosen for me was, but I bit my tongue and cracked it open. It smelled like it hadn't been opened in over a decade, but I told myself it'd be worth it if it held the answers I so desperately needed.

# 14
## Silence

*Echo*

**Echo waited three weeks** before attempting to perform the claiming ritual on her new sword. She'd lost nearly a week to travel, another to planning, and then a third to nerves that still plagued her.

She'd paid the swordsmith full price for the weapon and had then backtracked down the street to the bookstore, where she'd used a combination of her magic and natural stealth to read every book on the subject of claiming she could get her hands on.

She may or may not have stolen a couple, but she reasoned it was for a good cause.

Once she was done at the bookstore, she ventured back out into the streets in search of more coin to replace what she'd spent on the sword. Then, mercifully, she had turned towards home as the sun had begun to set behind the Shadow Keep atop the cliff.

Now, she was kneeling by the side of the brook in the glade a few minutes beyond her treehouse, staring at the sword balanced carefully across her legs. She tried to ignore how much she was shaking.

*It won't be the end of the realm if it doesn't work,* she reminded herself. *The only thing in danger is your optimism.*

Echo sighed.

*I don't have much left to lose, do I?*

She waited a few more moments, listening to the faint wind in the trees and the sound of the water running, before taking a deep breath and turning to the notes propped up against a rock beside her.

"Place the weapon you hope to claim in running water to cleanse it," she read aloud, "and recite the words of enchantment."

Echo leaned forward and carefully placed the sword in the brook, hoping the metal was sound enough that it wouldn't rust, though for the price she'd paid for it, rusting should never be an issue.

As the blade left her hands, sinking beneath the water, Echo spoke the enchantment. "I call on Fidal, creator of all things, to cleanse me as this sword is cleansed, to make me a weapon of peace."

She expected to feel something as she said it—a ripple through the air, even—but nothing felt different. Nothing *looked* different, and she tried not to let that deter her as she read through the next step.

Perhaps there was no sign of change until the ritual was complete.

Echo lifted the sword out of the brook by the hilt and then got to her feet. Water ran in rivulets along the blade and down her arm as she walked a few paces away from the edge of the brook.

Then she thrust the sword point first into the dirt in front of her, ignoring the jolt through her muscles as the earth resisted but eventually gave in under the force.

"I call on Fidal, creator of all things, to ground me as this sword is grounded, to make me a weapon of wisdom."

Again, Echo felt no change in the realm, no disturbance in the woods, nothing but the sound of the trees and her anxious breathing. She urged herself to ignore her misgivings and find calm amidst the storm in her mind.

*It's not over yet. Have a little faith.*

Echo pulled the sword out of the ground and approached the fire she'd left burning a few paces away, equal distance from the brook and the surrounding trees. She had debated building the fire in the pit outside the treehouse, but she was worried the enchantment would fade away if too much time lapsed between tasks, so she'd chosen to perform the entire ritual within the glade, to be safe.

She clenched her fist around the hilt of the sword as she plunged the entire blade into the flame, praying she wouldn't slip and catch her dress on fire.

"I call on Fidal, creator of all things," she said as she winced against the heat, "to test me as this sword is tested, to make me a weapon of strength."

*Now for the fun part,* she thought as she removed the sword from the heat and placed it carefully on a rock she'd set out.

Then she reached for the vegetable knife she'd grabbed out of the kitchen. It was the cleanest knife she owned and the sharpest—the best option she had to fulfill the blood bond requirement of the ritual without putting her in danger of getting an infection.

She took a few more deep breaths before pressing the knife into the palm of her left hand and slicing a shallow cut across her skin. She gasped at the sharp pain but pushed through it and squeezed her bloody hand over the sword, letting her life force drip onto the blade.

"I call on Fidal, creator of all things, to bless me as this sword is blessed, to make me a weapon of truth."

She waited the span of a few breaths, unsure exactly how much blood was required, and then quickly bandaged her hand with a scrap of cloth she'd brought with her. She would apply the proper herbs to it later.

The claiming ritual was almost done, and Echo was buzzing with a healthy mixture of nerves and excitement. If it was all for naught, she'd be disappointed, but she could always try again. If it worked… Well, Echo hadn't considered what that would mean for her exactly, only that she wanted it.

Finally, Echo picked the sword up again and walked into the centre of the clearing where she thrust the blade in the air above her head and spoke the final words of the enchantment.

"I call on Fidal, creator of all things, to free me as this sword is freed, to make me a weapon of hope."

For a moment, nothing happened, and Echo was about to lower her arm in defeat when she felt energy crackle through the air, and her hair began to stand on end. The energy built, growing warmer, almost becoming something she could hear, and then a single bolt of lightning cracked down from the stars. It struck her sword, and all the Edgewood faded into the blinding light of the flash.

•  •  •

Echo woke with a start to a splitting headache that drove itself like an arrow through the centre of her skull. All her muscles ached as well, but nothing felt broken. She didn't know how long she'd been unconscious, but night had fallen, and the air around her was chilled.

She couldn't remember what had happened, didn't know where she was or why.

The thought should have concerned her more than it did, but all she felt was a sense of curiosity underneath the throbbing pain throughout her body. It took her several minutes to gather the strength to sit up, and her head swam with the effort, blurring her surroundings until the pulsing stopped.

*By Wylla, what happened to me?*

She leaned forward to wrap her arms around her legs, and that's when she noticed the long sword lying on the ground beside her. There was something etched along the centre of the blade that hadn't been there when she'd bought it in Tamise.

Echo leaned in for a closer look and was able to read the word engraved on the blade, as if by magic.

*Silence.*

She reached for the sword instinctually, and when her hands closed around the hilt, her memories came rushing back. She'd come out to the glade to perform the claiming ritual for the sword, to have a named weapon like Isan and Sky. She'd executed all the steps and had thought it hadn't worked when...

*By Wylla, was I struck by lightning?*

Panic tried to grip her heart again, but Echo soon realized her pain was gone. It had vanished as soon as she'd touched the sword.

My *sword*, she reminded herself. *Her name is* Silence.

Echo grinned and rushed to her feet, feeling like herself again for the first time since her friends had left. She began to dance around the glade with *Silence*, swinging the sword expertly around her as if she'd been born holding it.

The exhilaration was breathtaking, and for the first time in months, Echo allowed herself to hope that her friends would return, if only so she could show Isan her new prize. In their previous duels, she'd given him a run for his money, but with a claimed sword, she would really make him sweat. She could imagine his exhilarated grin and determination lighting up his face, and she wanted nothing more than to share in the joy of it with him. It was a wisp of a dream, a shot in the dark, but Echo reminded herself that she was a weapon of hope now, and she prayed that would be enough.

# 15
# Trials and Triumphs

**That night, after another** long and tedious banquet dinner, Sky and I were holed up in my room, our faces still nose deep in the pages of our research books. I was about halfway through *The Life and Death of Queen Katheryn,* and it was a surprisingly interesting read.

Katheryn, unbeknownst to me, had been no ordinary Queen. In fact, she had been immortal and had married Henri, son of King Greenbrier and Queen Blossom—the first recorded monarchs of Summer—when he was eighteen and she was two hundred and seventeen. Twenty-seven years later, Henri died of an incurable disease, despite the best efforts of the kingdom's healer to save him, and Katheryn became the first sole Queen of Summer. She ruled for twenty years before she died at the ripe old age of two hundred and sixty four.

But of course, immortals didn't die of natural causes; they had to be killed.

The kingdom still hadn't solved her murder over three decades later, though the book said they suspected Winter was to blame. If I'd read the book a year ago, I'd be tempted to believe that, but after everything that had happened, I found myself questioning that logic.

Was blaming the Wyllans a crutch Summer leaned on to appease the masses? Was it easier to say Winter did it than to do a proper investigation for the truth?

All that aside, it was nice to finally learn about my family in depth, without the censorship of the magic ban standing in my way. I'd learned about Queen Katheryn in the past but only briefly, with all my scholars conveniently leaving out the part about her being immortal.

I flipped another page and noticed a note scrawled in the margin. Curious, I turned the book sideways and nearly went cross-eyed trying to read the tiny script.

Lea killed her.

I raised an eyebrow.

*Lea? As in Lea, First Queen of Winter?*

Who was this mystery writer, and if their words were true, how did they know for sure who Katheryn's killer was when no one else seemed to have a clue?

I shook my head and put the book down beside me, deciding I'd had enough mysteries for one day.

"Sky," I said, stretching out my limbs with a long yawn, "we should call it a night."

She didn't answer.

I stood up and found her sprawled across my bed, poring over *Into the Throes of Winter*.

"You're actually reading that?" I asked.

She nodded but didn't look up from the page.

"You know it's a romance, right?"

"So?"

"So, I didn't think you were into that."

She rolled into a sitting position and gave me a look. "Isan, all girls are into romance. Books like this give me an escape to a better world, a hope for my own future, however fragile."

"I see," I replied, my heart hurting for her, though I tried not to show it. Sky didn't want to be pitied. "I was thinking we should get to bed. All this reading is making me tired, and we have more challenges to sit through tomorrow."

She sighed dramatically and closed the book. "Fine. I suppose I can finish it tomorrow."

I raised an eyebrow. "Finish it? How much have you read?"

"About two thirds. How much have *you* read?"

I held up my book. "I'm only halfway through."

"Well, that's a start. Is it any good?"

"It's definitely more interesting than our history lessons," I admitted.

She gave me an impressed look. "It's weird to see you enjoying a book, but I'm happy you are. I'm sorry we haven't found anything yet, but we won't give up. The answers are out there somewhere."

I shrugged. "It's okay; I didn't expect us to find anything on the first day. Even the information about Darkenier came from pure luck. I wish there was someone we could talk to, aside from Echo. Someone in our family, or in Widonia. I can't be the only person walking around with magic."

"You know, I've been wondering… What *are* the chances that you're the only one with magic? My name *is* Sky. What if… What if I'm a Gifted Immortal too?"

I sat up straighter. "I didn't think of that."

"I can't stop thinking about it," she admitted. "Magic is hereditary and there seems to be a tell in my name, so what are the chances I'll be spared?"

"I suppose the odds aren't in your favour, but that doesn't mean it's set in stone. Besides, there's no use worrying about it now. If there's magic in you, there's no killing it. We'll just have to see what happens, and hopefully, I'll be versed enough in my own magic by then that I can help you."

She let out a breath. "You're right; one problem at a time. I just wish we could find you a teacher, but who would be brave enough or stupid enough to help you? No offense."

I sighed and replied, "None taken. It's going to be a long time before the people will accept magic users again, especially if they find out magic *was* used to kill our parents."

"All the more reason to get to the bottom of yours before something happens. You're already one wrong look away from a fight at the best of times."

"Oh, don't remind me. I'm still angry Jasper is second in the running to be your husband."

She raised a curious brow. "But you're not angry Asmund is first in line?"

"Yes and no?" I sighed. "Angry is the wrong word. Wary, definitely. I trust Asmund to a certain extent now, but it doesn't completely erase the past. I'd rather save you from him and be wrong in my judgement than let him have you and be proven right, you know? Though I suppose, if something terrible happened, I could expose him as a Magic Wielder and have him banished or something." I looked over at Sky. "What do you think?"

"Of what?"

"Asmund." I remembered their hand-holding the previous night and wondered if it meant anything more.

"He's...different than he used to be. Like you said, sometimes it's hard to look past how he used to treat me, to separate the boy who coveted me for power from the true man he is now becoming, but... I don't know if I want to be his wife. He wouldn't necessarily be a poor choice, and I'd definitely choose him over Jasper, but it still doesn't feel like much of a choice."

She paused.

"I keep asking myself what I would do if the Festival didn't exist, what romantic path I would want to take, but it doesn't matter, does it?"

She looked so sad and lonely at that moment, sitting on my bed with her feet curled up to her chest. I remembered when she used to do the same thing after a harsh lecture from our teachers or Darkenier himself, rocking back and forth slowly to keep herself grounded and stop the tears that wanted to spill forth.

I sat down beside her and wrapped an arm around her shoulder, halting her movement, and she relaxed a bit.

She sniffed and wiped at her eyes. "Fidal's breath, I feel so stupid worrying about my problems when you have so much more going on."

I squeezed her shoulder. "Don't say that. Being upset or worried isn't stupid, and my problems are never more important than yours. The magnitude of them doesn't make yours any less real or painful, okay?"

She nodded and said, "Okay."

Then she leaned into me and started crying, letting the stress of the past few days come flowing out. I offered words of comfort when I could but mostly listened as she detailed all her fears and the responsibility she felt weighing on her shoulders. Eventually, both emotional and physical exhaustion pulled her under, and I let her fall into my pillows, covering her up with my throw blanket.

I grabbed the books off the bed and slipped them into my wardrobe out of sight before blowing out the candles and climbing into the other side of the bed, careful not to wake her.

She would scold me in the morning for not making her stay awake and go back to her own room, but I didn't care. It was like a window into our childhood, when we had sleepovers all the time and told each other stories late into the night, before Darkenier had deemed us too old for such things.

I felt a twinge in my chest as I realized this was probably the last time we'd ever do something like this. Soon, our time would be monopolized by spouses and royal duties, and we would grow further and further apart.

And suddenly, the scariest thought about the Festival wasn't the worry that I'd be married to someone I hated, but that I would lose my sister, that one day I'd look back at these days in reverence but not be able to remember our last true conversation.

The thought stayed with me, and it was late into the night before I was able to close my eyes and fall asleep.

•  •  •

I woke with a start to the sound of someone pounding against my door, and I lunged across my bed for my sword on the nightstand, forgetting Sky was lying on that side of the bed. I nearly crushed her with my elbow, and she gasped awake.

"What's happening? Isan? Where am I?"

I rubbed at my forehead, cursing myself for ignoring what was best and still reeling from the nightmare. "You fell asleep, and you're too heavy to carry."

She gave me an indignant look. "You could've woken me up. My servants will have noticed my absence by now. What time is it?"

I ignored her and rolled off the other side of the bed, grabbing my sword before proceeding to the door. "Who is it?" I called out.

"It's Sir Quinton," the visitor replied, and I groaned, resting my forehead against the wood. "Her Highness is missing, so it would be in your best interests to open this door."

Sky looked over in alarm and hurried into a sitting position, smoothing out the wrinkled skirt of her dress and trying to tame her hair.

"Well, you can tell the guards I've found her," I said.

"You know where she is?"

"I'm looking at her right now."

"Open this door, and let me see for myself."

I scowled. "Why in Sancia's name would I lie to you about that? My sister potentially missing is not a joke to me."

I imagined him rolling his eyes on the other side of the door. "I'm not stupid, Your Highness. I know you would lie through your teeth for her if need be, so I'm going to ask you again. Where is the Princess?"

"Oh, for the love of…" Sky muttered, jumping off the bed and pushing me aside so she could open the door. "I am *right* here, you raving lunatic."

Quinton nearly fell into the room, clearly not expecting the door to open, and Sky shoved him away from her, taking a step back and closer to me.

"Are you satisfied now?" she asked him, crossing her arms. "Honestly…"

Quinton brushed off his coat and gave her a severe look. "Where in Fidalia have you been? Your servants reported you missing an hour ago."

She raised an eyebrow. "I've been missing for *an hour* and you're just now coming to see Isan?"

I coughed into my hand to muffle the snort that escaped me.

"And since when am I confined to my room at all hours?" Sky added.

"With the Festival of Honour underway," Quinton replied, "it is highly inappropriate for the Princess to be wandering around the castle at all hours of the night or morning. There are guards posted outside your room for a reason, and there are events you need to prepare for."

"So you don't trust Isan to keep me safe?"

"Oh, I don't doubt he'll keep you safe," Quinton allowed, "but he certainly won't keep you in line. Now come along, the second task will begin shortly, and you are far from ready."

He leaned over to grab her wrist, but we both saw the action coming a mile away. Sky pulled her arm away and stepped back, while I stepped in front of her and raised my sword.

"Try that again if you don't value your limbs," I snapped, certain a fire burned behind my eyes as I felt my hands heating up and the blood rushing through my veins. "I will take Sky back to her room, and we will arrive at the task on time, on our own terms. Don't you dare treat her like that again."

He said nothing, staring me down as if I was an insect despite the sword in his face.

"I'm warning you, Sir Quinton," I added. "This is your last chance, on my mother's grave. If you continue on this path, you won't live to regret it. Now get out of my sight."

I didn't give him a chance to answer as I retreated into my room and slammed the door so hard the walls shook.

"Lock it," I choked out to Sky seconds before my hands caught fire, the rage a living thing inside my bones and blood. The flames writhed in the air like a dragon seeking destruction, and I sat there and let them for a minute, let the anger run its course, let myself imagine running Quinton through with my blade, let myself be lost if only for a moment, my eyes unable to look away.

Then I took a deep breath and walked over to the fireplace, crouching down and laying my hands against the half-charred wood from last night. It took a few minutes, but the wood finally caught, and my fire slowly burned out into nothing, though my anger remained.

Sky had said nothing in the past few minutes, and I finally looked over at her, sitting on the edge of my bed once more. "Are you okay?"

She raised an eyebrow. "Me? I should be asking *you* that." She paused, wringing her hands in her lap. "I thought you were going to kill him."

I grimaced. "I thought I was too, but I guess self-preservation won out in the end. We better get going; I don't think I can hold myself back if he returns."

She didn't move. "Isan, are you *sure* you're okay?"

I clenched my fists, the fiery image of them still vivid in my mind. "It doesn't matter, does it? The world goes on whether you're ready or not, and the worst thing you can do is get left behind."

She gave me an agonized look. "That's not true. We can pause for a second. We can postpone the next task until tomorrow. We could say *to the stars* to all of it and send everyone home. Your problems may or may not be bigger than mine, but they definitely still exist, and I will not sit here and watch you fall apart while you bottle up all your feelings like nothing is wrong. It's not healthy, Isan. You're going to *quite literally* burn out."

I took a deep, shaking breath and walked over to sit beside her on the bed. "You make it sound easy."

"Only because you try so hard to make everything difficult so you have something other than yourself to blame."

The sudden silence in the room was stifling as her words pierced my heart like a longsword, plunging deep enough to cut bone and fast enough to steal the breath from my lungs.

*Why in Fidal's name is she always right? Why does she know me better than I know myself?*

She sighed. "Please say something. Your silence is going to be the death of me someday."

"I am so far from okay, it's laughable," I admitted. "I'm afraid of so many things. I keep seeing myself ruining everything, hurting or killing someone in a fiery fit of rage I can't control, someone who doesn't even deserve it. I keep imagining myself falling over an edge into darkness I can't escape, becoming as despicable as the man I killed for our freedom. I keep thinking about Icaria plotting her revenge, and about the curse I can't escape from.

"I wake up every morning gasping for air after watching myself burn Widonia to ash, and then I'm expected to go about my day as if nothing is wrong. I'm expected to sit down, to play nice, to choose a wife and start a family as if my world isn't still falling apart around me, as if I feel safe in my own skin, as if there isn't still an axe above my head waiting to fall.

"I'm not okay, Sky, and I'm terribly afraid I will never be again."

Another bout of silence took over the room, and we both sat in it, our thoughts racing as our hearts ached. I hated to drop all this negativity on her, but she had asked, and I didn't want to lie to her anymore. It was exhausting, and I knew how much it always hurt us both in the end.

Finally, Sky grabbed my hand and squeezed. "We will make this right, Isan. I promise you. I will do whatever it takes to make you feel all right again. If you want to call this Festival off, I will stand by you. If you want to try Quinton for crimes against the kingdom, I will support you. And if you want to see this through, as I suspect you do, I will be here for you every step of the way."

I squeezed her hand back. "You know me too well. Let's take it one moment at a time, but I feel like a change is coming soon, and it won't be long before my secrets are out, one way or another."

"We will deal with whatever comes. You and I are much stronger and smarter than you give us credit for. We survived a war. We survived Darkenier's repeated attempts on our life, a goblin horde attack, and a direct confrontation with the King of Winter himself. Our own kingdom will not be the end of us."

I nodded. "We will fight, with whatever power we have to our names."

"And we will not be alone this time," she added. "We have Asmund, Aramina, Aunt Mag, Sir Silas, and likely Tamsen and Penelope too. If we decide to take a stand, we will not stand alone, not by half."

"Then let's carry on and see what trials or triumphs today brings."

# 16
## The Beast of Burden

**The girls' first task** was abysmally dull and rather insulting compared to the boys' as we watched them waltz around the dining hall in their best gowns and demonstrate their prowess in etiquette and class.

They were made to walk like a lady, wave and curtsy like a lady, and talk like a lady who answered questions politely and appropriately. It was madness; as if I cared about any of that. I wanted a wife who was comfortable in her own skin and unafraid to be herself. And while all the girls put forth their best efforts, it was clear in their eyes that they weren't enjoying it and this wasn't how they truly conducted themselves most of the time.

Only Rosetta, Soleia, and Raina looked mildly comfortable, with the others looking completely out of place, especially Kainda and Gwyneth. Kainda looked like she wanted to rip the instructor's head off, making me smile for the first time since she'd arrived.

When Aramina tripped in her heeled shoes for the fifth time, I stood up and called a halt to the task.

Sir Kent gave me a look from his post at the end of the table. "Is something wrong, Your Highness?" Around the room, the girls had come to a stop and were looking at me curiously.

"Begging your pardon, sir, but this is *all* wrong. Understanding etiquette does not make or break a woman. It doesn't prove their ability to help lead this kingdom. What are the other tasks set out for my suitors?"

"They will be tested on their knowledge of history, geography, and mathematics, as well as their ability to read and write," Sir Kent replied, "and then the final task will have them planning and hosting an event for at least a dozen guests."

I rubbed at my temples while I tried not to show my frustration and disappointment.

"One of these girls will be *Queen*, Sir Kent," I said finally. "I need someone with strength, loyalty, and wisdom. Someone to stand by me in times of prosperity and peril. Someone who will not cave under the pressure of royalty and who will instill noble qualities into our future children. I need a *partner*, not a decorative centrepiece."

I turned away from Kent and approached the ladies, who were now huddled in a rough line facing the high table. "How many of you have ever cared for a child before?"

Only Kainda raised her hand, and I gave Kent a knowing look.

"I assumed as much," I replied. "It was your brother?" I asked Kainda.

She nodded. "I was only nine when he was born, but my ma had her hands full with both him and Gwyneth being young, so I helped out a lot. I know enough that children are only cute if you're not responsible for them."

Rosetta and the twins rolled their eyes, but Penelope and Aramina gave Kainda appreciative looks.

"And do any of you know anything about weaponry or strategy? Can you protect yourself if the need arises?"

Kainda's hand shot up again, along with Gywneth, Aramina, and Penelope, though she hesitated.

Rosetta crossed her arms. "This is ridiculous, Your Highness. Why would you want a wife who's learned such barbaric things as fighting?"

"It's not barbaric if you're protecting yourself," I replied.

"But why should I need to protect myself when you'll be there, along with countless knights?" Rosetta argued.

I cringed at her old way of thinking, at the harmful traditions her parents and countless generations before them had instilled in her. "I won't always be there to protect you, and you can't rely on other people your whole life. Mistakes and terrible circumstances happen. I want to know my wife will stand a chance against an enemy attack in the awful event that I am not there to save her. If someone found you alone and tried to hurt you, what would you do?"

She looked up at me, aghast, but didn't have an answer.

I walked back up to the high table and took my seat, noting Sky's proud smile. "These are the new tasks, Sir Kent. First, each lady will spend an entire day and night with young Master Euric, as long as Lady Katya does not object. Have her report back their aptitude for the task when they are finished. Second, each lady will demonstrate their abilities to defend against or attack an unknown threat. They will not fight anyone directly, but if Sky were in the running, for example, she would show her ability to hit targets dead on with her bow. The third task will remain as is; basic literacy and knowledge of the kingdom is important."

"Are you sure, sire?" Sir Kent said, keeping his voice low so the ladies couldn't hear. "Some of these ladies may struggle immensely."

"That's entirely the point," I replied. "Becoming Queen should not be easy, as *being* Queen never will be. If they cannot suitably complete the tasks, they are not fit to be my wife." I was not trying to be harsh, simply honest. After the tragedies this kingdom had been through, they needed a strong monarchy to set things right and pave the way for future generations.

Sir Kent gave me a resigned sigh and stood to announce the news.

I thought Rosetta would throw a fit where she stood, and the twins looked close to tears, but the others seemed relieved. Kainda even gave me a respectful nod, and I knew at that moment that I had done the right thing by my kingdom and my people. The mountain women were even harder to impress than the men, and Kainda had been looking down upon me since her arrival.

The girls were ushered out of the dining hall, with plans to commence the new first task in the morning, and Sky and I were left alone.

"That was an incredibly brave and risky move you made," Sky said, clearing the tension in the air.

I leaned back in my chair. "Oh, believe me, I know, but it was necessary."

She reached over and squeezed my shoulder. "I'm proud of you, and I think some of the girls are more than happy with your decision. They were looking at you like they could actually see a King in front of them, a leader."

"And what about the rest of them?"

"Rosetta, Raina, and Soleia don't understand you, but that's on them. I never thought they were Queen material anyway. If they can't rise up to the challenge, they don't deserve to sit beside you. Summer needs resilience now more than ever."

"And *we* need to use this free time wisely. Library?"

She grinned. "I thought you'd never ask."

• • •

The next week and a half passed like a Winter blizzard, the seconds piling up slowly until they suddenly accumulated into days, and I was left wondering where the time went.

Lady Katya agreed to let the ladies watch Euric for a day each, and the task carried on with no major disasters. Kainda emerged the victor, with Aramina surprisingly not far behind. Rosetta came last with Euric returning to his mother in tears and Rosetta looking like she'd been through a war zone. I had never seen her so disheveled.

Asmund was still leading the charge for the men, with their second task consisting of various strategy tests and scenarios. Jasper was close on his heels, however, with the other three eating their dust.

On the day of the combat demonstration for the girls, Kainda, Gwyneth, Penelope, and Aramina came out strong, with Aramina coming out on top, much to everyone's surprise. Her use of the staff was mesmerizing as she twirled it around herself and connected with a variety of targets.

The twins made a poor attempt at throwing daggers, barely reaching the targets at times, and Rosetta showed up with a bow, likely trying to win my favour but failing miserably when she couldn't even pull the string to half draw.

Sky couldn't even watch, and I felt terrible at the embarrassment Rosetta was experiencing, but I never said to choose a weapon you couldn't use. I wanted the girls to play to their strengths. Rosetta could've come out wielding a sharp-heeled pair of shoes for Fidal's sake. She might have fared better.

After the demonstration, Rosetta threw her borrowed bow down into the dirt and stormed out, her brother following in her wake after shooting me a dirty look. I didn't back down from his stare, and my eyes followed them both out. I wasn't afraid of him. I knew that if it came down to a physical altercation, he wouldn't stand a chance, and a part of me was happy to see him so flustered.

*Good people get what they work for, Jasper*, I mused. *Bad people get what they deserve.*

•  •  •

That night, I found myself at yet another ball, much to my annoyance. It was the fourth one we'd had so far during the Festival, and while my feet had adjusted to the onslaught of dancing, my patience had not.

Every conversation was nearly the same, each one of us confined to an unspoken bubble of topics and polite responses, dancing to the same music night after night.

Despite my best efforts to stay present, I kept imagining I was with Echo instead, kept hearing her laugh and seeing her easy smile. Every time *Whispers of Wisteria* rang out through the ballroom, I lost a piece of myself, feeling it drift back towards the Edgewood as if it was meant to be there instead.

And as the noble ladies of Summer attempted to court me, I began to wonder if I'd already given my heart to a Wyllan Princess, or if I just wanted to be anywhere but where I was.

"I beg your pardon, Your Highness, but are you even listening to me?" Raina's voice cut through the fog in my head like a knife, and I jolted back to reality.

I scrunched my face in discomfort at her tone and sudden volume. "Apologies, Mistress Raina. There is a lot on my mind."

She scowled. "Like what? What could be more important than giving your *honoured* guests the time of day? You don't even want to be here, do you?"

I bristled. "Look, I understand you are upset, and I am truly sorry for that, but insulting me is not going to turn the odds back in your favour. There are countless things more important in my life than this ball, I assure you of that. I might look like the same boy you berated your whole life, but I am now as good as King, and the fate of the entire kingdom constantly rests on my shoulders. Does that mean nothing to you?"

She bit her tongue, and I scoffed, stopping us in the middle of the dance and stepping away from her.

"Of course it means nothing to you. You're either here only out of duty to your parents or in the hopes of power and prestige that will make the people fawn over you like some pretty jewelled thing. You don't know what it means to be a leader, to have people rely on you to keep them safe, fed, and happy. You don't understand the concept of being willing to sacrifice everything you are for the greater good. Fidal's breath, *none* of you do."

"Your Highness, please," Raina said, reaching for my hand. "You're causing a scene."

I pulled my hand away from hers instinctively, feeling the heat rising to the surface of my skin. The sensation brought me back to my senses, and I took a deep breath to quell my anger, though a large part of me didn't want to. A large part of me wanted to give in, to show them all exactly what I was capable of.

But then another hand grabbed my arm from behind and pulled me towards them, snapping me out of my thoughts. I snatched my hand away and whirled on the person, only to find Aramina looking up at me with wide, terrified eyes.

"Mina?" I said. "What's wrong? What happened?"

"It's Sky," she replied. "Asmund saw—You better come quickly. I don't know what he's going to do."

My stomach turned over at her words. "Ara—"

"Now," she snapped, grabbing my arm and tugging me away. "I don't have time to argue with you."

I didn't give Raina the courtesy of a parting remark, as I let Aramina lead me away. I was sure she crossed her arms and gave me a nasty look behind my back, but I didn't care. My mind was racing with possibilities, hoping Sky was okay and worried we would be too late.

*Asmund is with her*, I reminded myself. *He'll keep her safe.*

*Unless* he's *the danger.*

I thought we'd come far enough that he wasn't a concern anymore, but at this point in my life, trust was a fragile thing that could easily shatter, and I couldn't afford to give people more chances than they deserved.

# 17
# Fire and Fury

**Aramina didn't let go** of my hand as she led me across the ballroom and out the far door, moving so fast I almost tripped over my feet. As the door banged shut behind us, it didn't take me long to locate the source of her distress.

Asmund and Jasper were facing off in the middle of the corridor, Asmund's axe drawn but held at his side. Sky was leaning against the wall beside them, seemingly unscathed, and Aramina rushed to her side, abandoning me.

"You're a scoundrel," Asmund was saying, an anger in his voice I hadn't heard since our last true argument before the war. "I should strike you down where you stand."

Jasper leered at him. "For what? Trying to take what's rightfully mine? If the King hadn't chosen Arran over you, I'd be first in line for her hand and you know it. If you weren't monopolizing all her time and sitting in the Prince's pocket, she would be mine by now."

The fire in my veins rose up again at his words and the violence in his tone, but Asmund moved first, his fist connecting with Jasper's jaw.

Jasper's head whipped sideways with the force of it, and when he recovered, he spit blood on the floor. "Feel better now?"

"I'll feel better when you shut your filthy mouth," Asmund replied, raising his fist again.

Neither of them had noticed me yet, but it wouldn't be long. I knew I should stop the fight, but I needed to make sure Sky was all right first.

I was starting to walk in her direction when I noticed she was leaning on Aramina for support as if…

Sky was wobbly on her feet, staring at Asmund and Jasper as if she couldn't quite focus on them, and the reality of the situation hit me as heat raced through my limbs, itching to be released.

I stormed around Asmund, pushing his raised fist aside, and stepped in front of Jasper. "Is she drunk?"

He didn't look troubled by my appearance. In fact, he smiled at me like he had won a war and said, "You're both *overreacting*. The Princess is fine; we were rather enjoying—"

I cut him off by drawing *Ember* and sticking the tip under his chin, just shy of the soft, vulnerable skin. "I am going to ask you one more time. Is. She. Drunk."

His eyes glared daggers into mine, and I was sure Sir Kent had noticed our absence by now and would soon intervene, but I didn't care. I didn't care if my magic spilled over and ruined everything because if he had tried to do what I thought he had, I wanted to watch him burn.

"Of course she's drunk, Isanfier," Asmund cut in. "Look at her! I caught this fiend trying to steal a kiss Her Highness was in no state of mind to consent to, given the fact that the wall he was pushing her up against was clearly the only thing keeping her upright."

Jasper shot him a look, nicking himself on my blade with the movement, but not seeming to care. Blood from Asmund's blow was already drying on his chin. "Your accusations mean nothing. You can *prove* nothing, but my black eye and bruised jaw in the morning will more than prove how *you* assaulted *me*. You should go back to the dirty military city you crawled out of."

"That's enough," Sky said, her voice slurred. She attempted to step between us, but stumbled instead and knocked right into me. That's when I noticed the angry red marks around her wrist, as if someone had tried to drag her against her will.

The fire roared in my bones.

I passed Sky over to Asmund and whirled on Jasper, sparks crackling beneath my skin. "You will pay for what you did."

"As if the Council will believe your claims against the favoured Heir of Mensden," he spat. "The Prince who doesn't think anyone is good enough for his sister and another suitor who wants the Princess for himself?" He laughed. "Face it; you're just causing a scene."

Oh, he didn't know the half of it. I was boiling, brimming with hatred, the fire calling out for vengeance, but I knew only diplomacy would save me.

I dropped my sword slowly and said, "Leave Widonia now, and I will forget your trespasses. Disobey me, try to so much as speak to Sky again, and I will follow through on my threat like *that*" —I snapped the fingers of my free hand— "and the only remnants of you will be the dust on this floor where you once stood."

He laughed. "I'd like to see you try! See, the thing about threats is that the other person has to be afraid. You may have returned from the war, but don't think you've fooled any of us into believing you actually fought in it, that you could've possibly had the guts or strength to kill the King."

The fire sizzled in my veins, raged through my arteries, and ignited my heart in a blazing inferno, sending heat radiating off me.

I wanted to kill him. I wanted to hack him into a million pieces. I wanted him to pay for his insolence, for his disrespect of Sky and the horrid intent he'd had for her. Fidal's breath, if Asmund hadn't seen him... I hated to think what could've happened. I wanted nothing more than to rip him apart, but I had to go.

Any second now, the fire would break through, and I sensed that this time it wouldn't be satiated easily. It wanted more than wood; it wanted to consume flesh and bone, and though I wanted Jasper dead, I couldn't let it.

I sheathed my sword, my hands shaking from the rage coursing through my every sinew.

"Restrain him, Asmund, and take him to the dungeons to cool off. Aramina, please see Sky to her chambers, and do not let her out of your sight."

"Where are you going, Prince?" Jasper drawled. "Aren't you going to make me beg for your mercy?"

I let my restraint waver for a moment and grabbed him by the lapels of his tunic, dragging his face within an inch of my own as I stared into his eyes, hoping he could see all the danger and anger in mine.

"You don't deserve my mercy," I told him, "but some day, you will realize how much it's worth."

Then I let go of his tunic, turned on my heel, and walked away, maintaining my composure until I rounded the first corner and broke into a sprint, the fire in me burning so hot I could see steam rising in the air around me.

I had never run so fast in my entire life. The halls were nothing but blurs of stone and glass as I raced down them, my boots echoing loud enough for the whole castle to hear, but it didn't matter now. I took the first servant's staircase I found and flew down it, my feet barely touching each step before I jumped to the next one.

I had to get out of the castle before my magic built into a terrifying crescendo and took everything down with it.

An outside door stood ajar at the bottom, and I breezed through it into the gardens, not bothering to look around to see if I had company. I took the fastest route possible to the gates, which meant jumping over some flower beds and cutting through others.

I whispered a silent apology to our gardeners but knew they'd be much happier with footprints than singed foliage if they had the choice.

When I pushed open the iron gates and ran out of the castle grounds, I tried not to think about how the metal burned red hot under my touch.

I sprinted through the streets of my city as if I were being chased by a flood and didn't know how to swim. Yet, the flood was one of magic, and I knew deep down that I couldn't escape it either.

I kept seeing Jasper's face, the marks on Sky's skin. Kept hearing his words and the reality that he *meant* them. There was no apology in his mind, no thought that he had done something wrong. My sister was nothing more than a prize to him, and he would cast her away when he grew tired of her, condemning her to a lifetime of loneliness and misery.

On Sancia's shining light, I wanted to take *Ember* and run her through his throat so he could never speak or grin again.

Inside me, the fire roared in answer, calling for blood, for vengeance.

*No,* I gasped in my head. *Don't think about the fire. You are* done *with vengeance.*

I had to be the bigger man, no matter how much it hurt.

*Don't think. Keep running…*

But my legs felt so weak. I hadn't exerted them like that in ages, and my lungs were leaden weights in my chest as I gasped for air and tasted a hint of iron on my tongue.

*I can't…go on…for much longer.*

*No.* Please *don't give up on me now.*

My legs burned. Every *inch* of me burned, like my body wasn't the coals of a fire but the flame itself; the only thing missing was the light.

But I had to keep going, had to protect my people and get out of the city before —

My thoughts were cut short as something crashed into me, and I was sent sprawling to the cobblestones, cutting my palms on some loose gravel as I reached out to brace myself. I had barely touched the ground before I was launching myself to my feet again in search of the culprit.

Only to come face to face with Sir Quinton, now standing between me and the quickest route to Widonia's gates.

*I don't have time for this.*

"Get out of my way," I snapped, making to walk around him, but he shoved me back, and I felt the anger in me raise one fiery claw in warning.

"I am not going anywhere until you tell me where in Fidal's name you think *you're* going. I always knew you were a coward, but I didn't think you'd run away after the stunt you pulled. Under whose authority exactly was Asmund taking Master Jasper to the dungeons?"

"Mine," I spit, hoping he could see the fire in my eyes and would leave before this interaction turned ugly.

He raised an eyebrow. "Oh, really? And since when do you have the final say around here?"

"Since a disgusting bastard got my sister drunk, dragged her away from prying eyes against her will, and attempted to claim her as his own," I snapped back. I could feel the heat of my fire in the air around me now, warming my face against the slight chill of the Summer evening. "Since you don't seem to care about anyone in this kingdom but *yourself.*"

I stabbed my finger into his shirt, hoping he wouldn't notice the singed fabric and tendril of smoke curling into the air.

"Now get out of my way, Quinton, or not even Fidal himself will be able to save you."

He smirked as he drew his sword. "You should be more worried about yourself, Prince, and what might happen to your poor, rebellious sister if she were to lose her knight in shining armour…"

Fury flashed in me like lightning, and I reached for *Ember*, but it was too late.

The fire had taken control.

It crept through my limbs like a thousand insects, bored into my veins, tapped into my energy, and lit the fuse.

*Please, no.*

Quinton lunged for me, but there was a flash of white light, and then all I saw was darkness.

# Part Two: Ashes

"Catch on fire if you must, sometimes everything needs to burn
to the ground so that we may grow."

—A. J. Lawless

# 18
# Smoke and Ash

**I woke to someone** shaking me and instinctively rolled away, raising my hands in a defensive position as my memory came back to me in fragments.

"Careful, Isan," a voice said. "It's just me, Aramina. I'm not here to hurt you."

I squinted at her, trying to get my eyes to focus, but every sense in me was off. My ears were ringing, and my nose burned as I breathed in the smell of cinders and looked around through the haze hanging in the air.

"What happened?" I wheezed. "What are you...doing here?"

She grimaced. "I was with Sky when we first saw the smoke, and she told me you were in trouble, so I...came to find you."

At her words, it all came crashing back, and I realized what I had done.

Widonia was burning.

I didn't know how far the destruction reached, but we were still in danger. I couldn't let myself believe Quinton had perished in the blast, and the assumption wasn't worth the risk.

"We need to move," I replied, trying to get up, but my bones ached. It was the kind of pain that seeped into every fibre of your being, sitting like a knife between your ribs.

Aramina knelt down and touched a hand to my shoulder. "Don't rush it, Isan. It's a wonder that much magic expulsion didn't kill you."

I looked up at her in alarm. "How did you...?"

She gave me a sympathetic look. "You were still on fire when I found you. It doesn't take a genius to put the puzzle pieces together, especially when your clothes are still fully intact."

I dragged myself into a sitting position and put my head in my hands. "Fidal's breath, you must think I'm a monster."

Smoke still hung in the air like a curtain of despair, and I shuddered at what I had done. Widonia's wooden houses and shops would've burned to the ground, going up in a chain reaction like the ones in Appalachia not so long ago.

The memory of that boy and his mother still burned bright. They had thought I was their hero, and now here I was, condemning so many more people to the same horrific fate.

Tears threatened at the edge of my already blurry vision, but then Aramina grabbed my hand and pulled it away from my face. She was crouched down in front of me now, her eyes level with mine and holding a wisdom far greater than her years.

"Magic is not monstrous unless you allow it to be," she said. "It is a gift, and it can be used to whatever end the user wishes. You did not want this to happen today, Isanfier. I know that. But magic can also be a curse if we let it control us. It's up to you to carve the right path, and we won't solve any problems sitting here bemoaning what is already done."

I wanted to pull my hand away from her, instinctively afraid I might hurt her, but she was right, and her words were the push I needed. With a shaky breath, I dragged myself to my feet, leaning on her for support like Sky had done only a little while earlier. Fidal's breath, it felt like days ago now.

"Lead the way," I said, but she smiled at me.

"Actually, I have a better idea."

Then she closed her eyes, spun her free arm in a circle at her side a few times, and the air started to change.

I watched in awe as what I could only describe as a tear opened up in the air beside us, growing in size slowly until it was a head taller than me and revealing what I recognized as Sky's bedroom.

"What in Fidalia?" I breathed, but there was no time to ponder further, because Aramina tightened her grip on my hand and stepped into the tear, dragging me along with her.

The next thing I knew, we were standing in Sky's room, and the tear revealing Widonia's cobbled street snapped shut behind us.

Aramina let go of my hand and dropped to her knees, holding her head as if in pain. I was still in shock from traveling in such a way, but Sky jumped up off her bed and stumbled toward us as fast as she could manage. She cradled Aramina against her as she seemed to lose consciousness for a second.

"Are you okay, Mina?" Sky asked softly. "Talk to me."

I sat down on the edge of the bed, feeling a bit dizzy myself as Aramina rubbed her head, trying not to wince.

"I'm fine now," she said slowly. "Traveling to a person takes a lot more energy than a place, I've discovered, and I don't typically do it twice in that short amount of time. I'm still learning."

"What exactly did you do?" I asked, trying not to sound critical.

She managed a devious smile. "That, my dear Isanfier, was a portal."

My eyes widened. "You're a Gifted Immortal too?"

"No," she replied, "just a Magic Wielder, as far as I know, though I haven't been able to access any of the other typical Magic Wielder abilities yet." She shrugged as if to say it was only a matter of time, and I marvelled at her nonchalance.

Sky glanced over at me. "I mean, it would make sense. Asmund *is* her brother."

Aramina choked. "I'm sorry, what?"

Sky and I shared an alarmed look, realizing we had spilled Asmund's secret without permission.

"Well, we're already dead now," I said. "We might as well explain it to her."

Sky sighed. "You better sit down, Mina." She helped Aramina to her feet, looking to be better herself, though I noticed she was squinting a bit in the light. She likely had a headache, and I hoped it wasn't too severe.

*Are you okay?* I mouthed to her when she looked my way.

She responded with a wave of her hand, and I rolled my eyes, not at all surprised.

She and Aramina joined me on the bed, and I started the conversation with, "Asmund discovered a couple weeks ago that he can shape-shift."

The story evolved from there as I detailed all our qualms to her, including my own magic and our quarrels with Quinton. A knock sounded on the door as I was finishing my tale, and the three of us stiffened, fear leaping into Sky and Aramina's eyes.

I stood up quietly and drew my sword, motioning for the two of them to get back. They retreated into the far corner of the room as I approached the door, Sky grabbing her bow from her desk on the way.

"Announce yourself," I called out, "or prepare to be challenged."

"Fidal's breath, Isan," Asmund answered. "We don't have time for this."

I sheathed my sword and let him in as quickly as I could manage.

He glanced at Aramina but said nothing to her before turning back to me. "What are you still doing here?"

I blinked. "What?"

"Isan, the entire lower town is on fire, and Jasper knows your secret. He's been screaming it to whoever will listen, and Quintion is definitely not going to keep him locked up in the dungeons whenever he gets back from wherever *he* disappeared to. You need to leave Widonia *now*."

I gave him a severe look, all the blood rushing out of my face. "How does Jasper know?"

Asmund scratched the back of his head. "I hate to be the bearer of bad news, but your eyes were kind of ringed with fire when you were trying not to bash his skull in. Oh, and your thumbs burnt a hole in his shirt too."

I winced. "It's honestly a miracle I held it back for as long as I did. I ran into Quinton before the fire took over, and I almost burnt him where he stood. I didn't see him after, but the blast must have taken him off his feet, if not killed him. I won't be too sorry if he *is* dead."

Asmund frowned. "You saw Quinton? But that's impossible."

"What do you mean? He was right there with me, without a doubt."

"He spoke to *me* two minutes before I noticed your column of fire going up in the lower town. There's no way he could've made it to you, let alone have had time to talk."

"Unless he didn't walk to Isan," Aramina piped up. "What if Quinton's a Magic Wielder? Like Asmund. Like…me."

I raised an intrigued eyebrow at her suggestion, but Asmund looked at her in shock, his eyes so round I feared they would pop out of his head.

"You're a Magic Wielder?" he asked her.

She nodded slowly.

"How long have you known?"

She wrung her hands together and didn't meet his eyes as she said, "Since about a week after mother died."

Silence fell in the room, and I could feel Asmund's pain as it spread through him, as he clenched his shaking fists by his side and tried not to show how badly he wanted to fall to his knees in guilt and grief. Despite their differences, Aramina was still his younger sister, and she had hidden the truth from him for over six months.

"You never said anything," he said softly.

"You never asked," she snapped back, finally looking up to reveal the tears running down her face even as her brown eyes blazed with anger. "Do you know what I would've gladly given up for you to have asked me how I was doing? For you to have noticed how much I was struggling? For you to have found it in yourself to *care?*"

He said nothing, and she barrelled on.

"*Everything*, Asmund. I would've given up everything to have not been so alone. Instead my grief tried to drown me, and when I hit rock bottom and wished to be anywhere but within the cramped, dusty halls of the citadel, I ended up in the Torrell River, miles from Skar. I almost drowned, and it took me two days to get home. But you know what happened when I finally returned?"

Asmund shook his head.

"Father scolded me for shirking my duties, and *you* didn't even know I was missing." Aramina's tears were flowing fast as a river now, but she made no move to dry the deluge. "My grief became an armour I wore to protect myself because I realized that day that no one was coming to save me. If I was going to survive in Summer with magic, I would have to figure it out on my own. And I did. No thanks to you, or Father, or anyone else."

She was on her feet now, gasping for breath, and for a minute, I thought she would strike him, but her hands stayed limp at her sides as she waited for him to say something.

I prayed he would choose the right words, and they could start working together to mend the rift between them.

Asmund leaned against the door, his eyes only for her as he said, "I know nothing I say can erase what I've done in the past and the pain I've caused you. I know I haven't been a good brother to you or Arran for years, and there's no excuse for that, but I am truly sorry. I want to make this right, Mina. I want to be someone you can rely on. So tell me what you need me to do, and I will do it, for as long as it takes to regain your trust. I don't care if I'm old and gray before it happens; I will become the brother you deserve and make our family proud."

Aramina wiped her eyes finally. "I would like to see that day, Asmund. I really would."

"I swear on our mother's grave that you will, whatever it takes."

"Well, you can start by telling us what we're supposed to do now. You said we need to leave?"

Sky stood up and walked over beside her, giving her shoulder a squeeze. "If Isan's secret is truly out, then it's not safe for him here, and it's only a matter of time before they find out about you and Asmund as well. We need a safe place to regroup and train, so that all of you can learn to control your magic completely before it consumes you."

She gave me a look, and I smiled. "We're going to see Echo."

Aramina frowned. "Who's Echo?"

"A dear friend of ours who lives in the Edgewood," Asmund replied. "You'll love her, Mina. She has both an incredibly kind soul and a no-nonsense attitude."

"The Edgewood? How did you meet her?"

"When the King left us to brave the woods on our own," I replied, "in the hopes we would die before ever reaching Winter, Echo saved us from a band of goblins. The three of us would be dead without her help."

"And you think she'll help us again?"

"I know she will. Echo is the kind of person who will go to the ends of the realm for those she cares about. There are few people in this world who have her determination, and she also has an extensive understanding of magic, so she's one of the only people who can give us what we need without fear of retribution."

"Well, we better hurry," Asmund said. "If Quinton lived, he'll be back—"

Three huge bangs sounded on the door then, as if someone was trying to break through instead of knock, and a disgusting, familiar voice broke through the silence of the room.

"Open this door now, Princess, or my men and I will force our way through. Your brother has committed treason against the kingdom, and you will be held for questioning until his return. If the Prince is in there with you, as I suspect he is, and you do not give him up, then you will face the same fate. The choice is yours, Princess, but you don't have long to decide."

The four of us shared a terrified look, and I glanced at Aramina.

"How many can you take at once?" I whispered.

She gave me a look I took to mean, *We're about to find out.* "Hold hands in a circle," she said softly.

We did as we were told, and she took a deep breath. A portal opened up slowly, revealing another room beyond, cloaked in darkness, and she motioned us toward it once it was large enough for us all to duck through.

She took up the rear, and just before the portal closed behind her, I watched Sky's door burst open and a group of knights rush into the room.

They wouldn't find much, but we *had* to hurry.

"Okay, where are we?" I asked, but it only took a quick look around to realize how stupid that question was. "Why did you bring us to my room?"

Aramina let out an exasperated sigh as she rubbed at her forehead and used my bedpost to support herself. "I didn't have much time to think, but I figured if they were coming to Sky's room, they'd already checked yours, and aside from that, I needed something close."

"You did good, Mina," Sky told her, giving me a look over her head. "We'll have to grab as many supplies as we can from here. What do you have, Isan?"

The four of us tore my room apart for supplies, under my direction, and we were able to scrounge up three sacks and four cloaks, though Aramina's would be a little big. I gave Aramina a set of daggers and Asmund an old sword I had sitting in the corner. Luckily, Sky had still been holding her bow when we stepped through the portal, and *Ember* was still strapped to my belt.

We also found a couple bedrolls, some extra blankets, and a tent. I shoved a bunch of extra clothes into one of the bags, hoping the girls wouldn't be too picky. The last touch was a pouch of food I'd had sitting around and a couple waterskins.

It wasn't much, sadly, but it would have to be enough. We were lucky I hadn't bothered to put my supplies away properly when we'd returned from the war a few weeks ago.

We could forage for berries and edible greens in the meadows once we were out of harm's reach, and Sky could hunt us a couple rabbits to give us some extra strength.

Ten minutes later, we were ready, and I looked at Aramina again. "What are the chances you can get us to the stables? We can find another way if your magic is spent. You've done a lot for us already, so I won't ask you to extend yourself anymore tonight if you don't feel comfortable."

"I'd take us all the way to this Echo woman if I could," she replied, "but I think I can manage the stables. It'll take a lot out of me, but it'll be worth it. Be prepared to carry me the rest of the way, though."

Asmund nodded. "We won't leave you behind."

"Then let's do this."

She sent us all through one more portal, leading us out of my room and onto the cobbled street in front of the stables. The night was dark, but fires still burned in the distance, their light revealing the smoke hanging above our heads. Thankfully, the stables remained untouched by the destruction.

*My destruction*, I reminded myself.

As she'd predicted, Aramina collapsed along with the portal, and Asmund rushed to catch her before she hit the ground. He slung her over his shoulder and followed us as we stole into the stables and hurried to untie and tack three of the best horses we could find.

Luckily, the stables had been left unattended as the men stationed there were sent to quell the fires.

Aramina came to by the time we were ready to go, but she was too weak to ride on her own, so Asmund hoisted her up in front of him, and she clung to the neck of the horse as we raced out of town, past the open gates, and into the fields beyond.

I glanced over my shoulder as we left Widonia behind, feeling the guilt seeping into me as I saw the fire still raging and the huge column of smoke billowing into the skies above.

I had destroyed so much in one night, and now Quinton would paint me as a traitor, would turn the citizens against me and attempt to take my crown, but if I knew anything in that moment, I knew he would not remain unchallenged.

I would return someday, armed with magic I could control and standing with three people who knew the true events of this night. Together, we would bring Quinton down and return Summer to its former glory. I just prayed to any of the gods who were listening that Summer would wait for us, that it would survive until we could come and save it.

# 19
# Into The Woods

**We didn't get far** that night, magical exhaustion keeping Aramina and me from staying awake. I put off stopping as long as I could, but after closing my eyes and nearly falling off my horse for the fourth time, I told Asmund and Sky it was time to make camp.

Asmund led us all into a copse of trees off the side of the road, steering his horse one-handed as he held a comatose Aramina in the saddle with the other. She'd been in and out of consciousness the whole ride, and my heart ached looking at her.

Had we pushed her too far? How long would it take for her to recover, and would she forgive us?

Despite my own magic trying to pull me into oblivion, I took Aramina from Asmund so he could get off his horse as Sky set up the tent. She was surprisingly sturdy in my arms, and I wondered if, on top of the magic, she'd been training with weapons in her spare time without her family's knowledge. Given how she'd fared in the trial, I wouldn't be shocked.

There was so much about her I didn't know—much like it had been with Asmund, I supposed.

"Asmund, can you help me with the rope? It won't pull tight," Sky said. There was a tired frustration in her voice, and I marvelled at how well she seemed to be handling everything. Emphasis on *seemed*, as I knew better than anyone how good she was at putting on a brave face and assuming the role of leader.

Asmund glanced at me. "Are you okay with Mina?"

"I'll set her down by that tree there," I said softly. "You help Sky. Not sure how much longer she can keep going either."

He nodded and turned away.

I walked over to the tree and braced my back against the trunk before sliding down it until I touched the grass, still cradling Aramina in my arms. I was glad she wasn't so heavy now.

I meant to move her over beside me, but I was tired, so I watched Asmund and Sky's progress instead. It was astounding how well they worked together now—a far cry from the last time we'd been on our own. Sky hadn't snapped at him once, and Asmund hadn't given anyone a dirty look, yet. It was strange but wonderful, the new dynamic between us, and I knew Echo would be biting back an *I told you so* as soon as we arrived.

I was excited and yet nervous somehow to see her again. It had only been a couple months since we had parted ways, but we were different people now. Each of us had seen and done terrible acts. I was a killer, for better or for worse, and I wondered if she would shy away from that, if she would refuse to help me.

I didn't know what worried me more—the possibility that I wouldn't learn magic, or that I would lose Echo as a friend.

Aramina mumbled something in her sleep then and nestled closer to me, bringing me back to the present.

I smiled.

*Oh, if the other suitors could see us now…*

Rosetta would be at both of our throats, and the sad thing was it wasn't even a romantic gesture—not to us, anyway. Asmund never would've left Aramina to my care otherwise.

The next thing I knew, someone was shaking me awake, and I struggled to react to their obvious intentions.

"Come on, Isan," Sky's voice said. "You can't sleep there, and I am *not* carrying you. *Get up.*"

She gave me another rough jolt, and my eyes shot open, my heart racing with adrenaline as I threw my arm out to defend against any threats.

Sky winced and drew back as I accidentally slapped her in the face. "Oh, for Fidal's sake, Isan," she groaned. "You are seriously more trouble than you're worth sometimes."

I blinked my eyes rapidly to try to get them to focus. "What happened?"

"Nothing," she replied. "You fell asleep again and scared yourself when you woke up. Now come on, let's get you to bed."

She held out a hand, and I took it, letting her pull me to my feet and lead me over to the tent we'd be sharing.

"Where's Asmund and Mina?" I mumbled.

"Already asleep. Asmund suggested I leave you under the tree, but I knew you wouldn't appreciate your sore back tomorrow."

"Thanks," I replied.

She held up the tent flap for me, and I all but collapsed on top of my bedroll. I felt her start to tug off my boots, but I was dead to the world again before she could finish the job.

•  •  •

I was not surprised the next morning to find I had slept soundly through the night without even a whisper of my latest recurring nightmare. It seemed the goddesses had been trying to prevent the destruction of Widonia this time, but they hadn't had the decency to explain what to do with the information they'd given me. Had they expected me to leave the city on a whim after having the first nightmare?

It might've prevented the fire, but it probably would've caused a slew of other problems.

As usual, the speculation left a sick feeling in my stomach, and I left the tent in search of fresh air, leaving Sky sound asleep in the bedroll beside mine.

I found Asmund sitting outside, poking at a small fire with a gnarled stick. There was a chilled mist in the air, but he wasn't wearing a coat. The grass was wet as I sat down beside him, keeping over a foot between me and the flame.

I watched it warily as it danced back and forth, crackling occasionally and sending tufts of smoke into the air. It was amazing how something so small could cause such destruction. Fire could be put out with a single bucket of water, but left unchecked, it could destroy entire forests. It could fool people well, but the truth was fire was always hungry.

Asmund glanced back at me and said, "How are you feeling?"

"I'm a little sore," I replied, "but my head is finally clear, and I no longer feel like I'm going to keel over."

He smiled. "That's good. If we keep a steady pace, we'll reach the Edgewood within a week. Then it should only be a few more days to get to Echo's, assuming we don't run into any trouble."

"Right," I snorted. "You know, I'm starting to think trouble runs into *us*, on purpose."

He huffed a laugh. "I can agree with you there. What are the chances that the three of us end up *blessed* with magic? It's a cruel joke when it's the one thing that can get you killed without question in our kingdom. Darkenier's absence is our only consolation, but I don't think it'll ever be enough with how well he ingrained his ideals into the people."

"There's no use thinking about that now," I reminded him. "We have to focus on controlling the magic first and then deal with whatever happens after."

"What will happen in Widonia, now that Quinton knows what you did, what you are?"

I sighed. "I'm loath to even consider the sinister possibilities, but I can't help thinking I handed him the throne by leaving. He'll stoke the fires of whatever rumours the people spread, and by the time we return, no one will have mercy for me. But I can't… I can't think about that if I want to stay sane."

Asmund reached out and put a hand on my shoulder. "We won't let him take your throne—not for long, anyway. When the time comes, we'll find a way."

I nodded. "Thank you for being here, for helping me these past couple months. I never realized how badly I needed a friend."

"You're welcome, but what about Sky?"

"A person's sibling can't be their only friend if they want to have any secrets," I replied.

He smiled. "I suppose that's true."

"Speaking of siblings," I went on, "I think it's time they woke up."

His smile widened. "I was thinking the same thing."

Five minutes later, the girls rushed out of the tent in a daze after Asmund and I banged our weapons together right behind their heads, startling them from sleep with the awful clattering noise of steel on steel.

"Isanfier Oaden!" Sky roared. "You'll pay dearly for that one, you sorry excuse for a brother! I thought we were being attacked!"

She rushed at me with her fists, and I ducked and dodged her blows until I tripped over an exposed root and sprawled onto the ground, face first.

Sky stopped short, and I spit out a mouthful of dirt, rolling over to face her with my hands outstretched. "I yield, okay? I yield."

She just grinned at me. "I hope you enjoyed that dirt, because I have decided I *won't* be cooking breakfast today." She turned away and barked at Asmund, "Pack up the tent; we're leaving."

• • •

Luckily, Sky's mood picked up over the next few days, and she let us have seconds when we stopped for dinner that night. The four of us travelled in companionable silence, each of us lost in our own thoughts, our own fears. Some days, it felt like time had reversed and we were still riding towards the war with Winter, but the silence was able to convince me otherwise.

We only passed a few people on the road—keeping our hoods up when we did so, in fear of possible spies Quinton had sent after us—and only traveled by villages in the dead of night, giving them a wide berth.

It was early morning on the seventh day when we once again beheld the Edgewood. One minute, the sunrise was sending orange streaks of light all around us, and the next, we were cast in shadow, the air seeming to grow colder with the presence of the wood.

I felt a weight settle in my chest as I laid eyes on its gnarled trees again, but it was a different weight. The forest had lost some of its menace in my eyes after the time spent with Echo, and I was more worried about leaving Summer behind because of my actions than I was worried something would happen within the trees.

Aramina, however, felt differently.

As soon as Asmund pulled their horse to a stop and she had time to take in the sight of the Edgewood before us, I watched her eyes widen. "What in Fidalia is that?"

"The Edgewood," Asmund said. "Our saviour lies somewhere within its trees."

"It looks as dangerous as the stories say it is," Aramina replied. "There's no way I'm stepping foot in that death trap." She crossed her arms.

Asmund sighed. "Aramina…"

I held up a hand. "It's okay. Look, Aramina, we all felt the same way when we encountered the forest for the first time, none more than I, but I assure you, it is no more dangerous there than it was back at the palace for us."

"As long as we don't run into any goblins," Sky added.

Aramina shot her an alarmed look, and I pinched the bridge of my nose. "Sancia's breath, why would you *say* that?"

She shrugged. "Because it's the truth?" She turned to Aramina with a bit more kindness in her eyes. "This forest isn't a walk in the gardens, and there are plenty of dangers to be afraid of, but the truth is, we have little choice. We have to trust Sancia will watch over us and that if we need help, Echo will be able to find us. I'm scared too, but I know this is for the best."

Aramina took a deep breath and then nodded. "I trust you, but if we die, I'm telling Fidal it was your fault."

Sky smiled. "Duly noted."

"Well, Isanfier," Asmund said, "will you do the honours again?"

"It would be my pleasure." I urged my horse into a walk again, and they followed me to the edge of the wood, close enough to see its brambles and the papery thin leaves that didn't move despite the slight breeze dancing around our horses' feet.

I closed my eyes as we came to a stop and tried to picture Echo's face, her white wispy hair and brilliant blue eyes, the curve of her smile and the way she'd moved with me that night, under the light of a full moon with the sound of—

Aramina's gasp cut off my thoughts, and I opened my eyes to find the path had already formed.

*Curious, I haven't even told it why I seek passage.*

Still, I shook off the unease and managed a smile as I turned to Aramina and said, "Welcome to the Edgewood."

She smiled back, and the four of us rode through the arch in the trees, following the path to Echo and the hope she represented. I prayed she would know what to do, that she could save us from ourselves.

• • •

We were growing weary from our travels when we stumbled into a clearing four days after the Edgewood had swallowed us up. Excitement flared in me for a moment before a quick scan decided that it wasn't Echo's clearing. The glaring absence of the treehouse confirmed it.

Disappointment showed on the others' faces too, momentarily masking their exhaustion, and they slid from their horses to fill their waterskins at the brook running through the space.

Sky groaned as she crouched down at the water's edge, nearly tumbling in. "How much farther do you think it is, Isan?"

"I'm not sure," I replied, dismounting my own horse. "A direct route should've seen us there already, by all accounts, but I have no way of knowing whether or not our path was straight."

I glanced around the clearing once again as I rooted around in my saddle bag for my water, and that's when I noticed the wisteria vine wrapped around the tree beside my horse.

"Fidal's breath," I gasped.

Sky immediately shot to her feet, hand going to the bow strapped at her back. "What is it?"

Asmund and Aramina followed her lead, albeit a bit slower, but I only laughed.

"I know where we are," I replied.

Seeing it in the daylight had altered my perception, but it was clear now we were in the glade where Echo and I had shared our waltz. I noticed the purple flowers at Sky's feet, though their petals were closed, and found the rock where we'd sat before Echo had realized the truth of the Curse.

Sky frowned. "You do?"

"Yes, tie up the horses and follow me. We'll come back for them in a bit."

She, Asmund, and Aramina looked confused, but they followed my directions and were soon tracing my steps between the thick trees as I navigated the final few minutes to our destination.

"Isan, where are we—" Sky started, but at that precise moment, the trees fell away, and we stepped into a familiar clearing, Echo's treehouse coming into view in the branches high above us.

A grin broke onto my face. "We're here."

Echo's clearing was exactly how I remembered it, as if we had departed only yesterday. There was the open space where we had sparred, the table where we'd eaten outside, and the stream that ran a few paces behind the treehouse. A brand new sword was leaning against the wood pile, beside the ladder ascending into the leaves.

I closed my eyes and took a deep breath; it was good to be back.

"Wow," Aramina said, breaking the silence. "This place looks amazing, like something out of a fairytale. Does this Echo really live up there?" She pointed to the trees, and I nodded.

"Her treehouse is like nothing I have ever seen, though a bit daunting if you're not fond of heights."

"Like Isanfier," Sky chimed in, a hint of a smile catching her lips.

I scowled, reaching over to smack her in the arm when we heard a rustle in the trees across from us. We reached for our weapons but were brought short once more as a familiar white-haired girl stepped out from between the trees with an armful of wood.

It took a moment for her to notice us standing there, but when she did, she dropped her bundle and stared at us with wide eyes like she'd seen a ghost.

None of us said a word for several heartbeats, watching each other like a bunch of scared animals.

Finally, Echo let out a breath and whispered, "By Wylla's wayward heart… Is that really you?"

I knew she was addressing Sky and Asmund too, but for a second it felt as if her eyes were staring into my soul, as if she was afraid I would disappear if she looked away.

Her words broke the stalemate, however, and Sky said, "Surprise?"

Echo's face lit up with the brightest smile I'd ever seen, and the four of us converged on each other, my arms finding Echo first somehow. I crushed her to me and found her doing the same, holding on to me with every ounce of her strength, though she relinquished me quickly and moved on to Sky.

The two started crying, and Echo was wiping at her eyes as Asmund dragged her into a bear hug, his braids swinging right around her head.

Echo stepped away from him afterward as if in a daze. "I can't believe you're all here. I thought... I thought for sure I would've lost one of you to the war, couldn't let myself imagine you'd return either way. I shouldn't... By Wylla, it's so good to see you."

Sky smiled. "It's good to see you too, Echo. There's not a day that's gone by where you haven't crossed our minds."

Aramina stepped around Asmund then, likely miffed to be left out of the conversation.

Echo raised an eyebrow. "And who is this?"

Asmund stepped forward, putting a hand around Aramina's shoulder. "This is my sister, Aramina. Mina, this is Echo, the Missing One."

Echo smiled fondly at the title. "Just Echo will do," she replied. "It's nice to meet you. Asmund said little about his family when he was here last, but I can tell you're kinder than he is."

Aramina laughed. "It's nice to meet you too. Are you going to help us with our magic?"

Echo's eyebrows shot up so fast I feared they would fly from her forehead, and I choked at Aramina's words. I'd been planning to break the news slowly.

Echo looked around at the four of us. "*Our?*"

I sighed. "I turned my uncle to ash, who turned out not to be my uncle, Asmund lost his face once, and Mina can show up in places where she wasn't five seconds previously."

Echo blinked at the rapid onset of information, looking at us like we'd grown second and third heads, but then her expression softened into one of concern. "You've been through some hard times since you left me, haven't you?"

I nodded. "The magic isn't even the worst of it."

She took a deep breath. "You better come inside, then. You can tell me all about it over some hot mugs of tea."

## 20
## A Bloody History

**A few minutes later**, the five of us were gathered around Echo's dining table with our hands curled around steaming mugs of tea. Echo had struggled for a few minutes to find an extra chair for Aramina, eventually grabbing an old tree stump she'd been using as an end table and shoving it towards Asmund before giving Aramina his old chair. Asmund frowned but said nothing, and she smirked at him.

Finally, she joined us at the table and said, "Out with it, then."

The four of us shared wary glances, unsure where to begin, but then I cleared my throat and said, "I suppose we should start by telling you that Summer won the war, if you can call what we did a victory. Both sides sustained severe casualties; our uncle, King Frost, and Prince Snowdon are dead."

She hung her head when I said Snowdon's name. "I felt his passing, like another part of my soul had been ripped away. As much as I know his death was for the greater good, it still hurts to lose a brother."

Sky reached over and rubbed her back. "He went painlessly; I can assure you of that much."

Echo nodded. "I'm glad your life was spared and Fidalia is one step closer to salvation. Now tell me how it all happened, sparing no detail. I need the full picture if I am to help you."

"You might need more than one mug of tea for this tale," I told her.

Over the next hour, we regaled every detail of our time in Winter, from the battles and travel to all of our discoveries.

Echo grew nervous when I reached the part about our encounter with Snowdon and then Frost, but she seemed more interested in knowing the dark figure's identity than she seemed upset about her father's death, which was to be expected, I supposed.

When I finally revealed the truth about the dark figure, she nearly choked on her tea. "He was your *uncle*?" she managed to say after clearing her throat. "You must be heartbroken."

"I had mixed feelings, to say the least," I replied, "especially after finding out he was never actually our uncle. And once he confessed to killing our parents, I didn't have a choice. He chose death the moment he brought it to our kingdom; he just managed to evade it for over a decade before the lies caught up to him."

Echo raised an eyebrow, and Aramina gave me a look. "What are you talking about, Isan?"

I sighed. "I guess you're in deep enough with us to know the truth. Our late King went by a false name and used a Magic Wielder to change his features during his reign. He was actually a Wyllan, posing as our uncle to steal the Summer throne and take his own revenge on Winter."

Aramina's eyes widened, but she couldn't find the words to respond.

Even Echo looked aghast. "A Wyllan? What was his true name?"

"Prince Darkenier of Winter," I replied, wincing inwardly as I voiced his true title for the first time.

Echo seemed a million miles away as she said, "So that's where he ended up."

"What do you mean?" Sky asked.

"I don't know much about that side of the family," Echo admitted, "but he was a bit of a black sheep, abandoning the palace for Tamise and then disappearing about twenty years ago. He must've gone to Summer then, and I might be able to shed light on why."

I nodded eagerly. "We'd appreciate any insight you can give."

Echo took a deep breath. "Well, sit back and relax, then. It's time for a story."

I smiled, remembering the warmth her stories had given me in the past, not to mention the knowledge. In another life, Echo could've been a scholar, tasked with memorizing our rich history and passing it on to younger generations.

The four of us settled into our chairs as Echo's voice began to fill our ears and minds.

*The first monarch of Winter that our records mention was Queen Lea, an immortal who was born in the year 103 to parents whose names and upbringing are lost to us now. She rose to her position through unwavering dominance and by instilling a profound fear into her subjects, becoming Queen of Winter at twenty years old.*

*She ruled the kingdom with an iron fist. Her wrath was unfathomable, and few dared to challenge their cold, dark Queen, despite knowing she had no magic to her name.*

*For centuries, the Wyllans endured Lea's heartless rule, until she fell for a young mortal man named Richard. He was one of her Royal Guards, and the two formed a bond over the many attempts on her life and his steadfast resolve to protect her, no matter what the people thought of her. The entire kingdom celebrated their marriage a few years after the two met and a royal birth the year following, as Queen Lea and Richard welcomed their son Prince Edmund. Two years later, Princess Rielle was born.*

*The two royal children of Winter grew up wanting for nothing and training to one day stand beside their mother. Edmund was the Heir Apparent, though Lea had no intention of succumbing to death or ever giving up her throne. She encouraged her children to marry well, which led to Edmund marrying Izabel, a noble girl with ice magic, and Rielle marrying Lord Izarr of Vendum a few years after that. Izabel later gave birth to Alice, and Rielle to Blizzard—two children who grew up to develop incredible gifts of their own.*

*However, the celebration of new life in Wylla's domain was not enough to quell the darkness that always spread throughout the land.*

*The realm was reminded of Winter's wrath and unpredictable cruelty when Queen Lea orchestrated the murders of King Greenbrier and Queen Blossom of Summer. The scholars claim it was retribution for a wrong they'd dealt her centuries before, but Winter and Summer were at odds even then, and everything was a power struggle between the two, a ploy to become the better kingdom or destroy the other completely.*

*And the bloodshed did not end there. Prince Blizzard was only a year old when a string of sudden murders rushed through the royal household, leaving him motherless and Princess Alice an orphan. The motivations behind Rielle's actions is still unknown to this day, but the fact remains that she killed Izabel, and the consequences of her doing so were felt for decades.*

*Edmund found Rielle standing over Izabel's body, murder weapon in hand, and was consumed with grief and rage. The two fought, and Edmund's sister was soon dead on the ground beside his wife.*

*Edmund tried to run, to escape the palace before the truth could spread, but it wasn't meant to be. Izarr was a powerful Gifted Immortal, and when he found out the truth of Rielle's death, it is said the whole palace shook with his anger and magic. Prince Edmund's body was found encased in ice and shattered into pieces.*

*Queen Lea took the orphaned Princess Alice under her wing, her new heir now that both her children had perished, and Lord Izarr was forced to raise Blizzard alone.*

*Decades later, peace had once again found the royal family. Alice was married to Colden, with her children Shiveera and Darkenier, and Blizzard was married to Iceclea with his son Frost, but death clung to Winter like a misty shroud, and the peace was not meant to last.*

*Iceclea was soon killed by Prince Foren of Summer, and Blizzard took revenge by killing his wife Meadow. Queen Katheryn of Summer also met her demise, and the blame was laid on Winter, though the claims have never been proven.*

*The death toll kept climbing.*

*Alice accidentally encased her husband Colden in ice and killed him. The next day, she committed suicide. Lea sentenced Blizzard to death for going against her orders and murdering Meadow.*

*Lord Izarr, devastated by his son's death, launched a long and bloody attack on the Queen, the likes of which the realm has never seen before or since. Izarr's magic was great, but the Queen had countless men to throw at him and plenty of Magic Wielders at her beck and call.*

*In the end, they both bled out together, lying on the floor of the throne room.*

*Queen Lea's reign came to an end after 472 years, and Blizzard's son Frost was crowned King of Winter.*

For a minute, I was so overcome by the horror of the tale that I didn't even realize Echo had finished it.

It was Asmund who broke the ensuing silence, bringing me back to the present. "I knew the Wyllans were volatile, but that… That is a brutal history. How did they ever hope to best Summer with that much inner conflict?"

Echo shook her head. "I wish I knew the motives behind what they did, behind their anger, but without proper records, we can only speculate. Edmund didn't let Rielle live long enough to explain her actions, and Lea would never be honest about her own, even if the scholars had asked her."

"I can't believe Frost wasn't the worst of them," Sky said. She looked sick to her stomach.

"My father, as cruel as he was," Echo replied, "was a product of the violence that came before him. He inherited a broken kingdom. He grew up in an empty castle, with few people he could trust to give him guidance. I don't want to condone anything he did, but sometimes I think he isn't entirely to blame. His ancestors failed him, and he was doomed from the start."

"Do you think this is the imbalance the Curse wants us to fix?" I asked. "Not just the one between Summer and Winter but the one *within* Winter as well?"

Echo furrowed her brows. "I suppose it could be, but I don't think we'll know for sure what the problem is until we solve it. We have to be open to whatever comes our way and dedicated to the well-being of the entire realm, not focused on a singular goal."

Aramina leaned forward, and I noticed her tea was untouched. "I don't mean to be rude, but I'm a little…concerned." She turned to Echo. "Did you say King Frost was your father? And what is this curse you keep mentioning?"

"He was," Echo replied, "but not necessarily in the way you think. Princess Icaria and I share a soul, for lack of a better explanation. I was raised in the Winter palace for six years until my mother died, and Icaria and I split into two separate people. As for the Curse…" Echo looked at me.

"There is an ancient prophecy," I told Aramina, "that speaks of the birth of royal twins in both kingdoms, at a time of great turmoil in Fidalia. The Elder twins and the Younger twins are cursed to fight each other to the death before their eighteenth birthday, or they will all die, and chaos will reign throughout the lands. Sky and I are one half of the Curse. Sky killed Snowdon, but I still need to defeat Icaria. Supposedly, whatever I do along the way to that goal will bring balance back to Fidalia and save us all from certain doom."

Aramina's face was grave as I finished my explanation. "So the fate of the entire realm is in our hands, then?"

"Well, my hands technically," I replied, "but yes."

"And how does your story help us?" she asked Echo. "You said it would shine light on the King's motives."

"Well," Echo replied, "at the time of Queen Lea's death, there were only three Winter royals left to take the throne: Shiveera, Darkenier, and Frost. Everyone else was dead. Shiveera had run off with her sweetheart nearly a decade before Lea's death and hadn't been seen since. The crown could not go to her, though she was the oldest and the rightful heir. It was between Darkenier and Frost, but like I said, Darkenier hadn't been seen in a while either, so Frost was crowned instead.

"I think your uncle—sorry, Darkenier—I think Darkenier felt cheated. He wanted the crown. He believed *he* should have been King. Thus, he did everything in his power to achieve that.

"He killed Frost's wife, my mother, so she couldn't oppose him, and your parents so he could present himself as your uncle and receive the Summer Crown. For twelve years, he built up his army, and then he went after Frost and the Crown of Winter that he thought was rightfully his. He killed Frost and realized his life's dream.

"Ultimately, killing him was the first step in solving the imbalance in the realm. You saved both Summer and Winter from his wrath, Isan. Now you must figure out your next step."

"The next step is obvious," I replied. "The four of us fled Summer after another betrayal. Our new Captain of the Guard has it in for me, and I wouldn't be surprised if he's sitting on my throne right now. He's been undermining me for weeks, leaving no stone unturned in his search for power, and now he's named me a traitor of the crown after I set fire to Widonia in a fit of rage. I need to learn to control my magic so we can go back and fight; right now, I'm a danger to myself and my people. We were hoping you could help me, help us."

Echo took a deep breath. "Fidal truly will not let you sleep. I am sorry to hear you've lost your kingdom to a vile man, but I know you'll win it back, and I will do everything in my power to help you. For now, it would be best for you all to get some rest. I will start your lessons in the morning."

I reached out to touch her hand. "Thank you, for everything you've done for us. I'm sorry for bringing our problems to your doorstep again, but we didn't have anywhere else to go."

Echo squeezed my hand. "I am glad to be your refuge, no matter what you're running from."

Asmund coughed, and we drew apart, the moment gone. Sky stood up, starting to clear the table of mugs, and Aramina followed suit. Echo left to prepare our rooms, leaving Asmund and I alone at the table.

He gave me a look. "Seems like someone is interested in you, Prince."

"What do you mean?"

"Oh, come now," he replied. "Didn't you see the look she gave you when she saw us in the clearing, or how she flung herself at you first? You'd have to be blind to miss that."

"Who, Echo?"

"No, Skiansy," he said with a roll of his eyes. "Of course I'm talking about Echo. She sees something in you, and I can sense you feel the same."

I scratched the back of my head. "It's not that simple."

He shrugged. "Love never is. Audria always makes us work for it so we know whether or not it's worth it in the end." He stood up and clapped me on the back. "You'll figure it out. Now let's get to bed. We have a big day ahead of us tomorrow."

•  •  •

I didn't get much sleep that night, my mind plagued by various nightmares, though they were all too disjointed to be visions this time.

In one, I was stumbling through the halls of the castle as it burned down around me, coming face to face with Quinton sitting on my throne. Suddenly, I was on my knees, blood coming out of a wound I couldn't see. Quinton started laughing maniacally, and then his face morphed into Icaria's, and she finished me off with an ice sword through my skull.

In another, I went through the motions of killing Darkenier, again and again, but every time he dropped dead, I discovered it was Sky's body on the floor in front of me instead.

The last nightmare I could remember had me chasing Echo through the Edgewood but never being able to reach her. The forest grew thicker and darker the longer I ran, the trees scraping my exposed skin with branches as sharp as knives.

I woke in a cold sweat in the early hours of the morning, my head pounding from the lack of sufficient sleep, and I decided I was done trying.

Asmund was still snoring in the bed across the room from mine, and I was glad I hadn't woken him. I didn't want to talk about what the nightmares could mean about my deteriorating mental state. What happened in Widonia was all my fault, and it would haunt me till the day my soul left this realm, especially if there was nothing left to save when I returned.

What would I do then? Who would trust me? Could I ever dare to show my face in Summer again?

I jumped out of bed and grabbed *Ember* from the bedside table, careful not to creak any floorboards as I made my way out into the hall. The treehouse was silent, peaceful, like there was nothing wrong in the realm at all. I remembered how we'd lost ourselves here last time, and I resolved to not stay longer than was necessary, no matter what happened.

Maybe I did like Echo, but I couldn't let that get between me and what I needed to accomplish. I needed to focus.

I walked through the quiet rooms to the ladder and climbed down it to the clearing below. Long streaks of yellow light streamed through from cracks in the foliage above, making the ground look striped, and standing on the far side, tending to our horses, was Echo.

She looked over at me as I hit the ground. "What are you doing up so early?"

I shrugged. "Couldn't sleep. I could ask you the same."

She grimaced. "I'm not surprised, after the story you told last night. You must be under a lot of pressure. Unfortunately, you're going to need to relax a bit if you truly want to control your magic. You can't be afraid of it, and you can't give it any emotion to latch on to."

"Well, that will be easier said than done."

"It will take more than one training session," she admitted, "but I have faith you will succeed. All of you. As for me... I guess I'm a bit nervous to be teaching, so I needed to occupy my mind with something else."

I held up my sword. "Would you care for a duel while we wait for the others? Swordplay always clears my mind. There's no room for anything else when you're focused on winning, and no better emotional boost than when you win."

She smiled. "But what if I win and you lose? How will you feel then?"

I grinned. "It'll make me that much more determined to keep practising so I can beat you next time."

"Deal." She walked back over to the treehouse and grabbed a sword, the same one I had seen yesterday when we'd arrived. It was a long sword that shone like polished silver with a midnight black hilt and a sapphire embedded in the pommel.

It was a breathtaking blade, and as the morning light caught it, I could see the name *Silence* etched into the metal.

"A claimed weapon?" I said. "You were busy while we were gone."

She blushed. "I made a trip into Tamise for supplies once I decided it was safe enough in Winter to venture out. I hadn't planned to buy a sword while I was there, but it caught my eye, in more ways than one. I also might have stolen a tome from the bookstore there which detailed every step of the claiming ritual. It was difficult doing it alone, but I managed. I remember when Icaria had her ritual, so I followed that as well."

"I wonder if you would be able to use each other's claimed weapons, if the sword and magic would be able to tell the difference?"

Echo frowned. "That's a good question. My heart tells me it would be easier than using your sword but still wouldn't feel exactly right."

"I'd be inclined to say the same."

"Well, let's hope I never have to find out." She pointed her sword at me. "Now, you promised me a duel."

# 21
# A Flicker of Hope

**We had finished three** duels and were at a stalemate by the time the others joined us outside. She won the first, and I won the second, but we were forced to declare the third a draw.

Still, I felt much better than when I'd first woken up. The exhilaration in Echo's eyes was contagious, and there was no better cure to depression than muscle exertion and the feeling of blood rushing through your veins.

Sky had brought out a tray of porridge and tea, and the five of us sat around the picnic table as we ate.

"Looks like you two have been busy," Asmund said.

"Isanfier is definitely much better now that he's completely healed," Echo admitted, "but I'm still keeping him on his toes."

I smiled. "It's nice to have a good challenge."

"I like your enthusiasm," Echo replied, "because these magic lessons are going to be far from easy." She looked around the table. "I'm going to do everything I can to teach all of you what I know, but most of the work must be done within yourself." She looked at Asmund before adding, "I am also not a Magic Wielder myself, as you and Aramina are, Asmund. All I know in that area I read in books, and they can only teach you so much without practical experience to bolster it."

Asmund nodded. "I understand, but any guidance you can give will be appreciated. We couldn't even find books on the subject in the castle."

Echo frowned. "It's such a shame that Darkenier stole that knowledge from your people. I can't imagine how many others are suffering. Are you all at least familiar with the different magic types?"

"I know Magic Wielders are mortals with a shared set of powers," Aramina piped up. "So, eventually Asmund and I will be able to do more than shape-shift and portal."

Echo nodded. "Magic Wielder powers are mental and physical in nature, like telekinesis and healing wounds. The first power you unlock is called your affinity, and it will always be your strongest magic. Some Magic Wielders never unlock more than one power, and it's said that some powers are so rare, they've been lost to time."

Aramina's eye lit up at the challenge, and I had a feeling that if anyone could master the entire set of Magic Wielder powers, it was her.

Echo turned to me then. "Gifted Immortals, on the other hand, are, of course, immortal and have a single Gift written into their name itself, though a parent cannot simply choose. The name is bestowed to them by the goddesses, in whatever form the realm needs at the time, or so people say. These gifts are typically elemental in nature, like your fire."

I frowned. "Everything else makes sense, but how are the names *bestowed*? What does that mean?"

"It's hard to explain," Echo admitted, "but as I understand it, the name just sort of comes to the parents. In a dream maybe or planted deep in their consciousness from birth, but your parents didn't decide to put fire in your name so that you'd develop fire magic. That's not how it works. Your soul was destined to have fire magic, so that's the name they thought of."

"Interesting," I replied. "Where do we start, then?"

"Each of you has a journey to go on," she replied, "something to forgive yourself or others for. Asmund, you wished to become someone else because you hated yourself. In order to control your shape-shifting and hone your other abilities, you need to accept who you are. You need to forgive your past self and dedicate yourself to the path you're on now.

"Aramina," Echo went on, glancing at her sitting beside Sky. "You wished to escape your family and your grief, but you need to stop running and face the adversity in your life. You've already done some of this, as you are able to create portals at will, but I sense there is still something holding you back from your full potential."

Aramina hung her head as if she knew exactly what Echo was talking about but didn't want to voice it, and Echo finally turned to me.

"As for you, Isan… You need to let go of your anger and forgive those who wronged you, even if you know they don't deserve it."

I clenched my jaw. Forgive Darkenier? Was she out of her mind?

"Echo, I—"

She held up her hand. "I know, but there is no other way. Magic requires balance, not only between life and magic but between your emotional highs and lows. It doesn't mean you have to avoid anger the rest of your life, but the more you confront what you're angry about and make peace with it, the less likely you will be to set yourself on fire without wanting to. Unintentional magic use can kill you, just as easily as using it for too long. You will all build a tolerance and be able to sustain your powers longer, but it will take time. Besides, it's not healthy for the mind to carry all that rage within you; it's a poison.

"Fear is *my* trigger, which is why I disappeared when I discovered the Curse was about you. I hadn't meant to, and the fear kept me from reappearing for a few minutes. I first discovered my Gift when I was attacked by a goblin horde, and it wasn't until I overcame my fear of them that I was able to properly use my magic."

I took a deep breath. "I understand the logic, but it's certainly not a simple task. How do you forgive a man who took nearly everything from you?"

Echo reached over and squeezed my shoulder. "Slowly, and one step at a time." She looked around the table at each of us and added, "We'll start with some meditation."

Ten minutes later, Asmund, Aramina, and I were sitting cross legged in the middle of the clearing in a rough circle, about six paces between each of us. Our eyes were closed, and Echo stood in the middle, encouraging us to empty our minds and focus on what we needed to overcome. Her voice was soothing, and it lulled me for a bit, but inevitably, my mind started to wander.

I had grown lost the last time I was here, thinking about only myself, so this time I couldn't help my thoughts from drifting to the Festival, to Quinton, to the people we'd left behind, and to Icaria and the Curse.

Even if I did somehow master my magic, how was I supposed to overcome all the obstacles in my path, let alone manage to kill Icaria? She'd had ten years to master her Gift already. What was I when compared to her?

"Isan," Echo said, "you're not concentrating." Her voice was right behind me, but I resisted the urge to turn my head and look.

"How do you know?" I asked, trying not to let annoyance leak into my words.

Her hands grabbed my shoulders and squeezed. "You're stiff as a board. You need to *relax*."

"I'm trying," I snapped, a little more harsh than I'd intended.

She let go, and I felt emptier without her touch.

"Stop trying so hard," she said softly. "Just let it happen. Let the emotions flow through you and out of you." She was speaking to all of us again, and I tried to lose myself in her words, her voice, but I knew I wouldn't make any progress that day.

• • •

We spent the next week following this path—meditating for an hour in the morning and an hour in the afternoon, attempting at the end of each session to call our magic forth. Aramina was the only one who met success, and she was allowed to train with her magic in the afternoon.

Sky helped each of us when she could but had read through most of Echo's small library by the end of the week.

Asmund and I spent our afternoon sessions in our shared room so Echo could train Aramina in the clearing without disturbing our meditation. The silence was unnerving to me, and I grew no closer to finding peace. However, just before the week was coming to a close, I opened my eyes during one of our sessions and found Aramina sitting on the bed beside mine.

"Mina?" I questioned. "What are you—"

Then Mina opened her eyes and gave me such an Asmund-like look that I was able to put the pieces together quickly.

"Sancia's breath," I told Asmund, "that's unnerving, and unfair."

He grinned, still wearing Aramina's face—and whole body, it looked like. Then he closed his eyes again and shifted one inch at a time into a near-perfect rendition of me, except for the eyes.

I smiled. "Nice try, but my eyes aren't brown. You need to work on your accuracy."

He raised an eyebrow. "And you need to take a better look in the mirror. You have the same eyes as Sky, though not as pretty."

I rolled my ice blue eyes and said, "Whatever. Who else can you do?"

It took another few minutes, but then it was Echo staring at me instead. "I'm sure you like this form the best?" Asmund-Echo said with Asmund's voice, and I cringed.

"Absolutely not. Change back right now."

"What, are you worried you'll start to fancy me?" He pursed Echo's lips at me, and I reached out and smacked him on the arm instinctively.

He recoiled, jolting back to his own form, and said, "Hey, it's wrong to hit a girl!"

I shrugged. "It's also wrong to be a show-off, but there you sit."

"You're just jealous I'm stronger than you now."

I didn't say anything for a minute, because we both knew he was right. I was slipping away from the pack, and I definitely wasn't special now—unless you called being useless at magic special. At this rate, Icaria would come to finish me off before I even learned how to light a candle.

Asmund sighed. "Like Echo said, Isan, you're trying too hard."

"Because it *is* hard," I snapped back. "I can't let go, I can't forgive him for what happened."

"Why?" he prodded.

"I don't know!" I shot back.

Asmund looked like he was about to push me further, but then someone cleared their throat behind us, and we turned to see Echo standing in the doorway—the real Echo this time. I was glad Asmund wasn't still wearing her face.

She gave Asmund a small smile. "Can I have a moment with Isan? Aramina can start showing you some basic steps for portal creation outside, if you'd like."

Asmund hesitated but then stood up and left the room. Echo took his place on the bed across from me, and I hung my head, feeling like a child who had been caught doing something wrong.

We sat in silence for a few moments before Echo said, "This isn't just about Darkenier, is it? There's something else holding you back. Why are you so afraid to let go?"

I swallowed hard and made a decision, though I shouldn't have been too surprised by my answer. Echo had a way with people...with me.

"Because if I do... If I let go of the anger, what will be left?"

She gave me a sad but understanding look. "You are not your anger, Isanfier. You lose nothing—"

"But it's not just that," I interrupted her. "Sancia's breath, it's stupid, but I think... I think I'm more angry at myself than at Darkenier."

I couldn't meet her eyes when I said it, but I heard her ask me why.

"I'm angry I didn't see his deception," I replied, "angry I let him destroy Summer, let him kill so many men, angry I let him put me and Sky in danger time and time again, that I still can't keep us safe, even after his death. I'm angry I didn't interpret the dream in time to prevent the war entirely. But most of all, I'm angry that I let it eat me away so much, and that I don't know how to forgive myself."

I put my head in my hands, and a few moments later, I felt the bed dip as Echo moved from Asmund's bed to sit down beside me.

"The first step to forgiveness is admitting to yourself that your anger has no merit," she said. "You can't keep blaming yourself for the actions of others, for situations that have come and gone. You can only try to be a better person going forward. You are not your anger, and it is okay to grieve."

I looked up at her. "Grieve?"

"Yes, Isan," she said. "You lost your uncle, despite his true identity. You lost your childhood to the war, and you nearly lost your life. You are allowed to mourn that. In fact, I think you need to let go of the anger in *favour* of grief to forgive yourself for what happened. You need to feel the pain and then let it go."

"I don't know…"

She squeezed my shoulder. "I think you do. We'll be outside when you're ready to join us, and I am here for you if you ever need to talk."

She left me alone then, and in the silence that followed, the walls around my heart started to crumble. I thought about who I'd been before the war—full of anger, even then, but also full of hope and excitement. Where had that boy gone? Would I ever see him again?

And Darkenier… He had betrayed us—that much I knew—and he didn't share our blood, but had it all been fake to him? Or had a part of him regretted all he had done and had yet to do when he'd declared war on Winter?

I realized at that moment that I had never been truly angry at him, just disappointed. I had worshipped the ground he'd walked on, and he had let me down. He had abandoned us, abandoned me, and now there was no one to turn to, no one to rely upon but myself…

My tears began to fall, and before I knew it, they were streaming down my face, cleansing me of all the negative emotion I'd been bottling up for too long.

When they finally ran dry, and I'd collected myself once again, I closed my eyes and searched within me for the supposed well of magic, and this time, I felt something. It was like a thread of energy, and as I pulled on it with my mind, I felt something unravelling within me. It took all my concentration, but I eventually followed the thread to a door inside my mind and gave it a tug.

A rush of power ran through me, a heat building up beneath my skin, and when I opened my eyes, a tiny flame flickered in the palm of my right hand.

I smiled despite my tear-stained cheeks.

Maybe I was special after all.

# 22
# Playing With Fire

**The next morning, the** five of us were gathered in the clearing again, but this time we would be training instead of meditating. We had each managed to come to terms with what emotions warred inside us, and now the real fun would begin.

I was equal parts nervous and excited to see what I could do.

"Aramina," Echo said, "we'll start with you. Please open a portal to Isan's bedroom, steal one of his shirts, and come back."

I scowled at her chosen task, but Aramina winked at me before summoning a portal in record time and disappearing.

"Now, Asmund, I want you to change into Aramina before she returns."

He nodded and closed his eyes, but Echo cleared her throat.

"Eyes open," she added. "Shifting should become as easy as breathing for you."

Asmund clenched his jaw but followed her orders, turning away from us to minimize distractions as much as he could.

"What about me?" I asked Echo, but Aramina's return muffled my words, and all eyes turned to her instead.

"Done!" she exclaimed, holding up one of my white tunics. "How was my time?"

"I think I could do better," came Asmund's voice as he turned to face his sister.

Aramina screamed at the sight of herself, and the rest of us doubled over in laughter.

"Sancia's breath, Mina, your face," Asmund gasped out, holding his stomach against the pain.

"Which one?" Sky added before dissolving into another fit of laughter so heavy she could barely breathe.

Tears began streaming down Asmund's borrowed face, which only served to add fuel to our laughter.

It was several minutes before we were able to calm down, and then Aramina faced us all with a terrible scowl. "You bunch are the meanest people I've ever encountered, and Lord Arrath is my father."

Asmund grimaced, shifting back into himself. "I'd prefer it if you *didn't* bring him up. I imagine he's dug us both graves by now."

Mina rolled her eyes. "As if Arran would let him."

"As if Arran would have a choice," Asmund shot back.

Echo clapped her hands. "All right, that's enough of that. I need you two to focus. You'll spend the rest of the morning honing these skills. Once you've mastered your affinities, we can move on to your other powers. Asmund, try to shift into as many people as you can remember, but check each one for accuracy in a mirror before you move on. Sky, if you could, I'd like you to help Aramina."

Sky stood up from her seat at the table. "Of course. What can I do?"

"I'd like the two of you to play an advanced game of hide and seek."

Aramina's eyes lit up. "How do we play?"

"Sky will hide in various places in the clearing and treehouse, and you have to portal to her, without opening your eyes or choosing a specific place to go."

Aramina smiled. "Challenge accepted."

Aramina sat down at the table and closed her eyes, while both Sky and Asmund headed up into the treehouse to complete their tasks.

I faced Echo. "Did you send them away to keep them out of harm's reach?" I uncurled my fists, imagining them full of fire, and tried not to flinch.

Echo walked up to me and took my hand in hers, cradling it gently as if it were a delicate piece of pottery. "I did no such thing," she replied. "They need practice, and you need the space to fulfill your full potential. Now, I want you to call the fire up, and then we can see what we're working with."

I slid my hand out of her grip and closed my eyes, taking deep breaths to calm my racing heart before reaching for the thread of magic once more.

*You can do this,* I reminded myself. *You are in control now.*

I felt the heat building and opened my eyes as the fire ignited, leaping to life in the palm of my hand. The flame was small, and I felt protective of it as I watched it dance in the breeze.

"That's great, Isan," Echo said softly. "Can you do both hands?"

I didn't dare take my eyes off the flame as I replied, "I'm not sure."

"Well, give it a try when you're ready, and relax your shoulders. You look like you're preparing to fend off a horde of goblins."

I scowled at her. "Maybe I am."

"There you go," she said. "It stays lit even if you don't stare at it."

I bit back my retort as I closed my eyes warily and tried to conjure a second flame. It took me ten minutes, and I lost the first flame several times before I managed it.

Echo laughed at the expression on my face. "It's not going to bite you, Isan. No one is safer than you when it comes to those flames. Now relax, and let them build."

I hesitated, and she gave me a small smile. "Your magic is a gift, not a curse, but it can fester if you allow it to, if you give yourself space to doubt. This fire is who you are; you can't separate yourself from that. You can only decide what you're going to do about it. I believe in you, Isanfier. Your kingdom needs you."

I sighed. "How do you always know the right thing to say?"

She shrugged. "I'm a good listener, especially to things people are afraid to voice. I've always been drawn to the space between."

"And you're not afraid of my magic? Of me?"

"I trust you," she replied. "Now trust me."

I wanted to protest, but I couldn't, not when she was looking at me like that, not when it felt for a second like we were the only two people in the realm.

"I trust you," I said softly.

"Trust yourself," she whispered back.

I eased my grip on the thread of magic inside me and watched as the fire grew.

"One step at a time," Echo reminded me.

*One step at a time.*

• • •

Two weeks later, Asmund, Aramina, and I were well versed in our magic, though I was a little jealous that they had an array of gifts while I had only one. They had each mastered the basics of both portalling and shifting, and they were slowly working on the other Magic Wielder abilities such as healing, telepathy, and telekinesis, to name a few. Echo often reminded them that some were more difficult than others, and a rare few, like prophecy, were almost unheard of.

Asmund took great pleasure in speaking to me via telepathy at the most inopportune times, which led to me setting something on fire accidentally on more than one occasion. It was fortunate, however, that he could only project his voice into my head and not read my mind entirely. Echo assured me daily that it was impossible.

While their bag of magic tricks was intriguing, I had to admit there were certain advantages to focusing my energy on one task. I was able to hone my gift much faster than they could, and as a result, I could set fire to my hands whenever I wanted and had learned to sustain the flame for an entire hour before exhaustion broke my concentration.

Echo was currently teaching me how to call the magic back to me after setting something on fire. I had been successful so far, and she promised she would teach me how to throw fireballs once I perfected it.

Asmund and Sky were inside somewhere, but Aramina sat against the treehouse trunk, practising her telekinesis on several different objects. She had come to life over the past few weeks, letting go of the masks she wore to protect herself. I was happy to see it but dreaded eventually having to take her back to the life she had spent years hiding from.

"Focus, Isan," Echo called out to me, bringing me back to the present. At my request, she stood at the other end of the clearing as a safety precaution. I'd singed the ends of her hair the other day, and I didn't want to invite any more incidents.

"Set fire to the woodpile, let it burn for a few minutes, then bring the fire back to your hands."

I gave her a thumbs up to let her know I understood, then I called on my magic. My hands caught fire, and I transferred the flames to the woodpile by laying my hands on it.

As Echo instructed, I watched it burn as I counted to one hundred. Then I held my hands against the flames—my instinctual human fear of being burnt long gone—and let my magic do the work. In an instant, my hands were burning, and the woodpile fire had gone out.

"How was that?" I asked Echo.

"Excellent," she said. "Now, here's your next challenge. Do that again, but this time, while the woodpile is burning, I want you to set fire to your hands again. Then take the woodpile fire without dousing your hands."

"Okay," I said, skeptical but willing to try anything.

Echo smiled at me. "I'm sure you can manage."

"Here goes nothing," I whispered to myself.

I did the same as before with little difficulty. While the woodpile burned, I tried the next step. It took considerable effort to set my hands on fire the second time, when I hadn't put out the first fire, but I did it without losing too much breath.

*Now for the hardest part.*

Once again, I placed my hands over the flames, but this time, I kept them suspended an inch away. I would have to bring the fire back without making contact, or I would transfer the second fire to the woodpile as well.

I closed my eyes as I let my magic seep into my surroundings, focusing on what I could feel instead of what I could see. The warmth of my magic radiated from the woodpile, and I could feel it calling to me, longing to be reunited.

Invisible threads of magic trickled out of me and into the air, searching for what had been lost, until they made a connection. The result was immediate, and I felt the magic retreat back into the reservoir inside of me while allowing my hands to continue burning. I opened my eyes and willed my hands to go out before looking to Echo.

She threw her hands in the air as a huge smile lit up her face. "I knew you could do it! How did it feel?"

I shrugged. "As easy as breathing; it's not stealing my energy as much anymore."

"Thank Madge for that," she replied, invoking the name of the goddess of magic. "The more intense the act, the more of a toll it will take on you, but the more you practise, the more you can withstand. Now, if you want to eventually learn how to throw fireballs, you will have to work on your distance."

"So repeat this task from farther and farther away each time?" I asked.

She nodded. "Exactly. You keep at it while I go check on Asmund and Sky. They've been awfully quiet today." She sighed. "I worry Sky feels left out, that I don't spend enough time with her."

I touched her arm. "Sky understands; you can't be everywhere at once, and she knows how crucial this training is to all of us." Her fears echoed my own, but Sky had told me on more than one occasion that she didn't need me hovering over her all the time. "Besides," I went on, "the two of you spend every evening thick as thieves. Personally, I'm a bit jealous of that."

Echo grinned. "Of Sky not spending time with you, or me?"

I half choked on my next breath. "What—What do you mean?"

She shrugged. "Oh…nothing. I'll be back in a bit; you keep practising."

She walked off without another word, and I found myself staring at the place she'd been long after she'd gone inside, my mind a mess of varying emotions.

Aramina laughed, jolting me out of my trance. "Asmund was right about you and Echo," she said. "You're completely smitten."

I scowled at her. "I am not, and since when do you listen to anything Asmund says?"

She played with the knife in her hand. "He may be my biggest annoyance, but he's actually pretty observant." She frowned. "Don't tell him I said that."

We stood in silence for a minute, and then she added, "It's okay, you know, if you like her. No one would blame you, and I personally don't think Echo would mind either."

I let out a sigh and walked over to sit down beside her, abandoning my practice for a moment. "It's not that simple, Mina."

"But it could be," she replied. "You're the Prince. You can change things. You can eradicate old traditions and build new ones. Isn't your happiness worth a little bit of conflict?"

"She's still a Wyllan," I reminded her. "Even if I could put an end to the Festival of Honour, I don't think the Council would look past where she came from, and she's bound to this forest until I kill Icaria, if I can even manage it. It would be cruel to tell her how I feel when she can't follow me, when this Curse might yet kill me. And besides, I don't know *how* I feel. Sure, she's pretty, and her smile lights up the room, and I love the way she looks at the world as if it's still full of hope…"

Aramina gave me a look. "It sounds to me like you know exactly how you feel."

"I suppose you're well-versed on the subject of romance?" I retorted.

She rolled her eyes. "I may be inexperienced, but I know love when I see it, and besides that… I'm an empath."

I frowned. "What?"

"Magic Wielders can sense and manipulate emotion, if they know where to look. Asmund can't figure that one out, but I find it simple."

I narrowed my eyes as I realized I couldn't hide from her anymore. "You're going to be a real terror when we return to Summer."

She smiled. "Oh, I plan to be a force to be reckoned with carefully."

I heaved a sigh. "So what if I *do* like Echo? What am I supposed to do about it?"

"Follow whatever path your heart tells you is true," she replied. "It's as easy and as difficult as that." She reached out tentatively and took my hand. "You deserve happiness, Isan, and you're immortal now, so... so marrying a mortal like the ladies back home would be cruel, for both of you."

I mulled over the truth of her words for a minute in silence, having never really dwelled on the matter of my immortality before now. The notion seemed so...ethereal, as if I was some kind of god. I could barely wrap my head around the idea of adulthood, let alone eternity, but Aramina was right. I couldn't resign myself to marrying just anyone now, couldn't bear to watch them grow old and wither while I remained in my prime.

But that didn't mean Echo was the one, and I couldn't risk pursuing that path when all our lives hinged on her continuing to help us.

I shook my head and repeated, "It's not that simple."

She sighed. "Love never is, but I'm told it's worth it. I mean, look at what Asmund and Sky are—" She stopped herself short, her face losing some of its colour, but the damage was already done.

"What did you say?" I asked, a sudden ire building up inside me, though my fire remained hidden.

Aramina put her head in her hands but didn't reply.

"You were going to say, 'Look at what Asmund and Sky are going through,' weren't you?" I said. "Are they..." My stomach twisted.

*I'll kill him. I swear, I'll —*

Aramina shot to her feet. "Isan, calm down for a second. They don't even know I know. I could... I could be wrong."

"But you don't think so."

She shook her head, not trusting herself to speak.

Echo had gone to look for them after their odd absence this morning, and when I thought about it, I realized how often they'd both been missing lately—Sky always volunteering to help him with his lessons, the two of them sitting beside each other at meals and laughing over some joke the rest of us couldn't catch, that one dance in the castle where they'd held hands for longer than was necessary...

The signs were all there, and I felt like a fool for dismissing them as inconsequential all this time.

I stood up and made for the ladder, but Aramina caught my arm.

"Isan, *don't,*" she said.

I turned back to look at her. "Why not?"

"Sky won't forgive you," she replied.

"Sky isn't thinking straight," I shot back.

"Are you sure Sky's the one not thinking straight, or is it you?" she snapped.

I clenched my fists against the flame simmering beneath my skin and then pulled my arm out of her grip, ascending the ladder before she could say another word.

She let me go, and somehow, that made me even angrier.

It was a miracle I didn't catch fire on the way up the ladder, but I remained in control as I stormed into the kitchen where I saw Echo fixing a pot of tea.

"Have you seen Asmund?" I asked, my voice barely hiding my rage.

She looked up and nearly dropped the kettle. "Isan…your eyes…"

I ignored the fear in hers, ignored the insinuation, and said, "Where is he?"

Before she could answer, I heard footsteps behind us and turned to watch Asmund waltz into the room, Sky nowhere in sight.

I scowled at him and said, "You bastard."

His smile faded. "What are you talking about?"

"You know *exactly* what I'm talking about. I trusted you. You broke the bond of brotherhood, and I swear to Fidal, if you're using her…"

Asmund's expression darkened further. "Don't you dare," he said. "Don't stand there and speak to me about trust when you're accusing me in the same breath. I care about Sky. I'm not trying to hurt her, but *you* will, if you continue down this path."

I glared at him in silence, my anger to the point of boiling over, but before I could retort, I heard footsteps approaching behind him, and Sky stepped into view, saying, "Oh, he already has."

"Sky—" I started.

"Who told you?" she snapped, cutting me off, moving to stand completely between me and Asmund.

"Aramina figured it out," I replied, "but don't blame her. She probably thought I knew, probably figured that either of you would've said something to me instead of sneaking around in the shadows. How long has this been going on?"

"Oh, like it's any of your business," she shot back. "Has it occurred to you that we kept our mouths shut because we knew that *this* is how you would react?"

"So you're the only one who is allowed to keep secrets?" I asked her. "Is that it? I'm expected to share everything with you but you're allowed to go behind my back like this?"

"At least I don't overreact when a secret *does* come out. Why can't you just be happy for me?"

"I want to be," I admitted, "but Asmund? Come on, Sky, months ago you said you wouldn't marry him if he was the last person in the realm, and now you're…courting him?"

Sky stared at me with an intensity I'd never seen and then told Asmund to go without turning to look at him.

"I'm not leaving you here alone when he's this unstable," he said, his eyes only for her. "Who knows what could—"

"*Go*," she repeated.

He clenched his jaw but opened a portal without another word and disappeared.

"So he's not even man enough to fight his own battle?" I asked her.

"We both know this isn't his battle to fight," she replied. "It's ours. Now, out with it; *what* is your problem?"

I raised an eyebrow. "*My* problem? You have to be joking. Please tell me this is an elaborate scheme to ruffle my feathers."

She shrugged. "It's not. It's exactly what you think it is."

"Are you out of your mind? This is the person who looked at you like you were a piece of meat for years, who threw you under the horse carriage multiple times, who nearly got you killed when he ran off by himself last time we were in the Edgewood."

"Yes, well, he's also the person who saved my life on the battlefield, who gave you counsel when you were too afraid to talk to me, and who initially saved me from Jasper's clutches, who—need I remind you—is a much worse human being than Asmund ever was. Asmund has been there for me, Isan, and for the hundredth time: he's *not* the person he used to be. For Fidal's sake, he's your *friend!*"

"A friend wouldn't go behind my back and court my sister without my permission."

"We don't need your permission!" she snapped. "I can't believe you, calling me a hypocrite. You're just as controlling, if not more so, than the men you're trying to keep me from." She pressed a hand against her forehead. "You know what? I'm done having this conversation. It's clear you're not listening to a word I'm saying."

She turned and started to walk away, and like an idiot, I followed.

"Sky, don't," I said. "I'm only trying to protect you."

She whirled on me, a lethal look in her eyes. "From what?" she cried. "From *what*, Isanfier? You're always looking for danger where none exists, always threatened by something, but being sheltered isn't the same as being safe. How am I supposed to grow if you won't let me move into a bigger pot? How am I supposed to breathe when you're suffocating me at every turn? I can't take it anymore! I can't keep making excuses for you because you're grieving, you're stressed, you're anxious, you're frustrated. I can't…"

Her voice broke, and I tried to fill the silence, but she held up a hand before I could utter a word.

"I'm not finished," she said, a mournful weight to her words, enough for me to know she hated saying them but meant them all the same. "How can you stand there and tell me it's about Asmund when we both know it's not? It's about me. It's about how I'm fragile, I'm naive, I'm a dreamer. How you don't want *anyone* to have me because deep down you're terribly afraid you'll lose me."

She wiped her eyes.

"How do you think that makes me feel? You're only afraid of abandonment because you believe I'm capable of it. You don't trust me."

"How can you say that?" I shot back, unable to stand the one-sided conversation anymore. "I don't think you'll abandon me because I don't trust you; I think that because I believe I might one day deserve it."

She scoffed. "See, there you go again, making it about *you*. Every single time it's back to *your* heartache, *your* pain, and I'm expected to stand tall and bear the weight of both our problems. I can't do it anymore. I won't."

"Sky—"

"No!" she snapped, tears starting to fall from her eyes. "When do I get to be happy? When do I get to be free? My whole life has been planned out for me, and the one time I make a decision for myself, it's my own brother who tries to stand in my way? What a cruel, Fidal-forsaken joke."

I knew then and there I'd gone too far and decided it was time to defuse the situation. No matter how angry I was, I didn't want to make Sky cry, ever.

I reached an arm out to her. "Hey… Let's take a second and calm down—"

She lashed out, and I heard her shout, "Don't touch me!" before the sound of a sudden rushing wind filled my ears instead, and I was lifted off my feet.

I heard a huge crack seconds later, and then pain shot through every nerve in my body as my vision went white.

# 23
# Solace

*Echo*

**Echo was about to** step out of the clearing to collect more wood for the woodpile when she heard an ear-splitting crack up in the trees. She whipped her head upward in time to watch Isan plummet from the sky.

"Fidal's breath," she gasped, her heart in her chest as she watched him fall, too far away to do anything about it. "Asmund!" she screamed, but Aramina reacted faster, jumping to her feet and throwing her hands out in Isan's direction.

She stopped his descent an inch above the ground, wincing as her mind warred against his weight and the force of gravity, and then lowered him gently the rest of the way.

Echo rushed towards Isan's prone body without a word and checked his neck for a pulse. It was there, but it was faint, and his every breath seemed laboured.

"What in Fidal's name happened?" Asmund asked as he dropped to his knees beside Echo.

Aramina hovered over his shoulder. "Is he okay?"

Echo shook her head. "He's alive, but that fall nearly killed him." She heaved a breath. "I was afraid this would happen, but I didn't think Sky would be able to hurt him. Serves me right for making assumptions."

Asmund's face fell. "Sky did this?"

Echo sighed and got to her feet. "Not on purpose. I'll explain everything in a moment, but right now, I need the two of you to focus all your healing magic on Isan while I go talk to Sky. She must be scared stiff."

Asmund grabbed her arm. "Echo, I don't—"

"You'll be fine," she said, pulling away. "Aramina is a natural, and I don't think Sky will want to talk to anyone else right now. Trust me."

Aramina was already on her knees beside Isan, her hands pressed to his chest as she spoke under her breath. Echo could feel the magic in the air, and even though she was loath to leave him, she knew Aramina wouldn't let him die.

Besides, Isan would put Sky first too, if he had the choice.

Echo took the ladder rungs two at a time up into the treehouse and then called out, "Sky, are you still in here? It's Echo. Isan is going to be okay, but I need to know you're safe. Sky?"

She didn't answer, so Echo started moving through the house, slowly so she wouldn't startle Sky, making sure to keep her footfalls heavy. Echo finally found her in the bedroom Sky shared with Aramina, her back pressed up tight against the wooden wall and her face buried in her knees as she sobbed, her whole body shaking with the effort.

"Oh, Sky..." Echo breathed.

Sky's head snapped up, and her red-rimmed eyes were full of fear as she looked at Echo. "Don't come any closer," she gasped. "I...I don't want to hurt anyone else." She looked down at her hands as if they would explode, and Echo felt a pang of sympathy in her chest.

Echo remembered how it had felt the first time she'd turned invisible, the panic that had clawed its way through her until the only emotion she could feel was terror. She had been alone then, and it was a wonder she had survived, but Sky wasn't alone. Sky didn't have to feel this way.

Echo crouched down in front of Sky and spoke to her softly, as if addressing a spooked animal. "Listen to me, Skiansy. You're going to be okay. We're going to help you through this, and you won't have to worry about losing control. Aramina and Asmund are tending to Isan as we speak, and he will recover."

Sky exhaled and started to reign in her sobs almost instinctively.

"What happened, Sky?"

"Sancia's breath, I was so *angry* at him, but I never wanted to hurt him. I just…wanted him to stop." She choked on another sob. "I tried to push him away from me, but… It wasn't just my hands; I felt air moving…out of me and towards him, and next thing I knew, he was flying through the wall, and I… I couldn't breathe."

Sky was gasping for breath again telling the story, and Echo finally closed the gap between them, pulling Sky towards her and stroking her hair.

"You're okay," she soothed. "This isn't the end of you. Just breathe."

It took several minutes for Sky to calm down, but finally she relaxed into Echo's embrace, and Echo felt relief wash over her. She hugged Sky tight for a moment and then let her go.

Sky rubbed at her eyes and said, "That was magic, wasn't it?"

Echo nodded. "You're a Gifted Immortal like Isan, but you have wind magic, hence the *sky* part of your name."

She paused to let that sink in before going on.

"If I'm being perfectly honest with you, I knew you had magic in you all along, but I didn't know what form it would take or when it would manifest. It's common for only one sibling to have magic or for two siblings to have different types of magic, but it's unheard of for one twin to possess magic and the other to be powerless. Twins are always crafted from the same branch; you have different gifts, but you are both Gifted Immortals."

Sky sniffed. "Why didn't you say anything before?"

"I didn't want to scare you, and I didn't know how to bring it up. I figured we would deal with it when the need arose, but I'm so sorry this is how it happened."

"It's not your fault," Sky replied. "I had a feeling I wouldn't be so lucky. Despite my jealousy of everyone else's powers, I knew there was a certain peace to being normal."

Echo squeezed her hand. "You'll find that peace again. I promise."

Sky gave her a look. "And I suppose my first task is to forgive my insufferable brother?"

Echo smiled. "I'm afraid so."

Sky sighed and rose shakily to her feet, gripping on to the bedpost for balance. "Then I guess we're both lucky I don't hold grudges."

# 24
# The Bond of Brotherhood

*Isan*

**When I came to**, my head was all fuzzy, and my back felt like I'd been helping Aunt Mag in the castle gardens for a week, but then the world came into better focus, and the pain sharpened until it took over all my thoughts.

*What in Fidalia* happened *to me?*

I squinted against the light filtering into the room and cursed the fact that I was once again bedridden in Echo's treehouse. I had the worst luck.

"Isan," a familiar voice called. "Can you hear me, Isan? It's Mina."

I tried to look for her, but it hurt to keep my eyes open.

"Just relax," she went on. "Asmund and I tried to heal you, but our magic is still weak in that area, so you're going to be in some pain until we can administer more traditional healing methods. Can you blink three times if you can hear me?"

I did as she asked and heard her sigh of relief.

"You'll be on the mend in no time. Asmund says Echo pretty near raised you from the dead once before and saved *his* sorry life, so I'm not worried." I felt the mattress dip as she sat down on the bed. "I don't know how much you remember, but Sky is doing all right. A little spooked but slowly coming to terms with things. She's still upset with you, but she's sorry about what happened. Personally, I think you had it coming, though not to this extent. I *did* warn you."

Her words started to stir up blocked memories, and as I listened to her mill around the room for a few minutes, I remembered what happened. I remembered arguing with Sky about Asmund and making her cry. I remembered falling.

*Did she push me?*

But that couldn't be right. We weren't near any windows at the time.

*Then how…*

"Mina," I choked out.

She squeezed my hand. "I'm here."

"I was…falling," I said through the pain.

"Yes."

"Why?"

She was quiet for a minute, and only the feeling of my hand in hers told me she was still there. "You and Sky had an argument about her and Asmund," she replied finally. "In a fit of rage, Sky unlocked her undiscovered wind magic and blew you through the side wall of the treehouse. I stopped you from hitting the ground, but you were already unconscious."

*Sancia's shining light…*

How was I still alive?

How many near-death experiences would it take before this forest claimed me for good?

I had so many questions, but I decided to go with the most obvious. "Sky has magic?"

"Indeed. Elemental like you but air instead of fire. Echo says it was inevitable; twins are born from the same energy, so if you were gifted and immortal, Sky had to be too."

I opened my eyes slowly so I could adjust to the light, the agony in my back becoming background pain, and found Aramina studying me with a look beyond her years.

"You're lucky, Isanfier. Sky's magic could give yours a run for its money."

I rolled my eyes. "I'll be the judge of that."

"Oh, will you now?" a new voice said, and I half turned my head to see Sky standing in the doorway, Echo hovering behind her.

I shrank back at her presence, remembering how awful I had acted. "Sky, I'm—"

She held up her hand. "Let me say my piece first. Echo, Mina, could you give us a few minutes?"

Aramina nodded, getting up and following Echo out. She squeezed Sky's shoulder on her way, and I noticed Sky wince at the contact.

She stood awkwardly in the doorway for a moment before coming over to sit on the far edge of the bed. I realized then how small and broken she looked, how scared. She usually sat with her shoulders back and at least a hint of a smile in her cheeks, but now she curled into herself, and her smile was more like a ghost.

"First of all," she said, "I'm glad you're okay. I had no intention of hurting you—not physically, anyway—and I'm sorry for putting you in danger. But I meant everything I said earlier."

This time, I had the common sense to keep my mouth shut and let her continue.

"You are just so *frustrating*, Isanfier. It's like you need to be the hero all the time, but you won't always be able to save me, and I won't always want or need to be saved. Asmund isn't the villain, and I know you know that. The villain, a lot of the time, is your own fear, your own worry about what *could* happen and what *might* go wrong, but we can't live like that."

She finally turned to look at me, and I saw she was tearing up again but not in the way she was before. "He makes me happy, Isan, and that's something I didn't think I would ever get the chance to experience. And maybe it won't last, but I want to see how it goes. I want to live in the moment, and I want you to accept that. I don't want to hide from you or constantly be paranoid about what you might do. If courting Asmund is a mistake, then let me make it."

I sighed. "He's a pain in the neck and not much to look at, but I suppose, if he makes you happy…"

She leaned over and smacked me in the arm. "Oh, you are such a nuisance!"

"Take it easy now," I replied, "I'm recovering here."

She rolled her eyes. "So, do we have your blessing?"

"Yes," I said, "but you were right, Sky; you don't need my blessing. Your choices belong to you, no matter what. Though if you ever announce you're courting Jasper, I'll end him on sight because you've clearly been duped."

She laughed and then squeezed my hand. "Thank you, Isan."

"So…you have magic."

She huffed. "Yeah, I guess I do. I won't need your protection from angry suitors once I can harness the full power of the skies."

"I guess not, but I'll always be there if you stumble."

"Will you help me practise?"

"Of course, but you're not allowed to do it indoors anymore. Echo likes her treehouse too much."

She winced. "I did a number on the place, didn't I?"

"I haven't seen the damage myself, but considering you put me through a wall…"

"I'm never going to live that one down, am I?"

I shrugged. "I kind of deserved it, and it can't be worse than incinerating a man."

"Do you ever…have nightmares about that?"

"Sometimes," I admitted, "but it mostly haunts my waking mind, this constant nagging notion that I'm dangerous, that one wrong move could leave me unhinged. Every new lesson with my magic gives me more potential, for both good and evil, but it's my responsibility to learn to keep the darkness in my mind at bay."

"You definitely stand a much better chance now of defeating Icaria. I wish I'd had magic in my fight with Snowdon. I could've redirected his snow and been done with it."

"I'm still a long way from being ready to challenge Icaria, but I'm grateful for whatever advantage I can get."

"When the time comes, you won't be alone. Icaria will have to stand against the entire might of Summer to get to you, against Asmund and Mina and me. She won't stand a chance."

I nodded, but it was a statement I couldn't get behind, something I didn't quite believe in, yet.

• • •

Later that night, I sat down on a log beside Asmund at the fire I had built so we could cook outside for a change. Echo had applied some kind of salve to my back after my conversation with Sky, and the only pain that lingered was if I bent over too long or too suddenly, though Echo warned me the effects would eventually wear off.

The five of us had roasted sausages over the open flame and then warmed some slices of sweet bread for dessert. Echo had said we were celebrating many things: Sky and Asmund's courtship, Sky's new Gift, Aramina's prowess with her healing magic, and the fact that I was still alive.

The girls had retired indoors for some tea, and likely gossip, around the kitchen table. I'd been sharpening my sword to clear my mind but knew it was finally time to address the bear in the barn. So I sat down beside Asmund and watched the fire crackle in silence for a few moments before I spoke.

"So, you and my sister," I said, unsure how else to start.

He let out a breath. "Yes."

"Before you try to redeem yourself, I want to tell you that you don't need to, and I'm sorry. You didn't deserve my accusations. I guess I was in shock—still am, if I'm being honest. But that's my problem, not yours."

He looked over at me. "So you're not mad? You don't want to kill me?"

I shrugged. "Not at the moment. Besides, if you screw up, I'm sure Sky will do it herself." I clapped him on the shoulder. "Best of luck with that."

He laughed nervously. "Oh, I'm well aware of the danger of dishonesty, and I was actually more afraid of Sky rejecting me than I was of your approval. I did a lot of bad things in my past, especially to her, but I desire her now for the right reasons. I *admire* her, more than anything. She's fierce and independent and won't let anything stand in her way, won't let anyone or anything hurt the people and places she cares about. She's everything I wish to be, and I hope that even a fraction of her kindness will rub off on me. She's everything I never knew I wanted."

"If I was a girl," I replied with a smirk, "I'd say, 'That was beautiful,' but I'll just say I'm happy for you, and if the time ever comes, I'd be proud to call you brother."

The expression that crossed his face at my words was something no man could truly describe, a sense of hope and pride and happiness all jumbled into one look, where his eyes said more than his cheeks ever would.

In that moment, I knew I had been equally worried about losing him as I had been about losing Sky. In that moment, I knew the sins of the past would never haunt us the way they once did, and so did he.

He grabbed my wrist and squeezed, the closest contact we'd had since childhood, and said, "When the time comes, I'll be proud to call you King."

I wrapped my hand around his arm and squeezed back, all the while trying not to let my emotions swirl to the surface and spill over. I never knew how important friendship could be, but now that I did, I never wanted to lose it.

Asmund cleared his throat awkwardly after a moment and let go, shifting away from me on the log. "Echo says we're nearing the end of our apprenticeships, that she's taught us nearly all she knows, and I doubt it'll take Sky long to get the hang of her own magic. It would be prudent of us to start considering our next steps. We can't hide in the Edgewood forever."

Oh, how I wished we could.

I found it ironic how the forest had become our refuge instead of the source of despair it had once been. I no longer feared the trees; they felt like home.

"As the only one of us who has been officially knighted," I replied, "I believe you should devise the plan."

"As the Crown Prince of Summer, I believe it is *your* responsibility."

Someone laughed behind us, and we both spun around to find Echo standing there. "Not fighting, I hope?"

I held a hand to my chest. "Fidal's breath, don't *do* that, Echo. I already *had* a near-death experience today."

Beside me, Asmund snorted and then stood up, stretching his arms over his head as he let out a huge yawn. "I'd love to stay and chat, but my bed is calling me."

I scowled. "Running away so you don't have to make the plan?"

He shrugged. "Something like that." He turned without another word, but I heard his voice in my head as he walked away. *I thought you and Echo could use some time alone.*

I fought to hide my blush and rising annoyance as Echo walked past him with a smile and sat down on the log across the smouldering coals from me.

"What plan?" she said.

I let out a sigh as I realized Asmund truly was leaving me alone with her. "Asmund says our time here is coming to its natural end, so it's time for us to think about our next move."

Her face fell, but still she nodded before saying, "If it's any consolation, none of you are a burden to me. You can stay as long as you need to, but I understand that Summer needs you too."

"The problem," I replied, "is that we have no idea what we'll be returning to, and I, for one, am nervous to find out. Our combined magic will be a formidable weapon, but it's useless without a strategy and more information. We could be walking right into a trap."

"You'll need to make use of your unique skills carefully. I would suggest Asmund and Aramina start practising their shifting abilities on you and Sky so you can all return with a reliable disguise. I would use their portal travel when necessary to gather information and their telepathy to reach out to possible allies. Of course, you will have to be careful who you trust, but this mission will be precarious no matter the precautions you take."

I sighed. "I wish you could come with us. You always know what to do."

She sank into herself. "Not always. I fear I haven't taught you all enough, that I've let you down, and you're not prepared for what comes next."

I gave her a look. "It's not your responsibility to keep us safe, Echo. We appreciate anything you can show us, but we don't expect you to know everything. That would be too much. Whether or not we succeed once we leave the borders of the wood is based on our actions, not yours."

Echo hung her head. "I know, truly I do, but… I wish I could go with you too, wish I could continue to offer guidance and be there for all of you. By Wylla, I wish I wasn't so defenseless, so weak, so trapped, so…lonely." She clenched her fists in her lap and looked up across the fire at me. The flames were fading now, barely more than an orange glow in the coals. "I was so lonely when you were gone, and I think… It's selfish, but I think I'm more afraid of you never coming back than I am of you dying. I don't want to be alone anymore."

Her voice broke on the last sentence, and she started crying, dropping her head into her hands as her whole body shook with the force of her sorrow and pain.

I moved before I even registered my desire to do so, going over and sitting on the log beside her, wrapping my arms around her and pulling her against my chest.

She leaned into me, and I stroked her head as she let the emotions flow through her. Her hair was even whiter up close and softer than I could've ever imagined, but I tried not to focus on that. She needed my friendship right now, my listening ears.

"It's going to be okay," I said softly. "I can't promise you we'll make it through whatever we have to do in the coming months, that would be cruel, but I want you to know I will do whatever it takes to get back to you, no matter how long it takes. I will never abandon you. I also want you to know that while killing Icaria is my destiny, I'm not doing it for the world or for myself; I'm doing it to save you. I want you to be free, to be happy, and I would go to the stars and back if necessary to see that happen."

Echo looked up at me in shock, tears glistening in her eyes. "You would?"

I nodded. "I will not let this forest be the end of your story, Echo. You deserve so much more."

She stared at me in disbelief for a moment, as if this was the first time she had seen me, and then she leaned forward and…

She was kissing me.

# 25
# A Deadly Encounter

**The kiss was slow** and soft and full of longing, but Echo pulled away before my brain had a chance to catch up and truly process what was happening.

I looked at her in a daze as she covered her mouth with her hands and said, "I am so sorry. I shouldn't have done that. I don't know why..."

I managed a short laugh. "I'm not upset, if that's what you're worried about. I... I've been wanting to do that for a while, if I'm being honest."

She started to smile and then stopped herself. "I'm sorry, Isan; I really shouldn't have done that. I feel this...pull towards you, but I don't want to ruin what we have with something that might not be real. I was confused, and my emotions were running high, and I don't want to give you the wrong impression. I hope you can forgive me?"

I took her hand in mine. "I'm not entirely sure how I feel either. All I know is that no matter who I danced with at the balls back home, my mind always brought me here, back to you. You're important to me, Echo, no matter what happens, and of course I forgive you, but there's nothing to forgive. You didn't do anything wrong."

"Thank you," she said, shuffling away from me and finally letting a smile through her defenses. "You're a good man, Isanfier, much more noble than you give yourself credit for."

I sighed. "Sometimes, I fear I'm darker than people realize." I held my fists out over the dying coals of the fire, studying every scar and blemish. "These hands are capable of so much destruction, so much pain. I've killed so many people now I've lost count, and I know it's only a fraction of the carnage I'll have to carve through this realm to restore the balance. Icaria won't go down without a fight, and the truth is, there's some part of me that revels in that thought. I crave the glory and the flames, and I'm so afraid I'll win the war but lose myself in the process."

Echo gave me a sad look. "If you spend all your time fearing the future, you'll never get to live in the present. And the more you dwell on the shadows in your mind, the thicker they'll become. You're not perfect, Isan, but I know those hands have saved people too, have hugged people, and have hesitated before taking a life. You are full of compassion, and if you focus on that, if you remember to love, the darkness will not take you."

We sat in silence then, and for a moment, I thought I could hear a wind whistling through the dead air of the wood, but it was gone again before I could focus on it. There was nothing but the clamour of my thoughts and the need to be rid of them.

"I set my own city on fire in a fit of rage and then fled like a coward," I told her. "The goddesses warned me about it for weeks, but I didn't listen. What if there's no way back from that? What if compassion isn't enough?"

Echo frowned. "What do you mean the goddesses warned you?"

"I dreamt about the fire happening, for weeks, the same way I did about Darkenier murdering my parents, though I didn't know it was him at the time. I guess I never told you about that. The dreams stopped the day before we met you. The new one started the first night we returned to Widonia." I paused. "Why are you looking at me like that?"

"You're telling me you saw the future in your dream?"

"Yes, though it didn't follow it strictly, seeing as I never dreamt about Quinton being there."

"But that's impossible," she replied. "You would have to—" She cut herself off, going deathly still as she whispered, "Did you hear that?"

I mirrored her stillness as I strained my ears and studied the forest around me. Even the Edgewood had its own melody, despite its apparent silence at first encounter, but the song of rustling leaves and swaying branches was gone.

Something was wrong.

I met Echo's eyes, and she caught the warning I sent her as we both reached for our sheathed swords at the same time.

Unfortunately, our mystery enemy was faster, and I heard the familiar sound of an arrow being loosed before we could even get to our feet.

"Look out!" I yelled at Echo as I attempted to push her out of harm's way, but I was too late.

I watched in horror as she gasped, eyes widening in shock and pain, and then slumped into my open arms. Instinctively, I tried to hold her, but then my fingers brushed the fletching of the arrow protruding from her back, and I recoiled.

*There is an arrow in her back.*

*How bad is it? Who is attacking us? Where are the others?*

*There is an* arrow *in her back.*

My mind was racing as fast as my heart, and I couldn't feel my body, like someone had doused me in ice water, simultaneously robbing me of breath and heat. Seconds were passing, precious seconds that couldn't be wasted in battle, but I couldn't move.

I couldn't think.

I was just sitting there, staring at Echo, at the girl who had kissed me mere moments before, now dead weight in my arms.

*She can't be dead.*

*Please Wylla, do not let her be dead.*

I sensed movement around me, sensed battle cries and clashing steel, but everything was muffled, blurry, inconsequential compared to the horror in front of me.

But then someone was calling my name, someone was touching me, pulling me away from Echo, and the world snapped back into place like a shot of lightning.

"Isan!" someone cried out. "Isan, come on, you need to *move!*"

"What—" I looked up to find Aramina pulling on my arm, her expression full of alarm and urgency, and then I finally noticed the soldiers in our midst, noticed their blue and black uniforms and shocks of white hair.

*Wyllans.*

*What are* they *doing here?*

But there was no time to ponder because Aramina spun, narrowly missing a sword to the ribs, and dragged me with her, right into the fray of the battle.

I drew my sword without thought, pulling Mina behind me in the same motion, and blocked the next blow, the impact reverberating through my arm and bringing my attention to the blood staining my hands.

Echo's blood.

And that was all it took. I called on my magic instinctively, my anger bringing it roaring to the surface. The fire leapt greedily to Ember's blade, like it had when I'd killed Darkenier, and I carved a path through my opponent with my flaming sword before moving on swiftly to the next one.

The minutes blurred together as I fought, my mind vaguely aware of the others around me, using both weapons and magic to push the Wyllans back or send them to their grave.

I alternated between sword tactics and fire, careful not to set the whole forest alight or harm my friends, even in my rage. All the while, I tried not to let my eyes wander to the firepit, to where Echo still lay, slumped and unmoving.

Finally, I ran *Ember* through another Wyllan's neck and was greeted with nothing but the heavy breathing of my friends as he dropped to the ground at my feet. I turned to see Sky standing behind me, hands on her knees as she bent over and caught her breath. She was still wearing her nightdress, which was now in tatters and splattered with blood I hoped wasn't her own. Aramina didn't look much better, but they were alive.

Just over a dozen Wyllan soldiers lay scattered around the clearing, bloody, broken, and singed, but there was no one left standing.

"What happened?" I asked the girls. "How did you know we were under attack?"

Sky grimaced. "You were screaming, Isan. The sound of it chilled us to the bone. Aramina sent the three of us through a portal, and she went to your aid while Asmund and I went to work on the Wyllans. Are you okay?"

I ignored her question, knowing she wasn't talking about my physical well-being, and posed one of my own. "Where *is* Asmund?"

"He's right here," came his triumphant reply as he marched back into the clearing, dragging an injured Wyllan soldier behind him. "I found a runner."

"Get off me," the man gasped as he struggled against Asmund's grip, but it was clear he was in too much pain to put up much of a fight. The left side of his face was caked in blood, and he winced with every jostling step that Asmund took.

Asmund finally dumped him at the base of a tree, letting the man prop himself up on the trunk. His shirt was soaked in blood as well, and I wondered how much longer the poor man would last—though I supposed it was what he deserved for attacking us unprompted at this hour of the night.

"Just...kill...me," the man choked out.

"Oh, rest assured, we will," Asmund replied, "but not until you tell us exactly what happened here tonight and why."

The man grinned, his teeth bloody. "You really have...no idea...what's coming. Oh, this is...beautiful." He coughed, spitting up more blood, though it didn't seem to bother him.

I could feel a chill snaking up my spine at his words. This wasn't some random attack. This was the beginning of a far more gruesome plan.

"Tell us what you know," I said, taking a step towards him. I had sheathed my sword, but there was still a threat in my eyes and fire in my heart.

"Ah yes," the man said. "The great Prince of Summer. I know *all* about what she's...planned for you."

I clenched my fists. "Icaria can make all the plans she wants, but if she thinks sending a small force to silence us quietly in the Edgewood is enough to put us down, she might need to go back to the drawing table."

"Oh, she wasn't...after you. Not this time. As for her reflection... I'd say we hit our mark."

I followed his gaze back over to Echo and felt the flames leap to life inside my chest. In moments, I had him by the neck against the tree, his feet barely touching the ground and my other fist on fire beside his cheek. "Tell. Us. What. You. Know."

If the man was fazed by my threat, he didn't show it, which only stoked my flames higher. "She's coming for you, Prince," he spat in my face. "You can't escape fate, and with her reflection vanquished, she'll be stronger than ever."

"Her name was Echo!" I snapped. "And if the Princess had done her research, she would know how grave her mistake in killing Echo was. Now tell me what you know before I shove my burning sword down your throat until you are begging for death."

The man only smiled. "I don't need…to beg, but you will. You will."

Then his eyes shut, his head slumped in my grip, and I knew he was dead. I let go and slammed my fist into the tree where his head had been only moments before, sparks flying in all directions. Pain shot through my arm at the impact, but I ignored it.

"How could you let this happen?" I screamed into the sky, my pain and anger and disappointment aimed at the goddesses, at the stars and Fidal himself, wherever he was. "What have we done wrong?"

Someone grabbed my arm. "Isan. Isan, stop!"

I clenched my fists to keep from lashing out at Sky and tried to listen to her words.

"It's not over," she was saying. "They haven't won. Look."

I followed her pointed finger back over to the firepit where Aramina was now cradling Echo's lifeless body in her arms.

"She's not dead," Aramina said, smiling at me through her tears.

I fell to my knees.

"What?" I gasped out, feeling like my heart was being torn open.

"I can feel her heartbeat," Aramina choked out, her voice thick with disbelief and joy. "It shouldn't be possible, but…"

Beside me, Sky squeezed my hand. "See? Miracles do happen. What can we do to help, Mina?"

"Well, we need to gather some supplies to help staunch the bleeding first, and then I'll need Isan to pull out the arrow while Asmund and I use our magic to keep her stable. Sky, you can oversee everything and run supplies. We won't risk moving her until we bandage the wound."

Sky clapped her hands. "All right, everyone has their orders. Let's do this. Isan and I will get some towels."

"What about all these bodies?" Asmund said.

Sky shrugged. "Not a priority at the moment. Isan can burn them later for all I care, but I'm not going to let Echo die."

• • •

The next hour and a half was a blur, much the same as the time Echo and Sky saved Asmund's life, but it was strange to not have Echo's calm and reassuring voice in the mix. She didn't stir the whole time—her consciousness stuck in a coma, Aramina figured.

There were a few times where I thought we might truly lose her, especially when I pulled out the arrow and she lost even more blood, but eventually we ceased the flow, bandaged up her entire torso, and moved her to her bed as the first rays of the sunrise were beginning to show above the trees.

Sky stayed to watch over her, but I couldn't bear to do the same, couldn't bear to exist in the silence without her, so I ventured outside.

I gathered the bloody rags and threw them into the firepit, filling it with more wood before I set it ablaze. Then I walked around the clearing systematically, setting fire to each body and keeping the flames contained until only ash and steel remained. It took me hours, but my mind was clearer by the end of it.

Asmund joined me as I threw the last sword into the growing pile beside the picnic table.

"You okay, Prince?"

I huffed a laugh. "Not particularly," I replied. "If Echo wakes up, I will be happy, but it won't put my mind at ease. Icaria somehow knows where we are, and she'll send more men once she realizes her first batch isn't coming back. She might even come herself. I don't... I'm not ready for that battle yet."

Asmund sighed. "I don't understand how they found us."

"Me neither, but it's clear we are no longer safe here — Echo especially, if they're targeting her."

"Maybe Icaria thinks she's dead. Her soldiers certainly did."

"I don't think she's naive enough for that, but it's possible. Echo said Icaria can't leave Winter for long until Echo *is* dead, so it's unlikely Icaria will endanger herself like that unless she's sure. She might send someone back for the body."

"So we leave," Asmund said. "But then what? What do you want to do?"

I took a deep breath. "I wanted to return to Summer, to take back what is mine and restore order, but... This attack only proved that Summer won't be safe until Icaria is dead. I need to confront her, and I'm not sure exactly what that entails right now, but I can't go back until it's done."

Asmund nodded. "To Winter, then."

"To Winter."

# 26
# Grateful Hearts

**That night, I was** sitting vigil in Echo's room, having a hard time keeping my eyes open even though sleep was the last thing I wanted to do. I wanted to be there if she needed me, and I certainly didn't want to deal with any nightmares the goddesses might throw at me. I had had enough excitement and heartache for one day.

I was nodding off again when I heard Echo cough.

I shot to my feet and was at her side in an instant, reaching for her hand. "Echo? I'm here. What can I do?"

She coughed again, and I grabbed the glass of water off her side table. Then I poured it into her open mouth, one drop at a time. I watched her throat as she swallowed it and felt my hands tremble with relief.

She was alive.

Her eyelids fluttered open a few moments later, and she stared at me in silence for the longest time, as if worried I would disappear or something. Finally, she blinked, and I watched the light return to her eyes when she realized I was still there.

"Isan," she whispered. "Is this…real?" She sounded pained, but I couldn't tell whether it was emotional or physical.

"Yes," I replied softly, squeezing her hand again. "It's real. You're alive."

"What happened?"

And so I told her everything. Her expression was unreadable by the time I'd finished, and she didn't say anything in return for a long moment.

Then she swallowed and said, "I can't die. Not…not like that. I'm a soul without a body, just like how the goblins live without hearts. It's the forest that makes me look like a normal person. If I leave the Edgewood for too long, I'll lose that 'body.' I'll disappear. So killing me is not as simple as running me through."

"Well, it looked pretty real to me," I replied, "and it's not something I ever want to go through again."

"I better keep my guard up, then."

"We've made plans to leave the treehouse," I told her. "It's not safe here anymore."

She frowned. "Where will you go?"

"*We,*" I emphasized, "will set up camp closer to the Winter border, and then we will plan our next course of action."

"You're not going home?"

I shook my head. "Icaria needs to be stopped. The man we caught implied she was planning something horrible, and we need to find out what it is, if not put a stop to it. I can't afford to return to Summer with a catastrophe on my heels."

Echo nodded. "You should go to Tamise. There is a sect of special soldiers stationed there called the Shadow Watch. If war is truly upon us, then Icaria will send word there before long. She will need their skill and numbers."

"We can discuss our options once we're a safe distance from here," I replied, tucking her suggestion away in my mind for later. "How are you feeling?"

She grimaced as she pulled herself up into a sitting position. "I feel weak but alive. I'm in no danger of dropping dead anytime soon, but I don't think I'll be able to make the journey on my own two feet in my current state, if that's what you're wondering."

"You can have one of the horses, then," I said. "We're bringing all of them with us anyway."

"How soon are we leaving?"

"Tomorrow morning, if you're up to it," I replied. "The Wyllans will return, and I don't want to be anywhere close to here when they do."

She looked at me with eyes full of concern, and I almost laughed at the absurdity of it, considering which of us was injured, but she always made time for others, even at the expense of her own needs.

"When was the last time you slept, Isanfier?" she asked.

"Nearly two days ago," I admitted.

"Well, that's a poor decision," she replied. "What happens if the Wyllans find us? How will you fight if you can barely keep your eyes open?"

"I'll manage."

"Isan, you can't—"

"I can, and I will," I snapped, clenching my trembling fists at my side. "I don't want to sleep, not right now. I... I'm afraid of what I might see, who I might lose."

I was afraid of what the goddesses might show me.

I took a deep breath. "I'll sleep once I know we're all safe, but it won't do me any good right now. I promise you that."

"I don't think Wylla would agree with that sentiment," she replied, "but I'll leave you be."

"Thank you."

We sat in silence for several minutes, neither one of us knowing what to say but not wanting to say goodnight either. I thought about our conversation around the fire before the Wyllans had attacked, about Echo's quick kiss and drawn-out apology before the concept of *us* had nearly been ripped away forever.

I wanted to ask her about it again, but I knew it wasn't the time or place to do so. Some things in the realm were more important than satiating a curious heart, and sometimes, knowing nothing was better than getting the answer you didn't want to hear.

"Well, I should leave you to rest," I said. "We'll be up at first light to get packed and will come get you when we're ready. Do you need anything before I go?"

"Some more water would be nice," she replied.

I nodded and grabbed her empty glass before heading to the kitchen.

Sky was standing by the counter when I arrived, nursing a cup of tea and staring into the lantern light as if she wasn't sure where she was. The creaking floorboards beneath my feet announced my entry, and she jumped, tea sloshing over the side of her mug.

"Sancia's breath, Isan," she scolded. "You scared the life out of me."

I frowned. "I wouldn't have if you weren't lurking in the dark. What are you doing?"

She hung her head. "I couldn't sleep. My mind keeps replaying the sound of your screams when Echo was shot, and I'm afraid we're being attacked again. I know Asmund is keeping watch, but..."

I took the tea from her gently and set it on the counter before pulling her to me in a hug. "I know how you feel, but I won't let that happen again. I won't let Icaria hurt any of us."

She sniffed back her tears. "Don't make promises you can't keep," she replied, but she hugged me tighter anyway, as if the realm would disappear if she let go. "How is Echo doing?"

"She's awake," I said. "I was getting her another glass of water, but maybe you should bring it back to her for me. You could both use each other's wisdom right now."

Sky laughed and pulled away, wiping at her eyes. "You're probably right. Fidal's breath, I'm so glad she's okay."

"Me too."

She took a slow sip of her tea and then filled Echo's water glass before saying, "I'm sure I won't be the first or last person to say this to you, but you should at least *try* to get some sleep, Isan. Even lying down in your bed will give your bones a rest. You'll be dead on your feet in the morning otherwise, and we have packing to do."

I sighed but didn't reply, and she left me without another word. I leaned against the counter alone for a few minutes before blowing out the lantern and heading to bed. I expected my thoughts to overwhelm me in the silence, but the steady rhythm of a light rain against my window soon lulled me into a peaceful slumber, and I was not granted a single dream that night.

•  •  •

We all woke early the next morning, to prepare for the trip ahead, and were on our way well before noon. The girls took the horses while Asmund and I took up the front and rear of our procession on foot. The journey was slow but calming, the tension and anxiety of the attack melting away as we traipsed through the silent trees, the wood's sturdiness and constant presence reminding us we were still here, that strength isn't so easily broken.

In the evenings, while the rest of us stayed warm by the fire, Echo worked on Sky's magic with her. Like we'd all suspected, it didn't take her long to get the hang of the basics. She only put out the fire once by mistake, which I thought was pretty impressive.

Aside from helping Sky, Echo was rather quiet throughout our trek, and I wondered if it was from the nerves of the unknown battles we had yet to face, or if she was feeling guilty for what had happened. We'd all assured her she wasn't to blame, but I had the feeling she didn't take our words to heart.

I knew how difficult it could be, to trust that those around you have forgiven you, especially when you can barely find it in yourself to do the same.

The events in Widonia still weighed heavy on me, and I couldn't bear to consider what might be happening in our absence. I could only focus on the next step in front of me and the promise that I would right whatever wrongs had been dealt in my kingdom, that I would return for the sake of my people and all they had suffered.

Finally, on the fifth night of our journey, Echo declared we had travelled far enough for the time being. The Wyllan soldiers shouldn't be able to find us, and we were still far enough away from the border that the chill of Winter wouldn't seep into our bones.

We set up camp in relative silence, and I made a fire — more to give us comfort and a sense of home than to give us heat. Sky and Asmund ventured off into the trees in search of some meat for dinner, and Aramina said she would fetch some water, which left me and Echo to our own devices.

She ignored the logs I'd rolled over to the fire, opting to sit on the ground in front of them instead, and I realized what she must be thinking about.

I mirrored her position but sat across from her. "It's okay to be scared," I told her. "Fidal knows I am."

She smiled. "*You*, scared? I thought you were the most courageous knight in all the realm."

I leaned back against the log. "Well, I'm not technically a knight yet, so there's that, and being courageous doesn't mean you're not afraid. It means you do the hard things anyway, because being safe isn't worth sacrificing a better future. I was scared to face the dark figure, even before I knew he was my uncle, or the man pretending to be my uncle, but I fought him regardless, and it was worth it, in the end, despite everything that happened after.

"Icaria scares me too," I went on, "but if I don't face her, we all lose. I don't know what will happen if she wins, but the entire realm will suffer if I don't even try. That's what keeps me going when the realm feels like too much. It's what keeps me on the right path."

She gave me an appraising look. "You know, you're wiser than you give yourself credit for, Isanfier. That was spoken like a true leader, like a future King. I'm proud of you. You've come a long way since we first met."

I shrugged. "Tragedy will do that to a person."

She rolled her eyes. "Oh, don't be so modest. Take the compliment for once and run with it. I. Am. *Proud*. Of you. I'm not saying it because I think you need to hear it. I'm saying it because it's true. Summer will be lucky to have you as their King when the time is right."

I allowed myself a small smile, and she returned it tenfold, her whole face lighting up.

"See, there you go," she replied. "A little self-appreciation goes a long way, you know."

I smiled wider. "I'm glad I was able to cheer you up. It's been hard to see you so withdrawn. You always find the silver lining in everything, and I was beginning to wonder if maybe this time there wasn't one."

"You know me so well," she replied with a sigh. "The past few days have been hard. It's exhausting holding on to hope sometimes when you don't have a lot to show for it. It seems…pointless."

I shook my head. "It's never pointless. Your hope has kept the rest of us going for a long time. We wouldn't be here otherwise. Optimism isn't a weakness, Echo. It's your strength, and I wish I had even half as much as you do."

Echo smiled again, holding my gaze across the flickering fire. "The girl who wins your heart someday is going to be the luckiest girl in Fidalia."

"Oh, she's not as lucky as I am," I replied, my eyes not leaving hers.

A blush rose to her pale cheeks as she realized what I meant, but the sound of sticks snapping behind us broke the spell of the moment, as something always inevitably did.

We turned to see Aramina trudging through the undergrowth with half a dozen waterskins bundled in her arms. "There's a stream about twenty paces behind us," she called out. "Purest water I've ever seen and the most stunning purple flowers growing along its banks. I didn't expect this forest to have even an ounce of colour, but I guess the stories were wrong."

She set the water down behind one of the logs as Echo and I shared a knowing glance.

I shrugged. "It's a beautiful place, if you know where to look."

Echo smiled at my words, her memory likely taking her back to the glade instead of this unremarkable patch of trees.

"Apparently," Aramina replied, sitting down on the log beside where Echo still sat in the dirt. "It's hard to believe we're here. Our father would lose his mind if he knew. Then again, maybe not. He probably wouldn't care if we were dead, especially if he found out we're with you."

I waved a hand. "Let him think whatever he wants, Mina. We'll prove him wrong when we take Widonia back with magic and might, and all of us equal. If he doesn't like what he sees, he can see himself out or face the consequences."

Aramina cracked a smile. "I'd like to see that."

Echo looked up at her. "Why would your father wish you ill?"

Mina shrugged. "It's complicated. He has extremely traditional views, and he expects perfection no matter what. I am only useful as a woman to be married off and nothing more, so coming out here...unchaperoned with the Crown Prince..." She sighed. "Few men would want me now. As for Asmund, well, he took Isan's side against our father and failed to be named our father's heir, so he's a huge disappointment now."

I hung my head. "I am so sorry for everything I put you two through. I never meant for any of this to happen."

Aramina held up a hand. "We made our own choices, and for what it's worth, I've never been happier. We'll handle whatever comes later, but I will never regret my decision, the knowledge I've gained, or the memories I've made. You set us free, Isan, and we're forever grateful, even if we don't always say it."

"We?" a voice behind Aramina piped up. "Who said I was grateful?"

Mina jumped, and Asmund burst into laughter as he came into view, three rabbits hanging from his hands and Sky trailing behind him.

Aramina smacked his arm as he walked past her. "Don't *do* that!"

He merely ruffled her neatly braided hair and walked off to prepare dinner.

I smiled at the exchange and realized Mina was right. Their lives might not be perfect, and I *had* put them in danger, but it wasn't all bad. The two of them had never been so close.

A sense of peace settled in amongst us as we cooked dinner over the fire, seasoning the meat with some wild herbs Sky had found, and ate our shares, each of us making several comments about how good it was. We were laughing and sharing stories by the time it was done, and I felt that seed of hope bloom in my heart again.

The road ahead might be tough, but I was confident we would make the most out of it and know the right turns to take when they came. Icaria was strong, but I wasn't alone, and maybe that was the difference. Maybe that was enough.

# 27
# The Fate of a Kingdom

**Our stomachs were full** and our eyelids heavy, but I knew it was time to talk about the future. We had put it off long enough. So I leaned forward and said, "Are we ready to start making our next plan?"

Asmund let out a long sigh. "As much as I'd like to live in this moment forever…"

The girls nodded their reluctant agreement, and I continued on. "Our first task will be to gather information about Icaria's whereabouts and her plans. Echo has suggested we travel to Tamise as Icaria will likely send word there if she requires more soldiers. Are we in agreement on that?"

Sky and Aramina nodded.

"It's a good place to start," Asmund replied, "but *how* do you plan on doing it? We don't exactly blend in." He tugged on the end of his black braids for emphasis.

"That's where your magic is going to come in," Echo said. "You'll have to shape-shift your appearances so you look like any other Wyllan: pale skin, short hair, and blue eyes. Sky and Mina can keep their hair long and the same colour, as long as it's unbraided. You would have to cut yours, Asmund, but seeing as that's akin to suggesting you cut off a limb, you'll have to shape-shift it."

Asmund made a face. "That much magic is going to take a lot of energy and concentration. I'm not sure I can manage it for all of us."

"Well, you don't need to manage it for me," I pointed out. "I already look like a Wyllan from head to toe."

"Not quite," Sky replied. "Your eyes are still brown, and that'll be a beacon to your true identity."

I frowned. "What?"

Sky sighed. "Honestly, Isan, do I have to spell it out for you? Wyllans have blue eyes and you don't. Your cover will be blown right away if Asmund doesn't disguise them."

I gave her a concerned look. "But… But my eyes are blue."

All four of them turned to look at me as if I'd just suggested we invite Icaria over for tea.

"How many times did Aunt Mag drop you on your head as a baby?" Sky asked after a moment. "Because your eyes have always been brown. I don't… I'm not really sure what else to tell you."

I wanted to argue further, but if they all truly thought my eyes were brown, what else could I possibly say to sway them? I'd always thought my royal portraits had been painted with brown eyes because the painters *assumed* I had brown eyes, but maybe this whole time that was simply the truth?

*Was* I crazy, and if not, why did I see myself differently than others did?

Asmund cleared his throat, diffusing some of the tension, and said, "So that still leaves me with limited magic…

There was a long pause as we looked around the fire at each other, and then Aramina took a deep breath and said, "I'll stay behind with Echo."

Asmund raised an eyebrow. "Are you sure?"

"It's not what I want," she admitted, "but it's the logical choice. Isan is going, he won't survive a day without Sky, and *you're* obviously going. Besides, three strangers entering the city will be less suspicious than four, and you can always call me telepathically if you need me. We can stay informed about each other's situation that way."

"If our thoughts will reach that far," Asmund said.

The two of them had yet to test the full range of their magic, but I guess there was no time like the present.

Aramina shrugged. "We won't know unless we try. I think it should be fine though, as it's a fairly passive ability. It shouldn't use too much energy."

"All right," Asmund replied, despite his unsettled expression, "that's settled then. What else?"

"Where exactly are we going, and what are we looking for?" Sky asked.

"Tamise is home to a group of Wyllan knights called the Shadow Watch," Echo replied. "They start their training as mere acolytes, learning all manner of weaponry and doing menial labour, but eventually they graduate to either Ebony or Ivory studies. Ebonies become royal assassins, and Ivories become royal guards. The three of you would pose as new recruits and hopefully be able to collect information once you're inside their ranks.

"You'll want to keep an ear to the ground for any rumours about visitors from the capital," Echo went on. "Icaria won't go herself, but if she's planning something, she'll send someone to the Shadow Keep to discuss assembling a raider unit with the Shadow Master."

Aramina frowned. "Who is the Shadow Master?"

"He is the leader of the Shadow Watch," Echo said, "and an incredibly powerful man, from what I've gathered in my limited research. He's a master at all forms of weaponry, and people say he wields a kind of magic few have ever seen. Of course, I've never met him, so I can't tell you much more than that."

"Is he a Gifted Immortal or a Magic Wielder?" Asmund asked.

"I've never heard either option confirmed," Echo replied, "but my gut tells me he's immortal. The way people speak of him… It's like he's *always* been the Shadow Master."

I rubbed my chin. "So would he be a friend or a foe?"

Echo sat up straighter, her eyes widening in distress. "*No one* in Winter is your friend," she replied swiftly, a sharpness in her tone that I'd never heard from her before. "I cannot stress that enough. If anyone finds out who you truly are, they will deliver you straight to Icaria, if they don't kill you themselves. Trying to find allies isn't worth the risk. They will be few and far between. Even those who may be sympathetic to our cause will be reluctant to defy the kingdom and incur Icaria's wrath."

I held up my hands. "I understand we have to be careful. I didn't mean to upset you."

Echo shook her head. "It's all right, I just don't want to lose any of you. This is going to be a delicate mission."

"Then we'll make sure we cover all possible problems we might come across," I replied. "Dying or getting captured is not in the plan."

She rolled her eyes at my confident answer, and I tried to give her a reassuring smile. I knew she was worried about sending us there alone. I was nervous about going, but there was no other choice, and Echo's limited knowledge of Winter's current state would have to be enough to keep us alive.

• • •

We spent the rest of the evening going over the plan, breaking it down into smaller steps as we went on. Eventually, we decided there wasn't much else to be said, and we were all having trouble keeping our eyes open by that point anyway. The fire had died down into a bed of orange coals—a good sign it was time to retire.

We still only had one tent, so Asmund and I laid our bedrolls in front of the fire while the girls squeezed into the tent. It wasn't the best situation, but at least we would all stay warm.

Breakfast the following morning was a quiet affair, as it had been decided that Asmund, Sky, and I would leave shortly after. There was no point in delaying the inevitable. We didn't know how much longer Icaria's plan would take before she acted, and we wouldn't be any more prepared if we waited another day or two.

We had to go before we lost our nerve.

Sky and I spent an hour after breakfast collecting food and water to take with us while Echo and Aramina worked with Asmund on his shape-shifting. Echo wanted to make sure he was capable of the magic required before she sent us off into the unknown.

"Well," Sky said as she shoved the last bundle of herbs into her satchel. "Do you think we're ready for this?"

I clenched my hands around the straps of my own bag. "I don't know what to think, but I have to believe we can do it. There's no other way."

Sky nodded and then was quiet for a minute, as if she was contemplating whether or not to say something else. A sudden breeze rustled through the leaves at our feet, and it took me a few seconds to realize it was coming from her, her fingers dancing nervously at her side and manipulating the air around us absentmindedly.

Finally, she found her voice again and said, "Do you think Aunt Mag is okay, back in Widonia? I know we're making the right choice, the logical choice, but I can't stop thinking about the people we left behind. They're counting on us to come back for them, and I'm so scared of letting them down."

I walked over and put a hand on her shoulder. "Aunt Mag is a lot tougher than she lets on. She can survive whatever atrocities Quinton commits, and she'll hold out hope until we return. If something were to happen to us... You know she won't resent us for it. She'll know we did everything we could.

"But nothing is going to happen to us," I assured her. "We have faced impossible odds before and lived to tell the tale, so we have to trust ourselves and the path we've been set on. I don't think Fidal is done with us yet."

She took a deep breath. "You know, that's what I'm afraid of, that Fidal has plans for us beyond what's already been discovered, and that we're not ready, not by half."

"Well, I haven't had any new dreams lately, if that makes you feel any better."

She huffed a laugh. "I guess that's a start."

"We'll figure it out, Sky," I said. "We always do, and even if we fail the realm miserably in our destiny, we'll try to make it a tale to be remembered."

She smiled. "It's been pretty eventful so far: battled goblins and ogres in the Edgewood, discovered a prophecy that could spell our doom, faced off against the Winter Prince and King, stopped the man who raised us from destroying Summer as we know it, and unlocked our own powerful magic." She looked over at me. "Did I miss anything?"

"No, that about sums it up."

"And we're about to add 'infiltrate a Wyllan stronghold' to that list."

I shrugged. "The stories definitely won't be able to say we were boring."

"Or wise," she countered.

"It's not a good story without a little bit of risk," I reminded her with a grin.

She sighed and massaged her temples. "Promise me you'll stick to the plan and not do anything stupid."

"I promise to do my best," I replied.

"Then that'll have to be enough."

We rejoined the others shortly after, the both of us feeling a bit more sure of our goals and what was at stake should we fail. Echo and Mina were pleased with Asmund's results, and though none of us could foretell how long his magic would last, we had to have faith it would be long enough.

"All right," Echo said, "remember what I told all of you. Wyllans are much more quiet and reserved than Sancians, so you have to pretend to be the same. When around authority figures, don't speak unless spoken to. Always be sure to address people by their formal titles where they exist. Eat slowly. Don't complain about the cold. And above all, don't mention Summer with any sort of familiarity, if you mention it at all."

Asmund, Sky, and I nodded.

"You are to return to us in three weeks' time, or sooner, if Asmund's magic seems to be weakening. There is nothing more important than ensuring your survival and keeping your identities secret."

"I'll check in on you through my telepathy regularly," Aramina added, "and if something goes wrong, I'll use a portal to get to you."

Echo took a deep breath. "Well, I believe that's everything. Asmund, if you'll do the honours?"

Asmund closed his eyes, and we all stood in silence as he shifted his appearance. Even after all these weeks of watching him train, it was still such a strange thing to witness as his hair slowly shrank to a couple inches longer than mine and his skin paled.

As a rule, Magic Wielders could only shapeshift into people they'd seen before, like they could only portal to places or people they'd seen before, but Asmund had discovered he could pick and choose which aspects of a person to use.

When he was done, he looked like he could pass for my brother, much more than Sky ever looked like she could pass for my sister. His hand reached up to touch his new hair absentmindedly, and he scowled in disgust, glancing at me. "How do you live like this?"

I shrugged. "I could ask the same of you."

He did Sky next, lightening her skin and changing her brown eyes into blue to match my own. She had already taken the braids out of her hair, and it hung around her face like a dark curtain.

Finally, Asmund turned to me. "Now for the easiest part. I suppose this is the only time your skin condition has been an advantage for you."

I rolled my already blue eyes but bit back my retort.

When he was finished, Echo and Aramina studied the three of us with a critical eye.

"As long as the magic holds, no one should question you," Echo assured us.

Mina rubbed at her eyes. "I'm not going to lie, it's kind of making my skin crawl, but it's a perfect disguise."

"Then we're ready," I said, attempting to let go of my nerves along with my breath.

"As you'll ever be," Echo replied. "By Wylla's wayward heart, *please* be careful. All of you."

I couldn't help but notice how her eyes lingered on mine, despite addressing all of us, and I knew she was thinking about the connection between us, the question that had yet to be truly answered. I hoped I would come back to put it all to rest.

Sky gave Mina and Echo a crushing hug each and then mounted her horse, wiping at her eyes.

Asmund gave Echo a nod. "Take care of my sister."

"Take care of yourself," Aramina countered. "Arran will never believe me about you if you're not there when I tell our tale."

Asmund smiled. "I'll do my best."

And then it was just me.

I took a deep breath. "We'll be back as soon as we can," I said, "and hopefully with good news. Don't you two get into any trouble while we're gone."

Mina grinned. "I make no promises."

"I expected nothing else," I replied.

Echo grabbed my hand, and I turned to face her. "Be careful, Isan," she said. "Remember, this is only a reconnaissance mission. Don't make it more complicated or dangerous than it needs to be. Icaria hasn't won yet."

I squeezed her hand. "I won't, and I know."

I walked away before I lost my nerve or did something unbelievably stupid, but I could still feel her hand in mine as I mounted my horse and the three of us rode away. I vowed I would hold it again, come what may.

## 28

## The Viridian Viper

**The sun was beginning** to set as the three of us came upon Tamise. The sky glowed red in the dying light with layers of pink and orange melting through, as if the sun had set the clouds on fire. For once, I let myself admire its beauty instead of convincing myself it was a bad omen.

The day's last rays shone down into the city. It sat nestled in a valley at the base of a cliff, the houses in the distance hugging its face. A short stone wall protected the rest, with a gate at each compass point.

At first glance, it didn't look like a strategically placed or well-defended city at all, but then my eyes inevitably shifted towards the black tower perched atop the centre of the cliff. The Shadow Keep. It loomed over the city, at least half again the height of the cliff, and I knew any enemy would be hard-pressed to plan a surprise attack on Tamise, let alone execute it.

Asmund let out a low whistle. "Now *that* is an impressive piece of architecture. It puts even the Citadel to shame."

"The Wyllans certainly don't do anything by half," I replied, remembering how impressive their palace and capital city were too.

"At least we won't be able to get lost," Sky pointed out. "Though that also means we won't have an easy time escaping, if we need to."

Asmund let out a nervous breath. "Let's hope I have enough magic left over to create a portal if we need one. Your disguises are still in place?"

Sky and I exchanged glances and nodded. It was strange looking at her, because although the shape of her face remained, it wasn't quite her. It was as if she was someone I'd met in passing once but couldn't remember where.

"Then let's get this over with," Asmund replied. "The sooner we get into the city, the sooner we can relax a little. We'll find some place to stay overnight and then make for the Keep in the morning. Lower your hoods so we don't raise suspicion from the guards."

We did as instructed as a gust of wind blew across the plain, scattering snow and sending my hair into disarray.

Beside me, Sky shivered against the chill and pulled her coat tighter around her. We'd prepared for the weather this time, and though Sky's coat was thin so as to not raise questions, she was bundled tightly in layers underneath.

"Lead the way, Garyth," I said to Asmund, using the false name we'd chosen for him. "I am eager for a hot meal and warm bed."

He rolled his eyes but urged his horse forward. Sky and I fell into step behind him as we rode toward the north gate and an uncertain future.

As we approached the gate, a pair of guards emerged from the adjacent wooden building and took up their posts on either side. They each held a crossbow, but they didn't raise the weapons, which did little to put my mind at ease.

I tried to remind myself that getting into Tamise was supposed to be the easiest part of the journey, not a lethal obstacle.

When our horses were a few paces away from the gate, Asmund motioned for us to halt and dismounted his horse to close the distance on foot. Sky and I watched his back, prepared to come to his defense at the first sign of danger.

One guard trained his bow on Asmund as the other came to stand in front of him, albeit on the opposite side of the gate. "We'll need the reason for your stay and the toll fee before we can let you through," he said, "and the names of all three of you." He was straight and to the point, which I liked, but the absence of pleasantries was off-putting nonetheless.

"My name is Garyth Tarian, and these are my younger brother and sister, Ewen and Cleantha," Asmund replied, his voice steady. "We are here to prove our strength and become members of the Shadow Watch."

The guard nodded his approval. "There is no greater honour than to be chosen. May Wylla guide you."

Asmund inclined his head but offered no words of gratitude. "How much is the fee?"

The guard held up four fingers, and Asmund reached into his pocket before pressing the coins into the guard's outstretched hand.

The two guards retreated back into the building without another word, and a few moments later, the gate swung open, the metal creaking in the wind.

Asmund mounted his horse once more, and we rode into Tamise without further fanfare, the gate swinging shut behind us with a note of finality. The easy part was over. All that was left to do was infiltrate a fortress of skilled Wyllan swordsmen and uncover the sinister plot of the ice Princess herself.

*Sancia save us.*

"So where to now?" I asked, once we were a good distance from the gate.

"Echo gave me the names of a few reputable inns and taverns," Sky replied. "I suppose we'll call at each of them until we find one that has room for us."

Asmund nodded in approval, turning his horse towards Sky's. "Did she say where we would find them?"

"The first one should be up here around the corner," Sky said, urging her horse along and motioning for us to fall into step behind her. "It's called the Crimson Hawk."

I shared a look with Asmund. "Well, *that* sounds inviting."

He cracked a smile but said nothing as we followed Sky down the road.

A few moments later, Sky pulled her horse to a stop in front of an immaculate building that looked almost *too* nice.

The inn was exquisite, with huge windows, a grand staircase leading to the double doors, and balconies for each third-storey room. I didn't doubt that, after the palace, it was one of the most beautiful structures in all of Winter, though it was hard to compare two buildings that were in such stark contrast to one another. The palace was made of ice, the colour of fresh snow, whereas the Crimson Hawk was painted a deep black with red accents dark enough to mirror blood.

Asmund jumped off his horse before I finished gawking and made for the stairs. "I'll see if there's room. You two wait here and keep an eye out for trouble."

I frowned. Though I knew he was playing the role of the older brother, I thought he was laying it on a bit thick. Still, I watched him go until he was safely inside the doors and then turned to Sky.

"Are you doing okay?"

She nodded. "I dare say this has been a much more enjoyable venture than our first trip to Winter, though I may yet eat my words."

"I pray that you don't."

We only waited a few minutes before Asmund came bounding down the stairs again, shaking his head. "They're full for the next fortnight," he called out, "and I think we'd find ourselves poor within a week staying there."

Echo had given us her life's savings of Copper Crowns and Bronze Buttons, gathered discreetly on each visit she'd made to Tamise in the past, but it wasn't a fortune by any means. We were praying we'd be able to join the Shadow Watch quickly and that we could earn our keep there without money.

I let out a sigh at Asmund's words, but I didn't expect to have much luck on our first try. "Next suggestion?" I asked Sky.

She took a deep breath to calm her nerves and led us away.

• • •

The sun had well and truly set by the time we came upon a tavern called the Viridian Viper in the south end of the city, the Shadow Keep much closer than I would've liked. We'd visited all of Echo's suggestions, and they were either full, too expensive, or took one look at the weapons we carried and waved us off.

I found it hard to believe that Wyllans would bat an eye at the potential danger, but I guessed they didn't want to invite any more trouble into their already miserable lives.

The Viridian Viper was a squat two-storey stone building that leaned on its neighbours with mortar missing between some of the stones and slate hanging off the edge of the roof in several places. It didn't look like the sort of place that reputable people frequented or even passed by. My senses were on high alert as we approached, and my hand dropped to *Ember*'s hilt on instinct.

"Are you sure this is our only option?" I asked Asmund.

"I'm not happy about it either, but we need to eat, and they likely have a room for a good price. Just don't let your guard down. And Sky?"

She looked up. "Yes?"

"Stick close to me."

I bristled but bit back my usual overbearing retort. Asmund was allowed to be protective of my sister, as much as I hated the idea of trusting her safety to someone else. Besides, it was nice to know he had our backs.

Sky nodded, and the three of us dismounted our horses together. We tied their reins to the post in front of the tavern, grabbed our meagre belongings, and made for the front door.

The Viridian Viper wasn't any more inviting on the inside than the outside. The ceilings were low, and lanterns swung in the stale air every few feet so even *I* had to duck under them despite being of average height. The floor was uneven, the wooden planks creaking and groaning under our boots. There would be no sneaking up on anyone in this place.

I took a deep breath to calm my nerves and gagged on the smell of stale beer and filth.

About a dozen patrons sat at the wooden tables spread around the room, nursing tankards of ale under the dull glow of the lanterns. The light didn't fill the space, leaving the corners in shadow. The tavern keeper stood behind the bar on the left side of the room. He was the only one who looked up when we came in, but I could sense someone watching us from the corner where the light didn't reach.

Instinct had me wanting to look in that direction, but I ignored it, knowing the likelihood of it ending well wasn't high.

Instead, I pulled off my hood and dusted snow from my cloak, making it look like I was comfortable in such a place.

Beside me, Asmund and Sky were doing the same. A few of the patrons looked over as soon as they realized a woman was in our midst, but a quick look from Asmund had them turning their heads again.

*Let them try something*, I thought, my hand going to *Ember*'s hilt again. They would lose their hands so fast, their heads would spin.

None of them made a move, but the night was still young.

Asmund started making his way over to the tavern keeper, though I knew he was none too eager to part with any of our precious coins for a tankard of questionable ale. Still, we had been travelling all day, and any food or drink would taste like a godsend at this point.

Sky followed close behind him, and I took up the rear, my eyes scanning each table for potential threats as we crossed the room.

The tavern keeper put down the glass he was cleaning as the three of us stopped in front of him, throwing the stained towel over one shoulder. "What'll it be, then?"

I blinked at him, put off by the lack of proper greeting, but Asmund didn't miss a beat. He dropped a handful of coins on the counter and said, "Three tankards of ale, three bowls of whatever passes for stew here, and a room for the night, if it's not too much of a bother. I trust this will cover it."

The tavern keeper nodded stoically, closing his hand over the coins and sliding them off the counter. "That should be enough, yes. Are you wanting a separate room for the lady or something more…cozy?"

"One room, three beds," Asmund replied, ignoring the insinuation beneath the tavern keeper's words. "Two beds at minimum."

"Very well," the tavern keeper said. He walked away and came back a few minutes later with a bronze key that he pressed into Asmund's hand. "Third door on the right up the stairs around back. If you have horses, there's a small stable there too."

Asmund nodded but said nothing more.

It felt like ages, but we were finally served our ale and stew. We took the closest table we could find, leaving plenty of space between us and the rest of the room.

I sipped the ale tentatively at first but was surprised to find it wasn't terrible. The stew, on the other hand, was probably the worst I'd ever had, but the three of us scarfed it down without complaint, knowing we had no other choice.

Finally, Asmund leaned back in his chair, the whole thing creaking with age, and said, "We're being watched."

I nodded. "Felt it as soon as we walked in. They're in the far corner."

Sky tried not to show her alarm, but I could read it in her eyes. "What do you suppose they want?"

"I should like not to find out," Asmund replied, "but I have a feeling that's not in the stars for us. Let's retire to our rooms and see if he follows. At least then we'll have space to maneuver."

"And less people will get in the way," I added.

The three of us stood in unison and made for the front door, pointedly averting our gaze from the far corner where our potential enemy lurked.

The fresh air of the Winter night was much preferable to the staleness of the tavern, and I took in several deep lungfuls as we collected our horses and led them around the back of the building.

The stable was nothing more than a horizontal post and half collapsed food trough under a lean-to that looked like it was about to disintegrate, but we tied the horses up anyway. We left their tack on, though, in case we needed to make a hasty escape, only loosening their reins and saddles a bit to ease their discomfort.

Our room was at the top of a steep, rickety wooden staircase along the back of the building that creaked and groaned with every step as we climbed it, saddle bags in hand. I was shaking with nerves by the time we finally reached the landing, which didn't look much sturdier than the staircase itself.

"Still afraid of heights, I see," Sky said with a knowing smile, and I stuck my tongue out at her.

In front of us, Asmund unlocked the door to our room and used his shoulder to shove the door open, sending a layer of snow down on top of our heads from the roof.

Sky shivered from the cold, and I smirked. "Still too delicate for snow, I see."

She scowled and pushed past me, joining Asmund in the room that looked more like a broom closet than anything else. The beds were cots only as wide as our shoulders, nestled so close together we could drool on each other in our sleep. A foot of space was reserved at the end of each bed for our belongings and boots.

"Well, I'd hate to see the cozy room," I said.

"Just get in here and close the door," Asmund retorted. "You're letting in the chill."

I did as I was told, and the three of us stood in the tiny entrance to the room, taking in our situation in silence for a minute before Sky said, "I don't know about you two, but I'm going to bed. This day has been a lot, and I'm too exhausted to care what the bed feels like."

She dropped her saddle bag at her feet, unstrung her bow from her shoulder, and yanked off her boots before flopping down onto the nearest cot, her cloak still around her shoulders.

Asmund and I shared a weary glance before following suit and taking up the cots on either side of her, leaving our swords within easy reach.

I was on the verge of nodding off when Sky's voice broke the silence of the room, albeit in a whisper. "Are you still awake?"

I opened my eyes blearily, not sure who she was talking to, but didn't roll over.

"Az," she prompted, followed by the sound of rustling, as if she had sat up.

I raised an eyebrow at the nickname but tried to keep my breathing even so she wouldn't realize I was listening.

"What's wrong?" Asmund replied after a second, sounding startled but exhausted.

"Are you awake?"

I could almost see his eyes roll. "I am *now*. Can't sleep?"

"No," she replied softly. "That mystery person is still out there, and we're in hostile territory. I'm glad to have somewhere warm to rest, but... I'm afraid to close my eyes."

"I know what you mean," he replied. "A part of me is astounded we even made it this far."

There was a moment's pause before she said, "You know, that...doesn't really make me feel any better."

I resisted the urge to snort. He'd walked right into that one. Sky wanted reassurance, not sympathy.

"Sorry," he said quickly. "I didn't mean—We're going to be fine. The identity and whereabouts of our new foe may be unknown, but the three of us can take on anything. They should be more wary of us than we are of them."

"Maybe," Sky allowed. "Do you think they're a member of the Shadow Watch?"

"I'd be more surprised if they're not, but I suppose we could use that to our advantage, if we play our cards right. They could lead us to where we need to go."

"Or lead us to our deaths."

Asmund heaved a frustrated sigh and then said, "Come here."

She didn't reply, but I heard more rustling blankets and figured she'd laid back down, probably closer to Asmund, judging from his request.

I bristled at the thought. Yet, I knew there was no point in rolling over and berating them for it. On the one hand, this room was much too small for a proper fight. On the other, I was probably overreacting.

"No one is going to die," Asmund said after a moment. "We're too strong and clever and determined for that. The road ahead may not be easy, but I won't let anything happen to you, I promise. Especially not tonight. So try to get some sleep, okay?"

"Okay," Sky replied, sounding more relaxed. I marvelled at how he was able to comfort her, how she was willing to let her guard down for him. It wasn't an easy feat.

Their breathing steadied a bit, and I thought that was the end of the conversation until Sky asked, "Were you able to reach Aramina with your telepathy?"

"I told her we were safe once we found the room," Asmund replied, "and she said to be careful, so I guess it works."

"I'm glad she's in the Edgewood with Echo," Sky replied, half asleep.

"Me too," Asmund said, "but I know she'd fight Fidal himself to save us if it came to it."

"Then let's pray she doesn't have to."

29

# A Shadowed Stranger

**I jolted awake from** a dead sleep sometime after midnight, my thoughts jumbled and heart racing as I tried to remember where I was while also discerning what had woken me. The details of our borrowed room came back to me as I saw Sky sound asleep beside me, her arms wrapped around her makeshift pillow of Asmund's cloak.

Asmund, too, was still sound asleep, his body curled protectively around Sky and his arm draped over her.

My instincts had me reaching to push his arm away and demand to know what he thought he was doing, but I stopped myself short, remembering their earlier conversation. Asmund might not be perfect, but he made her happy, and that was all that mattered.

I managed a smile at them, but then someone knocked on the door, and my fear came rushing back to the forefront of my mind.

I grabbed *Ember* as I got to my feet and hastily pulled on my boots before reaching over to shake Asmund awake.

"Asmund, Asmund!" I called out in the loudest whisper I could manage.

He rolled over, blinking his bleary eyes. "Wha—"

"Someone is at the door," I said.

He opened his eyes the rest of the way and followed my gaze to the door where the person was still knocking, and I knew he was thinking the same thing I was.

The mystery person had come back, and we were in grave danger.

I handed him his boots and took up a defensive position at the door. "What's our plan?"

"Shield Sky when I open the door, but don't leave yourself open for attack," he replied, still blinking the lethargy out of his eyes.

*Easier said than done,* I thought to myself.

Still, I drew my shoulders back, holding *Ember* in a ready position, and waited for Asmund to get up.

Finally, he came to stand behind me, one hand on the doorknob and the other gripping his sword tightly. "Ready?"

I nodded, and he thrust the door open in one swift motion, the two of us bringing our weapons up to draw as we were exposed to the world and whoever waited outside.

"Lower your weapons, strangers," a voice said, "unless you want the Fidal-forsaken meal you had earlier to be your last."

My eyes had adjusted enough to the darkness of the night to make out the figure of a man standing on the landing in front of us, dressed head to toe in black. His voice was soft but laced with a promise of pain if we stepped out of line.

"Introduce yourself first," Asmund said, "and we might consider your request."

The man smiled. "Smart man; I wouldn't concede to me either. The old man might be right about the prospects of this quest after all."

I frowned. "What are you talking about? Why are you here?"

The man sighed. "So many questions, so little caution. Fortunately for you, I've been instructed to be polite, but I'm afraid we don't have time for the full story right now. I will tell you my name is Cahir Tremont, and I am an Ebony soldier from the Shadow Watch. I am here to recruit you."

"How convenient," Sky's voice replied, making Asmund and I jump as she forced her way between us, her bow strung and nocked, an arrow aimed at Cahir's throat. "How do you know why we're here?"

Cahir shrugged, unperturbed by Sky's obvious threat. "I don't, but the Master knew you'd be here all the same, no matter if your intentions were what we assumed. He said one day you would walk into that tavern and that the fate of Winter would be in your hands when you did. I've been waiting in that dark corner for your arrival every night since. The old man's never wrong, but it still surprises me every time."

Sky and Asmund lowered their weapons and glanced warily in my direction, because although Cahir had been answering Sky's question, his eyes hadn't left mine the entire time.

I swallowed the nerves in my throat as I said, "The Shadow Master has been waiting for *me?*"

Cahir nodded. "He's quite eager to meet you."

"Why?" My thoughts were racing, but my curiosity was slowly winning over my suspicion.

Who was this Cahir truly, and what did he mean that the Shadow Master knew I was coming or that the fate of Winter was on *my* shoulders?

I lowered my sword. "If we go with you, how do we know we can trust you? How do we know this isn't a trick or a death sentence?"

"I'm afraid you don't," Cahir replied, "but I haven't made any attempt to unsheath my weapons thus far, despite the less-than-hospitable welcome I received, and the Shadow Master wants you alive. I can't guarantee your safety beyond that initial meeting, but the journey there will be more comfortable if you cooperate."

There seemed to be honesty in his words, and I exchanged a few looks with Sky and Asmund before sheathing my sword and straightening my stance. "We'll follow you, but we can't promise we won't retaliate against any danger we encounter."

Cahir smiled. "I would look down upon you if you did. A smart man looks after himself first. Take a few minutes to gather your belongings, and I'll see you at the horses." Then he turned on his heel and took the stairs two at a time, leaving the three of us in stunned silence.

"I don't like this at all," Sky said once Cahir was out of earshot, reluctantly stowing her bow away. "We could be walking directly into a trap."

"He didn't say they knew who we were," I argued, "just that we'd be here. Well, me specifically."

"And he could be lying through his teeth," she countered.

"Sky's right," Asmund said, causing a groan from me and a smile to light up Sky's face. "We don't know his true motives or extent of his knowledge of us, so we have to proceed with caution."

Sky gaped at him. "You think we should go?"

He crossed his arms. "I don't think we have a choice. It's either we go willingly now, or he knocks us out and drags us there. He said he was an Ebony of the Shadow Watch, an assassin. We might have our own skills, but it wouldn't be wise to challenge him in his own domain. We should take advantage of his restraint as long as we can."

"This was the plan anyway, right?" I added. "Get into the Shadow Keep, collect information, and escape unscathed. It looks like we might accomplish the first two right off the bat."

Sky let out a breath and walked back into our room. "Don't get your hopes up."

•  •  •

Ten minutes later, the four of us sat on horseback in front of the entrance to the Shadow Keep. I had expected stairs upon stairs to gain access to the tower high above, enough to make a person nauseous with exhaustion, but instead we were met with a deep chasm in the face of the cliff and a silence unlike anything I'd ever known.

Around us, a fierce Winter wind whipped the snow in all directions, rubbing our faces raw. Inside the crevice, the air was as still as death and filled with shadows.

"You want us to follow you in there?" I asked as Cahir urged his horse towards the gap in the ice and rock.

"Oh, for Fidal's sake," Sky said. "If you can brave the Edgewood, surely you can muster up the courage to survive this, or are you afraid of the dark as well as heights?" She nudged her horse onward and took my place behind Cahir as he disappeared into the crevice.

I followed begrudgingly with Asmund on my heels. I knew Sky was trying to lift my mood with a little tough love, but the truth was the dark *did* get under my skin these days. It reminded me of Darkenier, of the nightmare that had stolen my sleep for weeks, and of the day I nearly lost everything to a man who had lied to me my whole life for his own gain.

I wasn't afraid of the dark so much as what it represented; the unknown was a deeply grave concept, and I feared falling prey to it.

We followed Cahir deep into the crevice, for what seemed like eons, until light spilled around us again, and I spotted a torch wedged into the ancient rock walling us in. It was soon joined by others, and I began to feel like maybe we would make it out alive after all, or at least live to see the mysterious Shadow Master.

Eventually we reached what I assumed to be the official entrance of the Shadow Keep, a pair of ebony-coloured wooden doors that stood twice our height and cleaved the stone around them in two. A silver knocker the size of my fist hung from the centre of the left door, almost too high for any average person to reach, though I doubted anyone actually used it.

Two young boys in grey robes approached us, seeming to materialize out of thin air, and reached for our horses' reins.

"Dismount and grab whatever belongings you need," Cahir called out as he dropped to the snow. "The acolytes will take your horses to be tended to."

We followed his instructions without a word amongst us, and I placed a hand on *Ember*'s pommel for reassurance as he led us past the grand entrance and to a man-sized door in the shadows to the left of them.

It was such a well-concealed entrance that I never would've noticed it without him, such was the grandeur of the ebony doors.

I noticed the door didn't creak at all on its hinges as Cahir pushed it open and ushered us inside.

Immediately, I felt the temperature around us rise and watched Sky's shoulders drop, no longer needing to conserve her heat. The inside of the Shadow Keep looked much like some of the older wings of the castle, except without windows. The walls were made of thick stone blocks, and there was a maroon carpet runner beneath our feet, lit up by evenly spaced torch sconces.

No one else was in sight, but I supposed it was well into the night, and even the Shadow Watch had to sleep sometime.

Cahir turned to look at the three of us as we stood in the entrance awaiting further directions. "I will take you to see the Shadow Master," he said, "and then to your accommodations, should your meeting prove to be successful. Follow me and try to keep up. It's easy to get lost in the subterranean labyrinth of the Shadow Keep."

We nodded our understanding, despite whatever reservations we might have had, and he was off again without another word.

Cahir navigated the Keep with natural ease, as if he had grown up in the maze of tunnels, hallways, and staircases he led us down and up. I was entirely turned around within the first few minutes and knew I would not be able to find my way out alone. I doubted Sky or Asmund would fare much better either. Everything looked the same, from the colour of the stone to the angles of the turns and size of the intersections.

Eventually, we came to an open space at the end of a long passageway where another pair of massive black doors were set into the stone wall. They stood imposing before us, like two sentries in the night, sending nerves shivering down my spine.

Following Cahir had seemed like a good idea at the time, but at that moment, I wasn't so sure of my decision.

Cahir came to a stop a few paces from the doors and looked over at me. "The Master waits beyond."

I took a deep breath and glanced at Asmund and Sky. "Are we ready?"

"As I'll ever be," Sky replied, her anxiety showing in her eyes, though her voice was strong.

"Whenever you are," Asmund added, giving me a solid nod.

We made to step forward as a group, but Cahir held up a hand. "I apologize, but the offer only stands for one." He met my eyes again. "Your siblings will have to wait out here with me."

I scowled. "What does the Master want with me? Is this some sort of elaborate plan to get me killed?"

Cahir sighed. "I promise you I don't know, but it's highly unlikely the old man wishes you harm. Not after he went through all the trouble to get you here. You'll go in there alone or not at all, and I'll need your sword."

He held out a hand, and I gave him an incredulous look. "I'm sorry, but that is out of the question. I am not going in there alone to meet a man called the Shadow Master, who trains royal guards and assassins alike, unarmed. That would be foolish and suicidal."

Cahir massaged his temples in frustration, and then I heard Asmund's voice in my head.

*Easy, Isan. We need him to get out of here. Just do what he says. Worst comes to worse, you can use your magic.*

I gritted my teeth as I let out a resigned breath. "Fine," I said. "I'll leave the sword, but not with you." I unsheathed *Ember* and handed her to Asmund, who took the sword without question. "If I die, use her to remove Cahir's head."

Then I strode forward without another word, opened the doors, and left the three of them behind.

The doors groaned as they swung open, greeting me with a rush of stale air when I stepped inside. A few seconds later, I felt the unshakeable sense I was being sealed in a tomb as they banged shut behind me. It was a hollow sound that echoed in the emptiness of the space.

Two torches set into wall brackets illuminated the low stone room and the people waiting for me. A pair of guards stood in white uniform on either side of a grey throne that seemed carved out of the rock of the room itself.

It struck me as odd that a place such as this existed in a kingdom where the rulers basked in having absolute power. My knowledge of Winter was thin, and my time with King Frost had been short, but he didn't strike me as the type of man to let someone else claim a throne in his kingdom, no matter what it was made of.

The Shadow Master wore robes of the same colour as the throne in question and looked up from his seat as I came in, the flickering torch light reflecting in his dark eyes. My resolve wavered as I met his unflinching gaze, but then he softened, his shoulders relaxing and his eyes widening in surprise.

He stood from his throne as if in a trance and took a step toward me. "I didn't think this day would come," he said, "but here you are, in front of me, after all these years."

I swallowed the lump in my throat. "I don't mean to be impolite," I replied, "but I'm growing tired of these cryptic phrases concerning me. Who are you, and what do you want? I need answers."

The man shook his head, as if to clear it, and said, "Yes, of course. You must be confused with the manner in which I brought you here. Come forward and allow me to explain myself—as much as I can, that is."

He sat down again, and I walked towards him tentatively, eyeing the guards and the weapons they carried. There seemed to be an entire arsenal on their persons, while the Master appeared unarmed.

*Strange.*

One would think the Shadow Master would lead by example. I supposed he could have weapons hidden somewhere beneath his cloak, but something told me that wasn't the case. I had the sense his reputation itself was threat enough to most would-be attackers, and Cahir had already taken my sword.

Again, I wondered why King Frost would let a man like him live, but that mystery wasn't the reason I was here.

I stopped a few paces short of the Shadow Master's stone throne and waited for him to speak.

He took a long breath, as if to clear his mind and collect his thoughts, and then said, "I have known of your coming for centuries, young man, though we have never met. My powers of prophecy have painted your face many times in the future yet to come, for good or ill, but no matter the outcome, each path starts with you walking into the musty atmosphere of the Viridian Viper."

I arched a skeptical brow. "You can see the future?"

"Not all of it," he admitted, "and not all at once or when I want to. It comes to me in flashes, sometimes blurry, but my visions of you have always been clear as day."

"Cahir said the fate of Winter itself sits on my shoulders. Is he… What is he talking about?" I almost mentioned the Curse but caught myself at the last second, realizing it would give away my lineage if I explained it to him in any detail.

The Shadow Master clasped his hands together. "There is a prophecy, rather ancient, which I believe points to you beyond any doubt. It says that one day a *Prince* of Fire will rise to unite the Summer and Winter kingdoms once and for all and restore balance to Fidalia. He will endure many trials, but he cannot fall if this realm means to survive."

I gave him an incredulous look. "Prince of Fire? Unite the kingdoms? You think I'm… your champion?"

He nodded. "I believe you're Winter's only hope."

I massaged my temples, my mind reeling as I tried to figure out how to get answers without revealing too much. "Let's say you're right… What about Princess Icaria? Isn't she the hope of the people, the future Queen of Winter? Surely she could unite the lands, become a savior?"

The Shadow Master shook his head. "The branches on that side of the royal family tree have withered and decayed. There is no hope there. Her Highness will be the ruin of us all if gone unchecked. Even now, rumours circulate of a great and terrible evil brewing in Appalachia. No, she cannot be trusted, and the prophecy speaks of you, not her."

I struggled to mask my surprise at his words. I had never heard anyone so openly denounce the monarchy before, in Summer or Winter, and to hear it from such an influential figure was unthinkable. Had I somehow found an ally in our plight?

He was confirming our suspicions about Icaria's sinister plans, but whether or not he held further information on the matter was nothing but speculation at this point.

Still, I felt emboldened enough to say, "What of the fire part of your prophecy? What makes you think I fulfill that requirement?"

He smiled. "I have seen it. In my visions, you wield your magic like a sixth sense, protecting your allies and vanquishing your enemies with an unparalleled precision. You may not be an actual Prince, but you are a ruler of the element itself. Aside from that, I can feel it. There is heat in your veins and fire in your heart."

I swallowed my unease at his words, unsure of how to proceed. If he truly was able to sense my magic as he said, there was no point lying to him, but if he was bluffing and I showed my hand, it could have disastrous consequences.

"How do I know I can trust you?" I replied. "I don't want to denounce your claims, but I have been led astray by many people in my life, by family and friends. It is hard to trust, especially a stranger. I cannot afford to make any more mistakes of that nature."

The Shadow Master gave me a sad smile. "It is not easy being someone people rely on, is it? To always be two steps ahead of your enemies and sacrificing time and time again for the greater good… I understand. Trust is a slippery slope, and it is earned through actions, not bought by words."

I nodded.

"I'd like you to stay," he went on, "to learn the ways of the Shadow Watch and build trust in me. Think on my words, and should you decide I am worthy of your secrets, you know where to find me, but you are free to go if you wish. I will not keep you here if you are being called elsewhere."

I bowed low, surprised by his decision. "Thank you, Shadow Master. I am eager for the opportunity to prove myself in combat, though I would also ask that my brother and sister be allowed entry as well. They are waiting for me in the hall."

The Master waved a hand. "Of course. Any friends of yours are friends of the Shadow Watch, and please, call me Cadmus. Few do these days."

I smiled. "Cadmus, it is."

"And your name, son, if you don't mind me asking?"

"They call me Ewen."

He arched his brow. "But that's not your name, is it?"

I don't know why I felt so at ease with the old man, but I shook my head. "Sometimes a lie is easier to bear than the truth, and sometimes a lie can save a man's life."

"Indeed," he replied, leaning back on his throne. "Wise words for a young soul. I do believe you are exactly the saviour this realm needs. Now go, get some rest. Cahir will see you to your training tomorrow."

I bowed again. "Thank you for your time, Cadmus. I hope you can forgive my wariness."

He waved his hand again. "You know where to find me."

I turned on my heel and walked back to the doors, finally letting my bewilderment show on my face, if only briefly. Who was the Shadow Master really, and what exactly did he want from me? *Could* he be trusted?

I supposed only time would tell, but I had the sinking feeling we didn't have that luxury.

# 30
# Mystery and Master

**Asmund and Sky looked** sick with worry when I rejoined them in the hall, while Cahir leaned casually against a stone pillar, sharpening a dagger with a handheld whetstone.

Sky ran up to me as soon as she saw me and wrapped me in a crushing hug. "Oh, Fidal's breath," she gasped. "I was so worried. What happened? Did he hurt you?"

I hugged her back but shrugged as she relinquished me. "No, he just…talked to me. He is nothing like I expected him to be. Certainly not as stoic and malicious as his title suggests, though not without power of his own. He says we can stay, train to become members of the Shadow Watch."

I caught Cahir's eyes, and he said, "What else did he say, stranger? About you."

"Nothing I am comfortable discussing in the present company," I replied.

Cahir put away his tools and sheathed his dagger. "Whatever, stranger," he said. "I'm sure the old man will tell me himself, in his own time. Just know that whatever future he spoke to you about, you can't run away from it. It's less about *if* it will happen and more about how and when. Now follow me. It's late, and I imagine you could use some sleep after being roused from your beds in the middle of the night."

He walked off, and the three of us scrambled to follow him. Asmund hadn't said a word yet, but I assumed he was waiting until Cahir left us alone to interrogate me about what had happened. I was too focused on Cahir's parting remark to care.

If he was right, then I had no idea what that meant for me. I was indeed a Prince of Fire, but uniting the kingdoms, after everything we had done to each other? I didn't think it was possible as things stood, but *after* I killed Icaria? Fidalia would be in chaos, and the last person the Wyllans would ever listen to would be the one who killed their Princess.

It couldn't be done, even if I wanted to, and I wasn't sure that I did.

Cahir led us back through the winding halls and staircases of the keep, finally coming to a stop at an arched wooden door in the centre of a long stone corridor filled with doors of the same size and shape.

"This is your room," he said, "and this is the residence quarters." He spread his hands out to illustrate his point. "All of your fellow acolytes live on this floor. Meals are served two floors down, and the bathing chambers are at opposite ends of this hall. That way for the men"—he pointed to the left—"and that way for the ladies." He pointed to the right. "Any questions?"

"When does training start?" Sky asked. "And will I be permitted to join my brothers?"

Cahir gave her a look. "Women aren't treated differently in the Shadow Keep, if that's what you're asking. I assume you didn't come all the way here to sit in your rooms and count bricks. As for the training itself, it starts when the bell tolls, but I'll give the three of you the courtesy of ignoring the first bell you hear. You won't be any good to me half delirious with exhaustion. I'll expect you at second bell. Follow the other acolytes, and you shouldn't get lost. Goodnight."

He left us in the hall without another word, and Sky let out a frustrated breath. "Entitled bastard. Who does he think he is?"

"If I had to guess," Asmund replied, pushing in the door to our room, "he's probably one of the highest-ranked soldiers here, considering how he refers to the Shadow Master as 'the old man.'"

"He told me to call him Cadmus," I said as we stepped into the room. It was a much nicer space than our room at the Viridian Viper, though still small. A single bed each sat nestled in three corners of the room with a weathered wooden wardrobe in the other corner. A chest sat at the foot of each bed, and a tiny teardrop-shaped window across from the door spilled a sliver of moonlight into the space.

"This is cozy," Sky said, turning in a circle as she took in all the details. "We must be higher up in the tower now if there's a window. How many storeys do you think the Keep has?"

Asmund scratched his head. "Well, if it runs down through the entirety of the cliff… Could be close to fifty floors, but that's a wild guess. What's that you were saying, Isan?"

I sat down on the bed closest to the door, leaving them to claim the other two. "The Shadow Master asked me to call him Cadmus, said few people do these days. Do you think that's his real name?"

Asmund frowned. "Could be, though it's odd he would trust you with it."

I leaned back against the wall, letting my shoulders sag. "The whole conversation was odd. He spoke to me as if we were old friends. No formalities or threats. He was more polite than any Wyllans I've met before, aside from Echo, and even some Sancians. And he told me about a…prophecy."

Asmund's eyes grew round, and Sky looked up sharply from where she'd been unpacking her bags. "He what? Does he know about the curse?"

"I don't think so, but he knows I have fire magic. I didn't confirm his suspicions, but he says there's an ancient prophecy that speaks of a champion who will unite the kingdoms of Summer and Winter and bring peace to Fidalia once and for all, a Prince of Fire."

Sky's eyes were like dinner plates. "And he believes that person is you? Does he know who you are?"

"He's seen visions of me apparently, visions that give him reason to believe, without a shadow of a doubt, that I'm this *Prince* of Fire. He said he could sense my magic, but he assumes the prophecy uses the term 'Prince' in a more metaphorical sense than literal, so I don't think he suspects our lineage. I don't know what powers he wields himself, but it's like Echo said; it's not like anything we've ever seen before."

"But what does this mean for you, for us?" Asmund asked.

"I don't know yet," I admitted. "I can't tell if he can be trusted, and we have other objectives to meet right now, more important problems to solve. He might become an ally down the road, but we can't afford to lose focus on the mission right now. Summer is still in danger; even *he* said Icaria is up to something."

"Well, at least we know we were right to come here," Asmund replied, "or do you think he's already spoken to Icaria?"

I shook my head. "It sounded more like he had a suspicion than any details, though it also seems like Icaria is placing her hopes in the wrong person, if she is planning to call for his aid."

Sky frowned. "What do you mean?"

"He said the royal family was rotten, basically called Icaria a plague upon her own kingdom. That's why I believe he could be an ally. He doesn't sound loyal to the crown at all."

"That's an interesting development," Asmund replied, "but we'll have to wait and see. I'll relay the information to Aramina. Echo might be able to shed some light on the situation, but we should all get some sleep. There's nothing more we can do tonight."

Sky nodded and undid her cloak while Asmund stood up to lock the door. I unbelted my sword and set her on the floor beside my bed, within easy reach should I need her. Then I pulled off my boots and massaged my sore feet for a few minutes before crawling under the covers. Hopefully a good night's rest would ease my nerves, but I had a feeling I wasn't going to have the luxury of sleeping deeply, not with so many thoughts and anxieties vying for attention in my mind. Still, I closed my eyes anyway and waited restlessly for morning.

•  •  •

The loud tolling of a bell woke the three of us up from a dead sleep before dawn. Sky groaned loudly into her pillow as she rolled over and pulled her blanket over her head in an effort to muffle the noise.

She was sound asleep again in a few minutes, but I rolled into a sitting position to find Asmund already pulling his boots on.

I laughed. "I guess we're more alike than we thought."

He gave me an unamused look, likely fuelled by his lack of sleep. "Don't make me answer that."

The two of us got ready in silence, lacing up our boots and belting our weapons back into place. I noticed as we headed for the door that he looked like himself again.

I said as much, and he rubbed his temples as if in pain. "Right, I almost forgot about that. I let the illusion fall last night once we locked the door. I'm not sure if I can manage it again so soon. My head is pounding from the magical exertion and lack of proper sleep."

"Well, I'll go get breakfast for the three of us, then, while you rest up some more. I won't be long."

I turned to go, but he grabbed my arm, "Wait, your eyes. I have to at least change those."

I spun back around to face him, swallowing a rather exhausted sigh. "Do you think you can manage it?"

He scowled. "Do you think you can manage to sound more condescending?"

I crossed my arms. "You knew what I meant, and I certainly didn't say it with that tone of voice. Can you do it or not?"

He sighed and waved a hand across my face. "There. You should be fine for the day. Now please be careful out there. The Shadow Master might like you, but I doubt the other acolytes will hold you in such high regard. The three of us are on the bottom of the social ladder now."

I nodded. "Don't worry. I'm sure I can handle it after everything you put Sky and I through at the barracks." I ran out the door before he could return fire, laughing quietly to myself at the expression on his face.

He would get over it soon.

Maybe.

I made my way down the hall to the staircase slowly, not meeting anyone else on my way, though I supposed they'd all followed the call of the bell and that this floor would be abandoned until they returned.

The staircase wound down two floors and then opened up into a large dining hall; I could tell by the dozen long wooden tables filling the space. It was illuminated by large windows stained with a grey-coloured glass depicting weapons or figures dressed in dark cloaks, so although the light could filter through, I couldn't see the world outside.

"You're late," a rather disgusted voice called out, echoing through the empty room and making me jump. I searched around for the owner and finally spotted a stout middle-aged man with a splotched white apron standing at a counter along the far wall. He was drying dishes, and as I walked toward him, his disgruntled expression came into focus.

"What was that?" I asked him once I was properly in earshot.

"You're late," he repeated, pointing at me with a soup ladle. "Breakfast was served an hour ago, and I'm sure your lesson master is none too pleased by your absence at this point. I'd turn tail and go back where you came from if I were you."

"I'm new here actually," I replied. "My siblings and I arrived in the early hours of the morning, so we were instructed to ignore the first bell. I didn't realize there was a time limit for breakfast."

"Oh, you didn't realize," the man said. "In that case, I suppose I should pretend like I care."

I blinked at him. "Have I offended you in some way?"

He scowled. "All you pretty little soldiers expect the world handed to you on a silver platter, but I am not here to cater to your every whim. You missed breakfast. Try to be on time for lunch."

I opened my mouth to protest, but he waved his ladle at me menacingly and said, "I said get out!"

I held my hands out in front of me in surrender and left without another word, my stomach grumbling mournfully as I did. The stew at the Viridian Viper had been terrible, but I found myself wishing I'd had a bit more of it.

"Don't mind Vergus," a familiar voice said as I reentered the stairwell.

I managed to resist the urge to jump out of my skin and turned to see Cahir leaning against the wall, tossing a loaf of bread in his left hand.

"He's cranky because he has to work." Cahir grinned. "He always has to work." He tossed me the loaf, and I caught it despite my nerves being shot at his sudden appearance.

I narrowed my eyes at him. "Are you following me?"

"The old man asked me to keep an eye on you, and I figured you'd miss breakfast. I do it all the time, but it's easy to sneak into the storeroom and grab whatever you want when Vergus is busy with his dishes." He winked at me.

I eyed the loaf of bread. "You stole this."

He shrugged. "It's not stealing when you own the place."

"What?"

"The Shadow Master is my grandfather," he replied simply, as if it wasn't a big deal. "Now run along, and try not to get into any more trouble."

I watched him go, clutching the bread to my chest, and then headed back up the stairs to discuss my findings with the others.


"His grandfather?" Sky said incredulously. "But then, if Cadmus is immortal like Echo suspects, does that mean Cahir is too?"

Sky had been up when I'd returned, and I'd told her and Asmund what had happened in the dining hall while we split the loaf of bread between us. It was pretty good, though a little dry without anything to put on it.

"He's definitely strange," I replied. "I can't tell how he feels about us, if he holds Cadmus' views, or if the Master even told him the supposed *truth* about me. He's impossible to read."

"I suggest we keep our guard up around him," Asmund said. "Men like him are good at getting under people's skin and exposing their secrets, without the victim even realizing how or when it happened. Giving us this bread could be a way of building our comfort around him so he can pull the rug out from under us later."

I nodded. "That's exactly what I was thinking. We need to keep him at arm's length and keep our heads down through whatever training he throws at us."

Sky frowned at me. "You want us to pull our punches? I was excited to finally have a real chance to train and duel new opponents."

"I don't want you to pretend to be terrible or anything," I reassured her, "but if we show off, it'll paint a target on our backs that we don't need on top of Cadmus and Cahir's own curiosity. We can't have them guessing who we are if we don't know their true intentions."

Sky sighed, but she knew I had a point. The less we stood out, the better, especially when Asmund didn't know how long his shape-shifting could hold out.

She turned to him. "Have you heard anything from Aramina and Echo yet about Cadmus?"

"Echo is as surprised by his behaviour as we are," Asmund replied, "but she said she'll let us know if she thinks of anything new."

I nodded. "So what's the plan for today?"

"I guess we wait for the so-called second bell and play it by ear from there," Asmund suggested with a shrug. "There's not much else we can do until we figure out the schedule of our lessons and meals. Then we can work around them to dig for more information. Hopefully, the emissary from Appalachia arrives soon, so we can get what we came for and get out of here."

It wasn't long before the bell sounded again, and we rose from our beds to follow the tide of acolytes wherever they were going. We stuck close together, our weapons sheathed at our sides and back as the group of pale grey cloaks descended further into the tower. I realized then that we didn't have cloaks of our own, but maybe they were given at lessons or after certain milestones were met.

Finally, the group of about four dozen young watchmen and women stopped before a metal door at the end of a low ceilinged hall. Then they split seamlessly into two lines against either wall. The distinction between the two was hard to see at first with the cloaks, but then I realized men were on the left and ladies on the right.

I nudged Sky. "Join the other line. Asmund and I are right here if you need us."

She nodded and squeezed my hand before breaking away from us and joining the women. I was pleasantly surprised to see the female warriors almost numbered evenly with the men and hoped that, if nothing else, Sky could find a sense of freedom and belonging at the Shadow Keep.

"All right, listen up, soldiers," a gruff female voice called out from behind us. "Today we are working on sparring with swords. Two laps around the training room to get started, and then break off into pairs. Whoever wins each match will be paired off with another winner until we have our champion. Any questions?"

The woman had walked up between the two lines as she spoke, and now she turned to face us, standing at the door. She had broad shoulders but was of average height, the acolyte beside her standing several inches taller. Her dark brown hair was pulled into a tight bun behind her head, and though she wasn't a beauty by my standards, she was still pretty enough. Light freckles dotted her pale face, and there were dimples in her cheeks.

Across the hall, a female acolyte raised her hand.

"Yes?"

"What do we do if we lose the match while the others are still sparring?"

"Training circuit until you can't move your limbs as recompense for your disappointing performance."

There was a collective groan from everyone, and though I had no idea what the woman was talking about, I knew I didn't want to be a part of it.

"All right," she said again, pushing open the door to the training room and ushering us inside. "Two laps. Let's go."

Asmund, Sky, and I followed the lead of the acolytes around us, running two laps around the room, which was easily sixty paces long and twenty paces wide, and then formed a line in front of our lesson master.

Her eyes scanned each person in the room and then narrowed when she landed on Asmund and me. "All new recruits, step forward," she called out.

We did as we were told, and I was surprised to see two others step out of line as well.

"Welcome to the Shadow Watch," she said. "My name is Hally, and you will address me as such. May Wylla guide your hearts. May you keep your swords sharp and your mind sharper. Come to me once we're done here for your cloaks. Swords are on the far wall if you do not have one. Now, you may all begin."

The acolytes broke off into pairs and began their matches in earnest, ignoring me and Asmund.

I gave him a look. "Guess it's you and me, then."

He grinned. "I'll try to go easy on you."

"And I'll try not to embarass you too much." I lunged at him, and soon the sound of clanking steel was the only thing on my mind as *Ember* and I danced, coming alive with the familiar back and forth of basic swordplay.

# 31
## The Betrayal of Trust

**I bested Asmund, which** didn't surprise either of us, and proceeded to win every duel after until I made it to the final round.

Asmund wasn't too pleased. "So much for keeping our heads down," he muttered as the three of us sat on a bench against the wall.

Hally had called a break before the final match so everyone could catch their breath and have the presence of mind to witness the victory. The losers of the matches had been subject to a grueling rotation of running laps, target practice, and a variety of physical exercises, including lifting jugs of water above their heads and walking around the room.

I could tell Sky was exhausted, but she still gave Asmund an admonishing look. "You can't blame him, really. He could probably best half the room in his sleep without even knowing it. Holding back in the target practice was only doable for me because everything else already killed my arms. I'm not sure I could've held the bow steady if my life depended on it."

Asmund sighed. "There's no complaining about it now, I guess, but you better win after all this trouble. No brother of mine gets second place."

We all laughed, some of the tension of the day fading away, but then a girl approached us and said, "You've been lucky so far, new boy, but your streak won't last. You're up against Senya now, and I can't wait to watch her put you in your place."

She flipped her braided white hair over her shoulder and walked away without another word.

"Nice to meet you too," Sky muttered after her.

"Who is Senya, and what makes her so special?" I wondered aloud.

"She's slated to be the next acolyte to graduate to Ebony or Ivory studies," the boy sitting down the bench from us replied, "and she's arguably the best sword wielder here. No offense, but you're probably doomed."

Hally rang a little bell then, signalling the start of the final match, and I swallowed the lump in my throat. I was torn between keeping a low profile and showing them all exactly what I was capable of.

But then Sky gave me a look and said, "Go prove them wrong."

I smiled. "Oh, don't worry. I intend to."

If the duels had done anything for me, it was boost my confidence, and nothing, not even this girl Senya, could bring me down. I was going to win this competition. Sancia help whoever dared to stand in my way.

Senya had fire in her eyes, that much I knew for certain. I could tell mischief danced behind her cool and calm façade and that I was going to enjoy watching her bravado crumble.

The bell rang, and I let her make the first move, like any good gentleman.

She was lightning fast, but I was too, and I blocked her blow with ease.

I stayed on defense, allowing myself to get a feel for her form, and blocked and dodged as we danced around each other.

After a few minutes of this, she narrowed her eyes and said, "Why don't you fight back, you coward, and give them a proper show?"

*Coward.*

The word stung, and I felt the fire within respond to my sudden ire, but I sent it back, and it sizzled down to ash once more.

"If you insist," I replied, aiming a blow at her head, "I'd be happy to deliver." I grinned as she nearly fell for my feint, just managing to block her shins in time.

Gasps sounded from the audience.

I lunged again, doubling my efforts, and she struggled a minute before matching my pace.

*Interesting*, I thought, *but can you keep it up?*

I tripled the frequency of my attacks, and she stumbled a few times, my blade narrowly missing her skin on several occasions. Her return attacks, however, were just as fierce, my nerve fuelling her fury, and I relished it.

*I have you now.*

As her anger grew, her moves became sloppier, less effective. *Ember* continued to taunt her as I hid the rising smile on my face.

Slash, block, parry, jab, and swing.

The silence around us became deafening.

Lunge, dodge, stab, sidestep, and…

She switched her sword to her right hand.

*What?*

It distracted me for a moment, and I nearly lost the duel right then and there, but I recovered in time to parry her attack before dancing out of reach. She followed, and the intensity of our duel increased again.

It didn't take long for me to realize she'd switched to her better hand, and even less to know she'd made a grave error in doing so, because I'd had the same plan myself.

The switch to my right hand was easy, and the change was immediate.

She handled her shock better than I had but was not skilled enough to stand against my better hand.

The duel lasted one minute more. She blocked a few blows, albeit barely, and then with a simple flick of my wrist, it was over. Her sword fell to the ground with a definitive thud.

The training room exploded into cheers.

Senya seized her fallen sword and stormed out of the room, the girl from earlier disappearing along with her.

Asmund and Sky were by my side in an instant, wrapping their arms around me.

"That's the way!" Sky exclaimed.

"I'll admit," Asmund said, "this is definitely more fun than keeping a low profile."

I laughed and then watched as Hally approached us, beaming.

"Amazing work, acolyte," she said. "If you keep up performances like that, you'll be a full-fledged Ebony or Ivory in no time. Class dismissed."

I bowed my head at her praise, watching as everyone else filed out of the room.

Hally walked over with our new cloaks, handing over mine last. "Welcome to the Shadow Watch," she said. "You've more than earned it."

"I dare say he has," Cahir said from behind me.

I jumped.

*I wish he would* stop *doing that.*

I turned to scowl at him. "Do you take pleasure in removing years from my life?"

He cracked a smile. "Removing life is my job, but yes, yes I do. You're so easy to spook. More Ivory material than Ebony, but I still don't think that's why you're here."

I narrowed my eyes. "I'm sorry?"

"Just speculation, stranger, but I'm sure I'll figure you out someday. Vergus is serving lunch now. You better get some while it's still hot."

I shook my head in confusion as he walked away and then went to join Asmund and Sky again.

•  •  •

Over the next two weeks, the three of us worked hard day in and day out to prove ourselves and keep up our charade. We woke up at the crack of dawn to go for a run out in the cold dark crevice with the other acolytes. Then we had breakfast in the dining hall before sparring lessons around midmorning. Senya was promoted a week after we'd arrived, despite her devastating defeat at my hands.

In the afternoon, we were subjected to academic lectures on strategy and royal etiquette, which was way more complicated than my childhood Sancian lessons. It was all I could do to keep my eyes open and pass our daily tests, even with Asmund whispering the answers in my head.

Cahir was an ever-elusive presence around us, but we never got any answers out of him or any further summons from the Shadow Master himself.

Asmund's magic was growing weaker by the day, and we were all beginning to wonder if the endeavour was a huge waste of time when we finally discovered our first lead—a knight from Icaria's court.

• • •

It was the morning of our sixteenth day, and we were sitting in the dining hall eating our oatmeal when he walked in. He was dressed in silver armour from head to toe, with a black cape hanging from his shoulders. A broadsword with a massive black gemstone was suspended from his hip, and I decided that even *I* would not dare to cross him. He exuded an air of importance, and everyone looked up as he passed by.

The room fell into silence at his arrival, and something tugged at my memory, as if I'd seen him before.

Cahir stood up from his seat a few tables down and said, "Ah, Sir Kallen, to what do we owe the pleasure?" I still didn't know if he ate with the acolytes because he felt like it or because he was keeping an eye on us.

The knight's name sent off warning bells in my head, but I still couldn't place it. Had I faced him in battle before?

"I am seeking an audience with the Shadow Master, but I can see he is not here."

Cahir grinned. "The Master eating breakfast with the Shadow acolytes? I should think he isn't, no."

Sir Kallen scowled. "Do you know where I can find him?"

"What do you wish to discuss?" Cahir asked, dodging the question.

"That is for the Shadow Master's ears only," Sir Kallen replied with the hint of a growl in his tone.

"Oh yes, I forgot," Cahir said. "Our ears are too sensitive for the dark musings of Her Highness."

"Do you know where he is, Master Tremont?" Kallen snapped. "I am not playing your games today."

Cahir grinned, as if claiming a victory over Sir Kallen's emotions, and said, "Of course. Follow me."

The pair left without another word, and conversation resumed in the hall, but you could feel the tension in the air like a drawn bow about to be loosed.

"Who *was* that?" Sky whispered, breaking the silence that hadn't yet lifted from our table. "Why is he here?"

And suddenly, it came to me.

"He was close to King Frost," I replied, keeping my voice low so no one could overhear me. "He fought in the final battle against Summer. He spoke to me when I announced we would spare the Wyllans and turn the kingdom back over to them."

Asmund and Sky's eyes both widened as they realized what I was talking about.

"Will he recognize you?" Asmund asked.

"I don't think we should find out," Sky replied.

"Either way," I butted in, "he has the information we need. We have to infiltrate his meeting with Cadmus. It's the whole reason we're here."

Sky crossed her arms. "And how do you propose we do that exactly? He's heading there as we speak. There's no time to make a plan."

"There's also no time to lose. If we squander this opportunity, all the time we've spent here will have been for nothing. I'm asking the two of you to trust me."

Asmund let out a loud sigh. "We might not have succeeded in killing each other, but you're still going to be the death of me. What are you thinking?"

"Can you shape-shift me into Cahir?"

Ten minutes later, I was navigating the warren of halls towards the Shadow Master's throne room, wearing his grandson's face and praying that Cahir had escorted Sir Kallen to the meeting and then left.

My plan was still to sneak in, but if I was caught, Cadmus would probably let me stay—or at least not be too suspicious of my presence, given my disguise.

Getting in and out of the hall would be the hardest part of the whole operation. The hinges on the door groaned, and Sir Kallen and Cadmus would notice my entrance if they were looking in that direction. I would have one chance to get in undetected, and it was a slim chance at that.

The end of the hall where the black doors stood was dark, all the torches snuffed out. No light would be let into the room when I opened the doors, thank Fidal.

I walked up to them as quietly as I could and wrapped my fingers around the door handle. My heart was in my throat as I pulled it open ever so slightly, to lessen the noise, and peered in.

Sir Kallen stood before the Shadow Master. The single torch in the room lit up one side of his face. The other was cast in shadow, making him look twice as deadly as before. He reminded me of the dark figure, and I shivered with unease. Cahir was nowhere in sight.

I opened the door an inch more.

"You know why I am here," Kallen began.

Cadmus crossed his arms over his chest. "I'm sure I do not."

Two inches.

"The Queen has sent me here to recruit the Shadow Watch."

I stopped short at the mention of the word Queen.

*Has Icaria been crowned already?*

"Has she now?" Cadmus said, arching a pale eyebrow.

I pushed the door open a few more inches.

"With your permission, of course," Kallen replied, his tone implying the exact opposite.

"Of course," the Master repeated, "and what would she be doing with them?"

"They are to join her army. The Queen is in need of another battalion, and from what I've heard of their prowess, the Shadow Watch will be an invaluable addition to our forces."

"And why does the Queen need another battalion?"

A foot.

Sir Kallen didn't look like he wanted to answer that.

Cadmus laughed, a cold and empty sound. "My dear General, I cannot offer my aid if I do not know the objective. The Queen's request is not enough. Why does she need my watchmen?"

Kallen let out a breath. "She is planning an invasion of Summer, as soon as our forces are ready. I estimate in a month's time."

I froze where I was, his words knocking the breath out of me. I had always feared she would retaliate after everything we'd done, had never dared to hope I could bear the burden of her wrath myself.

"An invasion?" Cadmus scoffed. "We are at peace."

The General shrugged. "It's hardly a secret that Her Majesty wants all of Summer dead."

Nausea bubbled up in my stomach.

"Oh yes," Cadmus said, "it's evident that your Queen wants a war, but did she ever consider the people? What if *we* don't want a war? What if that's not the best course of action to take? Look what the last one did to us. Half of Appalachia burned to the ground. We lost our King and our Prince. We've barely found our feet, and now the Queen wants to knock us over again?"

"Whether or not we go to war is of no concern to the people. If my Queen wants a war, she shall have it."

"Your *Queen* does not have the power to decide that," Cadmus shot back. "In fact, she isn't officially Queen yet, is she?"

The General looked chastened. "No," he admitted, "but she will be. The coronation has been moved up to next week, in preparation for the war to come."

"Next week? She's not yet seventeen, let alone eighteen."

"Age does not matter. We need a monarch. We need someone to make decisions."

"No, we need someone to set us straight," the Shadow Master countered, "not an arrogant, temperamental little girl!"

My eyes widened at his tone and his courage to voice his hatred of Icaria in front of her own General.

In a flash, Sir Kallen drew his massive sword and leveled it at Cadmus. "You watch your tongue!" he demanded.

"Or what?" Cadmus said. "You know trying to kill me is more trouble than it's worth. I will say what I like because nobody else in this kingdom has the guts to stand up to tyranny but me. Your Queen is incompetent and unworthy. The Sancian Princess should have killed *her* instead of the boy. Prince Snowdon would have been twice the monarch Icaria could ever be."

Sir Kallen's eyes flashed with anger, and he raised his sword above his head.

Cadmus held up a hand and said, "Make an attempt on my life, General, and your precious Queen will never get the help of my watchmen in this war."

Kallen hesitated but let his sword drop.

"In fact," the Shadow Master went on, "make an attempt on my life, and my Shadow Watch will travel across the border and stand with Summer *against* you."

My jaw dropped.

*What?*

"That would be direct treason," the General said, his voice barely above a whisper in his shock at the Shadow Master's words.

Cadmus laughed. "General, do you know what treason means?"

"Of course I do! Do you take me for a fool?"

"Not at all, but you, of course, only know the second meaning: 'the act of overthrowing the kingdom to which one owes allegiance.' Few people know this now, but the first definition of treason is 'the betrayal of trust.' Thus, it is the Queen who has committed treason. For the people of Winter trusted her to keep them safe, to keep the peace, and she has betrayed that trust. Therefore, General, it is the Queen you should be threatening to execute, not me."

For a second, Sir Kallen didn't speak. He looked flustered, but that turned to anger in seconds. "Enough with the games!" he bellowed. "Will you or will you not give your men over to the Queen?"

"I will not," Cadmus replied calmly. "My men and women have nobler pursuits than fighting in a pointless war. Do you suppose the kingdom will protect itself?"

The General scowled and said, "Then you leave me no choice." He raised his sword once more and plunged it towards the Master's heart.

My own heart skipped a beat, but the sword was still an inch away when the blade bent, as if striking a wall, and snapped in half.

There was a blast of light, and the General was thrown to the ground.

Cadmus shook his head as if he pitied the man. "You are not the first to ignore my warnings, and I dare say you won't be the last. I have survived in this realm for centuries, have been faced with far graver dangers than you and lived to tell the tale. You think you are wise and mighty, but you are nothing but a fool. Run back home to your Queen now. Tell her she won't be receiving my help or the help of the Shadow Watch. Tell her that if she sends anyone to ask again, I will come to Appalachia myself and end her regime before it starts. She will learn to leave the Shadow Keep alone, or she'll have a revolution instead of a war."

"You have no right," the General forced out, his voice raspy as he struggled to breathe after the blow he'd been dealt.

"I have every right! My power exceeds anything the Princess could ever build. It would serve you well, General, to not test me! Now go. Leave my presence! Go crawling back to your Queen, and deliver my message."

The General dragged himself shakily to his feet but made no move to leave.

"Go!" the Master yelled, pointing towards the door.

Towards me.

# 32
# Fight or Flight

**The two stared at** me for a moment in silence, and I was afraid Asmund's magic had worn off, but then Cadmus waved me forward. "Just in time, Cahir," he said, as if the heated argument with Kallen had never even happened. "The General was just leaving."

Sir Kallen scowled at the both of us in turn and then walked towards the door as I ventured into the room, giving him a wide berth.

He stopped with his hand on the door and turned back to face the throne. "You will live to regret your decision," he said. "You and all the people in this Keep. I can promise you that."

Cadmus shook his head. "Regret is for those who live in the past, General. It does not touch me. Now, good day. Be grateful I am allowing you to walk out of here at all, let alone on your own two feet."

He looked at me then, dismissing Sir Kallen without another word or glance in his direction.

I heard the door slam shut behind him as he finally took his leave, and I turned to face the Shadow Master, but before I could say anything, Cadmus cleared his throat and said, "You can come out now, Cahir."

My heart dropped into my boots as the real Cahir stepped out from behind a pillar and walked over to stand at his grandfather's side. "It's not quite like looking in a mirror, is it?" he said to no one in particular as he studied me.

I held up shaky hands and replied, "Look, I can explain."

Cadmus let out a long sigh. "There is no need, my dear boy. I understand your motives, and your quest, and the sheer terror you must be feeling. You do not need to hide who you are anymore. I knew from the day I met you that you were not of this land, and it mattered not."

I blinked. "You mean…"

Cadmus smiled. "I have not talked with a Sancian in a long, long time. It is a wonderful change of pace, I assure you. Now, if you'll drop the illusion, we can discuss what this truth means for you."

I grimaced. "I can't. I'm not a shape-shifter."

It was Cadmus' turn to look confused. "You're not?"

"No, my broth—" I caught myself, deciding not to lie about it. "My *friend* is. He disguised the three of us as Wyllans so we could come here and gather information about Icaria's plans for Summer. I assure you I take no pleasure wearing Cahir's face at all, let alone while he's in the room, but I have no choice. The magic is not mine."

"Very well," Cadmus replied. "We cannot fault you for that. I suppose you'll have sufficient information for your monarch when you return, after what transpired here today. Rest assured I have no desire to turn you over to Icaria, nor do I have any wish to see her upon the throne of Winter for longer than is strictly necessary. Tell the Summer Prince—or King, if he's been crowned already—that the Wyllan people need his help. We have suffered for far too long at the hands of tyrannical monarchs, but we cannot prevail alone.

I took a deep breath and decided to tempt fate even further than I already had. "My name is not Ewen," I replied, "and I am not the Sancian Prince's spy. I *am* Prince Isanfier of Summer, and I swear on my parents' graves to do whatever I can to end Icaria's reign, whatever the cost." Then I lit my hand on fire and watched Cadmus' eyes widen as he realized his prophesied champion was an actual Prince after all.

"By Wylla's wayward heart," he breathed. "The gods are testing you, my boy."

I snuffed out the flames. "You don't even know the half of it."

"Why would you come here alone?" Cahir asked with a frown, finally finding his voice amidst all the revelations. "You must really have a death wish, stranger."

I opened my mouth to reply, but then I felt a jolt of magic go through me.

A few seconds later, I looked up to see Cahir nodding in approval. "See, you *can* do it."

I gave him a look. "Do what?"

"You shape-shifted your face back to your original disguise," he replied.

"That wasn't me," I said, my voice shaking as I realized what had happened.

Either Asmund had finally reached the bottom of his magic reserves, or something had happened to him.

"Asmund's magic must've worn out. And this isn't a disguise," I added, pointing at my face. "I had a disease as an infant, so my skin has no colour, but Asmund and Sky… Everyone is going to know they're Sancian now. I… I have to go."

I turned to run, but Cadmus said, "Let Cahir find them. He knows where he's going, and he holds a position of authority that you do not."

Fear and uncertainty lanced through my heart as I considered Cadmus' words. He was probably right, but could I trust their safety, *Sky's* safety, to a stranger, a Wyllan at that? I looked over in Cahir's direction. "Skiansy is my sister and the only true family I have left. If she doesn't return to me unharmed… Let's just say Winter will no longer have a champion."

He put a fist to his chest, grim understanding in his eyes. "I will value their lives above my own until the three of you are safely on your way back to Summer."

I nodded and watched him go with a tight-lipped expression, all my nerves standing on end as I put Sky and Asmund's lives in his hands. The door shut behind Cahir, and I looked back over at Cadmus, wondering if he could see the sheer terror reflected in my eyes.

But his own gaze widened as he looked at me, staring down into my soul. "You have blue eyes," he said softly.

I stopped short. My instinct was to correct him, but then I realized he was right and that he was the only person who had ever said that to me.

I stared at him. "You… You can see them?"

"As clear as day," he replied, emotion echoing in his voice. "I…" He stopped himself.

"I've been told my whole life that I was crazy," I said. "All my portraits have brown eyes. My sister thinks I was dropped on my head as a baby. Asmund shape-shifted my eyes so I could blend in here… They look blue to you?"

Cadmus smiled, his own eyes watery. "They *are* blue, Isanfier. It turns out I've been waiting for your arrival in more ways than one. I never thought the Prince of Fire would be *you,* but now… It makes more sense than most other things I've encountered in my long life."

I narrowed my eyes, his words circling around in my head with confusion. "What do you mean? What are you talking about? Who… Who am I?"

He gave me a sad look. "I'm afraid I can't tell you. It would destroy the sacrifices made to get you this far and put your life in grave danger, but I know where you can find answers. The palace in Appalachia holds countless secrets, but none more important than your own. Follow the sunflakes, and you will find the truth."

Before I could demand he tell me more and stop speaking in riddles, the door burst open, and Cahir came barrelling in, Sky and Asmund hot on his heels.

"I convinced them the Shadow Master wanted to interrogate them himself," Cahir gasped out, clearly out of breath, "but Hally is demanding she witness the punishment. The three of you need to leave *now*."

Sky rushed over to me, panic clear in her face. "Oh, Isan, I thought we were dead. What is going on? Why did he save us?" She looked over her shoulder at Cahir.

"It's a long story," I replied, "but we can trust them."

"I hope you're right, Isanfier," Asmund said, "because the entire Shadow Watch was tight on our heels, and I don't think I could summon a portal the size of my fist right now."

I looked at Cahir. "What are our options?"

"The halls are no good," he replied, wiping at his brow. "I can't smuggle you out that way, not without having to answer a lot of questions or slaughter my own men." He paused and looked up at Cadmus. "Grandfather?"

Cadmus took a deep breath and met my eyes. "I can take you as far as the Keep entrance, but you are on your own from there." His eyes conveyed a thousand emotions, and though I was angry at his cryptic answers, some part of me understood what he was trying to say—that he was sorry, and that he cared about me on a level I did not yet understand.

"We are grateful for any time you can spare. What do we have to do?"

Cadmus stood up from his throne and walked into the middle of the room. Then he raised his hands, spun them in a wide, perfect circle, and opened a portal as gently as if he was turning over a sheet of paper. "Hold onto each other's hands, and walk slowly," Cadmus said. "Then run like the wind, and don't look back."

Cadmus' portal brought us out into the crevice, in front of the grand doors we'd seen upon our arrival less than a month ago. It seemed surreal that we were leaving already, let alone with the help of the Shadow Master himself.

It was snowing outside, but the midday sun still trickled down into the crevice from high above, giving us enough light to navigate by. A part of me wished for the cover of darkness, but I knew the Shadow Watch would use that to their advantage much more than we ever could.

Asmund and Sky gave me looks of bewilderment as the portal closed behind us, but I shook my head. "No time to explain. We need to flee the city first. Asmund, do you have enough magic left to tell Aramina to be ready?"

He nodded despite his squinted eyes hinting at a brutal headache, and then the two of them chased after me as I started running down the crevice towards the city.

"We'll find a safe place to hide out, and then we'll call on Aramina," I went on while I could still breathe steadily. "It's too dangerous to call her now, and we can't risk running out into the open plains outside Tamise. They'll know it's us, or at least send someone after us to make sure."

"Less talking, more running," Sky chided as she pushed past me, moving her hands around her in a steady rhythm. It looked like she was using her wind to keep the snow from blinding us entirely, pushing it away and behind us to shield our backs.

We were fifty paces down the crevice, running faster than we ever had before, when an arrow shot past my head and landed behind the heel of Sky's boot.

"Fidal's breath," I gasped. "They've found us. Don't slow down."

Sky's wind picked up, whipping snow all around us, and I hoped it would slow our pursuers down or distort their aim, but I also knew the Shadow Watch had been training in these conditions since its conception. They were in their element, and we were vastly outnumbered.

"What's the plan, Isanfier?" Asmund gasped out. He was keeping pace with me, but the physical exertion on top of the magical exhaustion was clearly testing his limits. Sweat beaded on his face, and his breathing was ragged.

"Don't slow down," I replied, wheezing. "Don't get shot."

"Brilliant," Asmund muttered.

After that first shot, the crevice was rife with flying arrows and knives, the Shadow Watch closing the gap between us but not yet hitting their marks.

The three of us ran in a weaving pattern, never staying in the same line of sight for long, Sky redirecting as many arrows as she could, but I could tell we wouldn't make it to safety at this rate. We needed something to buy us time.

So as we rounded the next corner, I yelled at Asmund and Sky to keep going while I stopped to create a diversion. My mind was muddled, and my energy was low, but I managed to throw up a fire wall about three feet thick which would hopefully slow them down.

Then, with half of my brain focused on maintaining the magic, I turned back around and raced after Sky and Asmund.

The crevice straightened out again, and I could see the exit ahead of us, nothing more than a sliver of light a few dozen paces away.

Sky and Asmund were going to reach it in moments.

I could hear cursing behind me and knew the Watchmen had encountered the fire, but I also knew it wouldn't keep them at bay for long. I was sure they'd been trained to tolerate pain and had more than one magic user of their own to counteract my flames or at least dampen their effect.

Still, we were almost there.

I could taste it.

Asmund and Sky crossed into the city and turned right a minute before I did, but it made all the difference because as I tried to do the same, something cold and sharp bit into my right shoulder.

I cried out and stumbled forward, my mind going blank with the sudden pain.

"Isan!" Sky called out.

"Go," Asmund said. "I have him."

"But—"

"Go!"

The world around me was a blur when I felt Asmund slide his arm under my good shoulder and pull me back to my feet, eliciting a hiss from me as fire ripped through my upper body.

"Come on, Isan," Asmund urged. "Don't give up now. I have you. Mina will come get us soon. We're almost there."

My shoulder burned, but I ignored it as we shuffled through the city streets, down alleys, through taverns, and in circles until anyone following us would be hopelessly lost. Tamise was different in the daylight, much brighter and livelier with street markets and wayward children running after each other.

I expected everyone to be gaping in our direction, to gasp at the knife in my flesh and run away in fear when they realized there were Sancians in their midst, but nobody seemed to notice us at all.

"Why is…no one…questioning us?" I ground out through the pain.

"Break my…concentration," Asmund gasped out, "and they soon…will be."

A mix of gratitude and concern washed through me at his words. He had somehow mustered enough magic to restore at least some of his shape-shifting, which was probably the only reason we hadn't been sold out to the Shadow Watch yet, but he was playing a dangerous game. I prayed to Madge herself that his magic wouldn't kill him before we reached safety.

Finally, we came to a stop in the back alleyway of the Viridian Viper, and Asmund eased me down onto the steps before all but collapsing down beside me.

"How bad is it?" I asked, glancing at my shoulder. The blade was still wedged in my flesh, and I could feel it twist when I moved. The pain had faded to a dull ache with the adrenaline of our escape, but now it was rushing back to the forefront of my mind.

"I've seen…worse," Asmund replied.

"I could…say the same," I countered.

"Fidal's breath," Sky gasped from behind us. "The two of you are on death's door, and the best you can think to say is 'I've seen worse'? If we survive this, I'm going to kill you both." She gave Asmund a look that was both reprimand and prayer as she knelt beside me and reached for the hem of my cloak. "Let me see it."

I pulled away from her but winced at the movement. "We don't have time," I ground out through clenched teeth.

"I am not escaping Tamise only to have you drop dead a few minutes later."

Asmund reached over and put a hand on her shoulder. "Isan's right, Sky. We're sitting ducks out here, especially without my magic to keep us hidden. We'll fix him up once we're safely back in the Edgewood, I promise. He's not going to die."

She bit her lip and didn't argue, but I could tell she was on the verge of tears, for both of us. It was the first time I'd noticed the unspoken bond they shared. They hadn't shown much of the courtship between them since we left for Tamise, but it was there, under the surface, and I was happy for them.

We waited for a few minutes that seemed like eons until the air a few paces in front of us started to ripple, and then Aramina stepped out into the alleyway, immediately wrapping her hands around her bare shoulders.

"Sancia's breath, it's *cold* out here," she gasped.

"Oh, thank Fidal you made it," Sky said, running up and throwing her arms around her. "Isan's injured, Asmund overworked himself, and the Shadow Watch could discover us at any moment."

Aramina's eyes widened as she glanced at me. "What happened? Are you okay?"

"Just focus on…keeping that portal stable, Mina," Asmund replied, "and we'll discuss everything when we've…washed our hands of this place. Sky, you first."

Sky looked like she wanted to argue but did as she was told, jumping through the portal without another word.

Asmund dragged me shakily to my feet, and we shuffled in after her, Asmund reaching for Aramina's hand at the last second to make sure she didn't get left behind.

# 33
# Anguish



**Echo's hands were wrung** raw, and she had worn a deep groove in the dirt under her feet by the time Aramina returned with Sky, Asmund, and Isan in tow. Sky came through first, looking tired but none the worse for wear. Then Asmund walked into their small clearing, all but dragging Isan behind him, and Echo held a hand over her mouth to keep from crying out.

Isan looked awful, even paler than usual with his head hanging low and all his weight on Asmund, who looked like he was about to keel over too.

"Fidal's breath, what happened?" Echo gasped, rushing over to the pair.

Aramina closed the portal behind them and then braced herself against a tree with one arm as her other hand shot up to her forehead. "Oh, that hurts a lot," she breathed. "Should have worked on my distance more, I guess."

"Just take a seat, Mina," Sky said, walking over to support her if need be.

Asmund winced as he lowered Isan onto another log. "We were found out and had to flee on foot," he said, finally answering Echo's question. "Isan got a dagger to the shoulder on the way. We didn't have time to stop, and…I don't have enough magic left to heal him. My shape-shifting wore off; that's why we had to go and why Mina had to come get us. I… Goddesses, is the realm supposed to feel like it's spinning?"

A few moments later, he leaned forward in a daze, as if he was about to be sick, and Echo rushed forward to keep him and Isan from falling face forward into the dirt.

"Sky," she called out as the full weight of the pair bore down on her.

Sky rushed over and took Asmund's weight, slowly laying him down on the ground. He'd slipped into unconsciousness but was still breathing.

"Will he be okay?" Sky asked her as she brushed a stray braid out of his eyes, desperately blinking back tears.

"Sleep is the best thing for him right now," Echo assured her, shaking her head at the situation. "By Wylla, it's a wonder you three even survived without…" She trailed off as she felt the wetness on her hand and realized Isan's blood was dripping down her arm as she held him in place.

Her eyes finally landed on the dagger wedged several inches into his shoulder and had to take a deep breath with her eyes closed to maintain her ironclad composure.

"Sky, I need fresh water, clean rags, and woodroot right now," she managed to choke out. "And something to rest Isan's head on."

Sky looked up and sprang into action, spurred on by whatever emotion she saw in Echo's eyes.

Echos didn't look away from the wound until Sky returned with the supplies.

"What do you need me to do?" she asked.

"We need to roll him onto his stomach and keep his head elevated. Then you're going to need to be ready with those rags when I pull this knife out of him. If he loses too much blood…" Echo swallowed hard, not ready to face that possibility, but Sky knew what she meant. She always did.

"Do what…you need to do," Isan choked out through clenched teeth. His entire body was tense, and it pained Echo to look at him, but it was a good sign he was still conscious. He hadn't lost enough blood to impede brain function. Yet.

She took another deep breath. "This won't be pleasant," she told him.

"Never…is," he gasped.

She shook her head. Only he would try to be sarcastic at a time like this. It was one of the things she admired about him. Despite all his pessimism most times, he was calm and collected when circumstances were dire, making everyone around him feel better, even when he was on his deathbed.

*Possible deathbed*, she reminded herself. *I won't let him die.*

Echo and Sky slowly eased Isan onto the ground, propping his head up on a bedroll. Then they cut off his blood-soaked cloak and shirt, careful not to wiggle the knife in the process, until they had a clear view of the wound.

"I'm ready when you are," Sky said as Echo hesitated, afraid to start but more afraid to do nothing.

She wrapped her hand around the knife.

"Wait, let me help," Aramina called out, getting to her feet and stumbling over. "I… I can staunch the blood flow."

"Mina, no," Sky said. "You can barely stand. That portal was almost too much for you."

"Don't care," the girl muttered despite her obvious exhaustion. She made her way over and knelt down opposite Echo, placing her hands against Isan's ribcage. "I'm ready."

Echo knew using more magic could be lethal to Aramina if she wasn't careful, but she also knew that no amount of arguing would stop her. Mina cared about Isan more than she would admit, and Echo had a feeling they had all underestimated the wisp of a girl. She had portalled all the way to Tamise and back in the span of five minutes, and *still* had magic to use.

Echo took another deep breath and said, "On three."

The girls nodded, Aramina bracing herself against Isan and Sky grabbing a fistful of rags.

"One…two…three!"

Echo pulled the dagger out in one clean motion, throwing it aside as Sky moved in to soak up the blood that immediately began to gush from the open wound.

Isan cried out in agony, but Echo ignored how much it tore at her heartstrings as she focused on mulching up the woodroot against the log with the pommel of her own knife. It would disinfect the wound while also serving as a numbing agent so they could stitch him up.

"Sancia's breath," Sky breathed. "That's a lot of blood."

"Keep applying pressure," Echo urged her, "and try not to look at it. I'm almost done with the woodroot."

Sky used several rags before Echo was finished, but Aramina did seem to be helping. When Echo pulled the last rag away to administer the woodroot, the blood flow was a trickle despite the gaping hole in Isan's shoulder.

*Incredible*, Echo thought.

But she didn't know how long it would last, so they had to act fast.

She grabbed the waterskin Sky had filled and poured water gently over Isan's back, washing away some of the bloodstains and giving her a better view. Then she massaged the woodroot into the wound, careful not to prod too deep.

Isan shuddered under her touch but remained quiet, his body no doubt reserving his energy for recovery.

"Do we have any thread for stitches?" Echo asked, realizing she'd forgotten the most crucial part of the whole operation.

"In…my…bag," Aramina managed to get out. "Hurry."

Sky jumped up and returned with the needle and thread a few moments later, handing them silently to Echo.

"Keep Isan still as much as you can," Echo told her as she threaded the needle and disentangled the first several feet.

Sky braced her weight against Isan as Echo leaned forward and started stitching.

Ten minutes later, Isan was unconscious, but the wound was fully stitched. Echo leaned back, exhaustion creeping into her as the tension finally left her body. "He should make it," she declared. "All we can do now is wait."

At her words, Aramina finally lifted her hands from Isan's back and then collapsed against him as if she were a puppet whose strings had been snapped.

"Mina," Sky gasped, reaching for her.

Echo grabbed Sky's arm, shaking her head. "There's nothing you can do. She'll wake up once her body has restored balance between her magic and life. She was essentially giving Isan bits of her own life force to keep him on this side of the grave."

"And if she doesn't wake?" Sky snapped, snatching her arm back. "Isan's going to lose his mind."

"She knew the risk," Echo argued, a little frustration slipping through her calm facade amidst the stress of the situation, "and she made the choice. The consequences are hers to contend with. All we can do is watch over her and pray to the goddesses that she makes it through. Isan too. We've done everything we possibly can."

Sky hung her head, tears glistening in her eyes. "Then why doesn't it feel like enough?"

"Because you're too hard on yourself," Echo told her, keeping her voice gentle this time. "You can't save everyone all the time, and that doesn't make you a bad person. You can only do your best at any given moment, and you have to accept that. You have to believe it's enough. You have to give yourself permission to fail, or the pressure will kill you long before your time."

"You make it sound so easy," Sky sniffed, wiping at her eyes with her grey Shadow Watch cloak. "How are you always so calm?"

Echo laughed. "I'm an excellent actor, and it's anything but easy, I assure you. When I found you in the Edgewood sobbing over Isan's body that day, I offered my help because you needed it, not because I knew I could save him. I'd read lots of books but had never actually performed medical care on another person. Still, I knew I had to try because I was his best chance."

Sky looked taken aback. "You had no idea if he would live?"

Echo shook her head. "No, I didn't, but I did have faith."

"And now…?" Sky asked. "Do you think he'll be okay?"

Echo managed a smile. "I am almost certain of it. We've learned a lot since our first encounter, Sky. Isan is in good hands. Now, we should all get some rest. This situation will inevitably look better tomorrow."

The two of them set about putting the camp back into order—disposing of the rags, washing their hands in the creek, and laying both Asmund and Aramina down by the fire—before they unfurled their own bedrolls and sought sleep for themselves.

Echo laid awake for a long while, her head to the canopy above them, watching the light change as day faded into night.

She'd spoken to Sky with confidence, but it was waning as she laid alone with only her thoughts for company. She knew Isan would live, that much was true, but she didn't know if he would ever be able to properly use his arm again. If Aramina or Asmund had worked on it right away with their magic, they could've repaired the nerve and tissue damage until his shoulder was like new, but now…

Echo feared it would take a healer beyond their skill level to fix what had been broken, and to make matters worse, it was Isan's dominant side. How could he face Icaria with such an injury? She'd been nervous enough about an encounter between the two when he was perfectly healthy.

But like she'd said to Sky, there was nothing much she could do about it. Isan was stubborn, and there was no chance in the realm that he would back down from Icaria now. She didn't know what they'd discovered in Tamise, if anything, but if she knew Isan at all, he already had a plan, and it would likely test her resolve more than anything ever had.

# Part Three: Rage

"Where there is anger, there is always pain underneath."

—Eckhart Tolle

# 34
# Regret and Resolve

Isan

**I woke with a** splitting headache and a second heartbeat in my shoulder, but I was alive—thanks to Echo again, no doubt. I wondered how many more times she would save me before the events of the Curse had all played out, and whether or not I would ever find the means to properly repay her.

Every muscle in my body protested loudly as I struggled into a sitting position and looked around the camp. Asmund and Sky were nowhere to be seen, but Echo was poking at the small campfire, and Aramina laid a few feet away from me, fast asleep.

"Echo?" I mumbled, squinting my eyes against the pounding in my head.

Her head snapped in my direction, and her hands flew to her mouth as she realized I was awake. "Oh, thank Fidal," she gasped. "We were starting to worry. How do you feel?"

I rubbed my temples. "Like somebody dropped the entire Shadow Keep on my skull," I replied.

Echo winced. "That's to be expected. Here, have some water; it'll help." She stood up and walked over, handing me a waterskin as she sat down on the log behind me.

Or at least, she tried to.

My hand refused to close around it, and it tumbled to the ground in front of me, slipping right through my fingers.

"Are you okay?" Echo asked as she bent over to pick it up. "Does it hurt?"

"No," I replied. "I mean, my shoulder is a little sore, but... I, uh... I can't really feel my fingers." I winced as I tried and failed to make a fist with my right hand.

Echo's face fell. "I was afraid you would say that."

She passed me the waterskin again, and I took it with my left hand this time. I sipped the water tentatively, worried it might upset my empty stomach, but it felt so good in my parched throat.

"We did our best," Echo went on, "but Asmund and Aramina didn't have much magic left, and it's too late to heal it now."

I reached out slowly and touched her arm, trying not to think about how difficult the motion was or how I couldn't really feel her skin beneath my hand. "It's okay, Echo. I don't blame you for anything. I'm lucky to be alive. Thank you, again."

"It was mostly thanks to Mina, actually," Echo admitted. "I stitched you up, but she kept you from bleeding out with the last of her reserves. She's been out cold since but should come around soon. I hope."

My heart clenched as I followed Echo's worried gaze, noticing then how still Aramina looked, the rise and fall of her chest the only sign she was still alive. "She shouldn't have done that. I didn't..." Again, the sensation of my numb arm took my breath away. It was going to take a lot of getting used to.

"I tried to stop her, but she has a stubborn streak as long as your own and an unmatched concern for others."

"But will she be okay?" I hated to think of her in pain, because of me, because of anything. It was my fault she'd been forced to come out here and risk her life in the first place.

Echo sighed. "I don't know, but my gut tells me she will. She's strong, Isan."

We sat in relative silence until the sound of crunching undergrowth reached us and a voice said, "Oh good, you're awake. Are you finally going to tell us what happened now?"

"Oh, for Fidal's sake, give him a minute, Az," Sky replied.

I turned to watch Asmund and Sky walk back into the clearing, a pair of rabbits hanging from the snare in Asmund's hand. "Hello to you too."

Sky gave me an apologetic look. "He's just worried about Mina; we *all* are. I'm eager to hear your story too, but *mostly*"— she gave Asmund a sharp look—"I'm happy you're awake."

Asmund sighed as he sat down on the log across from Echo and me. "I'm sorry, I just..." He grimaced. "It should've been me, you know?"

I nodded in understanding. I would feel the same if Sky was in Aramina's shoes after saving Asmund. We both took our jobs as older brothers and protectors seriously—Asmund even more so after learning he'd neglected Mina for far too long.

"She'll be okay," I said, and he merely nodded, as if afraid that voicing his opinion would doom Aramina to the worst outcome.

"If it'll help us all feel a bit better," I went on, "I'll give you the details of my encounter with Sir Kallen and the Shadow Master. I am still not entirely sure how or why it all happened, but I'll tell you what I know."

The three of them nodded.

"I'll start with my first encounter with the Shadow Master, since Echo wasn't there. You were right about him possessing great magic. He had apparently foreseen my arrival in Tamise centuries ago, even had his grandson waiting for me in a tavern. He talked about a prophecy of a Prince of Fire destined to bring the kingdoms together and save Winter from demise. I wanted to dismiss his words, but now I believe his prophecy is connected to the Curse, because if I can kill Icaria, I *can* bring about balance and save Winter. That's the whole point."

Echo's eyes were wide. "If he can see the future, and he's telling the truth about how long he's been waiting for you, then he's an Immortal Magic Wielder. This is an unprecedented discovery, Isan. No one has recorded the existence of such a rare magic user in centuries."

"He hides it well, but I would agree with you. He was also able to sense my magic, deflect a blow from a Wyllan General without drawing a weapon, and create a portal for us to escape through. His magic is extensive.

"And not only that," I went on, "but he could see through Asmund's shape-shifting. He knew we were Sancian, though not who we were, as soon as we arrived, and he said it mattered not to him. In fact, he told General Kallen he would fight with Summer against Winter should he deem it necessary."

Sky and Asmund's expression of shock matched Echo's then.

"You must be joking," Sky said.

I shook my head. "Sir Kallen confirmed our fears about Icaria; she is planning to invade Summer as soon as she is crowned Queen. Sir Kallen asked Cadmus to supply men to the cause, and the Shadow Master all but spit in his face. Then, once Kallen left like a dog with its tail between its legs, the Shadow Master asked me to send a message to the Summer Prince for help in fighting *against* Icaria. He denounced her rule several times."

Echo was at a loss for words as she gaped at me, but Asmund said, "So Summer *is* in danger, then?"

I grimaced. "It's only a matter of time before Icaria attacks. Her coronation is in a week, and knowing her bloodline, she'll march for Summer straight from the ceremony. We have to stop her."

"How?" Echo asked.

I took a deep breath, knowing that none of them were going to like my answer, but it had to be done. The best decisions weren't always the easiest. "I intend to assassinate her at her coronation and put an end to the threat before it's truly begun."

Sky shot to her feet in protest. "Are you out of your mind?"

"What else do you propose we do?" I asked her. "Wait until her armies reach the border and try to keep them at bay then?"

"He has a point, Sky," Asmund butted in. "Under normal circumstances, I would agree with you, but we don't have much of a choice. With the way we left Widonia, we won't have time to muster up a force large enough to make a proper stand. There is no better time for the Wyllans to launch a full-scale attack on Summer than right now. Killing Icaria won't necessarily put a complete stop to the conflict, but it will buy us time, and without a monarch to guide them, Winter won't last long."

"But he can't face her now," Echo argued. "He can't feel his right arm. How will he wield a sword?"

Asmund and Sky looked over at me in concern.

"He what?" Sky said.

"My right arm is numb from the shoulder down," I admitted. There was no use lying or downplaying the truth. They would find out eventually, and it wasn't as if I could pretend everything was normal when so much was at stake. "But I can still fight with my left; I'm nearly as good with it, and I'll have my magic too."

Echo gave me an incredulous look. "That's your plan? Fight with your non-dominant hand against Icaria herself? Have you forgotten she's an expert at swordplay too and can encase you in ice with a single look?"

I sighed. "No, I haven't forgotten, but what choice do we have? Like Asmund said, we can't afford to wait for her army to reach Summer."

"We can't afford to lose you either," she shot back. "If you get killed pursuing this reckless plan, who will stand against her? Who will protect Summer? No offense, Sky."

"None taken," Sky replied, facing me with concerned eyes. "Echo's right. If you can't fight to your full potential… Confronting Icaria at her coronation would be a suicide mission, not an assassination."

"I didn't say I was going alone," I replied. "Surely we can triumph if we face her together?"

Sky sighed. "I don't know, Isan. It's still risky, and just because we're together, doesn't mean it isn't a stupid plan."

"We can't *all* go either," Asmund said. "My magic has recovered but not enough to disguise all of us."

"I was actually thinking you and Mina should head back to Summer," I replied, "to  start rallying forces in case Sky and I don't make it back."

Asmund frowned. "You do realize I have no power without you now, right? Arran is Heir Apparent of Skar, and Father won't listen to either of us, even if Mina and I manage to convince Arran we're telling the truth. Oh, and Sir Quinton wants both of us dead."

"We can't be entirely without allies," I argued. "Aunt Mag will help, and so will some of the knights, Sir Silas especially."

"If they're still alive."

My heart skipped a beat. "Don't say that. They have to be. I couldn't…live with myself if they weren't."

Asmund's expression was grave, but I could read the apology in his eyes. "I hope they're alive too, Isan, I do, but we have to consider all possibilities. This is way bigger than the five of us. The fate of the realm is at stake."

"You think I don't know that?" I asked, a tightness in my chest. "I'm trying to do what I think is best and keep as many of the people I care about safe as I possibly can. Icaria is *my* fight. I'm only letting Sky come because she won't let me go alone. I *need* you in Summer, Asmund. I need to know the kingdom is in good hands."

Oh, how far we'd come in so little time. Months ago, I wouldn't have trusted him with a spoon, but now I was trusting him with the safety and future of my entire kingdom. Yet, I knew in my heart it was the right decision.

I got to my feet and drew my sword as the others looked on in confusion. "Asmund Arrath," I said evenly. "I name you my heir, should Sky and I perish, and until I have children of my own to claim their birthright. This I solemnly swear, with Echo and Skiansy as witnesses." I brought *Ember* down upon his head and then both shoulders while he stared at me in disbelief.

"Isan, are you sure?" he asked.

I nodded. "Watch over our people, Asmund. Make Sancia proud."

He pressed a fist to his chest. "I swear on my mother's grave."

"Then it is done." I reached into my shirt pocket and pulled out the royal Summer seal I carried wherever I went. "If anyone questions your newfound authority, show them this. I'll even write a short letter to verify your claim."

An awkward silence filled the clearing for a few moments until Sky let out a long sigh and said, "So I guess we're doing this, confronting Icaria."

"I know, as far as plans go, that it isn't my brightest," I replied. "I know I'm asking a lot, of all of you, but I only ask because I know of no one else I'd rather have by my side. The fate of the realm rests in *our* hands, and I know of no better people to take up the challenge."

Sky met my eyes. "Then we will stand with you, to whatever end."

I turned to Echo next, and her expression was grave, but finally she said, "I don't like it one bit, but I know I can't stop you. I know you will do whatever it takes to end Icaria and save Summer, but promise me you won't be reckless. Promise me you'll tread with care and take every precaution to return safely."

"I promise to do my best," I replied.

"Then that will have to be enough."

Silence reigned as we all came to terms with the situation, and then Asmund said, "The only problem with this course of action is that we left our horses behind at the Shadow Keep, and you have no other means to travel to Appalachia. You'll never make it on time if you go on foot."

I grimaced as I realized I'd completely neglected to think of that. "I'm assuming you can't portal us there?" I asked him.

He shook his head. "I'm still spent from the prolonged shape-shifting, and I'll need to conserve whatever magic I have left to mask Sky's appearance."

"Any suggestions, then?"

"How much time do we have, Isan?" Sky asked, and I could tell her mind was working towards a solution.

"Sir Kallen said the coronation was a week away when he spoke to Cadmus," I replied. "We've lost a day since then, so we have six days left, and it's a seven-day ride to the capital under good conditions."

Echo nodded in agreement at my calculations.

"It's also a day's ride to Tamise," Sky mused, "but we don't have any horses to get there either... Asmund, can you portal us as far as Tamise and still have enough magic to disguise Isan and I?"

He narrowed his eyebrows. "I should be able to, but what good would that do?"

"We can retrieve our horses," Sky answered, "or steal different ones. You won't have enough magic to portal back, but you can ride your horse back to the camp to meet with Mina before making the return journey to Summer. Isan and I can head for Appalachia straight from Tamise, with only about a six-day ride left to go. It'll be tight, but if we keep the horses at a decent pace during the day, we should be able to make it. It's worth the attempt, anyway."

"That's not a bad idea," Asmund said with an appraising look. He glanced at me. "What do you think?"

"I think it's our only chance, and I'm up for it if you are."

The three of us exchanged a series of questioning looks and then nods of agreement before I stood up and said, "I guess there's no time like the present. Icaria's crowning will wait for no one, least of all us."

Echo shot to her feet after me. "You're leaving *now?*"

I nodded.

"But you just came back," she said. "Your shoulder is still healing, and your body hasn't recovered from your blood loss yet."

"I know, but we don't have a choice. We've discussed it at length already. I know you don't want to see me get hurt, even more than I already am, but nothing you say will change my mind. I'm doing this for you too, you know. If I succeed, Icaria will be gone, and you will be free to roam the realm once more. Don't you want that?"

Her eyes glistened with unshed tears. "Not if it means losing you, losing any of you. I... I wouldn't forgive myself."

My heart clenched at the pain in her words and the fear reflected in her eyes, but Sky reached out to touch her arm before I could say anything.

"This is our choice, Echo," she said. "We *want* to do this for you, for Summer, and for Fidalia. You are not forcing us, and if I *were* to die, the last thing I would want for you to feel is guilt. Death is an inevitable fact of life, and awful things happen to people every day, but it's not always someone's fault. Besides, there are certainly worse ways to go than fighting for the people and future you believe in."

Echo threw her arms around Sky, who held her tight while she started crying into Sky's shoulder. "What did I ever do to deserve friends like you?" she gasped out between sobs.

"You opened your heart and home to us without expecting anything in return," Sky replied, rubbing Echo's back. "If anything, *we* are undeserving of *your* friendship. Sancia's breath, Echo, this isn't goodbye. This isn't the end. And if it is… It was all worth it."

I nodded in agreement. "Sky's right, Echo. I don't regret a single thing, and if I die fighting for your freedom and Summer's, I would consider it an honour."

Echo peeled herself away from Sky and looked at me with watery eyes and tear-stained cheeks. She wasn't smiling, but I could feel joy and gratitude radiating from her, as if she didn't know how to process such deep emotion.

"Likewise," Asmund added before she could say anything. "You may be a Wyllan, and the late King's daughter at that, but you're still family."

She sucked in a shaky breath at his words, likely trying not to sob profusely again, and started wiping at her eyes with the end of her sleeve. "If I live to be a hundred, I don't think I'd ever find a better group of friends," she said finally. "You've reminded me what it means to be alive and how important it is to cherish that. May Fidal go with you, and may your swords be swift when the time is right."

# 35
# To Kill a Queen

**Less than an hour** later, Asmund, Sky, and I stood in the alley behind the Viridian Viper. We had said more tearful goodbyes to Echo, and Asmund had whispered a few words of encouragement into Aramina's ear before making the portal. She was still sound asleep when we left, but Asmund would return soon. They would be safely on their way to Summer by the time Sky and I reached the coronation.

Asmund put a hand to his head as the portal closed behind him, and he leaned into Sky, who immediately put her arm around him.

"Are you okay?" she asked.

"I will be," he said. "Just…give me a second." Thankfully, he had already worked his shape-shifting magic on us before we'd left the Edgewood.

"Promise me you'll take it easy for a while after this," she replied. "I don't want you walking around half dead all the time."

"Only if you promise to come back," he countered.

Sky pursed her lips but said nothing.

I scanned the area for threats while he regained his bearings, my eyes studying the upstairs windows of the tavern and the cobbled street beyond our alley. Flakes of snow were drifting down lazily from the sky, but the day was relatively warm for Winter.

Nothing looked amiss as far as I could tell, but when I turned around to check the makeshift stables, I almost jumped out of my skin.

Cahir smiled at the look on my face and pushed himself off the post he'd been leaning against. "Hello, Prince. The old man said you'd be back."

Asmund and Sky turned to face him too, Sky's hand going to her heart as she gave him a scathing look. "Are you *trying* to kill us?"

"Hardly," Cahir scoffed, "and you wouldn't know it if I did. I've been told you'll be needing your horses back, so I brought them here for you. Figured this would be the first place you'd look."

He gestured behind him, and sure enough, there were our horses tied to the makeshift trough, complete with the same saddlebags we'd brought with us the first time.

"The old man also said you could use this," he added, handing me a weathered piece of parchment paper, folded into a square.

I fumbled for it with my right hand before remembering to switch to my left. Then I unfolded the paper as gently as I could, revealing a detailed map of some kind of...building. I looked up at him. "What is this?"

"A map of the Winter palace. It might come in handy."

I met his eyes, not even bothering to hide the surprise and gratitude in mine. "You have no idea how much this means to us; thank you. I wish there was something we could offer you in return, but we are needed elsewhere, and if we succeed… Well, I think Cadmus and the Shadow Watch will be pleased."

Cahir smiled a knowing smile and said, "You don't have to explain yourself. My grandfather trusts you, and I trust his judgment above my own. You will do what needs to be done, and should you succeed, the realm will be better off for it." He turned on his heel. "Until we meet again."

He started to walk away, but I still had so many questions, so many doubts and fears about what was to come. "Wait!" I called after him, taking a couple steps in his direction. "Does Cadmus already know what will happen? Has he seen it?"

Cahir stopped but took the space of a few breaths before turning back around. "My grandfather has seen many futures, Prince of Fire, and the truth of the matter is that you don't always make it, but in the ones where you do… Let's just say it's worth every sacrifice you make along the way. The future isn't set in stone, so make each step count."

He walked away without another word, and the three of us stared after him in silence for the longest time until Sky cleared her throat and said, "I guess this is where we part ways, then."

Asmund glanced over at her. "I guess it is."

They stared at each other in awkward silence for a long moment before I rolled my eyes and said, "Oh, for the love of Sancia and Wylla, just kiss her already.

It was excruciatingly painful watching the two walk on eggshells around me, and while I realized it was mostly my own doing, I didn't want to experience it any longer. They deserved to be happy, and in the case they didn't see each other again, they deserved a proper goodbye.

They hesitated a second longer, and then Asmund cupped Sky's face in his hands and pulled her to him. She leaned into his touch, and the two of them kissed like no one was watching, like Fidalia was on fire and they were the only two people left in the realm. It was passionate and yet soft, and I knew in my heart then and there that if I didn't bring Sky back, Asmund would never forgive me.

I resolved to not let that happen.

Finally, the two pulled apart, breathless, eyes only for each other.

"Watch over Aramina," Sky said, "and Summer."

"I will," Asmund replied. "You stay safe, and don't let Isan do anything stupid."

Sky grinned.

"I am *right* here," I snapped, only half annoyed.

Asmund glanced over at me. "Oh, sorry, I didn't notice you."

I crossed my arms but said nothing.

Sky walked over to untie the horses, and Asmund held out his hand to me.

We clasped arms, and he said, "Make Summer proud, Isanfier, but don't get yourself killed, okay? I'm not sure I *want* to be King."

I laughed. "It's certainly not as easy as Darkenier always made it look."

He shrugged. "Nothing worth doing ever is."

"Are you ready, Isan?" Sky called from atop her horse. "We need to go before I lose my nerve."

Asmund and I nodded our understanding, and a few moments later, we said our final goodbyes and urged our horses onward—Asmund to the Edgewood and then home, Sky and I to Appalachia and a confrontation with the Princess of Ice.

• • •

We flew like the wind through the bitter plains of Winter, stopping only to eat and sleep, just long enough to maintain our energy. It took me the better part of a day to get used to holding the reins with my left hand, but I didn't fall off my horse, at least. Sky was understandably quiet as we rode, and the days slipped away like seconds. Before I knew it, I could see the spires of the palace in the distance. We had reached Appalachia, and with time to spare, if my calculations were correct.

The Wyllan capital looked different than it had the first time we'd seen it; less menacing somehow. There were huge gaps in the outer city where buildings once stood, now nothing but the faint scent of ash on the wind after falling victim to the fire Lord Arrath had started during the war.

If I closed my eyes, I could still hear the screams of the Wyllans who had died.

A shudder passed through me at the memory, and I hoped the boy I saved was still alive, that he had found peace despite the chaos. I hoped he would also survive whatever consequences were brought on by what I was about to do.

Somewhere in the palace, Icaria was getting ready for her coronation, unaware her breaths were numbered, unaware that the crown might never reach her head.

We tied our horses in a copse of trees outside the city and continued on foot, following a crowd of people flooding in through the open gates. I kept looking over at Sky to make sure Asmund's magic was still working on her appearance, but no one was denied entry or even stopped for questioning on their way in. I supposed it was due to the ceremony, though I did wonder how the guard expected to keep Icaria safe with such a policy.

It felt strange to walk the streets of Appalachia in the daylight with no immediate threat to our lives. Wyllans passed us by without a second glance as they made their way to and from small shops and chased after wayward children. I noticed their movements were more muted than the Sancians of Widonia. There was less laughter in the air, replaced by this lurking tension, as if one wrong move could spell disaster and destroy what little joy they carried with them.

There were snowflake banners strung through alleyways and over windows, becoming more prominent as we neared the palace, and though the festivities weren't obvious, it was clear that it was still a special day. It wasn't often a new Wyllan monarch was crowned. The kingdom had spent nearly five centuries under Lea's reign, and Frost had ruled for several decades before his demise.

I wondered if Icaria was as nervous about filling their shoes as I was about filling my father's someday soon. Did she stay up late thinking about everything that could go wrong, or did she believe it was her birthright through and through, not doubting herself for a second?

We followed a thick crowd of people through the city, the entourage growing by the second as people discovered the time, I assumed, and made haste for the palace. Everyone looked to be dressed in their finest clothes, and I worried it would make our plain cloaks stand out, but nobody seemed to waste a second concerning themselves with the people around them, so I tried to relax.

Finally, we reached the palace square, and though the rest continued on, Sky and I stopped at the base of the entrance staircase, memories resurfacing.

I thought about the battle that had been fought where we stood, of the lives lost and the blood shed. The cobblestones had been painted in red that night, and now not a trace of evidence remained. It was as if nothing had happened, but could the past ever be erased? Sure, the death of my parents had been the fault of one man, but this kingdom had raised him. This kingdom was full of thieves and murderers and power-hungry people like our so-called uncle and Icaria's father.

Even the Shadow Master himself had said Winter was falling apart, and though it pained me to add more blood to their history, I knew I had no other choice. Icaria would not hesitate to kill me if given half a chance. She wouldn't hesitate to kill anyone. I needed to remember that. If I didn't kill her, the entire realm would suffer for it, and Echo would never be free of the Edgewood.

*The Elder twins must fight to the death, and the Younger twins must do the same. The actions required to kill each other will restore the balance and save us all. For if they do not follow their quest, upon their eighteenth birthday, all four shall perish, and our realm shall plunge into chaos.*

Sky reached over and grabbed my good hand, squeezing it just enough to pull me out of my thoughts. "It's time," she said. "Icaria will wait for no one."

I nodded and let her lead the way up the icy stairs, her hand still tight around mine.

A line of guards in dark blue uniforms barred us from entry into the palace, but they simply looked us over once and then moved to let us through. Again, I marvelled at the apparent lack of security but ultimately decided that anything that made our job easier was better thanked than questioned.

The massive ice doors creaked open, inviting us inside, and with a deep breath, we took the final few steps towards an uncertain outcome.

# 36
# Nostalgia



**Appalachia was not how** Echo remembered it. The streets were colder, emptier. The air was tainted with fear, regret, anger, and pain. People were seldom happy there; she knew from experience.

She couldn't remember much of her early childhood, the time she'd spent in the palace, when she and Icaria were still whole, but she remembered how it had felt. She remembered the disappointment in her father's eyes whenever he looked at her; all because she'd dared to find the good in the realm, dared to *become* it.

She'd encouraged her brother's kindness, and he'd followed her lead, much to their father's obvious dismay. Their mother hadn't cared for their schemes either way, as long as they were healthy children, but she often pulled Echo aside to discuss her "bad habits."

All that had changed overnight when their mother was killed in cold blood—by Darkenier, Echo now knew. Something inside Echo had broken that night; she could still remember the pain of it, like someone had shoved an ice stake through her heart. The agony had enveloped every part of her, hardened her, split her in two. One half had frozen, becoming the emotionless ice Princess everyone came to know and expect, and a daughter the King could be proud of. The other half became who she was now, Echo, a lost soul fighting for life in a world darkened by the heinous deeds of the past.

Appalachia had only become more lethal in Echo's absence, and the realization broke what remained of her heart. She wondered if she could've saved it, had their roles been reversed, or if the city was always doomed to such a fate.

In the end, it mattered not. Echo wasn't there to change the past; she was there to change the future and to protect the two people she loved most in the world, Isan and Sky. She'd told them she would remain behind, but this was one battle she would not let them fight alone. So she'd used her invisibility to follow them through Asmund's portal and steal a horse of her own.

Echo had a score to settle with her other half too, and she would be damned if she didn't take responsibility for her own vengeance. She had hidden in the Edgewood for much too long, a coward in disguise while she encouraged others to stand up for themselves. She praised Isan's courage because she lacked it. Icaria stood between Echo and her freedom, and she'd failed to even look for her. She'd spent a decade accepting her fate, refusing to do anything about it, but no longer.

She would meet her other half that day, and she had a feeling neither one of them would walk away unscathed.

# 37
# Hatred at First Sight



**We followed the crowd** through the palace halls and up to the throne room.

Once more, I was struck by the cold beauty of the palace—the flawless ice floors and walls, the arched ceilings and doors, and its open spaces. I would have again marvelled at the throne room if not for what had happened there.

When I closed my eyes, I could still see the blood soaking the throne and Frost's head lying unmoving on the dais. I could still see my own men covered in frost and hear Sky's screams as she froze to death.

I shuddered; that room was a place of death and sorrow. Both of the past monarchs of Winter had died there, and if everything went according to plan, Icaria would too.

It occurred to me then that the Curse had the potential to end the royal families of both kingdoms. Sky had survived Snowdon, so Summer was now safe, but Winter was still vulnerable, and Icaria was the last of her line.

A multitude had gathered to witness Icaria's coronation, filling the throne room to the brim, and I tried not to think of the way my men had been crowded together like this, frozen as King Frost looked on with pride and glee. There was scarcely room to breathe, but a circle of space about three feet wide was left around the dais.

I had a feeling that anyone who stepped foot in that space would be quickly neutralized, accident or not.

Everyone talked idly amongst themselves until a few notes of music weaved through the chatter, growing in volume until they overpowered the voices, and we were hushed into silence. The lilting notes of the harp were soft and yet regal, signalling the start of the ceremony and the entry of its most critical player.

My whole body tensed in anticipation, and I felt Sky's hand grab my good shoulder as our enemy walked into the room.

A pair of flutes joined the harp in a heartstopping crescendo, and Icaria entered the throne room from the antechamber, followed by a train of royal advisors. Even I had to admit her outfit was stunning: a blue and white dress with huge crystallized snowflakes, and a cape that glittered in the afternoon sun streaming through the windows as if carved from ice. On her head sat a silver tiara with miniature sapphires.

She looked so much like Echo it was hard to believe it was truly a different person walking through the room. I know I'd been told the two looked identical, but to hear it and actually see it were two different things. They had the same face, down to even the most miniscule detail, and their hair was even the same length, though Icaria's hung in a single braid down her back.

If it had truly been Echo, I would've commented on how beautiful she looked, but Icaria wore the ensemble as if she'd been born with it, and I immediately felt resentment towards her. It wasn't hate, because I had nothing but stories to base my impression of her on, but she walked with such arrogance in her stride and expression that I couldn't help comparing her to the loathsome people I'd encountered in my short life.

Distaste rolled off her in waves, as if she despised the very thought of sharing air with the people in this room, as if she couldn't believe they needed something as dull as a ceremony anyway. She reminded me of Sir Quinton, Lord Arrath, and past Asmund all wrapped into one, with the lethality of her father lurking beneath the surface. On first impression, I wouldn't have guessed she and Snowdon were related at all, let alone twins. The only thing they shared was their shock of white hair and ice blue eyes like their father.

Icaria didn't spare a glance toward the waiting crowd, her eyes only for the throne as she walked up and knelt before it. The music faded into nothing, and silence fell over the room.

I gave Sky the signal, and she nodded.

One of the royal advisors came to stand in front of Icaria and began the ceremonial speech, opening with a dramatic account of the royal family's history. I started weaving through the crowd, pausing every few steps to alleviate suspicion.

Behind me, Sky nocked an arrow to her bow beneath her cloak, preparing to intervene if something went wrong.

The official droned on and on, while I slipped closer and closer to where Icaria knelt.

# 38
# Evanescence

*Echo*

**To say the palace** greeted Echo with open arms would be a lie.

Her anxiety increased the closer she drew, and it became a struggle to put one foot in front of the other. She held the hood of her cloak tight around her face as she trudged on.

The fear wasn't the only thing weighing her down; it had been six days since she'd left the Edgewood, and the effects of her absence were already tearing her apart. Every breath was pained, her limbs felt heavy, and her heartbeat was weakening.

If she didn't start the journey back to the Edgewood today, she wouldn't make it in time. She would dissolve into thin air, leaving nothing but a whisper behind as proof she was ever there in the first place. She would cease to exist, and Icaria would be more powerful than ever. She couldn't let that happen.

Echo tried her best to quicken her pace as she entered the Royal Square where the palace's grand staircase and main entrance awaited her. The square stood empty. A wayward wind swirled stray snowflakes around, but there wasn't a soul in sight, save for the two guards holding vigil at the doors.

Everyone who was anyone was already inside, watching the coronation with bated breath. Few would dare to miss the crowning of a Wyllan monarch; the results could be…bloody. Isan and Sky could be moments away from ensuring it was.

The thought of them in proximity to Icaria… It pained Echo, but she couldn't have stopped them. They were more stubborn than anyone she knew, and once their minds were set, they would do whatever it took to follow through. But this time, they wouldn't be alone.

This time, Echo would join the fight, and together, they would end Icaria's reign before it even began.

Echo stole into the palace through a back entrance near the stables. She remembered using it with Snowdon back when they were too young to leave the palace but did it anyway.

The entrance remained as unguarded as ever, and she slipped in without a trace, allowing her invisibility to take over. The transition was effortless, aided by the fact that she was already fading. Becoming visible again would be the real challenge. If she waited too long before switching back, she wouldn't be able to. She would be stuck until she returned to the Edgewood.

*I have to do this quickly.*

She headed towards the throne room, searching her brain for the memory of how to get there. It had been ages since she'd sifted through those.

It was difficult to find what she wanted but not impossible.

*Hold on, guys. I'm coming.*

# 39
# Challenge and Capture



**Finally, the official picked** up the royal Winter crown and spoke a few words. I stood at the front of the crowd, a couple paces away from Icaria. She took off her tiara and placed it on the vacant pillow. The official raised his voice and asked if anybody objected to the succession.

There was silence. The question was merely protocol. No one would ever defy a Wyllan royal's right to the throne, but the momentary pause was my window of opportunity. However, as I wrapped my good hand around *Ember*'s hilt and made to step forward, someone beat me to it.

"For Wylla!" a voice screamed from somewhere inside the throne room, and then a large axe came hurtling towards the dias, aimed perfectly at Icaria's head.

I held my breath, thinking it was all over for her, but the weapon reached the circle of space around the dias and bounced back into the crowd, sending people screaming and dropping to the ground for cover.

My eyes were as round as saucers as I watched the air around the dias ripple like water and then settle into nothing again. I reached forward with my left hand, into the empty space in front of me, but my hand stopped as if hitting an invisible wall, and I realized what had happened. Someone had built a magical barrier around the Princess.

That's why they didn't question people at the entrance or demand we remove our weapons. No one could touch her, and that meant my plan was worse than useless; it was suicidal.

I was still processing this information when a woman with long brown hair was thrown up into the air by some unseen force, as if an invisible giant was holding her up by her boot. She flailed around but to no avail.

"Put me down!" she screamed as people looked on in silent horror, too afraid to come to her rescue. "You have no right!"

On the dais, Icaria stood up and turned around, as calm and collected as if the woman had invited her to tea instead of making an attempt on her life, but the truth was in her eyes, where a cold darkness raged.

"Threatening a monarch is treason," Icaria said simply. "Surely you know this? Surely you know I have every right to do with you as I please. The moment that axe left your hand, your life was no longer yours to claim."

The woman turned her torso to look Icaria dead in the eyes. "You're a tyrant, just like your father and Queen Lea before him. Your family is a poison in this land, and I am better off dead than continuing to suffer in it."

Icaria smiled with lethal grace. "As you wish."

I felt the magic in the room change, and before everyone's eyes, the rebel woman turned to ice, the process almost instant. Then the Magic Wielder holding her up must have let go because she dropped to the ground and shattered into a million pieces on the ice floor. The people around her scattered, throwing their hands over their faces to protect themselves from flying ice shards.

I watched it all unfold with horror and dread.

She'd killed the woman with one look, reduced her to nothing but a whisper in the wind. Echo had warned us of her magical prowess, but this...

A rock settled in the pit of my stomach as doubt and fear rushed through me.

*How can I ever hope to bring her down?*

It was a question that lurked in the back of my mind at all times, this persistent feeling of inadequacy, this unrelenting fear of not being enough. Who was I when compared to her might, her magic, her skill? Echo had bested me in one-on-one combat more than once, and now it was clear that Icaria had a grasp on her own magic that few people could boast. She'd had ten years to hone it, after all, while I'd only had a couple months.

*What was I thinking?*

My racing thoughts were interrupted by Icaria's voice, calling out an order to her entourage. "Guards, search everyone here for weapons and confiscate them. If anyone resists, take them to the dungeon for questioning later. When I return in ten minutes, I expect this ceremony to finish without a second's pause, or all of you will be frozen statues for me to break. Understood?"

There was a murmur of agreement, and I stiffened. If they searched me, I was done for. I could no more hand over *Ember* than sacrifice my life, and even worse, somebody was likely to recognize me for who I truly was. My unnaturally pale skin may have helped me blend in, but it didn't disguise my face. At least Sky looked nothing like herself.

Icaria turned and walked away without another word, leaving all of us to our fate, and I knew I couldn't stick around to watch the chaos unfold. Already, people were in uproar, arguing with the guards and shoving each other out of the way.

I was jostled to and fro as I made my way through the crowd, searching for Sky's cloak amidst the sea of black and blue.

Panic set in as the seconds raced by with no sign of her and the circle of guards around us tightened.

*Where* is *she?*

Had she fled or been captured already? Was I too late?

And then I saw her, standing close to the entrance, as if ready to flee but clearly waiting for me. Our eyes met across the room, but the relief in them for finding me faded to fear as I faintly felt a hand close around my bad shoulder.

"And where do you think you're going?" the person asked me.

I whirled around, unsheathing my sword in the same motion, but the guard was fast, jumping away from my strike so the blade merely slid against the front of his uniform.

"I found another one," he called out as he drew his own sword, and though I was good, a whole group of them soon surrounded me.

I was assessing my best options for counterattack when another man walked up, a lazy grin on his face. He raised a hand towards me and a second later, *Ember* was torn out of my grasp.

*He's another Magic Wielder.*

I stared at him dumbfounded as the guards converged on me, pinning my arms behind my back. My right shoulder twinged painfully with the rough movement, and a fuzzy feeling travelled down my arm all the way to my fingers. I wanted to fight but knew it was useless and didn't want to call any more attention to myself than I already had. If Icaria confronted me in that state, I didn't stand a chance.

So I let the Wyllan knights restrain me, let the Magic Wielder toss my precious sword to the man that had questioned me, and let another knight drag me out of the room without further ceremony.

Sky's terrified eyes met mine before the doors closed behind us.

# 40
# Reunion

*Echo*

**Echo stepped out of** the spiral staircase into a familiar room. The antechamber was empty, but she could tell it wouldn't remain so for long. She could hear screams coming from the throne room. Something had happened.

*Am I too late?* Please, *let them be okay…*

Someone flew into the room in a flash of blue and white, nearly tripping over their ensemble.

"Oh, for Wylla's sake!" they cried out as they steadied themselves.

Echo stiffened, recognizing the voice as her own, though she was fairly certain she'd never used that tone before.

"The nerve of these people," Icaria spat, and Echo flinched despite herself. "To attempt an assassination on *my* coronation day? To think they could even come close to accomplishing such a task? *Fools.*"

Echo's heart fell. An attempted assassination? Had Sky and Isan failed? Were they discovered? Where were they now?

A pair of guards came rushing in after Icaria. "Your Highness! Are you all right?"

One moved as if to comfort her, but she threw up a hand over her shoulder to stop him, and the temperature in the room dropped. "I'm *fine*. Don't touch me."

The guard stopped short and crossed his arms over his chest instead. "The men are detaining any other suspicious attendees as we speak. The ceremony will be able to commence again soon, I assure you."

Icaria scowled but said nothing, her fists clenching and unclenching as she attempted to rein in her emotions.

It was so strange for Echo to watch her, as if looking in a mirror that was distorted somehow. Icaria's hair was in a long braid, and she was dressed in much finer clothes than Echo, but they had the same face, the same eyes, though Icaria's were much angrier, almost soulless.

Echo didn't know how to proceed. She had come all this way, with intense purpose, but now… It was almost too simple, to just close the distance between them and run Icaria through.

Would it hurt, she wondered, to kill this piece of herself? Would she feel the sword in her own skin, her own heart? Where did one of them end and the other begin?

Echo had raced to the palace fuelled by anger and fear, but now a heavy sadness was settling in her bones as she contemplated her next move, as she realized she would never be the same after this, no matter what happened.

Could a person forgive themselves for killing a part of them, even if that part was lost?

A single tear ran down Echo's cheek as she drew *Silence* and took a step forward.

Across the room, Icaria suddenly straightened, her eyes looking distant for a moment before they settled right on Echo. She knew Icaria couldn't see her, but for a second, it was as if they had locked eyes anyway.

"You," Icaria gasped.

Fear gripped Echo's heart again, sinking into her veins as she lost control of her magic and blinked into sight.

# 41
## Magic and Monsters

*Isan*

**The sounds in the** throne room grew distant as the pair of guards dragged me down the hall, my heart racing with dread as I tried to think of a way out.

The good news was that Icaria still didn't know I was here, but that wouldn't last long, not once she was crowned and paid a visit to the traitors in the dungeon. If I allowed them to take me that far, I would be doomed. I needed to make my escape before then.

*You'll only get one shot at this,* I reminded myself. *Make it count.*

I waited until we were a good distance from the throne room before I made my first move, pulling my arm up and elbowing the guard on my left.

He swore and cuffed me up the side of the head. "Try that again," he said slowly, "and I'll cut off your hands. Her Majesty will definitely kill you, but she'll watch you suffer first, and I'd be happy to contribute to the show."

I bristled. "I'd like to see you try."

The guard stopped us short. "Oh, would you? You think you can stand up to the might of the Royal Winter Guard? You like your odds?"

I shrugged, appraising him and the other man. "What? Two against one? Frankly, I fear for *your* odds."

The guard raised his hand to hit me again, but this time, I was ready.

I ducked the blow, and his momentum knocked him off balance, dividing his focus enough that I could pull my arm out of his grip. Then I kicked him hard in the ribs, sending him crashing to the floor.

The other guard, not fazed at all by my escape attempt, smashed his armoured arm across my face. The force of it knocked my head back and sent me reeling. I would have fallen over if he hadn't been holding me still.

The first man had recovered from my blow and regained his feet by then.

He stalked over to me with his fist clenched and shaking. "Filthy, traitorous scum," he spat, his eyes full of rage and disgust. "I would finish you off right now if it wasn't against Her Majesty's orders. Still, she won't mind if I give you a beating."

He wore a vicious smile as he swung at me, but I reached up and grabbed his arm, stopping his fist an inch away from my cheek. He stared at me in disbelief, and it was my turn to smile.

"I am no traitorous scum," I said calmly. Though anger radiated through me, I was in control. "I am Prince Isanfier of Summer, and they will remember me long after you're dead and gone."

Then I let the fire go.

It leapt up gladly, licking every inch of my skin with its tongues of flame.

The guard holding my other arm yelled out a curse and let go.

The first guard screamed horrible shrieks of agony as my hand began to burn his skin. He tried to pull away, but I gripped his arm tighter. His screams grew worse the longer I held on, and a few moments later, his eyes rolled back into his head as he went limp, the pain too much to bear while conscious.

I released his arm, and he collapsed in a smoking heap on the floor, sending tendrils of steam into the air as the heat collided with the ice beneath. The burn I'd dealt him was undoubtedly fatal. His skin was charred black and burned down to the bone. The blood leaking out of the wound boiled and hissed.

I wiped my hand on his coat before drawing *Ember* out of his belt and slitting his throat with her flaming blade. Blood spewed, and I heard a choking noise behind me. The second guard was on his knees, retching, a look of shock and terror in his eyes.

I put him out of his misery with a swift blow to the back of his neck, severing his head from his body.

I was about to sheath my sword and make my escape down the hall when I caught a glimpse of my reflection in the mirror-like wall of ice beside me.

I looked like a creature out of a child's nightmare.

Red and orange flames flickered along my skin, making my hair stand on end and illuminating the blood staining my hand. My black cloak looked like a burning coal, though the flames did not eat away at it. But it was my eyes that truly struck fear into my heart. They were dead eyes, eyes unfazed by the havoc I had wrought, eyes with pupils of blue rimmed with fire.

In that moment, I saw myself for what I was.

A monster.

The fire snuffed itself out in the blink of an eye, returning me to my normal self, but I couldn't forget what lurked beneath, couldn't shake the feeling that it was my fate to become the villain of my story.

# 42
# Loyalty

*Echo*

**For a moment, Icaria** and Echo stared at each other in silence, like a pair of rabbits cornered by a wolf, though in this case they were each both prey and victim.

The guards were looking in Echo's direction with disgust. "How dare you shape-shift into the monarch of Winter?" one demanded to know, brandishing his sword. "Show your true form at once, Magic Wielder, before we relieve you of your head."

Echo said nothing, facing him with her own sword held high.

Icaria held up a hand towards her guards. "Your assumption has merit, but is unfortunately inaccurate. This one is not a shape-shifter."

The second guard gave Icaria a confused look. "Is she a replica of yourself?"

"Almost, but not quite," Icaria replied, glancing in their direction. "Though I will say the resemblance is uncanny, we are not alike. Leave us."

The guards' eyes widened further. "Your Highness?"

"I said *leave us*," Icaria snapped, the temperature in the room plummeting even further, though Echo barely noticed the chill.

The men left the room without another word, and Icaria turned back to Echo, her eyes boring into what remained of Echo's soul, of *their* soul.

"So we meet at last," Icaria said. "I used to believe my visions of you were dreams, nightmares even, but it became harder to dismiss them as the years wore on, and now here you are. I'm surprised you would leave your sanctuary. I'm surprised you'd have the gall to show your face here, *sister.*"

Echo scoffed. *Sister.* It was so far from the truth as to be comical. "We both know what I am, Icaria," she replied, "but I believe you are in denial of *who* I am."

*I am you. You are me. We are* one, *and we can never escape that horrid truth.*

"You *dare* speak to me in such a manner?" Icaria demanded to know.

"Yes, I dare, because no one else will. They're too afraid of you, too afraid of dying, but I know death waits for us all, and I'd rather die fighting tyranny than exist in a world ruled by the likes of you."

"You have fire, but I doubt it'll last for long."

"I wouldn't underestimate me. I have powerful friends and the gift of light, of hope—something you will never possess."

It was Icaria's turn to scoff. "Hope. What is hope but a false promise made by gods who forsook us long ago? Look around you, *sister;* hope does not exist. This world was sewn in darkness, and its roots run black with the blood of innocents. As for your friends... If you're talking about the Sancians, then you're more delusional than I thought. Have you forgotten that Summer is the enemy? Have you forgotten what they've done to us, how they invaded our kingdom and razed everything we built to the ground? They're evil."

"They were misguided, same as you," Echo replied. "We've all been brainwashed into believing the other is entirely evil when that is simply not true."

"Summer killed our father," Icaria shot back, an untold fury in her eyes.

Echo shrugged. "I do not mourn him."

Icaria narrowed her eyes. "Well, what about the Princess, then? She killed Snowdon; surely *she* should pay for what she's done? Surely you *care* about our brother?"

"I think about him everyday, Icaria," Echo replied, unshed tears beginning to blur her vision, "but mostly I think about how you and Father treated him ever since you and I separated. I think about how lost and lonely he became, how he probably saw death as the only escape he would ever get. What happened to being best friends for life? I know when I used to swear that to him, I meant it with every fibre of my soul. What happened to it being him and us against the realm?"

Icaria gave Echo a severe look. "I grew up," she snapped, "and Snowdon...didn't."

"No," Echo countered. "No, you grew *afraid*. You grew complacent. You started bending to our father's will because it was easier, and you watched as Snowdon broke under the weight of it. You *let* our father break him." A single tear ran down Echo's cheek. "And I want to *hate* you for it, but I can't, because that would mean hating myself."

Icaria said nothing, and Echo wiped at her eyes with her free hand.

"Invading Summer will not fix what is broken in Winter," Echo went on.

"And I suppose you think killing me will?" Icaria asked, venom in her voice.

Echo shook her head. "I think it'll make life even worse, but even forests need to be reduced to ash sometimes in order to come back stronger, and the realm demands your death for its survival. Isan wanted to be the one to do it, but it's my responsibility, my burden."

"You're talking about the Curse," Icaria said.

The two of them could now see their breath in the air, it was so cold in the room.

Echo nodded. "You know one of you must die. I'm sure you also know I can't let it be him."

Icaria scowled. "Why? What makes his life worth more than mine? What makes him the better choice, and what makes you think you have the right to decide that?"

"I can feel it in whatever is left of my soul," Echo replied. "We are tainted, broken, nothing without each other. Isan is so much more. The realm needs him."

"Does the realm need him, *sister*, or do you need him? There's a difference, you know, or are your eyes so clouded by your own desire that you can't see straight?"

Before Echo could reply, there was a commotion outside, and a stranger entered the room, dragging someone kicking and screaming behind him. The man was familiar only in the way he looked at Echo with the same disdain as Icaria had, but Echo didn't recognize the girl he dumped on the floor until her eyes took in the blue dress, identical to the one she had given Sky for the coronation.

Sky's unnatural blue eyes met Echo's, and the two of them stared at each other in disbelief.

"Ah," the man said, "so the two of you know each other, then. Excellent."

"What is the meaning of this, Henrik?" Icaria spat out, as if she barely tolerated the man's presence.

"I brought you a gift, Your Highness," he replied. "I caught this one trying to steal in here and finish you off. I thought you'd want to see to her disposal personally." He kicked Sky in the ribs, and she curled up, wincing.

"No!" Echo cried out, lunging towards the man. "Don't touch her!"

"Echo, no," Sky choked out, reaching for her, but it was too late.

Echo felt her feet leave the floor and all the air rush out of her as she was slammed against the far wall of the room, ice shards shaking free of the ceiling and hurtling down around her.

She waited for the impact of her own fall, but it never came, and she realized she was being suspended in mid-air, an unseen strength continuing to force her against the wall as her body protested in agony.

Across the room, Henrik grinned at her, a manic glee in his eyes, and Echo realized two truths. One, he was a Magic Wielder, and two, he was enjoying her pain.

"Leave her alone, you sadistic monster," Sky growled, and then Henrik leapt back in pain as Sky slashed at his ankle with a knife.

Echo dropped to the floor and made to crawl towards Sky, but then Icaria screamed out, "Enough!"

Echo jerked to a halt, realizing she was frozen to the spot and that Icaria had done the same with Henrik and Sky.

Icaria stalked towards Sky and crouched down, grabbing her chin in one hand. Sky flinched and tried to jerk away, but Icaria's grip was like iron. "The magic concealing your true nature is strong, but I know who you are. There are only two people who would risk their lives to save the Missing One, and if *you're* here…" Icaria smiled. "Then your brother can't be far."

Echo's heart clenched.

*No.*

Icaria dropped Sky's chin and stood up. "Henrik, call off the ceremony, and have the guard search the palace high and low for the Summer Prince. No one leaves until we find him and I put him in the grave where he belongs. When you're done, I'll need your assistance with these two. I have a plan for my sister, and as for the Summer Princess... Well, she needs to pay for her crimes against the Winter Crown."

"If you so much as touch me, Isan will kill you," Sky snapped. "He will *burn* your kingdom to the ground."

Icaria's eyes lit up. "Oh, I'm counting on it, dear Princess. Your screams will lead him to his death, and if all goes according to plan, I won't even need to lift a finger."

# 43
## Safe Haven

*Isan*

**I left the dead** guards where they lay and found an alcove to hide in while I assessed my situation. Sky and I had been separated, the throne room wasn't a viable place for an assassination, and the guards were on high alert. It was only a matter of time before they discovered the bodies I had left behind and came after me too.

We were losing the element of surprise, but I knew deep down that if I abandoned the mission now, Summer would be done for. If I hoped to save my kingdom, I needed to stay the course. I needed to find Sky, regroup, and then forge ahead.

I reached into the inside pocket of my cloak and pulled out the weathered map Cadmus had given us, scanning through the various rooms and labels until I came across the one with *safe haven* scribbled furiously across it. I would wait there for Sky like we'd promised, and if she didn't show…

I swallowed hard.

I'd give her a good amount of time, but if she didn't turn up, I'd have to devise a new plan and face Icaria alone. Some part of me knew that was my destiny, but it didn't lessen the sting or the guilt of leaving Sky to fend for herself.

*There is no other way,* I told myself.

Then I memorized the first several turns on the map before shoving it back in my pocket, getting to my feet, and setting off.

The next ten minutes were full of tension and more close calls than I'd care to admit. I was dodging guards left and right, and it soon became clear they were searching for someone. Whether or not that person was me, I couldn't be sure, but I couldn't afford to be discovered either.

It took me twice as long as it should've to reach the hall Cadmus had indicated on the map, having to backtrack or wait for guards to pass by before I could move on. My nerves were frayed at the edges when I finally turned the right corner.

According to the map, the safe haven was in the middle of the hall on the left, but when I reached the spot where the door should be, there was only a wall. In fact, there were no doors in that hall at all.

I walked up and down the hall twice to make sure, but I couldn't see any doors or any cracks in the stone that would indicate a hidden one.

The map had lied.

A sudden anger and feeling of betrayal gripped me, and I slammed my fist into the wall, only to stumble when my hand passed through the stones. My hope reignited.

I slid my boot experimentally against the wall and watched as it slipped through as well, there one second and gone the next. Not giving myself any more time to question it, I closed my eyes and stepped through the wall into a hidden stone hallway, right where the map said the safe haven would be.

Not thirty seconds later, a group of guards rushed past. I felt the wind of their passage and watched as their eyes skipped right over my hiding place. I marvelled at the magic that kept the hall hidden; from the outside it looked like a wall, but from the inside, you could look right through. It was clever work, but there was the question of why.

Why was there a secret hall in the Winter palace? How many people knew of this so-called safe haven? What were they trying to hide?

In search of answers, I headed down the corridor.

The hall was dark and gloomy, no torches lighting the way, but for once, it wasn't cold. I was in a part of the castle not cloaked in ice, and the stone was a lot warmer and more welcoming.

There were no corridors branching off the hidden hall, and I kept going straight until I came to a spiral staircase. Still without a torch, I climbed up, letting the darkness swallow me further.

There was an alcove at the top of the stairs and a wooden door set into an archway, a symbol carved into its centre. I grabbed hold of the door's handle and pulled, but it didn't budge. I soon found that pushing did nothing either. With few other obvious options, I looked closer at the carving on the door's face.

What I saw gave me pause. It was a combination of two familiar symbols—the Sun of Summer and the Snowflake of Winter.

*What are they doing together?*

I placed my hand against the symbol absentmindedly and heard a sound like a soft sigh as the door opened. It must have been locked with magic, though I didn't yet know what I had done to make it grant me access. Three torches sprang to life, illuminating the space as I stepped into the room and closed the door.

I was stunned when I realized I'd entered a royal bedroom preserved by time. There was a four-poster bed, two wardrobes, a desk, two bookcases, and a few other furnishings. Everything was covered in a thick layer of dust, and I didn't doubt I was the first person to visit the place in decades.

Yet, it was the decorations that stunned me more—a combination of both Sancian and Wyllan. One side of the room was painted an ice blue, the other deep green. The sun and snowflake symbols were carved into the bedposts, and the sheets were also blue and green. Long-dead Summer ivy clung to the bookcase, and a lifeless Wisteria vine sat in a vase next to a Winter Aster. It was a peculiar sight, and I didn't know what to make of it.

Why would there be so much Sancian decoration in the Winter palace? Had there been a member of the Winter family who had sympathized with us or had a treasonous affair?

Still trying to process the whole situation, I drifted over to the bookcase and browsed through the titles. A few of them were Wyllan history books, but the majority were fiction novels set in Winter.

Then I came across a rather unusual title: *Sunflake*. It was a word I would use to describe the weird symbol on the door, and a realization hit me.

*Follow the sunflakes, and you will find the truth.*

That was what Cadmus had said when he told me he could see my blue eyes, when he alluded to knowing something about me that I didn't.

Curious and hoping for answers, I pulled the book off the shelf. As I slid it out, I heard a faint click, and the bookcase moved. I stepped back as it swung outward, revealing another hidden room. The place was one mystery after another.

Cautious, I stepped through the doorway, placing the book in the doorjamb in case the door swung shut and tried to trap me in there. The second room was small, about three paces squared, but it held four bookshelves, a window, and another desk. The shelves were home to countless Sancian books in addition to more Wyllan ones. The window didn't have much of a view, so I moved on to the desk.

There was an odd assortment of materials scattered across its surface—parchment, quills, empty ink wells, envelopes, seals, a dagger, earrings, and a ring. I picked up the dagger. Carved into its blade was the name *Regret*. The weapon was deeply personal with a name like that, and I set it down.

I took a closer look at the desk itself and found it had two little drawers on either side. One had the symbol of the sun, the other had the snowflake. I opened the sun-marked drawer first, placing my hand against the symbol to unlock it and pulling the drawer open. Inside the drawer was a plain white envelope with a name written on it.

*Skiansy.*

My heart stopped.

How could that be? Why was Sky's name on an envelope in a hidden room in the Winter palace? Was this another one of Icaria's traps?

I didn't know what to think, but I knew what I had to do next.

Holding my breath, I unlocked the other drawer and opened it to reveal another plain white envelope. My name was scrawled across it in the same handwriting.

Terror gripped me, and I dropped both the envelopes on the desk, taking a series of deep breaths to calm myself.

What was I so afraid of? They were just names.

*They could be for another Isan and Sky,* I thought, but deep down, I knew the truth.

I reached for the envelope with my name and tore it open. With my heart in my throat, I began to read.

Dear Isanfier,

    If you are reading this now, it means your father and I are dead...

*What? It can't be.*

I flipped through the pages of the letter until I found the closing signature, and my breath caught, a single tear running down my cheek. I read it three times to make sure I wasn't imagining it, but no, it was the truth.

The letter was from my mother.

# 44

Dear Isanfier,

If you are reading this now, it means your father and I are dead. It also means you reached the Winter palace and our plan has worked. And now, since both of these have come to pass and you are undoubtedly older, it is time you were told the whole story, every last detail.

This is the story your father and I would have told you, had we lived to watch you grow up. This is the story of our lives and love and sacrifice. You don't have to read it all at once, as I'm sure it will be a lot to take in, but I encourage you to finish it eventually, no matter the horrible truths it may reveal.

It is difficult to know where to start, but I suppose the sooner I tear out the arrow, the faster you can heal. Your father grew up as the Crown Prince of Summer, like you will—or like you did, I suppose. However, I grew up not as Areevia but as Princess Shiveera of Winter, second in line to the throne after my mother Princess Alice.

I know that truth will be a harsh one to swallow, but you deserve to hear it. I am Wyllan, and you are half Wyllan, and what I need to say—before you rip this letter to shreds and call me a traitor—is that there is nothing wrong with either of us because of it.

We may think the realm is divided evenly between Summer and Winter, good and evil, life and death, but nothing is ever that simple, my love. Corruption exists everywhere, and it is up to those who crave peace to fight for and protect it.

Still, when I was born, it was a difficult time to be a Wyllan, and a royal one at that. Queen Lea was still at the peak of her power, and I was looked upon by the townsfolk in both disdain and fear.

I wanted to be free of my family's reputation and dark expectations. I wanted to walk down the streets of a city without people cowering in fear or throwing food and rocks at my face. I wanted to leave that wretched land behind, but more than that, I wanted the hatred between Summer and Winter to end.

Once, after a particularly nasty argument with my mother, I fled to the Edgewood, to escape the burden of my family's legacy, and that's where I met your father. He also used the Edgewood as an escape from the strict life of royalty he led as an only child and heir to the throne. I craved freedom, and he craved adventure. Your father saved me from drowning in the murk, and that day in the Edgewood, he became my first friend. We knew we were from different worlds, but we didn't care. Oaden shared my hope that we could work together. And so we did.


       Annually, we met in the safety of the Edgewood for a month. Then, as our annual visit became monthly forays, we realized we were falling for each other, and it was time to reveal our royal identities.

We told each other the truth on the same night and agreed that it didn't matter.

We revealed many truths about ourselves that night. I told him I was a Gifted Immortal, that I could lower the temperature until someone froze to death, and it terrified me. He, in turn, told me he was a Magic Wielder and had so much raw power he thought he might explode.

When it was time for me to return home, Oaden came with me, disguising himself as a Wyllan with his magic—white hair, pale skin, and blue eyes. He was absolutely convincing, even fooling the Queen. Oaden wove a false life story that my family ate up, in which he had three older brothers, a sister, and a drunken merchant father back in his hometown of Desolace. He even gave a false name, Eznar, which matched the harsh sounds used in the bitter southeastern city. He amazed me.

For five years, your father made regular visits to see me, and neither one of our families suspected a thing. We often discussed our plans of running away together. He wanted to renounce his throne and escape to one of the less populated Summer cities, but I told him I wanted to meet and be a part of his family.

So eventually, we made plans to go to Widonia.

My family talked of marriage, and my mother was especially excited. I hated to disappoint her, but I couldn't stay in the palace anymore, not when our history was streaked with so much blood. The last straw for me was when I learned what had actually happened to my grandparents and great aunt Rielle. How they'd killed each other in cold blood.

We left at the end of that month, 589.

Oaden changed my appearance before we arrived in Widonia, giving me dark hair, brown eyes, and colour to my complexion. We also morphed my name into Areevia.

Shiveera. Iveera. Areevi. Areevia.

Oaden's father, Foren, and grandmother, Queen Katheryn, welcomed me into the family with open arms. It was the first time I felt like I belonged somewhere.

Oaden asked me to marry him at the end of that month, but we didn't get to celebrate because the next day, the Queen was found dead with a letter that read:

*I've been waiting forever to kill this miserable wretch, and you'll never find me.*

I would know the handwriting anywhere. It was Queen Lea's, but we couldn't tell anyone because we couldn't reveal my true identity. I despised my family even more.

Two years after Foren succeeded the Summer throne, your father and I finally married. It was a bright spot in what had become a dreary Sancian life, and after, the people were happier.

Several years later, when Summer was stable and wouldn't miss us, Oaden and I visited Winter. We became Eznar and Shiveera once again and travelled to Tamise to visit my brother, Darkenier. He was the only one who knew where I was, but he wouldn't tell a soul, for he hated our family even more than I did.

It had been a decade since I'd last seen him, since I'd been in Winter, and I had come to ask him how our family was. As much as they upset me and I didn't agree with their actions, I still cared about them and couldn't shake the guilt I felt for leaving them.

The news he gave me was devastating. He told me our parents were dead. Our mother had accidentally killed our father and was so guilt-ridden afterwards that she killed herself. If that wasn't painful enough, there were three other members of our family who had died that year: our great uncle Izarr, his son Blizzard, and Queen Lea herself.

Lea had killed Blizzard in sudden punishment for killing Meadow—Oaden's mother—twenty years previously.

Then Izarr—enraged at his son's murder—confronted her, and they fought to the death, dealing each other killing blows before they died.

Blizzard's son, Frost, had taken the throne.

I couldn't believe my parents' deaths, but the brutal murders of the other three did not surprise me in the least. They were cruel Wyllan people, and I was fortunate I had left when I had. Darkenier agreed with me and asked to escape with us back to Summer. Oaden changed his appearance, and he took up residence in Mensden. We didn't hear from him for several years.

Meanwhile, Oaden's father passed away, and we became King and Queen of Summer.


Now, Isan, this is the part where you're not going to believe a word I say, but I swear on my own grave this is the truth. Your father and I are going to be murdered, and my brother is going to do it.

It is such a cruel misfortune that even in Summer, my own blood will be my downfall, but my brother cannot let go of the past. He cannot live with the thought of being forgotten, of letting our distant cousin take the throne when it should've been him.

Once upon a time, it should've been me, but I suppose that, too, would've led to my demise eventually. I digress. My brother is going to kill us to take our throne, and then someday, he will go after Frost as well. He will stop at nothing to conquer the entire realm, but he will fall short, simply because you and your sister exist.

You will be his downfall, but if you are reading this letter now, you already know that. Whatever my brother has said, Isan, we _are_ proud of you.

I know you must be wondering why we didn't do something to prevent our deaths if we knew they were coming, but the truth is we need to die. If we don't, then Darkenier won't become King, Frost won't meet his end on my brother's sword, and you won't have the chance to bring peace to the kingdoms as the Prince of Fire.

There is an old Wyllan prophecy that speaks of a champion who will rise to save the realm, and that champion is you, Isan. You and your sister will put an end to the feud that has raged between us for too long. After Frost's death, you are the only one left with the right to the Winter throne. Sky is too, but you will be accepted with your pale skin and blue eyes.

You don't have to accept, nor do you have to make the decision right now, but this is our only hope for peace. With you on the throne of Winter, Skiansy will become Queen of Summer, and your bond will ensure peace. I'm certain Lady Magnolia raised you as loyal siblings who would never declare war on each other. You two will be the truce, and our salvation.

I know this is a lot to take in, and I never meant to pressure you, but you needed to know this.

There are a few more points I need to add.

You and Skiansy will be Gifted Immortals, blessed with two Gifts each due to your split heritage between the kingdoms. You have the Gifts of ice and fire. Isanfier: Ice and Fire. Your sister has the Gifts of air and water. Skiansy: Sky and Sea. If you work on these powers, they will help you defend your kingdoms.

Also, you are both half Sancian and half Wyllan, but you share more of my blood than Skiansy does. This is why your skin is pale and your eyes are blue, though others will see your eyes as brown. Your father disguised them soon after you were born to keep you safe, but when you come into your Wyllan powers, when you accept who you are, your true self will be revealed to all.

I have faith in you, in you both. <u>We</u> have faith in you. We know the two of you will do great deeds, even though we won't be there to see them, and I wish...

There, the paper was blotchy with ink smears, and I could tell she was crying as she struggled to finish her letter. I understood, for I was crying too.

...I wish I could see them. I wish we had more time, but this is my last night, and I know it's selfish, but I don't want to die. I want to be there for your first ball, your first duel, your first magic lesson...

I want to be there for you, but dying is the best thing I can do for you, and for all of Fidalia. It is the most selfless sacrifice. You might not agree, but one day, you'll understand.

After today, even though we'll be gone, you'll never be alone. All you need to do is look to the stars, and we'll be there, smiling down at you. One day, we might see each other again, but until then, your place is here.

I know it's not much, but I love you, Isanfier, and I miss you already. I never wanted to say goodbye. So I didn't. You weren't old enough to remember them, so I'll repeat my last words to you:

My Isanfier, always know that you are loved, and never give up, for anything worth fighting for is worth the wait and what it takes to get there.

Love always,
Mama

# 45
# A Final Duel

**My head was reeling** from the information I had received. Part of me expected to be angry, but I was actually relieved. Being half Wyllan was a shock, yet it made a great deal of sense. It was the reason why my eyes were blue and my skin was pale, not some unexplained childhood disease. It was the reason why I enjoyed wearing black and why I looked good in it. It was why the cold in Winter didn't bother me the way it should.

It explained so much that I couldn't believe I hadn't seen it sooner. My parents had worked hard to hide it well, but one detail still nagged at me. How was my father's magic still working, twelve years after his death, and why could I see through it? Asmund was still young, but he had exhausted his magic after only two weeks of disguising the three of us. I suppose there could still be aspects of magic we didn't know about, but if what my mother said was true, my father's power was reaching beyond the grave.

Not that I wasn't grateful.

What would Summer have done if they'd known? What would Winter have done? Both kingdoms would have been out for my blood, Sky's too. What we were, what my parents did, would be considered wrong by everyone.

I admired them. Their relationship showed their strength and wisdom, but most importantly, it showed their love. It takes a lot to marry a member of your mortal enemy's family. They risked everything to be together, and in the end, they died—for the kingdom, for the realm, for Sky and I.

Another tear fell down my cheek. "I won't let you down," I whispered to the room. "I promise. Your sacrifice will not be in vain."

The letter strengthened my resolve, and I felt like I could do anything. Killing Icaria did not seem impossible anymore. It didn't matter how many guards stood in my way. I would cut them all down to get to her.

*I will end her regime today.*

I pocketed both of the letters and left the hidden room, picking up *Sunflake* on my way through. I pulled the bookcase door shut behind me and replaced the book on its shelf, locking away the room once again. It hit me then, as I looked around once more, that I was standing in my parents' bedroom, the one they'd shared as Eznar and Shiveera.

The room had been their safe haven within the Winter court. Tears threatened again as I thought about the times they'd spent, as I realized my father's magic had saved my life, and as I wondered whether my mother would be devastated by the dust and dead flowers...

I fled the room before I started sobbing, leaving the past alone in its resting place amongst the dust.

• • •

The corridor outside the secret hall was quiet. Absent were the sounds of footsteps, clanking armour, and yells. I was safe. I still had no idea where Icaria was, but I remembered how Sky had said she'd felt an invisible pull towards Snowdon, even when he wasn't in her sight.

I closed my eyes and searched the palace for the invisible thread that connected us, the same way I had searched for my magic when I was first training my fire. It took a few minutes, but finally, I sensed it, a faint pull in my core.

A scream tore through the silence of the palace before I could follow the pull, grating my eardrums and tearing at something in my soul.

*Sancia's breath, what was that?*

I took a few more steps before it sounded again, and this time I made out a name somewhere within the agony of the person's voice.

*Isan.*

The person was calling for me, and a shiver made its way down my spine as I realized who was screaming.

Either Icaria had captured Sky, or she had someone in her court who was adept at mimicking voices. Both options were clearly traps, but they would ultimately lead me to Icaria, and if it really *was* Sky, I couldn't leave her to die.

Sky screamed again, and I set off, following her voice and the pull of Icaria deeper into the palace.


The pull eventually led me to an elaborate ballroom with a polished marble floor and a dozen crystal chandeliers. Sky's screams were a near-constant echo in my eardrums, and it took everything in me not to give in and run to wherever she was being held, but I knew I needed to be cautious now more than ever.

I fumbled with my sword for a second before entering the room, instinctually reaching for the blade with my right hand before catching myself. My fingers could still grip the hilt, but it felt weak, and the weight of the weapon pulled painfully on my shoulder.

I held *Ember* high in my left hand as I stepped into the light of the room, and across the space, Icaria stalked into view through another entrance, right hand wrapped around her own sword. She was dressed all in black, from her boots to her tunic—a far cry from the splendour of her ceremony.

She walked with purpose towards me, stopping a mere five paces away, her stance screaming anger and violence. I knew immediately that this duel would be slow and bloody.

Her lips rose in the slightest hint of a smile as she said, "I thought I might find you here."

Even her voice sounded exactly like Echo's, but I tried not to let that get under my skin.

"Yes, I suppose you did," I replied with my own smile, "what with my sister's screams reverberating through the walls. Your people are skilled in their magic, if she's not actually here, like I suspect. If that is her... I will burn this palace to the ground and feed your men to the Wolven."

Icaria shrugged. "She said you would say that, but I am not afraid. If she could fall so easily, your odds can't be much better."

I grinned. "The last person to tell me my odds didn't live long."

She lunged for me without another word.

I spun away and swung *Ember* back at her in one fluid motion, expecting her to lose her balance by my quick move and go sprawling, but as I looked back over at her, I realized the lunge had been a feint. It was I who was caught off guard as she came from behind.

I whirled to face her at the last second, not entirely escaping her sword. There was a sharp stinging in my cheek, and my right hand went to touch it as my left wielded *Ember* against Icaria, keeping her from doing any more damage. My hand came back wet and bloody.

She'd cut me.

My heart skipped a beat; we weren't even a minute into the duel, and she'd cut me.

Apprehension filled me, but failure wasn't an option. Sky's life depended on me, and so did the fate of Fidalia. I couldn't afford to fail.

I pressed on, ignoring the dull pain in my cheek, while she came at me with a ferocity unparalleled by any foe I'd faced before. She was fearsome, fear*less*, and lethal. There was an untold rage in her, and at first, I thought I could use that to my advantage, but even in her anger, she was in control. It did not distract her from the task at hand.

I admired her ability, as someone who struggled with such emotion, but it was frustrating. I had nothing to work with, and she blocked or dodged everything I threw at her. Of course, I did the same with her moves, but she did it with apparent ease, whereas I struggled. She was lightning quick—there and gone in an instant before I had taken a full breath. Each jab missed me by a hair's breadth, her sword whirring past, the wind of its passage giving me goose bumps.

In turn, my sword never came anywhere near her, and not for lack of trying.

I swung at her, feinting to the left, then towards the chest, and arcing around to her left side, which would've been exposed had she fallen for either of the feints.

Naturally, she hadn't, and her sword was already aimed at *my* exposed left.

Cursing, I barely managed to block her. My arm at an odd angle, I could only minimize the damage, and the tip of the blade ran across my wrist. I held my breath to keep from screaming as the cut burned like a line of fire.

Anger surged through me, blocking the pain as I attacked her with a fiery vengeance, doing my best to ignore the searing pain running through my good arm. I didn't bother to feint; I went for it, hacking at her multiple times in quick succession. She struggled a bit but still blocked every single one. The fire was near the surface, and I was tempted to let it go, but I was afraid that once I used my powers, she would too. I couldn't deal with magic *and* her impeccable swordplay. It would be too overwhelming.

Still, I kept that option open, stoking the flames as Icaria continued to beat me at my own game.

"Why don't you give up?" she sneered at me a few minutes later.

I hadn't expected her to say something, and it distracted me. My reward was a slash to my leg. It was shallow but hurt like hell, and I bit my tongue to keep from swearing.

Icaria laughed. "You're pathetic. You should accept my certain victory."

Gritting my teeth against the pain, I replied, "I don't think so. I will *not* let you win. I will not stop until one of us is dead, so quit toying with me."

"Fine, I won't, then." She smiled an evil little smile and raised her sword again, probably assuming I was on my last legs, what with the injury to my sword arm.

Little did she know, I had switched my sword to my right hand behind my back. Echo had said it was a bad idea, but desperate times called for desperate measures, and I didn't know what else I could do.

The fight began again in earnest. There was a flicker of unease in her eyes when she noticed I'd switched hands, but it was too late for her to recalculate as she was already swinging her sword at me.

I dodged it way before it reached me and slashed at her left. The movement tore out all of my stitches, and my eyes watered with the pain, but it was worth it, as I'd managed to open up a gash on her upper arm.

I had practically won the battle right there. Even with the blood trickling down both of my arms and the throbbing pain I was experiencing, she was doomed. I had the luxury of having gone through a lot worse before and was able to ignore the pain. It also helped that my right arm was still mostly numb.

Icaria, on the other hand, was having trouble coping with her single injury. Her eyes were pinched, her breathing had turned ragged, and her stiff expression hinted at clenched teeth.

I smiled.

*Good. She* should *suffer. I'm doing my fair share.*

We pressed on despite the pain, but it was clear I had gained the upper hand.

I dodged each blow almost before she decided to make them, and she barely blocked my blade at all, sustaining a few shallow slices to her side and leg. It wasn't long before worry reflected in her eyes. She could sense as well as I could that the battle was coming to an end, and she wasn't winning.

In desperation, she attacked faster, and I blocked every move with little effort.

Fear was making her sloppy, making her slow. It was the reason she made a mistake.

She fell for one of my feints and was unable to prevent me from twisting her sword out of her grip.

Time slowed as it flew through the air, clattering to the ground halfway across the room.

Icaria froze, realizing she wouldn't get to it in time to save herself, and I lunged forward, knocking her feet out from under her.

She hit the floor hard, her head cracking against the marble.

I wiped the sweat from my brow and walked towards her prone form.

When I reached her, she looked up at me in a daze, as if noticing I was there for the first time, but then terror raced into her eyes as I raised *Ember* up above her, holding the hilt in both hands.

"Isan?" she gasped out, a strange familiarity in her voice. "No, it's m—"

I plunged the blade into her heart before she could finish, not willing to give her the satisfaction of voicing her final words, and her eyes widened in horror and shock. I saw something in them—a flicker of hope, maybe—before they closed forever.

I pulled my sword out of her chest, and she crumpled, lifeless, to the floor.

I let out a huge shuddering breath as I straightened back up and wiped *Ember*'s blade on my already bloody pants. I had done it. I had killed Icaria.

*I am free of the Curse!*

So why did it still feel like I was carrying a huge weight on my shoulders?

*I must be in shock.*

I studied Icaria's lifeless body lying at my feet as my heart rate slowed and my limbs stopped shaking. She looked peaceful in death; with all her anger gone, she could be sleeping. She also resembled Echo even more, if that was possible. With her eyes closed, one could see how truly alike they were—the hair, the face, the...

The way she was fading before my eyes.

I blinked my eyes to clear them, but there was no denying what I was seeing. Icaria's body was disappearing, her legs already gone up to her knees. Why would Icaria be doing that? Why would she be...turning invisible?

I couldn't catch my breath as my mind put two and two together, coming to an awful conclusion. I felt dizzy, and the whole room tilted. I thought I might faint, but I had to make sure.

*It has to be a coincidence. It has to…*

Fear gripped me, and I stumbled across the marble floor to the sword she'd left abandoned a few feet away. I picked it up and read the inscription on the familiar blade: *Silence.*

My heart stopped.

It was Echo's sword, which meant….

She didn't just look like Echo, she *was* Echo. I had killed Echo, thinking she was Icaria.

*Sancia's breath…*

Echo was dead.

Echo, who had saved my life more times than I could count, despite barely knowing me. Echo, who had taught me everything I knew about magic and reminded me daily that my power was only a curse if I let it be. Echo, who had danced with me in the glade like there was no kingdom rivalry standing between us.

Echo, my friend, my teacher, my *hope* for a better realm and a better future.

My breath caught painfully in my lungs as I sank to the floor, despair pulling me down. I glanced back over to Echo in time to watch her fade away into nothing, with only an echo remaining as proof that she had ever been there at all.

*She's gone,* a voice told me.

"No," I whispered, my tears falling to the marble as guilt flooded me.

I killed her. I *killed* her.

"I'm sorry, Echo," I whispered to the empty room. "I'm so sorry…"

Maniacal laughter sounded behind me, and I raised my tear-stained face to see the real Icaria standing in the doorway.

"You!" I said, sheathing Echo's sword on my other side. "You did this!"

She laughed again. "No, you did this to yourself; I merely showed you the way."

Anger burned inside me, but I pushed it down. "You're a monster," I seethed.

"Hardly," she said.

"Then how do you explain this twisted turn of events?"

She smiled. "Well, when my *dear* sister showed up in my palace, she decided to pay me a visit. We had a little chat, and I was about to kill her when *your* sister showed up. I realized you couldn't be too far behind, so I decided I'd have a little fun before putting you out of your misery. Breaking someone's spirit is so much more rewarding than merely breaking their neck." Wickedness danced in her eyes as she circled me, and I couldn't believe I had mistaken Echo for her. "I have a few Magic Wielders in my court, and I had one of them manipulate her for me. She was nothing but a puppet on a string, though I'll let you in on a secret: she was fighting it the whole time, even succeeded in the end, but it was too late. The damage was done."

"You're sick," I spat.

"I'm strategic," she countered. "Now one of your allies is dead, I still have your beloved sister in my grasp, and you're injured. Finishing you off should be simple."

It was my turn to laugh.

She looked at me sharply. "What do you find amusing?"

"Your plan was flawed," I told her.

"How so?"

The fire raged up in me, and I let it. "You didn't kill me when you had the chance."

# 46
# Fighting Fire with Fire

**I flicked my hands** out, and they were aflame in an instant.

All other emotions left me until only anger remained, beating in rhythm with one thought: *Icaria is going to die.*

Her eyes widened in shock at my fire. "How did…?"

"You're not the only Gifted one," I replied as I threw a fireball at her.

Cursing, she retaliated with an icicle.

The projectiles met halfway, the fire melting the ice and the water putting out the fire.

"Is that all you have, then?" she asked, laughing breathlessly.

"No," I replied, my smile vicious, "and don't worry, I won't hold back."

I gave her no time to answer. I was done with the games, done playing around. I was changing the rules. I let my anger over Echo's death fuel my attack as I drew *Ember*, lighting the blade on fire and swinging her at Icaria despite the excruciating pain in my shoulder.

She tried to block it with an icicle, but it melted on contact, and she had to jump away at the last second, fire singing the ends of her hair. She drew her own sword and held it in front of her, as if she was ready for anything. I could read the letters carved along its length in the light of my own blade.

*Ruin.*

*How fitting.*

I swung my sword at her in dizzying patterns, becoming an unpredictable whirl of motion, impossible to track.

Icaria struggled to keep up, but she still insisted on goading me.

"What do you suppose Skiansy will think of you now, killing Echo and all?"

I gritted my teeth and said, "Shut up," as anger roared inside me. The flames on *Ember* rose higher in response.

Icaria took an involuntary step back and was silent as she struggled to block my sword and avoid its flames.

Whenever there was a lull in the duel, I felt my sorrow trying to claw its way back into me, but then I called upon the image of Icaria laughing over Echo's dead body, and the door to all other emotion slammed shut. I used my anger as a shield against the pain Echo's death brought me. I wielded it through my sword and through my fingertips as I hurled fireballs at Icaria with my free hand. She dodged them when she could and deflected them with ice when she couldn't.

However, even with the ferocity of my attack, she remained unscathed. This served to anger me more, and the rage inside me built, making my moves faster, stronger, and harder to block.

Despite my rage, I remained in control—a first for me. My movements were sure, sharp, and lethal. Icaria blocked every single one. The anger stretched inside me like a bowstring nearing its limit.

Just when I thought I couldn't take anymore, Sky's scream rang out through the palace once again, sounding closer than it ever had.

Icaria smiled.

The string of anger snapped inside me, and the fire rose. Icaria lunged for me, and I exploded into a pillar of light and heat.

The force of the blast threw Icaria across the room, and she crashed to the floor, letting out a scream of her own. I hoped she'd broken something.

I closed my eyes in dreaded anticipation; the last time I'd set my entire body on fire unintentionally, I had fallen unconscious. I stood there, waiting for the nausea, the dizziness, and for my senses to fade, but a few moments passed and I felt none of it, only this strange calm I'd never experienced before. My anger was gone, but the fire still raged.

I opened my eyes and found Icaria staring at me from her side of the room. She stood, but her right arm hung at an awkward angle, as if the bone was no longer properly attached to the shoulder blade. She was furious at the injury. I could tell by the burning in her eyes that she was livid, aching for my blood as she stared at me—no, *into* me.

She stared into me and smiled.

I felt pressure in my chest, and then…

I was encased in ice.

I screamed, panic-stricken, but I was still alive, and I soon realized why. The fire that covered me was melting the ice. However, the melted ice had put out the fire, and I didn't realize how exposed that left me until I looked at Icaria, smiling at my victory to see her smiling back.

*Why is she smiling? I thwarted her!*

Then I felt pressure in my chest and swore. I scrambled to bring the fire up again and felt the cold fingers of Icaria's ice when the fire seared my skin. I had saved myself but only just.

Icaria smiled at me once more, this time only in challenge. She was enjoying this, I realized. She could've pulled that trick on me from the start and ended the duel, but she didn't want to just win; she wanted to see how far I would bend before I broke.

We circled each other as we fought a battle of magic and wits, though I could only defend, not attack. I didn't have *time* to attack, for as soon as my fire melted the ice, she threw more at me, and I fought to bring my magic up again in time. It was an endless cycle, and it was getting us nowhere.

If neither one of us slipped up, we could go on like that indefinitely. Fire and ice were no match for each other; they cancelled each other out. You had to fight fire with fire. Or in this case, ice with ice. Then I remembered what my mother had said in her letter, that I supposedly had the gift of both fire *and* ice.

*Could I…?*

It would give me a fighting chance, but I couldn't call on it on a whim. Gifts required a severe emotional trigger and then a significant amount of training to control. It had taken me weeks to master my fire. I didn't have that long. In fact, I was pretty sure my existence was now measured in minutes.

I lost myself in the fight again, maintaining my fire the only thought on my mind. It was hard work, and I felt my strength waning. I felt dizzy, staggering every couple of steps, and once, when I called on my fire, it flickered and went out. I had never been more terrified than in that moment, thinking, *This is it*, but after the flicker, the fire had come back in full force.

Yet, the lapse had put me on edge. I was exhausted, not to mention bloody and broken. The blood had dried on my cheek, left wrist, and leg. The pain from those wounds had faded, dwarfed by the much worse pain in my shoulder.

I was experiencing the consequences of using my right arm. The blood from my torn stitches had dried, making my movements stiff, and if I so much as twitched it, a searing pain shot through my shoulder and nerves to my spine. My shoulder pain contributed greatly to the nausea and dizziness, and if I concentrated on it too hard, my vision blurred. I couldn't go on like this much longer.

As I continued the fight, I surveyed my options and came to a dire conclusion. I would have to fake a surrender and hope Icaria was unhinged enough to *not* kill me on the spot. If she threw me in the dungeons or something, I would have another chance to fight or escape. I could come up with another plan.

It was a desperate idea, but I knew I couldn't win the way things were going. I waited until I was at my weakest to put my plan into action, fighting on for five more minutes. Then my resolve withered.

*I need to stop, to rest, to…*

It happened while I was distracted by my exhaustion.

Icaria pulled out her sword and slashed at my leg, the same leg Echo had injured, and, I realized then, the same leg the goblins had stuck with a spear all those months ago.

My vision blackened around the edges, and I experienced a whole new level of agony as blood spurted and my leg gave out. Screaming, I collapsed to the floor, my limbs splaying out in all directions, and my injured shoulder smashing against the marble.

Then the blackness crept in, and I knew nothing.

I was out for a split second, but it was enough. When I came to, Icaria stood over me, her sword in both hands, ready to plunge it into my chest.

I let out a curse and scrambled away from her, leaving a trail of blood across the marble floor. "Stop," I pleaded, my voice barely above a whisper. "Stop! *Please*. I'm done. I surrender! Please… No more. No more…"

She stopped where she was and studied me, buying into my pathetic little show. She enjoyed watching me suffer.

Tears rolled down my cheeks as the pain returned. I half expected knives to be embedded in my leg and shoulder, but there was only blood and…ice. I was strangely cold, as if the blood in my veins was frozen, but I supposed it was the nerve damage in my shoulder and the shock of the blow I'd sustained.

Icaria sheathed her sword and put her hands on her hips, indicating that she no longer believed me to be a threat. I didn't blame her. I was a mess, but I hoped she would live to regret the decision.

The cold inside me built, and I trembled, goose bumps forming on my skin.

"Who would've thought?" Icaria said. "The great and mighty Isanfier of Summer, a coward." She laughed.

I wanted to scream at her that I was not a coward, but she wasn't entirely wrong, nor was she the first person to point it out.

Instead, I wiped my eyes, took a deep breath, and said, "I'm not the only one. You gave up on Echo, the one person who could've helped you. You discarded her like she was a piece of garbage. You were content to ignore her, but then she threatened your existence, and you were *afraid*, afraid you'd lose everything you had built, so you—coward that you are— killed her. You killed her, and now she will destroy you."

"How will she accomplish that, pray tell?" Icaria asked. "She's *dead.*"

"She lives on through me," I replied, "and I will make you regret giving up on her. I will make you hate what you've become. I will make you wish you were dead but never give you the freedom of dying. I will be the nightmare you can never wake up from, the shadow you see around every corner, the demon in the dark, and the monster under the bed. I will be everything you fear and worse, and, in the name of Echo, I will destroy you."

She didn't laugh at my words. She didn't even smile. In fact, for the first time in the whole confrontation, she looked nervous.

"Brave words from a boy who's on the cusp of death," she said, attempting, but not succeeding, to keep the emotion from her voice.

It was my turn to laugh. The motion should have made everything hurt even more, but the ice in my veins was sapping all sensation from my body.

"Oh, I'm not the one who's in danger of dying, Icaria. You are."

"How do you figure that?" she sneered, turning her nose up at me.

"Unlike you," I replied, "I don't want to be a coward anymore."

As the numbness set in, I flung out my hand and let my magic go.

I was expecting fire to singe her unguarded legs, a measly attempt to buy myself more time, but an icicle appeared instead, spearing into the muscle of her calf.

Icaria dropped to the floor, screaming, as blood began to trickle down her leg, and I marvelled at what I had done. I had manipulated the magic on instinct and hadn't realized I was playing with ice until it was already too late.

Icaria's shocked expression morphed into one of horror as the ice continued to creep up her leg before stopping short of her knee. "Impossible," she breathed through the pain. "How did you…?"

"There is a lot about me you don't know," I ground out as I grabbed *Ember* and pushed myself to my feet, careful not to put any weight on my injured leg, "and that will be your downfall."

My ice magic was still swirling in my veins, the cold soothing the pain of all my injuries enough to clear my head.

Icaria struggled to her feet as well, hissing against her own pain, and by the time I limped over to her and swung Ember towards her head, she had her own sword up to block it. The force of the blow shook us both, and it was a miracle either of us stayed standing.

"You'll never win, no matter the tricks you have up your sleeve," she growled at me as she took up the defensive, though her moves were as sluggish as my own.

"Then we'll both lose," I shot back, fighting the pull of oblivion as I blocked her attacks and looked for an opening to throw in my own.

We were both bloody and broken, our energy mere moments away from giving over to nothing, and I wondered, for a brief second, if we were destined to meet the same fate as our ancestors Queen Lea and Lord Izarr—bleeding out together on the palace floor with no one to save us.

But that wasn't strictly true.

Sky was still in here somewhere, needing to be saved. Asmund and Aramina were waiting for both of us to return. And I still hadn't avenged Echo's death or taken back my kingdom.

I couldn't die here.

Not yet.

I summoned my fire magic to the tips of my fingers again, steeling myself for a final assault with whatever strength I had left, when a voice spoke in the far reaches of my mind.

*Hold on, Isan. I'm coming.*

It sounded so far away that I couldn't discern who was speaking, but I trusted the voice, trusted I wasn't alone in this fight.

I let my magic go, what little was left, and Icaria and I danced in a whirl of steel, ice, and fire as our wounds threatened to pull us under and the room started to tilt and blur before our eyes.

Finally, she snuck through my defenses and tripped me again, but the sudden pain of the impact sent shards of uncontrolled ice flying away from me in all directions, sullying her short victory as they tore through her clothes and into her skin.

She hissed in annoyance and pain, faltering on her injured leg, and then she did something I never would've expected. She turned away and ran from the room—or at least, she tried to. She couldn't manage more than a desperate shuffle with her injuries.

I lurched in her direction, finding my way to my knees, but the fight was leaving me, darkness beckoning at the edges of my vision.

I was so close and yet so far.

*I can't let her slip away. She has to* pay.

My vision blurred again, and when I found my focus, someone was throwing an arm under my shoulder to support me. "Come on, Isan, stay with me. We have to get out of here. Sancia's breath… There's so much blood."

"Asmund?" I gasped out through the pain threatening to pull me under. "What…are you…doing here?"

"Saving your sorry life, again," Asmund replied. "I'll explain later, now move. I neutralized that Magic Wielder for now, but he won't stay unconscious for long."

"Where's Sky?"

"Safe," he replied, dragging me along beside him. "I sent her through a portal to the horses, but we'll have to go on foot."

"What about Icaria? I can't…. I have to…."

"You are going to *die* if we don't leave right now," Asmund snapped. "So shut up and walk."

I didn't have the energy to protest further.

We'd made it out into the hall when he spoke again. "Sky said Echo was here. Have you seen her?"

"Gone," I choked out. It was a pathetic answer, but it was all I could manage. I was fraying at the edges. The anger in me had dwindled, and sorrow was creeping back in through the crack in the door.

Asmund had the good grace not to answer, and we continued on in silence.

• • •

The next twenty minutes were complete chaos. The halls of the palace were full of guards. Asmund and I fought them off with magic and might as best we could, my body running on nothing but pure spite.

When we made it out of the palace, it was all I could do to put one foot in front of the other and keep up with Asmund's pace as he ran down the streets. I slipped a couple times until Asmund wordlessly threw me over his shoulder and kept running.

People gaped at us as we passed by but made no move to bar our path.

Mercifully, our horses were where we'd left them, and when I saw Sky standing on her own two feet beside them, I nearly started crying. "Are you okay?" I gasped out as Asmund finally put me down.

"I'm fine," she replied, though her voice shook a little. "The screams were exaggerated, but he did—" She stopped herself. "It's nothing I can't recover from, but you..." She hesitated. "Is that all your blood?"

I shook my head and bit my lip against the curses I wanted to spew for allowing Sky to get hurt. "Nothing I can't recover from," I repeated. Then I used the last of my energy to hoist myself onto my horse while Asmund pulled Sky up onto his.

We rode away from Appalachia without a backwards glance.

• • •

We rode for hours.

We rode until the day fell into night.

Then, as dawn's red hues bled into the morning sky, we stopped.

We slid off our horses and onto the ground, exhausted. Explanations would have to wait, for in seconds, sleep took us far away from our world of troubles.

• • •

I woke to the deep orange glow of sunset and Asmund kneeling over me, brows furrowed with sweat. I scrambled backwards. "What are you doing?"

He rolled his eyes and smacked the side of my arm. "Trying to heal you, for Sancia's sake. Sit still."

"Is Sky—"

"She's fine, sleeping. Do you really think I would heal you first?"

"Fair point."

My limbs were stiff, and all my wounds ached, though it was my shoulder that caused the most trouble. Every movement was a struggle, and when I managed one, I was rewarded by a brilliant flash of white-hot pain. It was not a good sign. My leg didn't look too good either. The gash was deep, and I shuddered to think of the further damage it had sustained running out of Appalachia.

"Will you be able to fix it?" I asked.

"Not all of it," Asmund admitted. "Aramina is much better at this than I am, but you'll live."

424

I nodded. "I guess that's all I can ask for. Why were you in the palace? What happened?"

He gave me a look. "I could ask you the same thing."

I stared at him in silence, unable to form the words, but then I heard Sky's voice say, "She's gone, isn't she."

I turned my head to find Sky sitting up in her bedroll, eyes damp with tears, and I could only nod.

Sky began sobbing with abandon, and Asmund sat down beside me. "She shouldn't have gone. Why did she go?"

"*How* did she go?" I asked.

"When I reached the camp after leaving you two in Tamise, Aramina was awake, and Echo was nowhere to be found," Asmund said. "We figured she must've turned herself invisible and followed the three of us through the portal to Tamise. She wanted to help, but obviously nothing went to plan. How did she die?"

I swallowed hard. "I killed her."

Asmund narrowed his eyes. "You better start from the beginning and leave no stone unturned."

So I did, mostly.

I told them everything exactly as it had happened, though I left out our mother's letters, deciding neither of them were in the right state of mind for that news, and tweaked the story so I stabbed Icaria with a hidden knife instead of an icicle. Asmund told his side of the story next, how he'd raced to the capital to help us at the behest of Aramina and had arrived in time to save both Sky and I from a vicious death.

When we were finished, a solemn silence ruled us, and we sat in it for a long time before Asmund said, "I know our wounds are still fresh, but we can't linger here. If Icaria has any brains at all, which I'm afraid she does, she'll send scouts after us. We need to move."

Sky and I nodded, following him reluctantly, Sky catching my arm before I mounted my horse again.

"What is it?" I asked her.

"I want you to know Echo's death isn't your fault," she said.

I frowned. "I didn't say it was?"

She sighed. "I know you didn't, but I know *you*, Isan. I know how your brain works, but you can't let this destroy you. Icaria is the one to blame, and rest assured, we will make her pay."

• • •

In the end, we returned to the treehouse one last time. I thrust *Silence* into the dirt beneath Echo's vast creation to mark her final resting place, and the girls picked a multitude of flowers from the glade to decorate her clearing.

Then we whispered her name to the wind and said our farewells.

Sky and Aramina wept as the short ceremony came to a close, but I did not. My heart had been shattered into a thousand pieces, and I had no tears left to shed nor any sorrow with which to shed them.

All that remained in my tiny sliver of a heart was revenge, and hatred for Icaria. She had broken my heart, and it would never heal. The relationship between Echo and I had never had the chance to blossom into love, but if there was one person in this realm who hadn't deserved such a fate, it was her. She had been a friend to all of us without ever asking for anything in return, and the realm had lost a beautiful soul with her passing.

Icaria had killed the person we all loved most, and in doing so, she had sealed her fate. I would stop at nothing to avenge Echo, would stop at nothing until Icaria was six feet under the frozen Winter ground. One way or another, the curse would end and free me from my life of pain and suffering.

War was coming, a war that would put an end to Winter. They had destroyed my past and future, and now they would pay with their lives in the present. I was done playing games, and I was done playing nice. Icaria had no idea of the monster she had unleashed.

Ice sealed my broken heart, burying it under eternal darkness. My curse of hatred and revenge would soon wreak havoc in all the lands.

Icaria would die, and if I had to burn down the entire realm to accomplish that, so be it.

# EPILOGUE

## *Icaria*

**Icaria glared at her** reflection in the mirror as one of her servants slipped her tiara on her head, hopefully for the last time. Her royal advisors had argued against crowning her before she came of age, but the King had been dead for months, and Icaria was young, not stupid. Winter needed guidance and strength, or it would crumble.

Weakness existed to be exploited, after all, and Icaria would not bow for anyone.

The servants finished her hair and left the room without a word from either of them, leaving Icaria to her dark thoughts. The coronation would begin again shortly, and Icaria prayed everything would go according to plan the second time around.

She didn't particularly feel like getting blood all over her glittering white dress, but if the moment called for it, she would do whatever was necessary to secure the throne.

It had been an entire week since the Summer royals had infiltrated her castle, an entire week since Prince Isanfier had made an attempt on her life and then fled. Icaria found comfort in the fact that she had brought him to his knees and nearly triumphed over him once and for all, but *nearly* wasn't good enough.

Nearly was a poor disguise for failure.

The truth was he had come so close to ruining everything, and she couldn't afford to let that happen again.

Her hand drifted absentmindedly to her leg. Henrik had healed the wound, once he'd recovered from his own brush with death, but Icaria swore it still pained her, a faint hint of cold seeping into her veins despite her Winter blood.

A large part of Icaria—the part her father had always cautioned against—wanted nothing more than to rush after the Summer Prince and beat him into the ground where he stood, but she couldn't risk it, not when Winter was still so unstable.

Besides, it would be too swift an end for the likes of him.

*No.*

Let him run back to his precious kingdom. Let him regroup. Let him believe he stood a chance against her.

She would soon follow with an army at her back, no longer held prisoner in Winter by the existence of that miserable forest dweller. She would face him on his own soil as Queen of Winter, and he would not live long enough to claim his own throne.

Yes, she was quite looking forward to planning his demise.

# To Be Continued in Season of Ruin

# THE NOBLE FAMILIES OF SUMMER

## Widonia

Prince Isanfier & Princess Skiansy(16)

## Mensden

Lord Byron & Lady Florence
Jasper(19), Rosetta(17)

## Fortude

Lord Maddix & Lady Elara (deceased)
Penelope(16), Tamsen(15)

## Laurel

Lord Lachlan & Lady Solana (deceased)
Soleia and Raina(15)

## Cargoff

Lord Caldwell & Lady Katya
Dorin(14), Orella(8), Diera(6), Elena(4), Euric(3)

## Skar

Lord Arrath & Lady Violette (deceased)
Asmund(20), Arran(15), Aramina(13)

## Ne-Trol

Lord Norwell & Lady Helga
Kainda(21), Gwyneth(17), Weylyn(12)

# MAGIC IN FIDALIA

## Mortal:

Mortals are people with no magic and a regular lifespan. 64% of the population

## Immortal:

Immortals are people with no magic, except for their immortality. They will not die of old age and are resistant to disease. They stop aging around twenty years old. 10% of the population

## Magic Wielder:

Magic Wielders are mortals that have access to the same set of magic abilities. So while they wield incredible power, they will die as nature intended. Some of their abilities include but aren't limited to: telepathy, telekinesis, talking to animals, creating portals, healing, and shapeshifting. 5% of the population

## Gifted Immortal:

Gifted Immortals have one power at their disposal that is unique to them. They stop aging at sixteen and cannot die unless killed. Their Gifts vary, from conjuring and controlling the elements, to illusions, invisibility, and more. 20% of population

## Immortal Magic Wielder:

Immortal Magic Wielders have the combined might of both Magic Wielders and Gifted Immortals, and are extremely rare. They are immortal, they have access to the Magic Wielder abilities, and they have their own unique Gift. No known cases currently exist in Fidalia.

# AUTHOR'S NOTE

**Thank you so much** for reading!

If you liked *Winter's Wrath*, it would mean the world to me if you could leave a review on your chosen vendor, Goodreads, social media, and/or anywhere else you share books. Reviews are essential to boost an author's reach and help new readers decide if they want to give the book a chance. Even a rating by itself or a single sentence review goes a long way. I can't wait to hear your thoughts!

If you are interested in more content from yours truly, I have a monthly newsletter, which gives you access to an exclusive community. I send updates on my writing, releases, and more, as well as excerpts of the books I'm currently working on, short stories, and early blog posts. You can sign up on my website which I have left below.

**www.emmacouetteauthor.com**

# ACKNOWLEDGEMENTS

**First, I want to** say thank you to my younger sister, Megan, once again. I want to say that I didn't bother her quite as much for this book as I did for Summer's Revenge, but she'll be the judge of that. Thank you again for helping me develop this word and these characters.

Second, to my significant other, Allan, who encouraged me to keep pushing forward whenever I was tempted to throw in the towel completely and give up on being an author. You always help me see that I've been here before and that I always find my way out.

Third, to my parents for supporting my author dreams and rooting for me every step of the way. Thank you to both of you for helping me carry boxes and set up events in the past year. I couldn't have done it half as well without you.

I am beyond grateful for my amazing Critique Partner, Ashley, who assured me multiple time that this book was not a dumpster fire. You were wrong, of course, but the peptalks kept me going and we were able to cobble this story together and create something worth sharing.

Thank you as well to my Beta Readers: Joy, Rachel, and Sandy :) I can't wait for you guys to see the finished version!

Big thanks to the members of my Street Team for spreading the word about the cover, pre-orders, giveaways, and more: Amber, Catherine, Crystal, Gurleen, Ilsa, Meg, Pearl, Priscilla, Robin, and Sarah.

Thank you to MoorBooks Design for creating another stunning cover. I can't wait to see what you come up with for book three!

Huge thank you to Nicki Richards for being my editor yet again. It honestly amazes me how many mistakes there still are when I send it to you. Thank you for helping me create a polished version and making a few suggestions that really increased the wow factor of this story. Ps I'm sorry I made you cry.

I would also like to thank Rachael Ward from CartographyBird who designed the stunning map at the beginning of the book.

Shoutout to the writing community over on Instagram who always inspire me and motivate me to keep going no matter what. I want to give a special thank you to Hidden Hollow Book Tours for the fantastic tours they ran for both *Winter's Wrath* and *Summer's Revenge*, Aubrey C. Sanders for the stunning character art featured in my release giveaways, and Hannah Drinkwater for being the best writer friend.

Last, but not least, thank you to my readers for following Isan and sky into book two. I hope you enjoyed *Winter's Wrath* and I can't wait to share the grand finale with you! Thank you for supporting me and my ever growing imagination.

# ABOUT THE AUTHOR

**Emma K. C. Couette** is a Canadian wordsmith born and raised in a small Ontario town. She has written a few award-winning short stories and dabbles in poetry when the inspiration strikes her. Her dreams include travelling the world, being a mom, and owning a small library. *Winter's Wrath* is her fifth novel, the sequel to *Summer's Revenge*.

Website: www.emmacouetteauthor.com
Instagram: @emmacouetteauthor
Facebook: emmacouette.10
Goodreads: Emma Couette